Total-E-E

SAVIOURS OF OESTEND

MARIE SEXTON

Saviours of Oestend
ISBN # 978-1-78184-512-7

Interior text design by Claire Siemaszkiewicz
Total-E-Bound Publishing

Published in 2012 by Total-E-Bound Publishing, Think Tank, Ruston Way, Lincoln, LN6 7FL, United Kingdom.

Total-E-Bound Publishing is an imprint of Total-E-Ntwined Limited.

SAVIOURS OF OESTEND

Dedication

For all the travellers who don't need a map.

Chapter One

The house still smelt of death. It was a horrible, cloying scent that filled the halls, permeating the wood and the curtains, and clogging the air. The house felt heavy with it. When Dante had first entered it, he'd had to turn on his heel and run right back out to vomit violently in the dirt. And even now, weeks later, the smell got to him.

It wasn't as if he was a stranger to death and its aftermath. He'd seen it before. He'd killed men himself. But this death that filled his new home, clawing at the back of his throat and tainting his every breath, was different, because one of the rotting corpses found in this home had been his younger brother, Brighton. No matter what else Dante had done in his life, no matter how stupid or irrational or selfish he'd been, he'd loved his brother with all his heart.

Another of the dead found in the house had been Brighton's wife, and two more had been their sons. Dante was ashamed now to admit how little regard he'd had for the woman and the boys. In truth, he'd always thought Shay an arrogant bitch, and although there was nothing inherently wrong with the boys, they'd constantly reminded Dante of his own failings in his marital bed. Yes, it may have been a sin that he grieved so little for them now, but he made up for it by grieving for his brother, each and every day.

Still, life in Oestend did not stop for anything as trivial as grief. The sun continued to rise. The wind continued to blow. Cows and horses gave birth to young. The cattle needed tending and fences needed mending. There was nothing he could do but rise every day and do his best to carry on.

"I hope they get here tonight," Frances said that morning, looking west at the sky. "Travelling tomorrow will be awful."

Dante didn't have to ask who he meant. He'd sent Simon to town several days earlier for supplies and to recruit new men. Their first group of hands hadn't lasted long, mostly because the stench of decaying bodies wasn't confined to the house. Several maids had died in the barracks on that fateful night as well. The building smelt as bad as the house. Possibly worse. And until Simon returned with the new men, it was just Dante and Frances, and one other young hand named Ralf who was as skittish as a colt, trying to get everything done.

Dante followed Frances' gaze. The sky to the west was pale and white, hanging low and heavy like the belly of a pregnant mare. Dante shivered just looking at it. "Too early for snow. Shouldn't be seeing it for another month or more."

"It's coming, early or not."

"You're right about that." Dante eyed the skyline, assessing the cold, clear brittleness of the horizon. He noted the way his breath was already coalescing in the air. Everything was deathly silent and perfectly still, except the tops of the trees, swaying in a breeze he couldn't feel. He shook his head. "Gonna be a damn cold night. If they don't make it back, you and that kid ought just as well come to the house." After all, there was no point in burning fuel to heat both the barracks and the big house when there were only three of them there on the ranch. "Easier for me to keep you warm."

Frances bent back to his work without a word, but Dante noticed the way the tips of his ears turned bright pink. It confused him, until he replayed his words in his head. *Easier for me to keep you warm.* He hadn't meant it that way, and he suspected Frances knew that, but he also suspected Frances would have jumped at the invitation if he *had* meant it that way. They'd certainly never discussed their sexual habits, but Dante was pretty sure he knew which side of the fence Frances stood on.

Of course, that made Dante think about what it would be like if he *did* take the boy to his bed. He thought about the two of them skin to skin under the covers while the snow fell outside.

No.

Dante wasn't about to let anything like that happen. He slammed a mental door on the thought and turned away, praying to whoever might hear that Simon would make it back before the snow came.

As it turned out, his prayer was answered. That evening, just as the snow was beginning to fall, just past when the supper bell might have rung, if they'd had one, Simon appeared, with a string of men and a full wagon behind him. And one other thing Dante wasn't expecting—a woman. She was tall for a girl, and slender, with deep brown hair that fell in her face, and huge, dark eyes that were guarded and wary.

Dante grabbed Simon's arm and pulled him aside. "What the hell you thinking bringing a woman here?"

Simon was only a couple of years younger than Dante, and just as big, and he clearly didn't appreciate being manhandled like a mere boy. He pulled his arm free from Dante's grip. "She asked to go to the BarChi, but when we got there, Aren said I should bring her here."

Dante clenched his jaw, biting back on the anger that always welled up in him at the mention of Aren. "Not enough he drives me off the BarChi? He thinks he can call the shots on my ranch now, too?"

Simon's patience was clearly wearing thin, and no wonder after so many days on the road. "Look," he said through clenched teeth, "I got no idea what went down between you and Aren and Deacon. All I know is, she's got nowhere else to go. She asked specifically for the BarChi, but with Olsa there, and Tama and Alissa, they don't have work for her. Aren thought we could use the help here."

Fuck, but Dante hated it when Aren was right. Dante knew how to run a ranch, but there were so many things the women at home had taken care of. He hadn't quite realised at the time just how much work they'd done. He'd already vowed more than once that he'd get down on his knees and thank Tama to the heavens next time he saw her.

Simon seemed to relax once he realised Dante was done being angry. He pulled his hood up onto his head and brushed at the fat, soft flakes of snow that dusted his shoulders. "She says she'll cook and launder." He shrugged, motioning towards the big house. "Not like you don't have room."

Yes, she'd have to be given a room in the house rather than the barracks. Dante wasn't sure if he liked that idea or not. He turned towards her and pitched his voice loud enough for her to hear over the hubbub of the new men.

"Go inside. I'll deal with you later."

She didn't thank him. She didn't say anything at all. She just picked up the blanket roll at her feet and went past him to the house.

Fuck, but women made life difficult.

Frances came out of the barracks to greet Simon, obviously pleased that the older man was back. Dante watched them together—the familiar way they gripped each other's hands, and the happy smiles they shared. He'd wondered many times if they were lovers. Most of the time he thought not, but there were occasions when he saw something in Frances' eyes that made him want to change his mind. He almost hoped they were. It would be just one more reason to not let himself give in to the dangerous temptation Frances offered.

Dante turned away from the two men to survey the five recruits Simon had brought back with him. As usual, the new hands were mostly young and green as the spring grass. Most of them were hugging themselves against the oncoming storm, looking with wide eyes around the ranch and watching the moody sky to the west.

"Do they know what happened?" Dante asked Simon. It was better that they be warned ahead of time about the deaths, in case any of them were superstitious.

"They know," Simon said. "And I warned them about the smell."

"Good."

One of the hands stood out from the others. He was still younger than either Simon or Dante, but older than the other boys. Dante guessed him to be twenty-five. He stood apart, with his arms crossed over his chest. His sleeves were rolled up despite the cold, and Dante could see multiple brands on them, proving he'd worked ranches before. One brand stood out, partly because it was still fresh enough to be puckered and red, but mostly because it matched the one on Dante's own arm.

"His name's Foster. He's from the BarChi," Simon said, confirming what Dante already knew. "Wasn't there long."

"Why's he here now?"

Simon shrugged. "No idea. Just said he wanted to come. Deacon said he's a good enough worker, but to keep your eye on him."

"For what?"

Simon shrugged again. Simon wasn't much of a talker and neither was Deacon. Between the two of them, it was likely that was all they'd said. Aren, on the other hand, was more straightforward. Dante hated to ask, but he swallowed his pride and did it anyway. "And what did Aren say?"

"Aren said he's trouble. He said, trouble for him, and maybe trouble for you for the same reason, but that maybe you could handle it better than him 'cause you're stronger." Dante raised his eyebrows at that, wondering what it might mean, but Simon waved him off. "That's all he'd say, so don't ask me to interpret."

Dante pondered Aren's words, wishing he knew exactly what they meant. He couldn't think of any rational reason a man would choose to leave the BarChi to come out here, to the furthest known end of the prairie, to a ranch that produced more grief than cattle.

It really did speak of trouble.

He waved Foster forward and the man came. Dante didn't see any reason to waste time with chatter, so he asked immediately, "Why'd you leave the BarChi?"

Foster stood up straight and squared his shoulders. "I won't work for men like them."

"Who you talking about?" Dante asked. "My father or Deacon?"

"Deacon and that dandy who warms his bed." Foster turned and spat pointedly on the ground. "Men like them disgust me."

Dante saw the flash of alarm in Frances' eyes at Foster's words. He saw the quick glance the boy threw at Simon. Simon seemed unalarmed, although it was clear he had no sympathy for Foster, either.

Well, at least the mystery of Aren's words had been solved. Aren knew that Dante was just like him in his sexual tastes. Except Aren had said Foster wasn't as much of a threat to Dante as he was to Aren, because Dante was stronger. Dante knew that was wrong. It took strength for Aren to face those other hands at the BarChi every single day, each of them knowing he was essentially Deacon's wife. It took strength to accept what he was, to stare unflinchingly into the eyes of other men and admit his proclivities. If there was anything that would save Dante from Foster's contempt, it was that Dante was weak. He didn't want the world to know what he was. He wanted to hide it away, like the terrible secret his granddaddy had made it out to be. It was that weakness that had cost him Deacon.

Dante turned away, not granting Foster a response. "Take them to the barracks," he said to Simon. "You know what to do."

Simon shouted out to them, telling them to follow him, and in the hubbub, Dante reached out and took

Frances' arm. The boy turned to look at him with his huge blue eyes.

"He gives you any trouble, I expect to hear."

Frances was like an open book, every emotion he felt showing on his face. Confusion then alarm, and then embarrassment as he undoubtedly wondered how much Dante knew about him. The answer was, not much, but it seemed he'd guessed correctly.

"I'll be fine," Frances said at last.

That was probably true. Simon may not have been his lover, but he was certainly his friend. He'd probably kill Foster himself if the man threatened Frances.

"In that case, you tell me if he makes trouble for any of them others, all right?"

Frances smiled at him, a big broad smile that lit up his face and his blue eyes and almost made Dante wish he was as strong as Aren and could reach out and claim Frances as his own. "I will," Frances said. "Thanks."

Dante let him go. He watched them all trail across the grounds to the barracks. When they were gone, he turned to look at the big, empty house that until now had sheltered nobody but him. Now it would be home to some strange woman as well. Somehow, he knew she was bound to cause trouble. Women always did.

He sighed and went to face her.

* * * *

Dante found her sitting in the living room. She had pulled the long sleeves of her sweater down to cover her hands, and she held one of them over her nose.

"Simon said he warned you about the smell."

She nodded and said through her hand, "He did, but it's worse than I expected."

"Wish I could say you'd get used to it."

She shook her head. "I can fix it."

He hadn't expected that. "We already burned the mattresses, and all the linens, too."

"I know," she said.

That was all. No explanation of how she intended to do it. Just silence, and her big brown eyes, staring at him over her hand.

Dante sighed and sat down in the chair across from her, trying to decide how to proceed. Were women really so much harder than men, or did he only imagine it? He wasn't sure.

"What's your name?"

"Cami."

"Simon says you asked specifically for the BarChi?"

Her eyes were still wary, but she finally lowered her hand from her face, crinkling her nose at the smell. She was just a bit off from being pretty. Her eyes were her best feature—deep brown and almond-shaped, rimmed with thick, black lashes—but her brows were a bit too thick. Full, pouting lips, but her jaw was a touch too wide. "I needed work."

"And why not the McAllen ranch, or some other ranch with maids instead of hands?"

She looked down at her hands, clenched in her lap. "I have my reasons."

"Where did you work before?"

She looked up at him through her lashes. "I don't want to say."

He sighed in frustration. No, it couldn't be his imagination. Women were *definitely* more work. After all, men in Oestend branded their work history onto their arms. It was easy enough to see. And when asked why, they answered, like Foster had, even if their answers were ignorant or cruel.

She took a deep breath and said, "Aren said—"

"I don't give a fuck what Aren said," Dante snapped. "Aren ain't here."

She flinched at his words. She pulled the sleeves of her dark sweater down further over her hands and wrapped her arms around herself, as if she could use the garment as protection against Dante's anger. "Do you want me to go?"

"I want you to answer my question."

She stood up and turned her back on him, walking closer to the fire. She was rail-thin, straight and lean like the long grass that grew in the prairie. "I worked at The Chalice."

The Chalice. Dante rarely heard it called that, but he knew what it was—Milton's one and only whorehouse. He'd been there once, years before, when he was still young enough to think he might be able to make things work if only he found the right woman. Even back then, he'd found it to be a vile, disgusting place. He could understand why she'd want to keep it secret. "I see."

She looked over her shoulder at him, and he could see how much the confession shamed her. She eyed him, as if judging his reaction, but whether she liked what she found or not, he couldn't tell. She sighed and turned back to stare at the fire. "You hear things, working in a whorehouse. I heard about the BarChi. I heard how Aren and Deacon are different."

Different. What a diplomatic way of putting it.

"I also heard how they had another woman at the BarChi who wasn't anybody's wife, but that they kept her safe just the same."

"But they didn't have room for you, and you figured better here than back to The Chalice? Tired of being a whore?"

She turned to glare at him. "I'm not a whore! Not anymore. The only reason I came here is because Aren promised me you wouldn't force me into your bed."

Aren promised.

And once again, Aren was right. It irked Dante to admit it, but Aren hadn't lied to Cami. "What else did Aren say?"

She shrugged, her anger gone as quickly as it had come, apparently satisfied that he wasn't going to try to prove Aren wrong. "Nothing. Only that he thought you might need help. Not more men, he said. A woman's help."

"I suppose that's true enough."

"So you'll let me stay?"

"Don't see why not."

"Will you protect me from the others, even though I'm not your wife?"

"I don't condone rape, whether we're married or not."

The smile she gave him was almost apologetic. "I don't care what you say to them. Tell them whatever will keep me safe. You can tell them I spread my legs for you every night, if you like. Just don't expect me to actually do it."

It was strange. She was so adamant about not being a whore, and yet she didn't care what the other men thought of her, as long as Dante kept them from her. It was a fair enough request. He thought about Tama, back at the BarChi. She'd been his closest friend for years. He thought of what he would have done to any man who had dared touch her. He didn't know Cami at all, but he didn't need to. She deserved the same protection he would have given Tama, or Olsa or Alissa. Or his own wife Daisy, once upon a time, if she'd ever wanted anything so simple from him.

He didn't need to drag Cami's honour through the mud to keep her safe, either. If the hands knew she'd been a whore, they'd be more likely to think she was fair game, so that had to remain a secret. And as for telling them she was sharing his bed?

"It won't come to that," he said. "They touch you, I'll kill them. That's as much as they need to know."

She flinched at his words. "That seems rather harsh."

"My ranch, my rules."

She stared at him, assessing him, and her lips curved up in the smallest hint of a smile. "Tama told me you were a good man. She said, no matter what anybody else says, and no matter how bullheaded and stupid you sometimes are, that underneath it all, you have a pure heart."

He found himself smiling at the words. He could hear Tama saying it. How many times had she scolded him—and rightly so—for some stupid thing he'd done while blinded by rage or by jealousy? "How is Tama?"

"She says she misses you. She says life is downright boring without you causing trouble every time the wind blows."

Yes, that definitely sounded like her. He missed her, too, but he didn't say that to Cami. It was one more piece of his life that was wrong. He'd lost Deacon. He'd lost the BarChi. He'd lost Daisy, and although he didn't exactly miss her, he did miss what she represented—a wife and a chance at someday having a family. And he'd lost his one and only friend, Tama.

It seemed as if it were all because of Aren.

He shook his head. He didn't want to dwell on that thought. He'd done that for too long already. Instead, he watched Cami. She'd turned away from him to hold her hands out to the fire. The odd sweater she wore only came halfway down her back, revealing a slim waistline that trailed straight down under her skirt to narrow hips. His daddy would have said she wasn't fit to bear children. He wouldn't have meant it in any kind of mean way, but having lost his own wife to childbirth, he'd been vigilant when choosing wives for his sons. Broad hips meant healthy babies, and more importantly, it meant healthy moms who survived the birth. That was one of the first things he'd said to Dante about the wife he'd chosen for him. "Daisy has good wide hips. Childbearing hips. You'll have a hoard of babies in no time."

Of course, he'd been wrong, but it hadn't been Daisy's hips that had been the problem.

Cami moved closer to the fire, wrapping her sweater tighter around her. A glance out the only window in the room showed him that the snow had stopped, but he could tell it was bitterly cold out. There was a luminescence to the air that spoke of more precipitation to come. The moan of the wind was low and ominous. Simon and Frances would be out in it, trying to get as many of the animals into the barn as they could, stocking the woodpiles and the coal, securing the feed. He should be out there helping them. But first, he felt he needed to settle things with her.

She was edging closer to the fire, her hands held out to its warmth. A skinny girl like her was bound to be chilly all the time to begin with. Cold like they had on the Oestend prairie might kill her, and that was no exaggeration. Dante eyed the clothes she wore—a skirt that looked none-too warm, a thin shirt, that strange short sweater with the overly long sleeves. Under the hem of her skirt, he could make out low boots—perfectly practical for working inside, but they'd never be enough to keep her feet dry when she had to leave the house.

"Gonna be cold tonight," he said. "And even colder tomorrow. Storm like this, we might not see much thaw for a week or more." He eyed the blanket roll on the floor that held her belongings. It was too small to hold much. "You bring any warm clothes?"

She glanced over her shoulder at him. There were spots of colour high on her cheeks, but she smiled a bit. "These *are* my warm clothes."

He rolled his eyes. "They ain't gonna do you much good." But as soon as he'd said it, he knew he also had the solution. "Come on," he said to her as he pushed himself up out of his chair. "Follow me."

He led her through the kitchen and up the stairs. It was significantly colder on the second floor. The heat from the kitchen and the living room hearth didn't reach that far. There were four bedrooms along the hall. The largest one, which had belonged to Zed Austin and his wife, held a fireplace. Logic dictated Dante should take that room, but he'd resisted. For some reason he couldn't quite explain, he'd wanted to be in the room that had held Brighton on his last night alive. Sharing the room with his brother's ghost reminded Dante each and every day of what had been lost and of how easily things could go wrong in the wild. Now, it seemed doubly provident that he'd rejected the main bedroom.

He led Cami to it and opened the door. "May as well use the room with the fireplace. I suspect you'll need it more than me." She was surprised, he could tell, but before she could say anything, he led her into the third of the four bedrooms. He opened the closet door. "Everything we found in the house, we put here. Most of the men's clothes have been taken by now, but nobody's had use for any of the women's things. And since Zed ran a maid ranch and had daughters, there's plenty of it. Go through it. Take whatever you like. Ain't nobody else around here going to need it."

She didn't answer, and he turned to try to read her expression. She was the tallest woman he'd ever met, nearly his height. She stared at the closet full of clothes, smiling like it was the most amazing thing she'd ever seen, her eyes huge and childishly excited. He was surprised she hadn't already pushed him out of the way to get to them. It made him laugh. "Tama always said the way to a woman's heart is through her closet door. She said, men are always trying to get women's clothes off. Too bad they don't realise the quickest way is to put clothes on them first."

Her eyes flashed towards him, suddenly full of alarm, and he thought about what he'd said. As usual, he'd spoken without thinking. He hadn't meant to make it sound like he was trying to get under her skirt, but he realised that was exactly how it had come out. He held his hands up defensively and took a step back. "I didn't mean it like that."

She relaxed at once, and her smile returned, as bright as before. "Thank you."

Her gratitude made him uncomfortable. He hadn't done anything. People had died. That was why he was here, in this house. That was why there was a closet full of unused clothing. None of it felt like his. Sure, he could have kept the clothing a secret, but to what purpose? He wasn't being nice. He was being practical.

He pointed to the closed door of his room. “That one’s mine,” he said. “But the rest of the house is yours as much as anybody’s.”

He saw the surprise and understanding in her eyes. “Thank you,” she said again.

The words made him as uncomfortable the second time.

“Enough talk,” he said. “We both got to work to do.”

Chapter Two

Simon hadn't wanted to bring the girl. He'd wanted very much to tell her no, but she'd looked at him with those giant brown eyes, so much like Lena's, and he'd given in.

Of course, he'd been kicking himself for his weakness ever since.

It wasn't Cami's fault. Not really. But the truth was, she made him uneasy. Yes, her eyes were like Lena's, but it was her demeanour that spooked him the most. She was still, silent and observant. He had the uncomfortable feeling that Lena was somewhere behind those eyes, watching him, trying to determine if he'd kept his vow.

The Saints knew he'd tried. They knew he'd failed, too, on a couple of occasions. But not recently, and on not this trip. No way could he have allowed temptation to get the better of him this time. Not with Lena's eyes watching him. Besides, when they'd reached the McAllen farm, there hadn't been as many willing maids as there were willing men. Simon had seen the way some of the boys had begun to turn their eyes towards Cami. He also noted the way she'd huddled in the corner, her eyes huge and scared.

In the end, he'd taken Cami into his stall instead of a maid. "I won't touch you," he'd assured her. "I won't let them touch you either." It was apparently what she'd needed to hear. He'd barred the door, and the two of them had bedded down on opposite sides of the stall. Neither of them had spoken a word. And if the moans and gasps of the lovers in other stalls had seemed harder to deal with that night than ever before, Simon had chalked it up to his own guilt. He'd called the memory of Lena up in his mind and reaffirmed the vow he'd made to her so many years before.

The next morning had dawned with a barn full of smiling young men. Simon's heart had been heavy, but at least it was with the comfortable familiarity of ancient grief, and not the sharp, hateful pain of self-recrimination and regret. He'd held onto that thought like a talisman.

He'd thought to be rid of Cami at the BarChi, but it wasn't to be. He'd figured her getting back to town was her own problem, until Aren had tracked him down in the barn and asked him to take her to Dante's.

"You have any idea how pissed Dante'll be if I show up with a woman in tow?" he'd asked Aren.

Aren had raised his eyebrows at him, laughter sparkling in his brown eyes. "Are you afraid of Dante?"

"You're not the one has to work with him!"

"True enough." Aren had smiled innocently at him. He'd turned away, as if he were giving in. But Simon hadn't really been off the hook. "So, how's the food there?" Aren had asked. "Are you getting three square meals a day?"

Simon had found himself cursing, thinking of the day they'd eaten nothing but pickles because it was what some fool hand had dragged up from the cellar and the rest of them were too tired to argue. The truth was, Simon had worked cattle drives back in Lanstead. He knew how to cook a bit. Mostly beans and flatbread, but even that was better than pickles. But his skills were always required outside the house. It didn't make sense to have him working in the kitchen when there was so much other work to be done. And so far, none of the other men they'd recruited had known cornmeal from dust.

Aren had taken Simon's obscenities for the answer they were. "What about laundry?" he'd asked. "When was the last time your shorts were washed?"

"My shorts aren't your concern!" he'd snapped. He'd always thought Aren a bit of a know-it-all. The annoying thing was, Aren really did seem to know it all.

"And how about canning?" Aren had asked next. "Deacon says the Austins had a big garden. Are you going to be able to put any of it away for winter?"

Of course they weren't. Simon didn't know a blessed thing about canning, and he was pretty sure Dante didn't either.

"All right!" Simon had conceded in frustration. "I'll take her!"

And so he'd had to deal with Lena's eyes watching him for two more days. And because after the McAllen ranch, Cami apparently trusted him not to take advantage of her, she had stuck close to him the entire time. Of course, the fact that she'd needed to resort to such measures was one of the other reasons Simon didn't want her along.

Women caused trouble.

Simon was level-headed enough to recognise that it often wasn't their fault, but the truth of the matter was, once a woman was in the picture, men could usually be counted on to do stupid things. Some of the new recruits continued to ignore her. Some treated her with the careful politeness young men usually reserved for their meanest aunt. But a few had watched her the way a mountain lion watched a deer, and that worried Simon. Foster especially seemed to follow her movements with an almost predatory awareness. The girl was no fool, though. She knew to steer a broad path around Foster.

They finally arrived at the ranch. Simon breathed a mental sigh of relief when Cami took her pack and went into Dante's house. She was Dante's problem now. Simon planned to avoid her and her haunting eyes as much as possible.

"Do you think Dante will marry her?" Frances asked that night, after the chores were done and they were back in the barracks.

"I doubt it," Simon said. "He didn't seem all that pleased to have her here."

"I don't know why not. Saints, we might actually get a real breakfast tomorrow morning. My mouth's watering just thinking about it!"

Simon had to admit he'd be happy enough to see some real food at the ranch. Still, he couldn't help but think having a woman around might be more trouble than it was worth. Especially one who watched him with Lena's eyes.

"You all right?" Frances asked.

"Right enough," Simon lied. He looked around the barracks. The new boys were all jockeying for space. The barracks at the BarChi had held rows of cots, but it was different here. There were four bunk beds, one in each corner of the room, and a big, round, open fireplace in the middle. It meant the men had to pair up, but it afforded each pair a semblance of privacy. There were four curtains too, ceiling to floor, allowing the different quarters of the room to be sectioned off. Even now, with the curtains all open and the entire room visible to all, they could sit side by side on the lower bunk with their heads together and hold a conversation without the whole blessed world hearing. Simon tilted his head to the side, indicating the empty space on the bed next to him, and Frances took his hint. He sat down next to him, close enough that their thighs were touching. Simon had never flat-out asked Frances about his sexual habits, but he'd suspected for a while they were more in line with Aren's than with his own. "You heard what Foster said about men like Deacon and Aren?" he asked quietly.

Frances' face flushed red, but he didn't turn away. "I heard."

"That going to cause trouble for you?"

Frances' blush deepened. The boy was so easy to read. He was embarrassed to have Simon ask and nervous about how Simon would respond. "Not if he doesn't find out."

Simon nodded. "Fair enough. But if you end up behind the hay stack with any of these boys, be sure to watch your back. Got it?"

If possible, Frances' cheeks turned an even deeper shade of red. But Simon also saw the relief that it was now out in the open and with nothing more said about it than that. "I will."

"You let me know if he gives you any trouble. 'Cause I'll string him up from the nearest tree."

Frances' smile was shy and grateful. "I will."

There was something else there in his eyes, too, and in the solemn tone of his voice. Simon had always chalked it up as a bit of hero worship before. Now that he knew for sure about Frances, he realised it might be more, but he chose to let it go. It didn't matter, one way or the other. Frances was the same boy he'd always been, and he was Simon's friend. The boy was the only companion he'd had since Garrett had died.

"You watch him around Cami, too. He had his eye on her the whole trip, and I don't think she appreciated the attention."

Frances was clearly relieved that the conversation was moving away from his own sex life. "She might have a lot of that to deal with."

Simon shrugged. "She might." He thought about Daisy, who had been Dante's wife, and about Sawyer, the man who Dante had killed for rolling with her. He thought about the maids at the McAllen ranch—the ones who were willing, and the ones who had probably stayed in the barracks, out of sight, in order to keep from being mauled. He thought of Alissa, alone on the BarChi and dependent on Deacon to keep her safe, just as Cami was now dependent upon Dante.

Simon was glad he wasn't a woman.

"Guess we'll see what kind of man Dante really is."

Chapter Three

It may have been cold outside, but it was downright hot on the second floor of the big house. It seemed Cami was making good use of the fireplace in her bedroom. Dante wondered if she was burning through their entire woodpile. He would have opened a window if it hadn't been night.

At another point in his life, he might have been annoyed, but now it amused him more than anything. He thought he'd enjoyed having the house to himself, but he found that he liked knowing she was there. Occasionally, he heard a bump or a door closing. He heard her wandering the hall, going upstairs to the third floor, checking the other rooms, taking stock of the closets. He found her presence comforting. He hadn't quite realised how lonely he'd been.

When he rose the next morning, she was already in the kitchen. The entire room was rich with a scent that was sweet and warm, and yet so simple and familiar. It made Dante's stomach grumble. "What's for breakfast?"

"Just oatmeal," Cami said.

Just oatmeal. Dante thought he'd never been so happy to hear those two words in all his life. For the last few weeks, it seemed they'd mostly been living on baked beans and salt pork. Yes, there'd been the pickles, and once, two weeks prior, Frances had brought up some jars of carrots, which they'd eaten cold. But more often than not, it was baked beans and salt pork. The thought of eating anything that *wasn't* baked beans and salt pork was a relief.

"I'm still taking stock of what's here," she told him, "and there wasn't much I could do on such short notice. I guess I could have stayed up all night—"

"No need for that."

She smiled at him. "Glad we can agree on that. Anyway, there wasn't time for bread to rise, but I made some biscuits, and I found some jam in the cellar."

"The boys will love you for it. Assuming I leave them any." At that moment, he thought he could eat everything she put in front of him, and to the wraiths with those other men.

She'd changed her clothes. She still wore her dark sweater over her blouse, but the skirt she had on was different. It was some kind of heavy dark fabric that looked thick and warm. "Looks like the clothes will work."

She was in the process of pulling a cast iron pot from the fire, but she smiled sideways at him. "I'll have to alter most of them but these fit." She laughed. "Well enough, at any rate." She nodded downwards towards her feet, and Dante followed her pointed glance. The skirt stopped a bit short of where it should have. At least four inches of ankle showed below her hem, revealing a pair of heavy boots she'd found somewhere.

"Can you fix it?" he asked. Seemed like she probably could, but Dante sure as hell didn't know the first thing about sewing.

"I could, but honestly, this way seems better. I don't have to worry about the hem dragging in the mud. The sleeves are a different story." He couldn't see the sleeves of her blouse because of the sweater, but he could imagine that they ended a bit short of her wrists. She shrugged. "I'll fix them once I have a few minutes. I'll either pull them off and start over, or add cuffs to the cuffs." She said this in a lighthearted way that told him it was a joke, although he wasn't sure he understood why it should be funny.

He didn't have time to ask, though, before the door burst open, and eight men came crowding through it, hurrying in from the cold. Frances was at the front of the bunch, and the eagerness on his face as he tried to see what they were having for breakfast was enough to make Dante laugh out loud.

Then it was time for the day to really begin.

It hadn't actually snowed in the night. It seemed more as though water had poured from the sky and frozen on everything it touched, blanketing Oestend in ice. It covered each and every tree branch. Green leaves were held captive, still and fragile in its grip. Evergreen branches drooped against their trunks. The barbed wire fences sagged under the weight. The sky was low and grey, and it was still bone-chillingly cold. Dante treaded carefully on his way to the barn, at least an inch of solid ice under his feet. On the bright side, the wind wasn't blowing, which was a rare blessing on the Oestend prairie.

"Can you believe this?" Frances asked as he came across the compound towards him. He slapped his hands against his arms for warmth, smiling like a kid. "I've never seen anything like it!"

Dante had seen it before, but not often and never quite to this extreme. He shook his head, but the movement caused him to lose his footing on the ice and he had to flail his arms to keep from landing on his ass, which made Frances laugh. "It's something, all right," Dante agreed once he'd regained his composure.

"I had ice skates back in Lanstead. Kind of wish I had them with me."

"Ice skates?"

"Yeah. You know…"

No, Dante didn't know, and Frances must have seen the confusion on his face.

"They're like boots, only with blades on the bottom, like a sleigh."

"Sleigh boots?" Dante tried to picture such a thing. He couldn't imagine why anybody would want them. Sure, sleighs were useful things for hauling hay or coal, but on your feet? The ice was slippery enough with plain old boots on. Putting sleigh runners on your feet had to make it worse. Just went to show how crazy those fools on the continent were.

Dante had a bitch of a time breaking through the ice on the troughs in the barn. The animals stood huddled together, snorting and blowing steam in the frigid air. They turned their mournful eyes on him, as if cursing him for being human.

"Don't look at me," Dante said. "I ain't the one decided you don't get a fire of your own." In the towns, some barns were kept warm with coal furnaces, but the livestock on the prairie had no such luxury. Coal was heavy, and a pain in the ass to cart so far into the wild. What they did have was kept in store for the generator. And checking the generator was his next order of business.

Like most Oestend ranches, the Austin ranch had only one windmill, large enough to protect the buildings nearest to it—the main house, the barn, and the barracks. The BarChi was the only ranch Dante had ever seen to have multiple generators, but that was because Deacon and Jeremiah weren't men who left things to chance.

The windmill of the Austin ranch was situated between the big house and the barracks, and it towered over them all. Its gears had frozen up in the night. Icicles hung from the unmoving propellers. The generator stored excess power during the day, so the ranch residents had slept safely, but only a fool would depend on reserve power two nights in a row.

"Better check the coal," Dante said to himself. "And the wood piles."

But it turned out the coal and woodpiles had already been stocked. In truth, Dante wasn't surprised. Simon had taken on the role of foreman without ever being asked, and as usual, he'd set the hands to work early that morning, without having to ask Dante what needed to be done. Dante found himself shaking his head. He thought of Deacon, back on the BarChi, who'd always run the ranch. Deacon may have acted as if Jeremiah was in charge, but everybody knew who the real boss was. There'd never been room for any of Jeremiah's sons. Of course Brighton and Jay hadn't cared, but Dante had. He'd always dreamed of running the ranch with Deacon, side by side with the man he loved.

Side by side. And yet, with their love somehow held secret.

Now Deacon really did run the BarChi with the man he loved. But that man wasn't Dante, and there was nothing secret about the way he lived or about how he felt about Aren. The ugly but familiar sting of jealousy throbbed deep in his chest as it always did when he thought of Aren. Dante remembered with painful clarity the day Deacon had kissed Aren in front of everybody. Dante had already known the two were sleeping together, but nothing had hurt him the way that kiss had. Up until that moment, he'd convinced himself Deacon was just using Aren—scratching an itch—but kissing him as he had, right there for all of the BarChi to see? That spoke of more than sex.

That spoke of love.

So now here he was, running a ranch that reeked of death. Aren had Deacon, and Dante was left with nothing so tangible. Sorrow and regret were his constant companions. He grieved for his brother and for the loss of his marriage, if not for the loss of Daisy herself, and he grieved with every fibre of his being for the loss of Deacon.

Of course, he realised now that Deacon had never belonged to him in the first place. Maybe that was the fact he grieved for most of all.

Dante pushed his fingers hard into his eyes, swallowing hard against the familiar lump in his throat. He hated being lost in the past.

He turned and slammed his fist into the cold metal at the base of the frozen windmill. It hurt, but that was the point. It distracted him from his heartache and from the treacherous sting behind his eyes. It was better when he managed to stay busy. Maybe he'd see if Cami needed anything.

He hung his head as headed for the Austin's big house. That was still how he thought of it. The Austin house. The Austin ranch. The big sign over the far gate still had the Austin brand on it, as well as the Austin name.

It wasn't really Dante's ranch, any more than the BarChi had been. It sure as hell didn't feel like home.

Well, he thought with a sigh, *maybe it does.* He hadn't ever been needed back home, and he was hardly needed here either. He'd never been needed anywhere, and the only person who'd ever really wanted him at all had been Daisy. Too bad he hadn't been able to return the favour.

* * * *

Cami wasn't in the kitchen. The room itself smelt heavenly, in a way it hadn't since he'd taken over the ranch. A thick vegetable stew simmered over the fire, and balls of dough sat rising on the counter, so fat and round and tempting Dante had to still his hand from reaching out to pinch them as he'd done when he was a boy. He wondered if Cami would smack his hand with a spoon the way Olsa had.

"Shit," he grumbled to the empty room. "I'll have to thank Aren for sending her." The idea irked him immensely. Yes, Aren had sent Cami. But Aren had Deacon. No matter how well she cooked, it hardly seemed like a fair trade. Dante would have swapped places with the boy in heartbeat, if only Deacon would have had him.

He found Cami on the stairs, trying to manoeuvre an oversized chair he knew had come from her bedroom down the stairway by herself. The passage was narrow, with a ninety-degree turn at the midpoint landing, and she'd somehow managed to wedge the chair in sideways, right where the stairs turned. No matter how much she tugged, it didn't seem inclined to move.

"Why didn't you get one of the men to do that for you?" he asked, as he moved up the stairs to take the chair.

She looked a bit frazzled, her hair flying loose all around her head. Her cheeks were flushed. She stood up and wiped her hand across her brow. "I'm not helpless."

"I didn't say you were. I asked why you didn't ask for help."

"Everybody else was busy. I didn't want to be a bother."

"I was raised on the BarChi," he told her as he grabbed the chair and began to try to yank it free. "It may be true that women had their chores and men had others, and they rarely overlapped, but you better believe if one of those gals needed something, all she had to do was ask. The hands are hired to work. Whether that means working for the ranch owner or working for the wives, it makes no difference."

"I'm not your wife."

"You're missing my point by about a mile." The chair finally came free, and Dante dragged it to the bottom of the stairs. "Where the hell you want it now?"

"Outside, on the front porch."

Why in the world did she think anybody would want to sit on the porch? It wasn't as if they'd be having a nice glass of ice tea or a cool mint julep anytime soon. "You have any idea how cold it is out there?"

She put her hands on her hips and cocked her head back and to the side, the same way Tama always had when he'd challenged her. "You want me to fix the smell or not?"

He knew better than to argue with a woman when she gave him that look. He took the chair to the porch as instructed. The chair from his own room was already there.

"Are there more?" he asked.

She shook her head. "The others are just wood. It's the upholstery on these that's holding the smell. I'll put some saleratus on them and let it sit for a while. That'll help."

"Saleratus? I thought that was for stomach aches. And baking."

"It helps with odours, too."

"How do you know that?"

Her gaze slid away from his, and she pulled the sleeves of her sweater down over her hands and hugged her stomach. "Everybody knows that," she said. He recognised evasiveness when he saw it. Interesting that such a simple question would make her feel threatened. "At any rate, I'll take the curtains down and launder them in it too eventually, but"—she gestured out at the frozen world—"may as well wait until I can hang them out to dry."

"Fair enough. You need help with anything else while I'm here?"

"No, thank you."

"Are you lying?" Partly he was teasing but partly he was thinking how helping Cami would probably mean working in the nice, warm house, which sounded far less miserable than working outside in the freezing cold.

She laughed. It was a sweet, light sound, and once again he was reminded of Tama. "I promise, I'm not."

It figured. She didn't need him either. He tried not to be bothered by it and went back to the barn. There was always shit to be shovelled from stalls, and the barn was the only building on the damn ranch that didn't reek of death. Even manure was preferable to the smell of decomposing bodies.

Once there, he fell into a rhythm that was both familiar and depressing. His daddy had always said that cleaning stalls was a good way to clean one's mind, but Dante had long fostered a love-hate relationship with barns.

As boys, he and Deacon had been inseparable. Jeremiah had raised them as brothers, whether Old Man Pane approved or not. They had shared everything, and so it had seemed only natural that eventually, they shared themselves as well. As boys, they'd discovered each other in the BarChi barn. That was exactly the way Dante labelled it when he looked back—discovered. It had been so innocent, and so pure. Just two boys, two brothers, sharing everything and learning what they each had to give. It had seemed like the most normal thing in the world. Up until his mean old granddad had caught them at it.

The aftermath had been horrible. He'd been so ashamed for so long, and yet he'd never quite understood why. The wounds were old, nothing to show now but a few scars on his back, but barns were the worst. They were all the same—the quiet nicker of horses and the snorting of cows, the soft mew of the kittens in the corner or dogs scruffing in the straw. The smell—not just animals and manure, but also hay, and saddle oil, and the leather tack hanging on the wall, and underneath it all, the earthy musk of birth and milk and new life. It was a smell others associated with warmth and comfort and safety, but for Dante, it meant secrets and shame. If he was busy, birthing a colt or talking with the hands, he could keep his mind on the present. But if he was alone, if he allowed himself to fall too deep into the rhythm of his work, his mind would begin to wander. And inevitably, it would turn to the past, whether he wanted it to or not.

* * * *

For the next two days, things were much the same. They did their chores in a frozen wonderland. For two nights, they ran the generator on coal. Finally, on the fourth day, things began to melt. The wind started to blow at last—not the frozen north wind Dante had expected, but a nice warm breeze from the south. Midway through the morning, the propeller on the windmill broke free of its ice with a crack that echoed across the ranch like a gunshot. The blades creaked and slowly began to turn.

"Thank the Saints for that," Simon said to Dante when it happened. "I was starting to worry about our coal."

Simon wasn't the only one who'd been worried. Zed Austin had let the stocks run a bit low to begin with. Dante had been remiss about restocking them. It was so rarely needed, and especially so early in the year. But if another freeze hit them, they'd all breathe easier with the coal bins full. Dante kicked himself for not realising sooner how low they were.

"Someone'll have to go to town." Dante turned to look at Simon. "You and Frances want to do it?"

Simon scowled at him. "I just got back."

"I know. I'm sorry." It was an eight-day trip to town, round trip. Still, most every hand loved to go, because it meant stopping twice at the McAllen ranch. It was a chance to roll with a woman. Women being in such short supply out on the prairie, men were usually jumping up and down to be the one chosen to make the trip, but he'd found over the last few months that Simon was the exception to the rule. It was another reason Dante sometimes wondered if he and Frances were lovers. "You don't have to go. I sure as hell won't try to make you. But *somebody* has to, and you have seniority. It's up to you."

Simon shook his head. "Nah. Take Frances if you need, but with all these new hands, I think it's best if I stay."

Dante wasn't sure he liked the idea of going to town himself, and especially not with Frances. First of all, it meant going home for the first time since he'd left, and while he missed Tama and Jay and his father, he wasn't looking forward to having to face any of them again. He especially wasn't looking forward to having to face Deacon or Aren.

Going to town also meant two nights at the McAllen ranch. As Jeremiah's son, he was afforded a room in the house for the night, which was better than being in the barn, but he knew damn well Frank McAllen would try to talk him into marrying one of his two remaining daughters. Dante winced at the thought. Uma was too young, and if there was one woman in the world he disliked more than Daisy, it was Beth.

And last but not least, going to town with Frances meant two nights in a shack alone with the boy and his big broad smile and his bright blue eyes. It meant two nights of trying not to think about how easy it would be to lose himself in Frances' young, fit body. It meant two nights of pretending that he wasn't randy as a three-peckered billy goat with a possibly willing partner within arm's reach.

And why not? Why shouldn't he have a couple of nights to take care of things? He'd had a few encounters with men over the years—different hands who'd come and gone. He didn't even remember their names. He only remembered the frantic need that had driven him to it.

But afterwards, he was always plagued by the deep, hateful feeling that he'd failed. At what, even he didn't know, but he knew if he took Frances with him, he'd end up having that feeling again.

He sighed. Maybe he could take one of the other boys instead, even if they were green. Or he could take Foster, although the idea of spending time with that man wasn't exactly appealing either, albeit for different reasons.

The obvious answer was to go alone, but he was afraid he'd be tempted to do what he'd done before. That didn't bear thinking about.

Cami wasn't in the kitchen as he expected. He could hear a strange, rhythmic thumping sound, and he followed it out of the kitchen, through the living room, and onto the front porch, where Cami was using a broom to beat the last of the selaratus from the cushions on the chairs.

"You need anything from town?"

She turned to look at him in surprise. "Somebody's going back already?"

"Looks like it."

She put the end of the broom on the floor and leaned on the handle, the way he'd seen a billion hands do with pitchforks over the years. "Who's going?"

"Looks like it'll be me."

She looked a bit alarmed at that. "Is Simon staying?"

"He is." His answer seemed to come as a bit of a relief, but she still seemed uneasy. "Something wrong?"

"No." But she was suddenly trying to tug the longs sleeves of her sweater down over her hands—a habit that was made significantly more difficult by the broom she held.

"I can tell you're lying."

She stilled her hands with obvious effort. She glanced towards the barracks, and although she still didn't answer, he realised he didn't need her to.

"You don't trust the men."

"Not all of them, no."

"You don't think Simon will protect you?"

"I'm sure he'll try."

He didn't need to ask for clarification. Yes, Simon could try. But there were six hands, not counting him and Frances, and there was no way Simon could do the work that needed to be done while babysitting all six of those men every hour of every day.

"Would you rather come with me?"

She frowned, not as if she didn't like the idea, but as if it hadn't occurred to her. "But there's the cooking," she said. "I don't know if I should."

"I didn't ask if you should. I asked if you'd rather."

She looked at him, chewing thoughtfully on her lip. A slow smile spread across her face. "I think I would rather."

"Good," he said, smiling back, "then I think you should."

Chapter Four

They left the next morning, just after breakfast. Cami left behind a giant pot of oatmeal, another of stew, several loaves of bread, some ham and cornbread, and a fresh-made batch of cottage cheese that Dante bet had been gone about five minutes after he and Cami were out the door.

"I hope they don't get too hungry," she said.

Her concern for a group of grown men made Dante laugh. Yes, the meals were better with her around, but it wasn't as if they were incapable of feeding themselves. "Don't worry. There's always pickles."

She wore a pair of the wide-legged trousers that maids often wore, although like her skirts, they ended a bit short of her ankles. She hugged her strange sweater around her and closed her eyes, leaning back to let the sun bathe her face. She seemed happy. Then again, she usually did.

She was quiet early in the day, but as the sun made its way across the sky, she began to talk. Shyly, at first. Seemingly random things.

"See those flowers?" she asked at one point. "The purple ones? They're not native to Oestend."

"Then where'd they come from?"

"They came across with the settlers. Not on purpose, but they started growing shortly after the settlers arrived. They're kind of pretty, but not really very useful. The Old People tried to weed them out, but it's a hardy little plant. Now it's everywhere."

"How do you know all that?"

She didn't answer. She shrugged and turned away to stare off into the prairie.

It went on like that. She'd start talking, telling him something, and then suddenly, it would be as if she'd hit upon a story she didn't know how to tell, and she'd just stop without a word. Still, he began to piece together a clearer picture of her past.

She was an only child. She'd been born in Oestend and had grown up in the eastern port city of Francshire. Her mother had died giving birth, and her father never spoke of her. She'd had a stepmother who she'd adored, but who had died of the fever when Cami was ten. Her father ran Francshire's largest fish market.

"That's how I knew about the saleratus," she told him. "The only thing that smells worse than dead people is dead fish."

It sounded as if her father was one of Francshire's more respected businessmen. It seemed he had a decent amount of money, which made Dante wonder why she was out here on the prairie, taking care of ranch hands instead of set up in a nice comfortable house in Francshire. She talked a lot about cooking and about household things. It seemed she'd spent a lot of time in the kitchen with the maids, learning to cook and helping with the sewing, but her father hadn't liked that.

"Why not?" Dante asked. "What else would he have you do?"

She shrugged again and turned away, and he had the feeling of having walked into a wall. He could have prodded, but he didn't. She had a right to her secrets. The Saints knew he had a few, too.

They arrived at the shack that served as the halfway point between the BarChi and the Austin ranch. It was small, equipped with bunk beds, a table and a few simple wooden chairs. A pot-bellied wood-burning stove provided heat, and a small generator in the back kept the wraiths at bay. There was no well, and no privy except the woods.

She'd brought dried beef and biscuits along for supper, as well as a jug of water. After they finished, he went outside to start the generator.

The last time he'd been here, he'd been sick with heartache. Banished from the BarChi, shamed by his own jealous actions, betrayed by his wife, hated by the man he loved. When he'd left the BarChi to claim the Austin ranch as his own, he'd made sure to go alone. He'd sat in the small, silent cabin, all by himself.

And he'd let the night come.

He'd waited for death, hoping for that ultimate release from the mess he'd made of his life. He'd wondered if it would be fast or slow. He'd wondered if, as he took his last gasping breath, he'd regret not having turned on the generator. He'd wondered how long his body would lie in the cabin and who would finally find him.

He'd wondered if Deacon would mourn him.

Eventually, he'd fallen asleep, and much to his dismay, he'd woken again the next morning, very much alive.

He should have gone on then, but he hadn't. He couldn't face those men at the Austin ranch. He didn't know how much they knew. More importantly, he couldn't face a future away from his home. The BarChi brand seemed to burn on his arm as it had so many years ago when his brother had pushed the scalding metal to his flesh. He'd wear that brand for the rest of his life, a reminder of what he'd lost.

If he'd had a gun with him that trip, he would have used it. He would have walked out into the woods, so as not to make a mess in the cabin, and he would have put the barrel in his mouth. But there was no such easy way out.

That night, he hadn't even gone inside. He'd dug out the jug of whisky he and Brighton had stashed in the wood pile only a year before. He'd sat on the ground in front of the cabin. And he'd waited.

Still, the wraiths hadn't come. Finally, when the bottle was long empty and the moon had set, he'd walked into the woods. He'd raged at the heavens and the Saints. He'd sworn and screamed and begged the wraiths to take him. But once again, they'd refused to oblige.

In the end, he'd fallen to the ground and wept. He'd wept as he hadn't done since he was a boy. Not since that fateful day so long ago when his granddaddy had caught him in the barn with Deacon and beaten him bloody. He'd wept for that boy, who had lay bleeding in the straw, wondering what exactly he'd done wrong. He'd wept for Deacon, who he'd always loved, but never had the balls to claim. He'd wept for his father, who had been hurt, and for Brighton, who was dead. He'd thought about Aren. Dante wanted to hate him, but when he'd thought about the things he'd done in an attempt to drive him off, he was ashamed. He'd gone into Aren's house. He'd destroyed Aren's things. He'd shredded Aren's art. And the worst part was, it had felt so justified at the time.

That was what Dante had wept for the most—for what he'd allowed himself to become. There had been so many factors at play—his rage and his jealousy and his inadequacy as a husband. His impotence with women and his fear of allowing himself to be with men. His shame. More than anything, the shame of it all.

He'd finally accepted that the wraiths weren't going to come. Dante had dragged himself inside and fallen, exhausted, into one of the beds. When he'd woken the next morning, he'd been wrung out. Resigned. Empty.

It had been months since the wraiths had denied him his death. He'd started to rebuild his life, but he still ached every day for what he'd lost. Could he stand to face Deacon again? To look him in the eye after what he'd done?

"Are you going to start that thing or let the wraiths take us?" Cami called from inside.

Good question. If he'd been alone, he might have decided to tempt them once more, but Cami was here. She was depending on him. "The wraiths don't want me," he said to himself.

He started the generator and went inside.

It turned out Cami had brought one more thing with her—a small, metal flask. She was sipping from it. Her cheeks were already a bit pink. She offered it to him, and he accepted. He expected whisky, which might have brought back even more painful memories of his last night here, but it was something else—something fruity, but still strong enough to burn all the way down when he swallowed.

"We could play poker," he told her as he handed it back. "Except the deck's been missing three cards for a few years now."

She shook her head. "I always lose."

He sat down in one of the chairs. It creaked under his weight as he leant back and stretched his legs towards the stove.

"Are you happy to be going home?"

He shook his head. "Not really."

She sat with her legs folded in front of her. She picked absently at the hem of her pant leg. "I feel like I should tell you something." She glanced up at him, her eyes wary. "I know Daisy."

Whatever he'd expected her to say, it hadn't been that. He hung his head and covered his eyes with his hand so he didn't have to face her. "You know her how?"

"From The Chalice. She works there now, you know."

"Spreading her legs was the one thing she was good at." The words were out of his mouth before he had time to think about what they might mean to Cami, who'd worked as a whore herself, but when he looked over at her, she didn't seem upset.

"She's the one who told me about Aren and Deacon and the BarChi." She hesitated. "And about you."

"So you talked to Daisy *and* to Aren, and you still wanted to come out to the Austin ranch and work for me?" He shook his head. "You must have been desperate."

She scrunched up her nose, pursing her lips in confusion. "Aren had nothing bad to say about you."

"Really?"

"He didn't say much, really, but he promised you wouldn't rape me."

It surprised him. It proved once again that Aren was a better man than Dante. "Certainly Daisy wasn't so kind."

She laughed. "No, she wasn't, but I learned right away I couldn't trust everything she said. It wasn't as if she lied, you know, but I had the impression she embellished things." She looked at him, as if trying to decide how much more to say. "She said she loved you, but that your marriage ended because you couldn't quit loving somebody who would never love you back."

"That's true."

"Who was it?"

"She didn't tell you?"

She shook her head. "I think that would have been admitting some kind of defeat. She wasn't exactly proud of having been rejected by you."

Dante was relieved she'd kept that detail to herself, no matter her reasons.

"She said you beat her."

He sighed and put his head in his hands.

"Is it true?"

"Yes," he said. "And no."

"It's one or the other, Dante."

"Twice."

"Twice, you beat her?"

"Twice, I slapped her." The first time had been early in their marriage, when he'd first caught her lifting her skirt for a ranch hand. When he'd confronted her, she'd laughed in his face. "At least *he* knows what a cock is for," she'd said. He'd smacked her, and he'd regretted it right away. He hadn't been raised to mistreat women, and he hated that he'd let his rage get the best of him.

After that, he'd learned to keep his distance. He'd learned through the years how she liked to goad him and bait him, so he'd turned his rage on other things. Mostly furniture. Every chair he broke, his daddy made him replace. He'd become an expert at building the damn things.

The other time he'd struck her had been near the end, when she'd nearly blurted out the secret of his desire for Deacon. He'd regretted that, too.

Just one more regret to add to the list.

Cami hadn't responded. When he looked up again, he was surprised to see a bit of amusement on her face.

"How long were you married?" she asked.

"Nearly eleven years."

She laughed. "Hell, I knew her three weeks and I wanted to slap her at least that many times."

He wanted to laugh too, but he couldn't. "It was wrong."

"It was," she agreed. "The world is full of wrong."

* * * *

Driving into the BarChi the next day was the hardest thing he'd ever done. There had been no way to send word that they were on their way, so everybody was bound to look out to see exactly who was coming down the road. No doubt Deacon and Aren would both groan and turn away. The hands? He had no idea what they knew. Jay would be pleased. His father would be kind, but perhaps distant because Dante had brought so much misery on them all. He was tempted to turn around and go right back to the Austin ranch.

The one thing that kept him headed forward was the thought of seeing Tama.

As he pulled his wagon into the courtyard, he saw Deacon coming out of the kitchen. Deacon's jaw clenched, and he turned away without even a nod. Dante tried to pretend that didn't hurt. Deacon ducked his head back into the kitchen, talking to somebody inside, and the next minute, Tama was running out the door, practically knocking Deacon over as she pushed past him.

Whatever reservations Dante had were eclipsed for the moment by the joy of seeing her. He jumped out of the wagon and caught her in the air as she threw her arms around his neck.

"You're here! I was so afraid you'd never come home!"

"Didn't exactly want to, but here I am anyway."

"Holy Saints, I hate you so much for leaving!"

He laughed and hugged her tighter. He kissed the side of her head. Years earlier, when their friendship had first begun, Jay had been jealous, but he'd quickly realised he needn't be. Tama was a perfectly faithful wife, and Dante had never desired her anyway. Their relationship had always been close, but also innocent.

"How's life up on that ranch?" Tama asked.

He wanted to say a thousand things at once, some that were true, and some that weren't—it's lonely, it stinks, it's fine, it's perfect. But what popped into his head first and foremost was how quickly he'd learned to appreciate the work the women on the BarChi did. He laughed as he let her go, but he did exactly as he'd vowed. He got down on his knees and pulled her close, although it meant bumping his head into her stomach and knocking his hat backward onto the ground. "I want you to know, I'll never sit down to a meal again without thanking the cook. And I thank the Saints for you every time I milk the damn cows. And I think of you every single time I have to put on dirty shorts."

She laughed and smacked playfully at the top of his head. "Well, it's about time for that first one, and the second, but the thing about your shorts is just disturbing."

He laughed and stood up to hug her again. It was amazing how something as simple as laughing with Tama could take away so much of the anguish he'd been living with. He hadn't quite realised how empty he'd felt.

Jay appeared next to shake Dante's hand, and their father was close behind. Jeremiah surprised him by pulling him into a strong bear hug. "I'm awful glad you're home, son."

It all felt more natural than he'd expected, and Dante sighed in relief. He'd expected to feel like an outcast, but really, it felt just as it always had. Tama's boys were there, although only for a moment before they went back to whatever game they were playing. Some of the hands stepped in to say hello. Not all of them, of course, but a couple, like Red and Ronin, who'd been around for a while. They shook his hand or slapped his back and moved on.

Dante noticed Aren come out of the barn. The young man glanced warily at Dante, but didn't approach him. Instead, he went straight to Cami. She'd been standing off to the side, looking lost and awkward and completely alone. Dante felt bad for having forgotten her, but Aren hadn't. Cami smiled when she saw him. She hugged him, and he put his arm around her waist and led her away, towards the main house.

Deacon was nowhere to be seen.

"How long are you staying?" Tama asked. "Just here for a few days."

"Just tonight and then a night on our way back. Headed to town for supplies."

They all looked surprised at that, and he couldn't blame them. Simon had been through less than two weeks before. "Coal got low," he explained. "That cold snap froze the windmill solid. Just about burned through what we had."

His father and Jay stared blankly at him, obviously confused, but Tama laughed and swatted him with the towel she had in her hand. "Now, really," she said. "The truth this time."

Now it was his turn to be confused. "I'm serious. That freeze had us running on reserves for one night, and on coal for two more. Still have a bit left, but not enough to last if we get another storm like that."

Now they were more than confused. They were beginning to glance awkwardly at each other, as if asking, "*Do you know what he's talking about*?"

"Ya'll didn't have a freeze here?"

"This time of year?" Tama asked.

"I sure as hell didn't imagine it! We were walking on ice for three days! Frances started talking about some fancy boots he had back on the continent with sleigh runners on them!"

Clearly, the wrong thing to say. Now they were looking at him as if he were downright crazy. "Ask Cami!" he said at last. Except, unfortunately, Cami was already inside with Aren.

"Well," Tama said finally, "whatever the reason, we're glad you're home."

He had supper in the dining room with his family. The room seemed so much bigger now than it had before. In years past, it had held Jeremiah, his three sons, their wives, and the four boys. On occasion, Deacon had joined them, depending on his frame of mind. On Sundays, even the hands squeezed in at the table with them. But this time, there was only Dante, Jay, Jeremiah, Alissa, who sat without saying a word, Tama, and her two sons.

The two boys were begging to be allowed to work the ranch with the hands, but were recalcitrant about doing the chores they'd actually been assigned. That was ever the way of small boys on ranches. Jay talked of an elk he'd brought down while hunting two weeks before. There was gossip from town—about Daisy working at The Chalice, about some of the hands who'd been kicked out of the tavern in Milton and told to never come back, and about a man visiting from the East who was offering a ridiculously large reward for the return of his missing son. Alissa and Tama also hinted that they suspected their sister Beth was in a bad way, because Frank McAllen was desperately trying to marry her off. Jeremiah laughingly told Dante how Frank had promised everything he owned as dowry if Dante would take the girl off his hands. He was glad his dad had known well enough to turn the man down.

They talked more of the ice storm. Dante was stunned to learn that the BarChi had experienced nothing out of the ordinary.

"A bit less windy than usual," Tama said. "But it was nice."

"How could that be?" Dante asked. "I'm telling you, it was cold! We had ice everywhere. The windmill was frozen solid!"

But nobody had any answers.

They'd long since finished their meal and the boys were trying to hide their frequent yawns when

Deacon came in. He looked as he always did—big and strong, his hat pushed low on his head and his long dark hair in a queue down his back. The room fell silent when he entered.

He looked right at Dante. "I need to talk to you."

Everybody else stood up, whether out of respect for Deacon or because they didn't want to witness an argument Dante didn't know. Chairs scraped across the floor and dishes clanked together as they quickly cleared the table and headed for the door. Jeremiah stopped and said a few words to Deacon, too low for Dante to hear. Deacon shook his head and said something back. Jeremiah seemed pleased with the answer. He clapped Deacon on the back, then gave Dante what was probably supposed to be a reassuring wink.

And then they were alone.

In the past, Dante would have been thrilled to have a few moments of Deacon's time, but not now. Not after everything Dante had done.

Deacon sat down in a chair facing Dante. He leant back and crossed his arms over his chest.

"I didn't come to cause trouble," Dante said.

"I figured as much. Thing is, seems like trouble comes along with you more often than not."

Dante didn't answer that. What could he say? He looked down at his hands, clenched between his knees.

"Jeremiah says you need coal."

"That's right."

"That it?"

The question confused him. "You mean, is that the only reason I'm here?"

"No, I mean is that all you need from town? Just the coal?"

"That, and whatever Cami needs—"

"Aren's talked to Cami already. He's got that all squared away."

Aren. Of course Aren had it covered. Aren was always working to make Dante obsolete.

"Look, we'll be out of your hair tomorrow—"

"Stop being defensive and listen. Aren and I were already fixing to go to town tomorrow. He's got stuff he's got to do with the bank and the merchants." He waved his hand as if whatever it was Aren was doing was a bit beyond him. "Account things to settle regarding money Zed Austin owed, and something to do with a dowry that ain't a dowry for Alissa, and the Saints know what else. Stuff he don't trust me to do right, so he wants to go. We're also taking about two dozen head in to sell, but Aren ain't no help at all when it comes to driving cattle, so I have Red and Ronin set to go with us."

Dante was surprised to hear a ghost of a smile in Deacon's voice. When he looked up, he found Deacon had relaxed a bit. He was still leaning back in his chair, away from Dante, but he'd taken his hat off. It hung on the arm of his chair.

"With you gone, and Simon and Frances too, Red and Ronin are about the best hands I got, and you know those fools, so you know how sad a statement that is. But they got seniority, and they're both so damn randy I'm starting to fear for my cows. If I tell them no now, I won't hear the end of it 'til next spring. That means the only person here to watch the men is Jay." He smiled a bit, and Dante found himself tempted to do the same. "And we both know he's soft."

"So what do you propose?"

"You stay here. Ride those hands. You can be a hardass better than Jay. Keep them in line for me. I'll take your wagon. Saints know Aren can barely ride a horse to save his life, but he has learned to drive a team a bit. We'll bring back your coal, and the things Cami needs, and you can have a few days to catch up with your kin."

It was a generous offer for him to make. Sure, he probably had his own reasons, specifically his desire to not having Dante tagging along with he and Aren for their days away, but nonetheless, he could have been a jerk about it. Instead, he seemed to be trying to make peace.

"I'd appreciate that," Dante said. "What about Cami?"

"She says Olsa gives her the creeps, but she'd rather stay here with you than spend four more days bumping down the road. So," he said as he stood up, "we got a deal?"

Dante stood up too, so he wouldn't have to strain his neck to look up at Deacon. As always, he found himself a bit in awe of the man. He had to force himself to speak. "Deal."

"Good." Deacon picked his hat up and pushed it onto his head as he turned to go.

"Deacon?"

He stopped, turning halfway to look back over his shoulder.

"Thank you."

"Don't thank me. It was Aren's idea."

Chapter Five

Simon had felt the weight of Frances' gaze upon him for two days. Ever since Dante and Cami had left. "Why didn't he send you?" Frances had asked.

"Because I didn't want to go."

Frances hadn't asked why at the time, just as he hadn't asked so many times before. The boy never prodded. It was one of the things Simon loved about him. It was why he'd allowed their friendship to grow. But it seemed they'd reached the point in their friendship where evasion was beginning to feel like betrayal. This was a topic Simon had avoided too emphatically and for too long. He felt he owed Frances an explanation, yet he had no idea how to go about giving one.

"Will you stop looking at me like that?" he finally snapped. It was the end of the day and they were in the barracks. The other hands were all there, but none of them were paying attention to Frances and Simon.

"Looking at you like what?" Frances asked, and Simon could tell from the boy's expression that he didn't realise exactly how obvious he'd been.

Simon sat down on the bed. He put his elbows on his knees and leant forward to stare at the floor. "Just ask already."

A moment of stunned silence, and then Frances asked the question Simon had known was coming. "Why don't you like to go to town?"

Simon put his head in his hands. Even though he'd known what the question would be, he still wasn't sure he was ready to answer it.

"The thing is," Frances went on, "if it were just since we'd been here, I'd get it. It's a long trip. But you were like this at the BarChi, too, and…"

It wasn't silent in the room, but Simon felt Frances' silence like a weight on his back. "And…?" he prodded.

"Well…" Frances' voice was quieter than before, pitched low so nobody else could hear. "It seems like it's not town. It seems like it's more about what's in between."

What's in between. The McAllen ranch. Frances had hit the bull's-eye with that one.

Simon propped his chin on his hands and looked up at Frances. "If I asked you to drop this, would you do it?"

Frances' cheeks turned red. Simon could read his eyes—hurt at first, as if he'd been slapped, but then thoughtfulness.

"Yes," he said at last, turning away. "I'm sorry I asked."

If he'd dug in his heels and pushed, Simon would have been able to be defensive, but that wasn't Frances' way, which was why Simon valued his friendship as much as he did. He sighed. "Come here, kid. Sit down."

Frances did, sitting close to him on the bunk as he always did so they could talk. "I'm sorry," Frances said again. "It's not my place."

"Not always easy to figure out where the line is between friendship and privacy."

Frances took a moment to digest that. It seemed to give him confidence. "I've noticed how even when we're there, you never go with any of the girls. You always share a stall with me. Of course, I never go with them either, but I'm pretty sure our reasons aren't the same."

Simon wasn't looking at Frances, but he heard the tiny note of hope in the boy's voice. "No. They're not the same."

"I figured." His disappointment probably wouldn't have been detectable by anybody who didn't know him so well. "So then, what is it?"

It took Simon a long time to figure out how to say the words. He wasn't a man who was used to sharing. Especially not anything so personal as this. He'd only told the story once before. That had been to Garrett, and he'd been sensationally drunk. But now, he felt the need to pick his words carefully.

Frances waited, not saying a word. That was another thing Simon had always liked about him. He was infinitely patient.

Where to begin? The answer, it seemed, was at the beginning. "There was a girl."

Four words. How could four words hurt so much to say? If he'd had to do it again, he wasn't sure he'd have been able, but it seemed as if now he'd begun, he had no choice but to go on.

"I was young. Only eighteen when I met her. Her father owned the mercantile in Holtshire." He stopped short. "You know where that is?"

"On the coast, I think? South of Francshire?"

"Right. It's a fishing town. I was fresh off the ship from Lanstead. Didn't know a soul, but I got a job on a fishing boat. Went in the store to buy a new knife, and she was there. The minute I saw her, I said, 'That girl's going to be my wife.'"

He remembered it clearly—Lena's big eyes alight in her face, and the innocently flirtatious look she'd given him when he'd asked if she had a beau. It had seemed so simple at the time.

"I courted her for several months, and we were stupid in love. But she was a good girl, wore her Saint's medal on a chain around her neck every single day, so it was just courting. We kissed, but she never let me go no further than that." And if at times his desire for her had seemed like more than he could bear, it had also been part of what made her so alluring.

He had to take a deep breath before he could say the next bit. "We got engaged, and I can't tell you how happy I was. But then three weeks to the day before we were supposed to be married, she was raped." He had to hold very still as he said the words. He had to hang onto the edge of the bunk, just to keep himself grounded. "My ship was due in, and she went down to the docks to meet me, but we were late and three dockhands got her first."

He shook his head, remembering the helplessness and the rage he'd felt. Three men, gone before anybody found her huddled and sobbing in the alley. "My eyes were closed," she'd said over and over, when they tried to ask who'd done it. "My eyes were closed." Like a mantra, as if it might have protected her.

"Oh, Simon, that's so awful!"

Simon nodded, because it was all he could do. At the time, he'd known about rape in theory, but he hadn't realised the ruthless horror of the act or its brutality. It had never occurred to him how some men used their desire as a weapon, or how they looked at women as tools rather than people, just something to be used. He began to realise then how vulnerable women were, just living day to day. How they were dependent upon men, at their mercy, and instead of helping, some men took advantage in the worst ways. And the damage it did was more than he could ever have imagined. "That kind of thing," he said to Frances, making himself move on, "it does something to women. They may walk away, but I think it kills something inside of them. Maybe not all of them, I guess, but it did for her. I didn't know right away." But he'd learned. He'd had plenty of time over the years to think about it.

"Did they ever catch them?"

Simon shook his head. "When we went to the magistrate to ask for help, he said, 'She was on the dock. Everybody knows what kind of woman loiters by the shipyard.'"

Repeating those words made the horrible anger rise up again in his breast, as hot and strong as it had been that day. He'd flown at the man, determined to wring his flabby white neck, but his shipmates, the ones who were trying to help, had stopped him. They'd had to drag him away.

He sighed, swallowing the anger. He was heading down the wrong path, he knew, letting his rage at what had happened distract him from the real story. He rubbed his temples with his fingers, making himself move back to what mattered most.

"Her father had no idea what to do. Neither did I. It wasn't just that she was hurt. She was embarrassed. And *ashamed*. I never understood that, but she was."

"Did you still marry her?"

"I did. She swore she wanted to go through with it, but things were never really the same."

Lena had never been the same. That was the point he couldn't quite bring himself to expound on. She was like a flower that had wilted. As if the light inside her had gone out. She turned in on herself. She'd sit, lost in her head for hours. He'd try to talk to her and realise she hadn't heard him at all. "I'm fine," she'd say, if he dared to ask. "My eyes were closed."

"Simon?" Frances asked quietly, and Simon realised he'd been sitting silent for too long, lost inside his head as Lena had so often been in those days.

"I don't know what I thought would happen. I guess I didn't think about it much at all. I loved her, and she said she wanted to be married. I thought I'd be able to protect her after that. It sounds stupid, but it seemed so right in my head. We'd be married, and after that, everything would be fine."

It was hard to admit how naïve he'd been. He'd honestly thought being married would fix it. He'd thought the light would come back into her eyes. He thought she'd remember how to laugh.

"Our wedding night was…" He found his hands were shaking, and he had to stop and breathe deep. She'd been stiff in his arms as he'd kissed her. He'd been so gentle, and so patient, but when he finally began to undo the buttons on the back of her gown, she'd become hysterical. She'd screamed in terror and flailed at him with her fists. "No, no, no!" she'd cried over and over again. Her blows had been weak at best. Her fear of him was what hurt.

"It was a disaster," he said at last. "But I understood. I swore I'd be patient. That it was fine if we took our time. We moved into the house her father had bought us as our wedding present. It was tiny, but it was more than I could afford on my own. There were two bedrooms, one for us, I thought, and one for the babies we'd have. But it turned out she'd had one set up for her and the other for me. After what had happened, how could I argue? I figured, it was just a matter of time before she started to feel safe. I could be patient."

Yes, he'd wanted to be patient, but days had turned into weeks, and weeks had turned into months, and still he'd been barred from her room every night. But that wasn't the worst of it. The worst was the way she'd pulled even further away. It was as if she hated him for desiring her. She wouldn't look at him. She'd barely speak to him. At supper, they'd sit at the table together, and she'd stare silently down at her plate. She rarely ate. He began to notice how her clothes hung on her frame.

In the weeks leading up to the wedding, he'd imagined comforting her, but he'd assumed he'd be allowed to touch her. Not sexually at first, but at the very least to hold her in his arms. But as the days of their marriage ticked by, she began to pull away from the simplest of touches. If he tried to kiss her, she'd get angry. Even a hand on her wrist would cause her to pull away as if stung.

"I'll be patient," he'd told her again and again. "I can wait."

But waiting was easier said than done.

"The thing is," he said, finally picking up his story, "I was barely nineteen. I know that's a flimsy excuse, but Saints, I was getting desperate." He thought suddenly about who he was talking to, and he almost laughed. "Hell, you're about that age now. You know what I mean."

"Boy, do I ever."

Frances' answer really did make him laugh, if only for a moment. It helped him face the truth of what came next.

"Well, there was this girl, Jin. She and Lena had been good friends before it all, but by this point, Lena didn't really have any friends. She didn't talk to anybody, and Jin stuck around the longest, but she didn't know how to help any more than I did. They'd been friends since they was girls, and Jin told me how she couldn't bear to see Lena just sitting there, like an empty shell.

"Anyway, one night, Jin came over and we talked. And then another night. And another night, too."

"Oh," Frances breathed. It wasn't even a word so much as a sound of realisation. A sigh that meant, "Oh no, I see what's coming."

Simon went on as if he hadn't heard, because he was near the end now. He was almost through to the other side where he'd be able to breathe again. "Well, then one night she came over with this bottle of cherry wine. We drank that, and when it was gone, we started on some whisky. And then…"

It hadn't even been that he'd desired her. She wasn't attractive. What had done him in was simply the fact that she was so unbelievably *willing*. After so many times of Lena pushing him back, turning away, closing the door…suddenly, there had been Jin. She could barely get her skirt up fast enough. He could remember so clearly the way she'd clutched at him, the way her legs had been wrapped tight around his hips, the way she'd panted into his ear, "Take me, Simon. Take me, take me, take me."

And he had. And it had been glorious. That was the part he hated the most. If he could look back and say he hadn't followed through, or that he hadn't enjoyed it, or even that he'd had a moment of guilt before he lost himself in her flesh, it might have been different. But the truth was, he'd been nineteen, horny and frustrated as hell. Fucking Jin had been momentous. For the first time in weeks, he'd felt vital and alive. Jin hadn't been a virgin. There was no doubt in his mind. She'd lain back, panting and crying his name as he'd fucked her, and he'd loved every single second of it.

Right up until Lena walked through the door.

"I was drunk, and I was a fool, and I wasn't noticing how much noise we were making until Lena caught us. The way she looked at me. It was pure hatred, not just 'cause I'd broken my marriage vow to her, but like what I was doing with Jin was the same as what those men had done to her.

"I spent the whole next day outside her door. I apologised, and then I begged. And then I got defensive and angry. I can't even tell you all the awful things I said, telling her it was her fault I'd cheated. Calling her frigid." He shook his head. "I'm not proud of that. Finally, I went to bed. Thing is, my boat was leaving the next morning. She'd quit working at her father's shop, and we were barely getting by on what I made. I sure as hell couldn't afford to miss it. So I left. It was a three-day trip, out and back, and when I finally got home, I went to her door, and I knocked. And for the first time ever, she said, 'Come in.'" He shook his head. He'd shed his tears long ago, but it still caused his heart to ache. "She had the fever. Seeing her there, I realised how much she'd changed from that girl I'd vowed to marry so many months before. I'd known she was barely eating, but seeing her there wearing just a nightgown, I realised she was just bone."

"It's not your fault," Frances said. "I know that's what you think, but what happened with Jin has nothing to do with the fever."

"It *was* my fault for not being a better husband. It was my fault for not realising how weak she was. It was my fault that I hurt her, and then I left, and she just lay there in her bed, wasting away of fever. If I'd done better, she might not have got sick at all."

"She died." It wasn't a question.

"Two days later. I missed my next boat and lost my job, but I didn't care. I sat there, and I apologised until my voice was gone. I begged her to stay. I begged her to get better. I promised her the world—everything I could think of. We'd leave Holtshire. I told her we could leave Oestend, that I'd take her back to the continent, because she'd always wanted to see Lanstead. And at the very end, when I realised she was never going to get out of that bed, I sobbed and I told her I'd never love another woman again."

"Simon—"

"I told her I'd never be with another woman again."

He took a deep breath and let it out, relieved to finally be done. He felt torn up and wrung out. He would have killed for a drink.

"You were nineteen," Frances said at last. "I don't think she would expect you to—"

"It doesn't matter! It doesn't matter what she expected! What matters is what I vowed. What matters is what was in my heart when I said the words. Don't tell me I have a right to break that vow just 'cause I get horny."

Frances didn't answer. They sat in silence for what seemed an impossibly long time. Finally, Frances stood up. He went to the rough wooden cabinet that held his things. He reached way in the back, digging behind shirts and worn boots, and he pulled out a bottle of whisky. He put it gently in Simon's hands. It was as if the boy had read Simon's mind.

He sat back down where he'd been, and Simon took a swig from the bottle. Then another. "So?" Frances said cautiously. "*Never* since you were nineteen?"

Simon wanted to smile at that. But he also wanted to cry. "Not 'never.' I've failed. More times than I want to say. But not for quite a few years. And not since I found the BarChi."

"It's no coincidence you're out here on the back end of nowhere with no women in sight, is it?"

"It sure ain't."

Simon took another drink. He knew Frances was trying to figure out how to put his thoughts into words. He could tell by the way Frances sat, next to him on the bunk as always, but turned towards him, one leg tucked underneath himself.

"It was my fault when Miron died," Frances said at last. His tone was matter-of-fact. He never balked at the dark stain on his past. He faced it head-on, every time it arose. "I don't know where I'd be in this world right now if weren't for you. You saved my life."

The words sounded dramatic, but Simon knew Frances meant them. They'd had this talk before, and Simon knew not to argue. But then Frances surprised him by veering into a new conversation.

"Simon, I think you know how I feel about you. I know it probably makes you uncomfortable, but I don't want to lie." His voice shook as he said the words, but his eyes remained steady on Simon's. "I know you don't feel the same way about me, and you probably never will, and that's all right. I don't expect that to change. I guess I just want you to know that I think the good you've done far outweighs the bad."

Frances' smile was shy. He hesitated a heartbeat, then leaned closer. Simon held very still, a bit afraid of where things were going, but unwilling to do anything that might make Frances regret what he'd just said. Frances touched the side of Simon's head, gently pushing his hair back out of the way, then Frances leaned closer still, and Simon felt the boy's lips against his ear. "I love you," he whispered. And then Frances kissed him there, just in front of his ear. "I'm awfully glad you came to the back end of nowhere."

The confession caused a small lump to form in Simon's throat. It wasn't because Frances was admitting his feelings so much as because the boy was exposing his soul, exactly as Simon had just done. Simon had given Frances his deepest, darkest secret, and Frances was responding in kind. He was letting Simon know that they had equal stakes in their friendship.

Frances sat back slowly. Simon saw the way his hands shook. He saw the fear in Frances' eyes. This secret was the greatest gift Frances had to give, and he was afraid it would be rejected, or worse, that it would cost him their friendship.

"Thanks, kid," Simon said. Frances was right. Simon wasn't in love with him and he knew he never would be, but he cared for him more than Frances probably knew. He appreciated having somebody he could trust with his secrets as well as his life.

He looked down at the bottle of whisky in his hand. It was tempting to drink it all and spend the day being numb, but he knew from experience it wouldn't help.

He'd end up lost in the past, thinking of all the things he should have done differently.

"Come on," Frances said suddenly as he stood up. "Let's get out of here."

"And go where?"

"Swimming."

"Are you nuts? There's still chores to do, and—"

"Fuck 'em."

It was so unlike him, it made Simon laugh out loud. "Are you serious?"

"We're always the responsible ones. We deserve a day off. Nobody will even know." Frances smiled at him, his blue eyes bright with a challenge. "I bet I can skip a rock twice as far as you."

Simon laughed. "Not a chance, kid."

"Only one way to find out."

Simon weighed his options. Frances was right. Nothing too bad could come from him taking an afternoon off, and it sure beat the idea of getting drunk and letting ancient regrets get the best of him.

"You're on," he said to Frances. "Lead the way."

Chapter Six

Dante's old bedroom felt full of ghosts.

It was still the same room. The same bed he'd shared with Daisy, usually both of them trying to ignore the person on the other side. There was an armoire, now mostly empty, and a rocking chair he'd built for her when they were first married. He remembered her saying, "It'll be a perfect place to rock the baby to sleep."

Except, of course, there hadn't ever been any babies. Not for he and Daisy, at any rate, but she'd sat in that chair many times, listening to their nephews cry in the neighbouring rooms. Dante had felt the weight of her gaze on him.

He left the room and its ghosts behind. He went down to the kitchen, hoping to find Tama. He did find her, but just as he stepped into the kitchen from the hallway, Cami and Aren walked into it from the outside.

Dante stopped dead in the doorway. It would be rude to turn around and walk away. Then again, they both knew they didn't want to see each other. Why pretend otherwise?

Aren's normally golden-pale skin turned pink, and Dante had a feeling he was thinking the same thing, wondering if he could bolt and have it appear casual. The two women stood there watching—Tama tense and Cami seemingly confused at the sudden awkwardness in the room.

"Hello," Dante said at last.

"I'm sorry," Aren said.

It was a strange thing for him to say, and the sudden deepening of his blush indicated that he thought so too.

I'm sorry, too, Dante thought. But not for the same things.

Aren cleared his throat and turned to indicate Cami, standing behind him. "Last time Cami came through it was only for one night, and she stayed downstairs, in Gordon's old room. But since this time you'll be here for several days, I thought maybe we could find her something more comfortable."

Aren's suggestion annoyed Dante at first—not because it didn't make sense, but because it *did*. Because, as always, Aren seemed to be ahead of him. Dante's gut instinct was to tell Aren it was none of his damn business where people slept while visiting Jeremiah's ranch, but he knew his reaction wasn't rational. Aren was right, of course. Gordon's old room was downstairs, and it was cold and oppressive. Olsa seemed to like it down there in the basement, but nobody else would choose that if they had another option.

"Of course," Dante said. He looked over at Tama, who shrugged.

"Alissa took Brighton's old room, but Cami could sleep in the one that belonged to the boys. I'll get some fresh sheets."

Not her boys, but Brighton's boys, who had died with their parents at the Austin Ranch.

"Come on," Dante said to Cami. "I'll show you the way." He was relieved to have an excuse to leave Aren and the kitchen behind. He suspected Aren felt the same.

Cami followed him upstairs and into the boys' room. If Dante had thought his room held ghosts, this one seemed worse. It was clear nothing had been changed since the day the boys had left it, heading off to visit their grandparents at the Austin ranch—a trip nobody had come home from.

Cami walked silently through it, her fingers trailing through the dust on the footboard of the bed. She stopped to eye the items sitting as if on display on the windowsill—an assortment of things that would have been strange to anybody but a young boy—string, rocks, the skull of some rodent-like animal. There was the torn piece of a playing card, and a small, clumsily carved piece of wood that was probably supposed to be a horse, or a dog, or maybe a deer. There was a stick, one end worn smooth by young hands, and a dried snake skin, and a piece of antler that had probably come from an elk. It was a collection much as Dante himself had once had. Cami touched each thing in turn with the tip of her finger, as if to acknowledge them. These things had been treasures, the grand total of two young lives spent in the Oestend prairie. Now, they were forgotten. Cami touched each one, as if to wake it from its sleep. As if to say, *"I see you. You're still here."*

On the small table by the door was a pocketknife. Jeremiah had given one to each of his grandsons. They were short, but plenty sharp. Tama had laughed, but Shay had been mad, sure the boys would hurt themselves. Of course she'd been right, but nearly cutting one's finger off with a pocketknife was just part of being a boy.

Dante smiled and shook his head as he looked down at the scar on his own finger where he'd done just that, so many years before. Where the other three knives were, only the Saints knew, but one was here, its small, sharp blade still out. The wooden table top bore four sets of initials—all four grandsons had carved on it. They probably all would have been strapped for it, too, if things had been different.

"Funny, isn't it?" Dante said. "All little boys are the same."

"No," she said quietly, shaking her head. "A few are different."

* * * *

Ghosts or not, the next few days were some of the most enjoyable he'd had in a while. Not that there was anything particularly fun about working the BarChi—after all, work on one ranch was much like work on the other—but it was nice to see his brother's smiling face. It was nice to have time with Tama. It was nice to feel like he was *home*. By the second night, his room no longer felt a tomb. It felt peaceful, in a way it never had during his marriage.

On the third day, Dante sat in the kitchen talking to Tama while she peeled potatoes at the table. At the other end of the kitchen, Alissa and Cami worked next to each other, talking quietly as they kneaded fat round balls of bread. Dante found it amusing to watch them. Alissa was obviously smitten with Cami. She laughed at everything Cami said. He watched as she reached up and brushed a smudge of flour off Cami's cheek.

For her part, Cami was friendly towards Alissa, but Dante couldn't tell if she shared Alissa's feelings or not. He wished he could hear more of their conversation.

He was distracted from watching them by Olsa shuffling into the kitchen. Cami's smile immediately faded. She glanced quickly back down at her work.

"Don't worry, Scia'loh," Olsa said. "I won't tell them your secret."

Dante had never seen Cami so spooked. She dropped her ball of dough, glancing around the room as if see who had heard. Tama, Dante and Alissa were the only ones there, but they were now all watching at her, unabashedly curious.

Cami's cheeks flushed bright red, and she turned without a word and left the room.

"Skittish as a hare," Olsa said, moving to take Cami's place at the counter. "That one doesn't trust a soul."

"What secret won't you tell?" Alissa asked, although her tone indicated she didn't really expect an answer.

"Don't be stupid, girl," Olsa said. Nothing more was said after that.

* * * *

On Dante's fourth afternoon home, as everybody waited for the men to come back from town, Tama found him outside and they sat together in the sun on the side of the well, watching the long grass of the prairie dance to the song of the wind.

"How's your sister doing?" Dante asked.

Tama sighed and shook her head. "Not well. She wanted to come here, but now that she *is* here, I think she's lonely."

"She has you."

"Yes, but I have Jay, and the boys. For her, there's nobody else. I don't think she'd really thought that through. Neither of us had, I guess."

Dante couldn't help but laugh. "What do you mean, there's nobody else? There must be nearly twenty people living at the BarChi!"

"But nobody she can count as a friend. There are the hands, but they're busy, and most of them have no use for her once they find out she won't lift her skirt for them. There was one who might have courted her, but of course she's not interested in that, either. She's scared of Olsa and Deacon. Jeremiah's nice to her, but she needs a friend, not a father. Aren's the only other adult here who has time for her, and he doesn't seem to have any interest in being her friend. Kind of keeps his distance from her." She shrugged. "She's alone, and depressed, and I have no idea how to help her. She's happy right now, with Cami here, but that'll only last until you leave."

"I think Alissa has a bit of a crush on her."

"I think you're right. Maybe you should take Alissa back to the Austin ranch with you."

Dante couldn't tell if she was serious or not. He also wasn't sure how he felt about having another woman at the ranch to look after. "Let's not get carried away. If Cami wants her there, then we'll see, but let's not go putting the wagon before the horse."

"She'd be happier there than here."

"I don't suppose going back home is much of an option."

Tama shook her head. "No. She's gone to town a couple of times, looking for a job, but the only place a girl can get work in Milton is at the whore house."

"Nothing else? The shops or the hostel?"

"We asked. They both have all the help they need between their wives and their kids. She asked at that new fancy inn, too. They said they hire maids, but we found out the maids there are expected to do a bit more than clean rooms, if you know what I mean. Apparently Mr Tucker likes to take liberties with his employees."

"So she'd basically be a whore there, too."

"Seems like it. It's tough, Dante. If she wanted to get married, it would be different, but for a land-owner's daughter to stay single out here is unheard of. Her only option is to go south and get a job as a maid on some other ranch, and that's not much of a life." She smoothed her hair back against the wind and looked out at the waves of grass. "The prairie is no place for women."

Her words made Dante think of Cami, running alone to the far reaches of Oestend. It seemed he wasn't the only one whose thoughts turned to her, because Tama's next question was, "Is Cami working out?"

"She is. I think the Saints themselves must have sent her."

"Not the Saints," Tama corrected. "It was Aren."

"Fuck, don't remind me."

She laughed. "I told him it was a bad idea."

"It wasn't, though. Wish I could say he'd been wrong, but she's made things there easier by a long shot."

"I'm glad." She suddenly turned serious, and he knew she was working up nerve to move onto her real questions. "How are you?" she asked finally. "Are you doing all right?"

He shrugged. "Well enough."

She stood up and walked a few steps away, hugging her arms around her against the wind. When she turned back, he could see the anger and the pain in her eyes. "I thought I'd never see you again!" It was an accusation, the way she said it. "I saw that look in your eyes, and the way you said goodbye, like it was the last time, and then you rode off over that hill, and I knew you'd never make it to the Austin ranch!"

He hung his head. She'd always known him too well. It was tempting to keep his head down rather than face her, but she deserved better than that. He made himself look back up at her and tell the truth. "You're right. That's what I planned. But the wraiths didn't cooperate."

She moved fast. Three steps, and then she slapped him hard across the face. It surprised him. He put his hand up to his stinging cheek.

"You stupid, arrogant fool! Is it not enough that your father has to lose one son?" She pointed up the hill, towards the Austin ranch. "Is it not enough to know that two of his grandchildren died out there in the wild? We all lost people we love, Dante! Not just you! My sons lost their cousins. They were their best friends, and their only playmates. They still ask when the boys will be home. And you want to add to that? Your pain is no worse than theirs! Do you think you have the right to bring more grief to us all? Or did it even occur to you the damage you'd do to your family? Are you really so selfish as that?"

Her words hurt, not least of all because they were true. Yes, he realised, he was that selfish. Not all the time, he hoped, but when it came to Deacon he was, and when he'd lost Deacon, he'd lost all sense of the big picture. He'd sat in that cabin and hoped for death, and although he'd wondered who would find him, it had never occurred to him how much pain his death would have caused his father, or his brother, or Tama. He'd spent the last few months grieving for Brighton every single day. Did he really want to cause them to carry that much grief for him as well?

"I'm sorry," he said.

She slumped, all the anger draining out of her in one sigh. "Every time somebody comes over that hill and down the trail, I hold my breath. Every time, I'm sure they've come to tell me that you're dead."

He shook his head. "It won't happen that way. Not now. I wanted it then, but..." He shrugged. "Can't say as I'm happy, but I guess it's not so bad I don't want to go on. Not anymore, at least."

She put her hand on his shoulder. "Find somebody else to love."

He shook his head. "I don't know if I can."

She was silent for a minute. Finally she said, "Dante, look at me." It was an order, the same tone she used on her sons right before she scolded them good.

Dante obeyed. She was looking down at him, her hand still on his shoulder, her face solemn. Her voice was firm. "He'll never be yours."

It was almost as if she'd smacked him again. He jerked back from her words, closing his eyes, trying to believe she hadn't said them.

Her grip on his shoulder tightened, and she shook him, forcing him to open his eyes and face her, and to face what she was saying. "Listen to me—he's never been happier. I know that hurts you to hear, but it's true, and it's time you learned to face it. I've never seen him be the way he is with Aren. He *loves* him, Dante. He's head over heels. He belongs to Aren, heart and soul. He will never, *ever* be yours."

Dante felt the sting of tears behind his eyes, a lump in his throat, his chest aching at her words. "I love him."

"I know you think you do. But you don't. Not really."

Her words confused him. After all the years they'd been friends, he didn't understand how she could doubt him.

She cradled his face in her hands, her calloused fingers gentle on his cheeks as she looked down into his eyes. "You love a dream, Dante. A dream you have where you were able to grow up as brothers and lovers and partners. A dream where Daisy never existed and Aren's coming here didn't matter. You love a dream where you didn't waste half your life being ashamed."

He couldn't stop the tears now. He put his head in his hands, trying to hide them. Tama put her arms around him, pulling him against her breast, comforting him like a child, and he held on to her tight. "He's the only future I've ever wanted."

"He's not your future. He's your past. Think about it. Even if he had a sudden change of heart and sent Aren away, would it be the way you've imagined? Your dad would still be here, and all the hands. Would you climb out of his bed each morning and walk down here to face them? Would you see him running this ranch the way he does and feel as if you were partners? After all these years, would you ever be able to call him your brother again?"

It hurt. It hurt so much to hear, but he knew it was true. What he longed for was a fantasy. He'd hung on to it for years. He'd nurtured it and cherished it, the one beacon of hope he had as he'd watched his marriage and his life and his dream of having a family fall apart. But it was no more tangible than the wind.

"Old Man Pane did a lot of damage, Dante, but he's long since cold and in the ground. Find another man to love, or a woman if you like, but don't let that bastard ruin even one more day of your life."

He shook his head. "I wish I could. I just don't know how."

She rocked him a little, and kissed the top of his head. "Let go of the dream, Dante. Wake up. Look around at the world. I promise, you'll find a way."

Chapter Seven

On the morning Dante and Cami were to leave for home, Jeremiah followed Dante to the barn to help hitch the team to the wagon. It was a job Dante could have easily done himself, but he could tell by his father's quiet reserve and nervous habit of clearing his throat that he had something to say. He seemed to be having a hard time working up the nerve, though. They had almost finished the job by the time Jeremiah finally spoke.

"I hope you're not angry at me."

The horses were between them, so Dante couldn't see his father's face. "Why would I be?" he asked.

"Well, the ranch, for one. Seemed logical at the time to let Deacon have the BarChi. I thought you'd be happy for a chance to start fresh, but I worry now it was wrong."

Dante shrugged, although his father probably couldn't see it. He'd always wanted Deacon more than he'd wanted the BarChi. Being sent away had hurt, but not for the same reasons his father was alluding to. "It's fine." He tightened the last buckle on his horse and when he looked up, he found his father watching him over the team's back. His cheeks were red with embarrassment.

"I remember the day my pa caught you and Deacon together in this barn."

Dante felt his own cheeks begin to burn. His father had never mentioned the incident, and Dante wished he hadn't brought it up now. "So do I," he said, and he hated the way his voice broke on the words.

"I was angry at him for making such a fuss. You were just boys." Jeremiah ducked his head and pushed his hat down low, much as Deacon often did when something made him uncomfortable. "The thing is, I never realised how much damage he did. I was busy with the ranch, and with your brothers. You and Deacon had been inseparable your whole lives, causing me no end of trouble, and I thought for sure you'd be back to it in a matter of days. It was months before I realised you couldn't even look at each other."

Dante ducked his head. He swallowed hard against the lump in his throat. Why did his father want to dig it all up now? "It's over," Dante said. "It don't matter anymore."

"It does." Dante was surprised to hear the strain of unshed tears in his father's voice. Jeremiah came around the horses to face Dante, although Dante couldn't quite make himself meet his father's eyes. He kept his gaze on the straw at his feet. "I should have realised," Jeremiah said. "I should have seen how hurt you were, and how confused. I should have seen how much you were struggling. I should have told you then it was all right. I should have told you and Deacon both, but the time I realised how bad things were, it was too late. I let my pa take something innocent and turn it ugly, and I hate myself for it. You should never have been separated, you and Deacon…"

His voice caught. His words stumbled to a halt. Dante looked up in surprise. Jeremiah's head was down. The wide brim of his hat hid his face, but it was obvious he was crying. He sniffled and put his hand up to wipe his eyes. Dante had only seen his father cry one other time, the day Dante's mother had died giving birth.

"It wasn't your fault," Dante said.

"It was. I should have protected you. I should have had the balls to stand up to my pa, but he was so mean—"

Dante laughed. "Don't I know it!"

Jeremiah looked up at him. His eyes were red, his cheeks still damp. "I'm your father, and I should have been there. And I'm sorry."

The words touched Dante. It was an old wound, one he'd learned to ignore, but his father's words soothed it a tiny bit. "All this time, I thought I'd failed you."

Jeremiah reached out and put his hand on Dante's shoulder. "Never. The Saints know you caused me enough trouble over the years. You've always been impetuous and hard-headed and downright ornery. But you're my son, Dante. I love you with all my heart. The fact that you think you let me down only proves that I'm the one who failed you."

Dante shook his head. He wanted to say no, that Jeremiah hadn't ever let him down, but the words wouldn't quite come out. How much different might things have been if Jeremiah had stood up for him all those years ago? How much might it have mattered to know that his father understood?

"I can forgive you," Dante said, his voice a hoarse whisper, "if you can forgive me."

Jeremiah pulled him into a tight hug and pounded him on the back. Dante hugged his father back, feeling like the child he'd once been. If only his father had hugged him like that the day Old Man Pane had horsewhipped him for daring to love another boy.

"I want you to be happy," Jeremiah said. "Promise me you'll find a way to be happy."

Dante nodded. "I'll do my best."

* * * *

On the way back from the BarChi, Cami asked if he minded going slower than normal so she could walk along through the prairie collecting plants and flowers.

"Can't you do that at home?"

"No," she said, in a tone that told him he was being a fool. "The ice killed them all, but here, they're still green."

They had plenty of time, so he obliged her. She gathered armfuls of plants, which she stuffed into a burlap bag she'd brought from the BarChi. He was confused by her choices. Some were flowers, but none of them were particularly bright or pretty. "What the hell do you need them for, anyway?"

"Different things."

"Like what?"

"Well, for one, I'm going to make potpourri. It might help with the smell."

Dante didn't have a blessed clue what 'potpourri' was, but he decided it was worth accommodating her, if it would ease the foul odour in their house.

Dante had failed to see the difference in the landscape on the way from the Austin Ranch to the BarChi, but on the way back, he was forced to see it.

By the second day, Cami's bag was full, and so they travelled faster. Dante noticed how green plants gave way to brown, the long grasses of the prairie lying flat and dark, mouldering in the sun rather than blowing in the wind.

"It's sad," she said. "It came too soon."

Dante wasn't sure about sad, but it was going to prove downright problematic. How much of his hay had been ruined? He had some in reserve, but he'd been counting on one more harvest to get them through the winter. And it wasn't just the cows that had to eat. "What about the garden?" he asked.

She shook her head. "About half of it was lost. Everything leafy is dead, except maybe the kale. Tomatoes are hit and miss. The ones closer to the outside are ruined, but some of the others were sort of sheltered underneath them, and should be usable. We'll still have potatoes, turnips and carrots. Peas, peppers and beans, I'm not sure about yet. My guess is, I can still use them in stew. They'll be mushy and won't taste as good, but it's better than going hungry."

"We won't go hungry. We might eat nothing but beef all damn winter, but at least we've got plenty of that." And without feed, he might have to slaughter some of them sooner rather than later anyway.

He was so busy worrying about cows and feed, he didn't notice anything unusual ahead until Cami put her hand on his wrist.

"Dante, look!"

She pointed ahead of them to where the ranch lay just out of sight over the hill. What he saw made the blood run cold in his veins.

Buzzards. Dozens of them. Probably more than a hundred. More of them than he'd ever seen in one place. Some circled high in the sky, and some much lower, but they were all clearly centred over the ranch.

"Holy Saints," he breathed.

"Do you think everything's all right?"

He wanted to say, "I'm sure it's fine," but he couldn't. In truth, he was picturing something like what Deacon had discovered so many months before, but he didn't want to alarm her.

He quickly judged the distance to the farm. The wagon was full of coal. It was far too heavy to make the horses pull it faster. He could get there quicker on foot, but they were still too far out for him to run the whole way without killing himself in the attempt. If he'd used quarter horses, he could have unharnessed one and ridden it bareback, but he'd brought the sturdy drafthorses, and they weren't trained to carry a rider.

He grimaced. There was nothing to be done but bide his time, as much as it pained him to do so.

They rode in silence, but he could sense Cami's unease. She was tense and fidgety, and it grew worse as they drew closer.

"Part of me wants you to go faster, and part of me doesn't want to get there at all," she said at last.

"I know what you mean." The more he thought about what might lie ahead, the more he felt he didn't want her to have to see it. Things as gruesome as he was imagining weren't easily forgotten. "I can get there quicker on foot. You know how to drive a team?"

"Only in theory."

"I could tie them here, and send somebody out once I know everything's all right."

"And what if it's not all right?" she asked. "Who will you send, then?"

Dante cursed. She was right. If the worst case scenario were true, and everybody was gone, they'd have limited to time to figure out what had gone wrong. If it was a problem with the generator again, he'd need every minute to work on it. He wouldn't be able to waste time running back to get her.

At least this close to the ranch, he didn't have to worry about conserving the horses' energy. He urged them to speed up as much as he dared.

When they were finally within sight of the ranch, he watched for movement. He'd been prepared to see more buzzards on the ground, feasting on death, but below the funnel of circling birds, everything looked normal. He could see men walking around. The dread inside Dante's chest abated some. Beside him, he heard Cami sigh.

Although the last hundred yards seemed to take ages, they finally pulled into the ranch. Simon came out to greet him. He was wearing a long duster with the hood pulled up. The weather didn't call for such a thing, but the spots of bird dung on it gave away its true purpose.

"Hey, boss. We meant to watch for you and send somebody out to ease your mind, but you caught us during supper."

"What the blessed hell is going on?" Dante asked as he jumped down from the wagon.

Simon shrugged. "Don't rightly know. They started showing up three days after you left. They been circling overhead ever since." He looked up into the sky. "Think there might be fewer today, to tell you the truth."

"No idea what's brought them?"

Simon shook his head. "Thought at first there must be something dead out in the fields, but we haven't found anything. Got the men spooked, though. Cattle and horses, too. Had a bitch of a time feeding the last two mornings, 'cause the horses don't want to leave the barn." He frowned. "Another thing—I don't know if it's the birds or what, but that milk cow in the barn quit producing, too. She's been dry the last three days."

It was the damnedest thing Dante had ever seen, but there was nothing to be done about it. He breathed a sigh of relief it wasn't something worse. He wasn't sure what he would have done if he'd come back to find all of his hands dead.

It was eerie having the birds overhead. They cast a strange, ever-moving shadow over the entire ranch that was surreal and a bit unnerving, but other than having to be careful about looking up, it didn't change the day-to-day running of the ranch. There was still livestock to be fed and chores to do.

On his third morning home, he came into the kitchen to find Cami standing in the doorway, looking up at the sky.

"How're our feathered friends?" he asked.

"They're gone," she said. "Every last one of them. And the cow must be making milk again. She's been fussing all morning."

"Thank the Saints for that. Maybe things will finally start being normal around here."

Somehow, he doubted that would be the case.

Chapter Eight

For a while at least, things did seem to be back to normal. Cami spent all of her free time playing with her plants. Some she simmered on the stove. Some she crushed. Some she even put in an old still she'd found somewhere. She dried others and mixed them in big bowls. Dante had no idea what all she was doing with them, but he had no reason to mind.

He found out potpourri was a mixture of dried plant pieces. Pretty soon, every room had little bowls of the stuff. She made packets of it that she burned in the fireplaces. She wrapped some of it in loose cheese cloth and hung them in the doorways to catch the breeze. Dante was constantly bumping his head into them, and they made him sneeze more often than not, but he had to admit, the smell of death was slowly being eradicated.

He asked Simon about the barracks and learned things were better there, too. Cami had given Simon pots full of liquid and plant pieces to boil over the fire in the barracks. She'd also washed the curtains from the barracks in saleratus, and scrubbed down the wooden floor with the water she'd boiled the plants in.

He had to give the woman credit. She'd told him she'd fix the problem, and it seemed it hadn't been an idle boast.

"I still can't figure how a freeze like that could hit us, but not the BarChi," Simon said to Dante one day as they were restringing barbed wire where a group of cows had pushed their way through. "You think it's something to do with the mountains?"

"Hell if I know."

They'd hashed it over more than once since Dante's return, but they were no closer to having an explanation for the ice than they were for the buzzards.

"Strangeness all over," Simon said. He gestured to the cattle grazing in the field. "They're acting odd the last few days. You noticed?"

"I did." Dante had hoped it was only his overactive imagination, but having Simon say it confirmed his fears.

"Not just the animals," Simon went on. "The men, too. Some of them are nervous, but a couple are getting mean. We've had fights in the barracks three nights in a row now."

"Somebody in particular I need to—"

"Dante!"

The shout came from the direction of the house, and Dante and Simon both turned to see Frances running across the compound towards them.

"Something wrong?" Dante yelled back.

Frances pointed towards the house. "Cami needs help!"

Dante ran. Frances was out of breath, and his words came tumbling out at a frantic pace as Dante rushed by him. "I tried to stop him, but he said to either help and take my turn after him, or get out of his way."

Anger was too simple of a word for what Dante felt. Frances' words about going second with Cami stoked the fire in his blood. Rage had always dwelled just below the surface for him. It took little for it to boil over and blot out all reason. By the time he burst into the kitchen, he was beyond thinking. His wrath blurred the periphery of his vision, narrowing his sight to one clear, brilliant focus.

In a fraction of a second, Dante took it all in. Foster was in the kitchen. His back was to Dante. He had Cami bent over the supper table. She was fighting hard, which was good, because it meant Foster needed both hands just to hold her down. He hadn't yet managed to lift her skirt.

Dante grabbed the nearest thing without even quite knowing what it was and bashed it over the man's back. Foster reeled backward, letting go of Cami, and Dante hit him again. The wooden chair burst apart at its joints. Foster fell to his knees. One chair leg was still intact in Dante's hand, and he hit Foster with it again.

And again.

And then again.

"Stop!" Cami yelled.

Dante did. He took two deep, ragged breaths, waiting for the rage to subside enough that he could think.

Foster lay on the ground, trying to protect his bleeding head with his hands. He wasn't dead. That was a bit disappointing. Dante was halfway tempted to kill him and be done with it, but then he'd be down a man. He threw the chair leg down in disgust and looked up, thinking to check on Cami, but as he did, he realised he had an audience. It seemed every hand on his ranch had come running, and they all stood by the door at the opposite end of the room, watching, their eyes wide.

Maybe he could make his point without resorting to death just yet.

Dante pulled his knife from his boot and stood over Foster.

"Dante?" Cami said from behind him, her voice low and shaky, but he ignored her. He addressed the men in front of him.

"You all are new to the prairie. Maybe you don't know how things are done, so let me be the one to fill you in. See, back before there were wraiths, when the settlers first came here to the Wild, they met the Old Ones. And the Old Ones taught them that all living things have a place. Wolves. Bears. Prairie dogs and badgers. They're all part of the whole. They all have a right to be.

"Then one night, something happened. A man like Foster here took another settler's daughter into the woods and had his way with her. When they caught him, her daddy wanted to string that man up by his balls, but the chief who was there said, 'How will the whole be served?' And that man realised the chief was right. 'Cause you see, wolves have got to eat too.

"So that night, they came up with what we call Wild Justice." Dante leaned over. He grabbed a handful of Foster's hair and lifted him partway off the floor, far enough that he could lean over and put the tip of his knife against the man's throat. He spoke into the man's ear, although loud enough that the other hands could hear. "First, we cut off your hands. Now, that may seem bad, but that ain't even part of the punishment. That's just to make things easier. 'Cause once a man's hands are gone, he tends to quit fighting back."

He moved the tip of his knife to Foster's gut. "Second, we open up your belly. Not deep enough to kill you, though. Just deep enough to make you bleed. Makes you smell real good to all those hungry things in the Wild.

"Then, we take you out to the woods, and we tie you to a tree."

He looked up at the boys in front of him, letting his gaze fall on each one of them in turn, forcing them to hear what he had to say. "There's lots of hungry things out there. You all hear them in the night, I know. You hear the wolves howling, and the coyotes when they try to get the hens. That ain't all, either. There's bear. Mountain lion, too. They mostly leave you alone, but when you're tied to a tree with your intestines hanging out, they just might be tempted enough to come in close.

"'Course, that ain't all. We got the wraiths now, too. Wild Justice may be the only time a man prays for the wraiths, 'cause if you're lucky, they'll find you first. If you're lucky, they'll steal your breath before the wolves show up to steal your meat. If the wraiths get you, we'll never even hear you scream." He grinned, and he hoped it looked as evil as it felt. "But if you're *not* lucky, and some hungry animal finds you first? Well, let's just say, you *will* scream then. You'll scream a long, long time."

His ranch hands were mostly young, green boys, and right at that moment, they really were green. One looked close to tears. Even Simon looked a bit shaken, which was surprising. Only Frances remained nonplussed. He actually seemed amused.

That was fine. Dante wasn't worried about Frances.

Dante dropped Foster back to the floor and stood up to face the men.

"Now, maybe this is my fault. Maybe I ain't been quite clear on exactly what is or isn't allowed on my ranch, but you may have noticed, when I get pissed off, I don't waste time asking for an explanation. So while I have your attention, let me lay it all out for you, clear as can be." He pointed behind him to Cami. "Any one of you touches this woman without her permission—hell, you even look at her in a way that pisses me off—I guarantee you'll only have 'til nightfall to regret it. And believe me when I tell you, this is the only warning you'll ever get. We clear?"

Wide eyes were his only response from most of them. A few bobbed their head. Nobody said a word.

Good enough.

Dante stepped back and kicked Foster hard in the ribs, just because it felt good to do it. "Somebody get this piece of shit off my floor."

Simon and Frances came forward. Not, he knew, because they gave a damn about Foster, but because they knew somebody had to do it. The rest of the hands were still frozen in place.

"Storytime's over, boys," Dante said. "Get your asses back to work."

* * * *

"Stop bleeding on me!" Frances griped at Foster as they dragged him into the barracks. "This is my best shirt!"

"It *was* your best shirt," Simon amended.

Foster's response was a string of obscenities. A few seemed to be aimed at Frances, but mostly they seemed to be about Dante. Simon laughed as they dropped the man unceremoniously into his bunk. They stood back to eye him. It was difficult to tell exactly how bad the damage was. Foster's scalp appeared to be split open from one eyebrow to the back of his head. He had his hand against the gash, but it did little to stop the massive flow of blood.

"I suppose something should be done about his head," Frances said.

Of course he was right, but Simon didn't feel like doing the man any favours. The incident had shaken him more than he liked to admit. Cami had obviously fought hard. She'd had a split lip and the beginning of a black eye. Still, she hadn't been beaten. She'd stood there and told Dante to stop.

Had Lena fought like that? Would she have begged mercy for her attackers?

But nobody had been there to help Lena. The fact that Foster had been thwarted didn't change the fact of his intentions.

"Let him bleed," Simon said.

Frances shrugged. "Works for me."

"The question is, can we leave him here like this, or should one of us stay with him?"

"I don't think he's going anywhere."

They were interrupted by a tentative knock on the barracks door. It surprised Simon. Nobody ever knocked on the door. Any of the ranch hands or Dante would have walked right in. He was even more surprised to open the door and find Cami there. She had a pan of water, and bottles and bandages tucked under one arm. She looked up at him with Lena's big dark eyes. "I came to check on him."

"Are you sure you want to do that?" Simon asked.

"No," she said in a shaking voice. "But somebody has to."

He held the door open and let her come in. She stopped though, just inside the door. She glanced over at him. "Will you stay while I do it?"

"Of course. We'll tie his hands for you, if you want."

She bit her lip, obviously considering it. "Let's see how he behaves, first."

Foster was absolutely cooperative. She gave him whisky for the pain, first, and Simon noticed how her hands shook as she handed him the bottle. She used vinegar and water to clean his wounds, which had him screaming, and finally, she wrapped his head in bandages. By the time she was done, he seemed to be only half conscious.

"After a head wound like that, there's a good chance he won't wake up," Simon said.

She hung her head. "I don't want anybody to die because of me."

Her words saddened him. "If he dies, it'll be because he made a horrible decision. Or it'll be because Dante is one ruthless son of a bitch. But it *won't* be because of *you*. Don't for a minute think this is your fault."

She nodded, although she clearly wasn't convinced. It reminded Simon again of Lena. She'd blamed herself afterwards, too. As if it wasn't enough for women to be abused by men, they somehow felt the need to bear the guilt of it, too.

"This was not your fault," he said again.

She shrugged. She glanced hesitantly over at Frances. He hadn't spoken since she'd come in the door.

"Thank you," she said.

Frances hung his head, and mumbled something unintelligible. Simon could tell by the boy's demeanour that he was blaming himself as well. Simon could have smacked them both.

Simon had her leave the vinegar and extra bandages and promised he'd tend to Foster himself. It didn't seem fair that Cami should have to do it. He could tell as he let her out the barrack's door how relieved she was to be able to leave to task to somebody else.

He turned back to find Frances still in the same spot on the bunk, looking down at his boots.

"Stop grousing and tell me what your problem is."

Frances sighed in frustration. "I should have been able to do something!"

"You *did* do something!"

"Yeah. I ran away."

"You went for help. That's not the same thing as running away."

Frances hung his head. "It feels the same."

Simon sighed and put his hand on Frances' shoulder. "Your first instinct isn't to fight, that's true. But that ain't a bad thing."

"It makes me feel weak."

Simon could understand that, and yet, he knew Frances had strength, too. He'd grown immeasurably since the incident with Miron. Countless times they'd been in situations as dangerous as the one with the bull had been, and not once had Frances balked. He'd covered Simon's back in a fight, and although he'd come away with a black eye and his nose broken for a second time, he hadn't backed down. And today, he'd tried to stop Foster, and when it hadn't worked, he'd gone for help. Simon didn't want him to be ashamed of that.

"Look, kid. You're never going to be Deacon, who keeps men in line with his fists. And you're never going to be Dante, who bashes people's heads in with a chair as easy as breathing. But if you ask me, that ain't necessarily a bad thing. I'd take you at my back any day over a wild card like Dante."

"You're just saying that to make me feel better." But he could tell by Frances' voice that he was pleased to have Simon say it.

"I wish somebody had been there to go for help when it was Lena."

Frances looked up at him in sudden realisation, his eyes big and full of embarrassment. "Oh, Simon. I'm so sorry! I didn't even think—"

"It's all right," Simon said, cutting that conversation off before it had a chance to drag him down. "You did well. A lesser man would have pretended he'd seen nothing. A lesser man wouldn't have wanted to risk having Foster as an enemy."

"I couldn't let him do that to her."

"I know." He gripped Frances' shoulder tighter and shook him until he smiled grudgingly. "Quit beating yourself up. It's 'cause of you Foster wasn't able to do what he wanted. Count it as a win."

"On the bright side, he'd have to be a fool to try again."

"You're right about that." But Simon wasn't as confident as he let on. In his experience, when it came to women, men were fools far more often than not.

Chapter Nine

Foster didn't awaken that day, although Simon assured Dante the man was still breathing. Dante didn't care. He'd never been one to waste sympathy on men like Foster. He noticed, though, how Cami wouldn't look at him. She was pale, and her hands shook as she served him lunch.

"Are you sorry I did it?" he asked her.

"I just don't want him to die because of me."

"It won't be because of you." Dante had no trouble admitting to himself whose fault it would be. One more death meant little to him.

"I feel like I've caused you so much trouble, and after everything you've done—"

"You *are* trouble," he said, but he smiled to soften his words. "Don't you apologise for it. You're worth a hundred of him and don't you forget it. I won't put up with garbage like him. This is your home, and he's nothing more than a dime-a-dozen ranch hand."

"A ranch hand you need, though."

"Not that bad, I don't. I'll string up every man here and work this damn ranch myself if I have to."

As it turned out, the issue of who was to blame for Foster's death ended up being moot. He awoke the next day, although he stayed in the barracks. On the third day, he disappeared.

"He was here this morning," Simon told Dante. "I sent him to muck the stalls, but looks like he took one of your horses and left."

"That's too bad," Dante said. "Good horses are hard to come by." Bad men though, he could do without.

A few days after Foster's disappearance, Dante took Frances with him to ride the fences. On the furthest end of the pastures, they found a deer caught in the fence. It had tried to jump over, but its foot had caught in the barbed wire. It had obviously struggled a great deal to get free but had only managed to tear up its leg on the wire. It lay panting and helpless, too tired to fight, its eyes rolling with fear as they approached.

Living on a ranch had inured Dante to the death of animals, but the deer made him sad. Life on the prairie was cruel.

"Think we can cut her free?" Frances asked.

Dante pointed at the odd angle of the deer's leg. "Pulled it right out of the socket. She won't be able to walk."

"Can't leave her like this."

"True enough."

Dante pulled his knife. She tried to buck as he knelt next to her, but her strength was gone. He put his hand on her neck and made soft, calming noises, the way he did with the horses. He remembered a story from his childhood, told by Olsa, of the Ainuai and how they could soothe an animal to sleep before they killed it. He wished he knew how to do that.

"It'll be over soon," he whispered.

He made the cut fast and deep. For some reason, he'd expected Frances to turn away, but he didn't. They sat in silence, watching her struggles end. Dante hadn't lied. It was quick. Then they had to cut her free from the fence.

"You know," Frances said, "I kind of feel like an ass saying this, but the salt pork ran out a while ago. It's been a long time since we had meat on the table that wasn't beef."

That was true, and Dante knew the Ainuai would have asked, "How will the whole be served?" It was a sad thing, but there was no sense it letting fresh venison go to waste.

They took the deer as far from the pasture as they dared and made quick work of butchering her. Dante silently said a prayer, both in apology and in gratitude, not to the Saints, but to Olsa's ancestors. It was something he'd never done before. He had no idea if they heard him or if they'd accept a prayer from a man like him. He only knew it felt right.

The strapped the meat to their saddles and then walked down to the stream to wash the blood from their hands. They were midway back to where the horses waited when Frances put a hand out and stopped Dante dead in his tracks. He didn't say a word, but pointed to the west.

Dante looked. He saw what Frances was pointing at, but he couldn't quite put words to what it was.

"What the blessed hell is it?" Dante asked.

His confusion was echoed in Frances' voice. "I have no idea."

It was like a misty grey curtain, from the heavens to the ground. "Looks like rain," Dante said. "But no rain I ever seen."

"It's not monsoon season."

Monsoon season or not, the grey wall was moving towards them at an alarming speed. He could hear it now, too. It was louder than a stampede. The two horses bucked and reared, then bolted together back towards the ranch.

"Son of a bitch," Dante swore.

The cattle in the adjacent field began lowing loudly, with an urgency usually reserved for predators in the fields. Beyond the grey veil of the oncoming storm, the Oestend prairie was nothing more than a dull smudge of brown.

"Dante?" There was a hint of fear in Frances' voice. "I think we better get out of here."

"It's just rain," Dante said. But he sounded far more confident than he felt, and the storm bearing down on them was so loud, he doubted Frances had heard him anyway. The storm was close enough now that Dante could smell it. Not the rich, clean aroma he associated with rain, but the sharp tang that hinted at lightning and the earthy smell of battered grass. It seemed ominous.

Frances grabbed Dante and pointed to the nearest building. It was a small shack a couple of hundred yards away. "Let's go!"

It's just rain Dante wanted to say again, but even he didn't believe it. The suddenness of it was unnatural, and it was moving faster than any storm he'd ever seen. Whatever it was, it was damn spooky.

"Dante, *let's go*!" Frances yelled again, and this time Dante went.

They were halfway to the shelter of the shack when the storm overtook them. It wasn't just rain. There was hail, too, some of it as big as peas. They ducked their heads against the onslaught and ran faster, squeezing through a barbed wire fence, and finally they were inside the building.

It was even louder inside than out. The hail on the roof was deafening. The building was for storage only and had obviously never been wraith-proof. What had once been tarpaper windows were now just empty panes, allowing them a bit of light. They stood for a minute staring out at the downpour. The ground was already covered with piles of hail, some of them so deep they looked like drifts of snow.

"I've never seen anything like this," Frances said. He glanced at Dante. "Have you?"

Dante slowly shook his head. Yes, he'd seen hail. Hail bigger than this, even. But the way it had come out of nowhere, descending upon them as if it had a purpose, had him unnerved.

"You're bleeding," Frances said.

Dante looked over at him, and Frances pointed at his right shoulder. "On your back. You must have caught it on the fence."

He hadn't felt it when it happened, but when he flexed his shoulder, he felt the sting. "Doesn't feel like much."

"Let me see." Frances tugged on the back of Dante's collar, and Dante unbuttoned his shirt so the boy could pull it off his shoulder. He felt Frances' fingertips on his back. "It's not deep, but it's pretty jagged. It'll be a nasty scar, unless you have Cami sew it up."

"It'll be fine."

"Hope it wasn't rusty. You don't want to get lockjaw."

"It'll be fine!"

Frances laughed. "All right. Don't get uptight."

Dante wasn't actually paying much attention to Frances. He was staring out the window. The hail was giving way to rain. The drum on the roof had become a dull roar. The piles of hail were slowly being washed away in the downpour.

"How long you want to stay here?" Frances asked.

Dante shrugged. "May as well wait 'til it lets up a bit."

Frances blushed a bit. He scuffed his toe in the dirt and bit his lip. When he glanced back at Dante, his smile was shy and unnervingly flirtatious. "You know, it's just us here. You interested in being entertained?"

Dante felt his pulse speed up. He instinctively took a step backwards. He didn't want this to happen.

Frances' smile grew. "I'd never tell, you know. Not even Simon."

Dante felt his own cheeks turning red. Frances continued to watch him, completely unembarrassed, waiting for an answer.

Dante wasn't sure what he was feeling. Saints knew it had been ages since he'd any kind of release he hadn't granted himself, and now here was Frances, making an offer. Dante had to admit, he was tempted. He found himself wondering exactly what Frances would look like bent over in front of him in the low light that fell through the windows. He couldn't deny the way the thought made his pulse race and his blood head for places south of his belt.

Still, he was sure he'd regret it in when it was over.

"I'm not sure it would be wise," Dante said.

Frances shrugged, still smiling, as if wisdom were inconsequential. "Well," he said as he turned to look out the window at the rain, "you know where to find me, if you change your mind."

Yes, Dante did know where to find him. At that moment, he really wished he didn't.

* * * *

The rain let up soon afterwards, and they walked back to the ranch in silence. They found the horses in the barn, the venison still strapped to their backs.

Frances seemed unconcerned about what had passed between them in the shack, and Dante tried to act the same. He refused to think about Frances as a valid option. He did the rest of his chores. He intentionally avoided the kitchen while the rest of the men ate. And all along, he refused to think about it.

Which of course meant he was thinking about it every single damn moment.

When the hands had all left, he wandered into the kitchen. The wind had picked up again, and a light rain pattered ineffectually against the window. Dante poured himself a very large drink as Cami put a plate of food down for him and turned back to her work.

And he continued to pretend that he wasn't thinking about it.

He'd hated himself for years for wanting men, and yet, when he thought about it rationally, he couldn't explain why. It wasn't as if it were unheard of. Men like Deacon and Aren who lived as a married couple were unusual, but out here in the prairie, where women were in short supply, it was common knowledge that turning to men was an obvious answer. "What's a hand job between friends?" he'd once heard a ranch hand say, and although he'd been too young to understand it at the time, he could see the practicality of it now.

Still, he couldn't quite bring himself to embrace it. And yet, he couldn't embrace women either.

Over the years, he'd tried to have sex with various women—mostly maids at the McAllen ranch, and Daisy, of course, and a whore or two in between. He'd even succeeded on occasion. But for the most part, he found it was more trouble than it was worth. Although he knew he should want women, in truth, when it came to sex, he found them borderline repulsive. The moist gap between their legs seemed foul. The cloying odour of their sex made him reel. When he compared his experiences with them to his time with Deacon in the barn, and the pure, bright joy of their pleasure, he knew he'd never, *ever* find what he sought with a woman. He'd married Daisy because it was what he was supposed to do, and because he hoped to someday have a family of his own, but their marriage had been a disaster from the start.

Yet somehow, he'd always felt that he *wanted* a wife. How that fitted with not wanting to fuck her, he didn't know.

He watched Cami as she moved around the kitchen. Her back was to him. She wasn't what most men looked for in a woman. She was tall, with no curves to speak of, and yet, she wasn't at all unattractive. She was slim and willowy and graceful. More importantly, she was pleasant and bright and practical. What would happen if he asked her to be his wife?

The real question was, what would happen when they got to the bedroom? He couldn't imagine undressing Cami, or touching her. There was no way he could kiss her. He couldn't bear the thought of what he'd see in her big brown eyes when he couldn't perform as a man. Would she be hurt or disappointed? Or would she laugh, as the whore back at The Chalice had done when he was eighteen?

No. Marrying Cami was definitely not an option.

He sighed. He closed his eyes again and tried not to think about Frances.

"Is everything all right?" Cami asked.

He nodded but didn't look up at her. "I'm just tired."

He heard her step near. He felt her hand on his shoulder, and heard her pour more whisky into his glass. He wished her touch stirred something in him.

"That was one hell of a storm today."

"It was."

"Frances said you cut your back."

"It's nothing. Just a scratch."

He heard her steps as she crossed back to him, and then felt her fingers on his neck. He jumped and swatted her hand away.

"I'm just going to check it."

He sighed. Of course that's all she was doing. Still, would it have killed her to warn him? "I'm sorry. I'm just tense."

"I noticed."

She began massaging his shoulders through his shirt. It felt good—not in a sexual way, but just in the simple way it was meant—and he was tempted to give in to her touch and let himself relax, but he was also scared of what her intentions were.

He reached up and gripped the fingers of her right hand. "Cami, I don't mean to be cruel, but…" *How to put it*? "I don't want you to touch me."

"I know." She pulled her hand free. She didn't sound hurt by his words. Just practical, as always. "If I thought you wanted me to touch you, I probably wouldn't. Now quit being ornery and hold still." She pulled his shirt off his shoulder then he felt her gentle fingers testing the skin.

"I'm sorry," he said, feeling for some reason he couldn't quite understand that he had to explain himself.

"Shut up, Dante. It doesn't hurt my feelings that you don't want to fuck me. Frankly, it makes things easier." She pulled his shirt back up over his shoulder. "The wound doesn't look bad. It's scabbed over. No sign of infection yet. You want me to wash it out, just to be sure?"

"It's fine."

She shrugged. "All right. Let me know if you change your mind."

He turned to look up at her, almost wishing he hadn't stopped her from rubbing his shoulders. He wondered if it would be rude to ask her to do it again. He didn't need to, though. She seemed to read his thoughts. She rolled her eyes at him, but then she put her hands back on his shoulders and began to knead them. It felt amazing. He could almost have purred. He let his head fall forward. He quit worrying about what she wanted from him and finally let himself relax.

She was quiet for a long time. The only sound in the kitchen was the quiet crackling of the fire in the hearth, the rain on the window, and the gentle song of the wind blowing across the prairie as it always did. "I worked in a whorehouse," Cami said at last, her voice quiet. Her hands still moved in a rhythmic, hypnotic way on his shoulders and neck. "Being desired sexually doesn't feel like a compliment. It feels more like a chore. It's not like that here, Dante. I like working here. I like living in this house with you. And what I like most about it is that it's easy. There's nothing complicated about it. It doesn't ever feel like a chore."

Dante took a deep breath and let it go. It felt cleansing. Yes, the doubts about Frances were still there, but at least he knew where things stood with Cami, and it was right where he wanted them to be. He and Cami had created a haven together, without ever meaning to—a place where they were both safe from their personal demons. A fortress against the storm, both literal and symbolic.

And although it felt childish and simplistic, he said what was in his heart. "I like having you here, too."

It really was as simple as that.

Chapter Ten

Somehow, their simple confession in the kitchen seemed to set them free. She moved easier with him and laughed more, and over the next couple of weeks, they fell into an easy routine. In the evening, after the generator had been turned on, but before it was time for bed, they'd sit together in the living room. She always had mending to do, and she'd sit by the lamp where she had the best light, and one of them would tell a story.

"Tell me about your brother," she said one night. "The one who died here."

And so Dante told her all about Brighton, who had always been happy and carefree. He'd had the ability to let every slight or difficulty roll off his back, and to laugh about it later, and yet, he'd never been a pushover. He knew what he wanted and had no qualms about pursuing it. He'd been a bright spot in the family—balancing out Dante's sullen hostility and Jay's lazy disinterest.

"He was the best of us," Dante said. "It should have been me."

"If it had, I'd still be a whore."

Dante couldn't argue with that.

She asked about his parents, and his childhood, and he found himself lost in memories he hadn't revisited in years. Memories from before the incident in the barn, before his grandfather had made him so ashamed of himself. Memories of what it was like to be a boy growing up on the prairie. The BarChi had seemed huge back then, and magical, and he and Deacon had prowled over every inch of it together. Sometimes Brighton or Jay would tag along, but many times they'd intentionally ditched the younger boys. They'd pretended to be kings and hunters and warriors. They'd unearthed what seemed like forgotten treasures in the outbuildings and done their very best to dam the river at least a hundred times.

"All this time I thought it was Tama you were in love with," Cami said. "But it's really Deacon."

Somehow, he didn't even feel ashamed of it. She made it sound the way it felt—natural. "It's always been Deacon."

He tried several times to turn the tables and ask about her past. Sometimes she'd share bits and pieces.

"Have you ever been in love?" he asked her one evening.

"I thought I was once."

"What happened?"

She thought about it a bit, and he knew she was trying to decide if it was a story she could tell or not.

"He could only love me in secret," she said at last.

Dante thought about Deacon, and the hope he'd held onto for so many years. "Is that so bad?"

"I don't think you can be ashamed of somebody and really love them, too. He was embarrassed of loving me. How could I feel good about that?"

For the most part, though, she evaded his questions, and Dante found he liked it best when she did, because she'd distract him with some other story.

"Do you know the one about Rider, who fought the giant?" she'd ask. Or, "Do you know the one about Seamus and the lost island of gold?" Or, "Have you heard the story of Joseph and the magic horse?"

No matter which story it was, Dante's answer was always, "No".

They were fairy myths and fables, and he realised they were tales most kids probably knew, but he'd never heard any of them.

"How do you know that story?" he'd asked the first few times, and the answer was always a shrug. "Everybody knows it," she'd say.

The more stories he heard, the more Dante realised how much of the world he'd missed. He'd lived his entire life on the prairie. His mother had died when he was six, and his memories of her were hazy and dim. After her death, there'd been only his father and his grandfather, Olsa, and a hundred hands who'd come and gone. Olsa had told them stories, but they'd been few and far between, and they'd all been about the Ainuai.

Cami's upbringing in the busy port city of Francshire had been so different from his own. She remembered her stepmother fondly, but she rarely spoke of her father.

"He had high aspirations," she told him one of the few times she shared something about herself. "We always had maids and cooks, and I had private tutors."

"So they taught you the stories?"

"Not really. The stories were always there, although sometimes there are different versions."

"What do you mean about your father having high aspirations?"

"He was always on the upper end of the working class, and he wanted so much to be one of the bourgeois."

"Why didn't he marry you off to some rich bourgeois brat, then?"

She smiled without meeting his eyes. "Do you know the story about Rasp and Raif and the magic flute?"

"You know I don't."

And Dante would close his eyes and get lost in the tales she spun, where heroes rescued princesses and magic was ordinary. It quickly became his favourite part of the day.

* * * *

One evening, as he sat in front of the fire, Cami surprised him by bringing him a giant roll of parchment.

"I found this," she told him. "It was in the back of my closet."

It was a map, and it was unlike anything he'd ever seen. He'd seen hastily scratched charts at his father's house, showing only the BarChi land. There was an illustration on the wall of the general store in Milton that showed the railroad lines in Oestend, from Francshire to Milton. There was another, in the bank, that showed Lanstead and the sea, but it ended just west of Oestend's eastern coast. But he'd never seen anything like the map he was looking at now.

It was Oestend—not the eastern parts, but the real Oestend. It started in the grain belt and stretched west of Milton farther than Dante could imagine. There were mountains, and grasslands, and lakes and rivers.

There was forest to the northwest, and desert in the south.

"Unbelievable," he said. "I had no idea such a thing even existed."

She pointed to the bottom right corner. "See the year? It's from before the wraiths. And see here?" She pointed to a strange circular mountain sketched onto the map. "That has to be the mesa Redmond talked about in his memoirs. This map must be from his expedition."

He turned to look up at her. "Who?"

She blushed. "You know. Paulus Redmond. He'd heard stories about a mountain of gold in the west, so he put together an expedition. They spent four years wandering around, but never found anything."

"Is that another one of your fairy tales?"

She laughed. "No, silly. It's history."

"How do you know?"

He saw the sudden elusiveness in her eyes. It was much as it had been on their trip to the BarChi, when she would suddenly seem to decide she didn't want to tell any more of a particular story. She shrugged. "I just do. Anyway, look. Milton and the ranches were drawn in later."

She was right. Milton was marked with a pencil instead of ink. There were also brands marking the various ranches, with property lines sketched out around them. Out in the plains, there was another brand—at least that's what it looked like to Dante—an A in a circle.

"What do you suppose those are?"

"I don't know, but look at this." She took the map and flipped it over to show him the back. There were signatures there, and although Dante couldn't quite read the names, he recognised the brands scratched next to them—the McAllens, the Ralstons, the BarChi, and the Austins. "This was their contract."

It was a strange piece of history, and one Dante felt he had no claim to. "We'll send it to the BarChi, next time somebody goes into town. Possible my dad or Aren will have a use for it."

"All right." She didn't say anything else, but he could tell there was something else she wanted to say.

He turned around and raised his eyebrows at her. "What is it?"

She glanced away from him, biting her lip in thought, as if debating what to say. Finally, she sighed. "I found these, too." She said it as if she were confessing a terrible sin. She pulled something from the pocket of her skirt and held them out for him to see.

They were combs. Not the kind used to actually comb hair, but the decorative kind women wore in their hair like jewellery. He thought maybe they were ivory, carved with an intricate floral pattern.

It amused him that she would feel compelled to give them to him. "What?" he teased. "You think I want them?"

"They were in a box, up on the shelf in the closet of my room." She shrugged. "It felt wrong for me to keep them."

Maybe so, but she liked them. He could tell by the way she held them, and the way her thumb brushed over them as they rested in her palm. She reached up and absentmindedly touched her dark hair, as if imagining them there.

"No reason for them to be stuck in some box when you like them so much."

"Really?" she asked, her eyes bright. "I can have them?"

"I sure can't think of any other use for them. They'd look awful silly on my cows."

The smile she gave him was huge and contagious, and for the first time, Dante found himself thinking she was pretty. She went to the window. With the lamplight inside, and the dark out, it served as a mirror of sorts. She spent what Dante thought was a silly amount of time arranging them in her hair. When she turned to face him again, her cheeks were pink.

"They look nice," he said, more because he felt he should than because he actually cared. Still, the smile his compliment elicited was worth it.

He went back to studying the map, and she went to her usual spot by the lamp, where she always sat in the evenings as she mended.

"So," Dante said, "tell me about Paulus Redmond and his mountain of gold."

* * * *

If Dante thought the storm had been strange, or the ice, or the vultures, they were nothing compared to what Oestend had in store for him the next day.

He was just coming down the stairs from his bedroom to the kitchen when Simon burst through the door. "You better get out here, boss."

At first, Dante saw nothing amiss. The same ranch. A bull in the corral, lazily chewing his cud. The milk cow lowing in the barn. Cami's chickens pecking the ground in search of breakfast.

Simon pointed to the left, towards the pasture. Dante turned, and stopped dead in his tracks.

Every single cow was dead.

"What the fuck?"

"I don't know, boss. I came out, and found them like that."

Dante strode out into the pasture with Simon at his heels to get a closer look. It was eerie. Nothing in the pasture was moving. He didn't even hear any birds. Each of the cows lay on its side, unmoving, eyes open and tongue lolling.

"Not a mark on them," Dante said. "Wasn't predators."

Simon shook his head. "Damnedest thing I've ever seen."

"It's not the froth, either. They were all healthy yesterday."

Simon leaned over and put his hand on one's flank. "Still warm. No flies yet, or smell. Like they just fell over dead at sunrise."

"Did you all hear anything in the night?" Dante asked. He hadn't heard anything in the house, but the barracks were closer to the field.

"Not a thing."

Dante whistled and shook his head. "Must be fifty head out here."

"Give or take."

"Don't dare use the meat when we don't know what killed them." Dante looked north, towards the further pastures. He could hear cows lowing in the distance, which meant his whole heard hadn't been affected. "Round up a couple of the men. I'll meet you in the barn. We'll ride out and see how many of the rest it got."

Dante was relieved to find that most of the rest of his herd was alive. It seemed the pasture next to the barracks was the epicentre of whatever had killed the cows. They found more dead in the adjacent fields, but only a few cows on the near side. Most of the herd they found huddled together on the far side of the pastures. The beasts were obviously agitated, their eyes wide and rolling in panic, but they were otherwise unaffected.

The next question was, what to do with more than fifty dead cows.

"Can't burn them," Simon said. "It'd take half the damn field and more firewood than we have."

"Sure as hell can't bury them, either," Dante said. The cows were big, and digging a hole deep enough to hold them all was out of the question. But leaving them to rot in the field less than fifty yards from the house wasn't much of an option either. It was also a waste. He didn't want to use the meat, in case it was tainted by whatever had killed them, but their hides were still good, and their fat could still be used to render tallow. They'd have to make sure to not use it for lard, but it would work fine for candles and saddle oil and to oil the gears on the generators. Maybe soap, too. If the fat were dangerous to the touch, they'd find out long before Cami was able to turn it into soap.

"How many of the hands know a thing about butchering?" he asked Simon.

"Me, Frances and Ralf. The rest of them will just make a mess of it. And one of them refuses to go near the carcasses. Thinks he'll catch a plague or something. I threatened to dock his pay, but he's practically pissing himself, he's so scared."

Dante sighed. He was probably lucky to only have one like that. "Tell him he better handle every other chore here himself. That'll keep him plenty busy while the rest of us do what needs to be done."

It took them the better part of two days. Dante, Simon, Frances and Ralf worked on skinning as many of the cows as they could and salvaging what they could from the corpses. The rest of the men used wagons to haul what was left of the bodies to a spot past the far edge of the ranch, upwind of the house and barracks, but as far from the river and the fields as they could get. They left them there for the scavengers. It was a gruesome solution, but the only one they had.

The next couple of days were spent rendering the fat and drying the hides. It was a struggle to do all of it and still stay on top of the regular chores. In the meantime, Dante pondered if there was anything more to be done.

His father and Aren needed to be told. After all, Jeremiah was technically the owner of both ranches, even if he let Deacon and Dante run them, and Aren kept the accounts for both ranches as well. It also made sense to get the hides to market as soon as possible. Dante also wanted to know if any of the BarChi cattle had been affected. And when it was all said and done, two of his hands decided they'd had enough of ranching and wanted to head back to civilisation as soon as possible.

In the end, he sent Simon with express orders to only take the men and hides as far as the BarChi and to hurry back after that. That would have him back in four days. For him to go all the way to town, sell the hides and round up new men would have meant him being gone at least eight, and possibly up to ten, and Dante didn't feel he could spare Simon that long. Frances had volunteered to go in Simon's place. He'd been surprisingly enthusiastic about it even, and Dante had debated taking him up on it, but Frances was young, and although he'd grown a lot over the last year, he was still a bit green. Dante knew his father and Deacon would have questions about the cattle, and they'd trust Simon's seasoned judgement more than Frances'.

"You still need a name," Cami said to him that night after dinner as they sat in the living room.

Dante had been lost in thought, staring into the fire as he thought again about the dead cattle, and her comment confused him. "What do you mean?" he asked, looking over at where she sat next to the lamp, sewing.

"Didn't I tell you? When we went to the BarChi, Aren told me to tell you that you should name the ranch."

"'Aren said,' huh? I suppose if Aren says it, it must be so."

She didn't react to his snide tone. She smiled, instead. "He said 'the ranch formerly owned by Zed Austin' didn't fit too well on the line of his ledgers."

"It's still the Austin Ranch to me."

"Well, better than what they call it in town."

"What's that?"

"Dead Man's Ranch."

Dante leaned his head back and closed his eyes. "Seems accurate."

"I don't like it," she said. "This is the first place I've ever felt at home. I don't like people calling it something so awful."

"Dante Ranch sounds damn stupid. Guess it could be the Pane Ranch." He laughed. "That's good. Pain. Ranch of Pain. How about that?"

Something small and hard smacked into the side of his head, bouncing sharply off his temple.

"Ow!" he said, sitting up to rub the spot. It stung like hell. He looked down to see a spool of thread rolling under his chair. He looked up at Cami in surprise. "Did you throw that at me?"

"Yes! Serves you right!"

"For what? Holy Saints, lady, that hurt!"

She didn't act a bit apologetic though. Her sewing lay forgotten in her lap, and she was glaring him with a hard, angry expression he knew all too well from his days with Tama at the BarChi. It was a look that told him he was in trouble. As if the spool to the side of the head hadn't been warning enough. "Didn't you just hear me say I don't like people calling it something awful?" she asked.

"All right then." He bent over and retrieved the wooden spool. "If you're gonna be so damn sensitive about it, what would you call it?"

Her anger fell quickly away. She ducked her head and picked her sewing back up. "I think you should call it Brighton."

Dante had been about to throw the spool back at her. He'd been debating whether or not it was bad manners to aim for her head, but her words brought him up short. He sat frozen, his arm cocked back.

"Brighton?"

"It works two ways, you know? You can honour your brother, for one. But also, it just sounds nice, doesn't it?" She smiled shyly at him. Her cheeks were red, and he knew she was afraid of his reaction. "Brighton," she said again, as if tasting the word. "It sounds sunny. And happy. Like a place people would want to live."

It was so simple, and so obvious, and so utterly perfect. Dante forgot all about hitting her with the spool. Instead, he stood up and walked over to her. He held the spool out for her. She took it, looking up at him in surprise.

He wasn't sure what to say. There was something so special about what she'd done, and yet he had no idea how to put it into words. Instead, he sank to his knees in front of her.

"What are you doing?" she asked.

"You're brilliant," he said. He took her hands in his and kissed the backs of them, first one then the other.

"It's not a big deal," she said. Her voice shook.

"It is." He lay his head in her lap, the way he remembered doing with his mother when he was only a boy, wrapped his arms around her hips and hugged her. "It's perfect."

She put her hand on his head, her fingers stroking his hair. It was simple, innocent gesture, but it felt good. It soothed him, and he sighed, content in a way he hadn't been in years. "Thank you," he said.

It took her a long time to answer, but finally she whispered back, "You're welcome."

Chapter Eleven

Simon wasn't looking forward to travelling to the BarChi with two scared green boys, but he was glad he didn't have to go any further than that. Two days there, one night at the BarChi barn, two days back. Then he'd be back in the barracks with Frances. Seemed easy enough.

The night before he was to leave, though, he had a dream. It started out as dreams often did, with Lena. He was kissing her, only this Lena wasn't afraid. This Lena had never been dragged behind a warehouse by three dockhands, and when he reached for the buttons on her blouse, she let him undo them.

In some part of his brain, he knew it wasn't real, but he didn't care. Lena changed, and the dream became more erotic in that slow, distorted, surreal way of dreams. He let it carry him, and he was temptingly close to climax when he was rudely awakened by somebody kicking the leg of his bunk.

"Wake up, Simon!"

Simon groaned and rolled over. He'd been so close. Why hadn't Frances let him sleep just a few more minutes?

"Must have been one hell of a dream."

"It was," Simon sighed. "You ruined it."

Frances laughed. "You were moaning. It was making all those hands blush and squirm."

"Fuck if I care."

Frances laughed again, and Simon debated the appropriateness of finishing things by hand even though Frances was still in the room. It only took him a moment to decide against it. He dragged himself out of bed and into his clothes, then to breakfast where the rest of the hands were just finishing up. He sent them off on their chores, sent the two who were leaving with him to pack their things, and he went to the barn to hitch up the team. Dante caught him just as he reached the barn.

"I almost forgot to give you this." He handed Simon a rolled piece of parchment. "Maybe my dad will want it, or Aren."

Simon unrolled it enough to see that it was some kind of map. "I'll get it to them."

"Good." Dante shook his hand. "Be safe, all right?"

"You got it, boss."

He tucked the parchment under the seat of the wagon, which was full of cow hides. He went into the barn, into the back room where the tack was hung. He shifted himself in his pants. He couldn't get the dream out of his head. It had left him surly and horny as hell.

"What are you doing in here?" Frances asked from behind him, startling him out of his thoughts. "Jacking off?"

"Fuck," Simon swore. He turned around to smile at Frances. "I was thinking about it. It's gonna be one damn uncomfortable ride."

Frances' normal friendly smile faded a bit. It changed, from something carefree to something that made Simon a bit uneasy. He reached behind himself and slid the door to the back room closed. Simon found that his mouth had suddenly gone dry.

"I could help you with that, you know."

It took Simon a moment to register what Frances had said. And what he meant. And when he did understand, he almost wished he hadn't.

Simon shook his head. "I'm not like you, Frances. I don't mean that in any kind of mean way. Believe me. Sometimes I wish I were. It'd almost be easier." And it was the truth. He'd wished many, many times that he could find some kind of release amongst the men. It happened all the time out here on the prairie, where women were few and far between, but he'd never had the opportunity or the desire.

Frances didn't speak at first. He just continued to stare at Simon, and for possibly the first time ever, Simon had no idea what he was thinking. Finally, he moved closer. He stepped to within a few inches of Simon, and Simon did his best to look nonplussed.

"I know how you feel about me, Simon. I know it's not how I feel about you, and that's all right. But we're partners, right?"

Such a simple question, but Simon had the uncomfortable feeling he was walking into a trap. "Yeah."

"And as partners, we help each other."

"Right."

"If you were out of water in your skin, or run short on pay, I'd help you."

"Sure."

"And when there's a chore I can't do because I'm too small, you help me."

Again, Simon wasn't sure he liked where this was going, but he nodded.

"The thing is," and with that Frances moved even closer, "this is the same. Just think of it as a favour."

"That's crazy! I can't—"

"It's something you need. And it's something I can give. It's as simple as that."

Simon almost laughed. "No, it ain't! Saints, Frances, it's anything but simple!"

"You moved out here so you'd be away from women, so you wouldn't break your vow. But your vow didn't say anything about men."

"No, but—"

"Your cock don't know the difference. Only your brain."

"Well, yeah. I mean, maybe. But—"

"Shut up and close your eyes."

Holy Saints, he wanted to argue. He wanted to say no. He wanted to walk away and pretend this embarrassing, awkward conversation had never happened.

Then again…

When he thought about how long it had been since he'd let anybody touch him, he wavered. Even when he had allowed himself a quick tryst with a girl, he'd always regretted it. But Frances was right about one thing—Simon's vow to Lena hadn't included men.

Still, he wasn't attracted to men. When he looked at Frances, he saw a young man. He saw his friend. He saw somebody he cared about, yes. But certainly not somebody he wanted to fuck. He'd had plenty of opportunities to see Frances naked, but he hadn't ever bothered to pay attention. In all the times they'd had casual physical contact between them as they worked, Simon had never felt even a stir of desire.

He was torn, but in the end, it didn't matter that his brain was confused. His cock wasn't. It understood that there was a possibility of joyous things about to be done. His cock began to rise despite his mental dilemma.

Frances smiled at him, and Simon knew beyond a doubt that Frances knew what was going on in Simon's pants.

"Close your eyes," Frances said again.

And this time, Simon did.

He felt Frances' fingers tug at the fly of his pants, and immediately, his brain rebelled. "No—" he started to say, but Frances cut him off.

"Shh…" His voice was quiet and gentle, the way it was when he approached a spooked mare. "It's not about me, Simon. It's about you."

Simon felt warm fingers wrap around his cock, and he moaned despite himself, because it was, after all, a hand on his cock—a hand that wasn't his own—and no matter how he felt about Frances, it felt damn good.

"You don't have to think about me," Frances said. "Think about Lena. Or some maid at the McAllen ranch. Think about anybody else you want. I don't care. Let yourself enjoy it."

Simon took a deep breath and slowly let it out, trying to relax. He wouldn't think about Lena. Not ever. He wouldn't sully his memory of her like that. But his mind did turn to women. Not any woman in particular, but the general idea of them. Somebody was touching him, stroking him, rubbing the head of his cock, and while he knew it was Frances, it was easy to keep that thought in the back of his mind. It was easy to concentrate instead on the fantasy in his head. He thought about a warm soft breast cupped in his hand, the hardness of an erect nipple against his thumb. He thought about the smoothness of their skin. He thought about the alluring slit between their legs. He called up the feeling of touching the folds of flesh there. The mystery of it. The moist heat of their sex. He thought about how it felt to slide his fingers into a woman's wet, hot slit. He thought about the rich, ripe smell of it, how it would cling to his hands for days, and the thought made him moan.

The next thing he knew, his cock was engulfed in something warm and wet and absolutely divine. He opened his eyes despite himself and looked down. Frances was on his knees, and that wonderful erotic warmth on Simon's cock was the boy's mouth.

Simon closed his eyes again. He didn't let himself think about Frances. It felt far too good to turn back now. He gripped Frances' head, and he began to thrust. As he did, he imagined a maid at some unknown ranch. He'd never seen her before as far as he knew, but in his mind, she was lush and curvy. Not too skinny, like so many of them were from working every day, but full and soft. But most of all, she was unbelievably willing. He could see her lying there in front of him with her knees up and her legs spread wide, the moist pink heat of her sex swollen and open and ready. And he thrust his way inside her without a hint of guilt.

Her hips were broad, her stomach pale and plump. Her breasts were big and spread out across her chest the way breasts did when they were unbound and the girl was on her back. They slid up and down on her chest as he moved in and out of her. Her nipples were hard pink nubs in big, round, dimpled aureoles. She was a woman unlike any Simon had ever actually fucked, and in his mind, he fucked her hard. He pushed her knees up towards her shoulders, and he fucked her like he'd never, ever fucked anybody in his life. He rode her. He smacked her flank. He squeezed the thick, soft flesh of her thighs and grabbed handfuls of her ample ass. And when he finally came, it was like a dam bursting. It was like the heavy, grey clouds before a monsoon when they finally opened up and poured their burden onto the earth.

It was a relief he hadn't known in years.

He almost laughed with the joy of it. He was still gripping Frances' head, and Simon barely noticed when the boy pushed his hands away. Simon ran his fingers through his own hair and breathed hard, trying to catch his breath, his body thrumming from the pleasure of his climax. He was surprised he could even stand.

"Holy Saints, I needed that," he said, and this time, he really did laugh. "Oh, Frances, you have *no idea* how much I needed that."

Frances laughed. "Yes, I do."

And of course, it was probably true.

Frances stood up, buttoning his own pants as he did. He was scuffing the floor with his foot, and Simon realised he was kicking the dirt over the puddle of his own cum.

Simon quickly looked away. Somehow, knowing that Frances had pleasured himself at the same time was disturbing. Frances had said this was nothing. Just helping out. A favour between friends.

But if Frances had enjoyed it too, did that change it?

Simon didn't know, and at that moment, he wasn't sure he cared, because the truth was, he felt better than he had in ages. His body was loose and relaxed. He could have laid down and fallen asleep in a heartbeat. He laughed out loud again at the thought.

"See? Told you I could help," Frances said, and when Simon looked at Frances again, he found nothing to make him uncomfortable. Just his friend standing in front of him. Frances' pants were done up again. He was smiling, a friendly, casual smile like he always did. He clapped Simon on the shoulder. "Come on," he said, turning towards the door. "Daylight's burning, and you got a long way to go."

* * * *

The trip to the BarChi with the two boys was tense, although thanks to Frances, not for the reasons Simon had originally anticipated. He felt a bit odd about what had happened, but mostly, he just felt unbelievably relieved. Still, the other boys were young and nervous as squirrels, and Simon was happy to arrive at the ranch.

Jeremiah and Deacon were stunned to hear about the cattle. Nothing strange at all had happened to their own herds.

"It had to be the froth," Jeremiah said.

Deacon shook his head. "Dante's no fool. He would have known if they'd been sick."

"There's no other explanation!"

"If it had been the froth, they would have died over several days," Simon said. "It wouldn't kill them all at the same time like that."

"What else is there?" Jeremiah asked. Simon knew he didn't expect an answer. He was just trying to reason it through. "Some new disease? Some kind of bovine plague?"

"We sure didn't see any sign of disease, sir, and none of us has come down sick, even after butchering, but I don't have an explanation any more than you do."

Jeremiah and Deacon both shook their heads, at a loss for words.

"So nothing strange is happening here?" Simon asked.

Neither of them answered right away, but Simon saw the way they glanced at each other.

"What?" he asked.

Jeremiah sighed. "Nothing odd here at all," he said. "And that seems to be what's odd."

The statement didn't make any sense, and Simon looked to Deacon for explanation.

"We been hearing rumours," Deacon said. "Between travelling to town and back, and the men visiting the taverns while they're there, we been hearing all kinds of strange things."

"What kinds of things?"

"Stories like yours," Deacon said. "Strange weather. Lots of lightning and hail. Every morning, the folks in Milton find birds and cats and dogs dead in the street. Tama heard the cost of milk and butter in town is sky high 'cause every cow in the Milton dairy quit producing. Eggs too. Ronin heard the tavernkeeper's wife say every one her hens have laid is missing the yolk." He shook his head. "We don't have pigs here, but Fred McAllen says they're all damn spooked—and horses, too."

"That ain't all," Jeremiah said. "The Ralstons had so many strange things happen, they up and left their farm. We had a group of their hands show up here, looking for work. They said there'd been a swarm of locusts who took out their crops, and their house and barn were overrun with rats. Horses started catching a plague. They torched their whole place before they left. We hear it's burned right to the ground."

"Odd," Simon said. He ticked the locations off on his fingers. "Milton, the McAllens, the Ralstons, and the Austin ranch. Yet the BarChi sits right between them all, and it's doing fine?"

Jeremiah and Deacon looked at each other as if debating an answer, but it seemed neither of them had one. Deacon shrugged.

"I've got extra men right now, because of those Ralston hands," he said. "I'll send a couple north with you. Seems like Dante could use them more than me."

"I think he'll appreciate that."

It wasn't until after Jeremiah had dismissed him and he was walking with Deacon back to the barn that he remembered the map. "Bring it on up to the house," Deacon told him. "We'll make use of Aren's whisky."

Deacon seemed spectacularly unimpressed by the map, but Aren more than made up for it.

"It's beautiful," he said, as he spread it out on the floor. His movements were gentle and his tone somehow reverent.

"It's just a map," Deacon said.

Aren shook his head. "It's art."

"No. It don't have the magic at all. Not like your art does."

Simon barely knew Aren, but even he could see the way those words pleased him. He glanced sidelong at Deacon and smiled. "It's a different kind of art." Aren turned back to the map. He pointed to the strange A marks scattered across the Wild. "What are those?"

"Probably tribes of Ainuai."

Aren traced the property lines with his fingertip. "The McAllens', the BarChi, the Austins'." He pointed to a mark southwest of the McAllen farm. "What's this?"

"Ralston homestead," Deacon said. "Daisy's kin. Or used to be."

"This shows the border of the BarChi being further west than it actually is."

Deacon leaned over to look at the map, and Simon followed suit. Sure enough, the loop around the BarChi ran far to the west, encompassing the chunk of land directly south of the Austin ranch.

"Old Man Pane's daddy thought to expand that way," Deacon said. "He claimed that land years ago, when people were first moving west. Later on, Zed Austin's father wanted to buy it, but Old Man Pane refused. Said his sons and their sons would need it eventually. Forced the Austins to go north first, up over the ridge. Made it a two-day trek from their home to here instead of one. Austins never really did forgive the Panes for that."

"But what's there?" Aren asked.

Deacon shook his head. "Nothing. Good land, but nobody ever wanted to homestead it. Brighton talked about it once, but Shay wouldn't hear of it. Said she didn't want to be all alone in the wild."

Aren pulled a pencil from his pocket and used the tip to measure distances on the map. "Wouldn't that have made her closer to her family? Looks like maybe only half a day's ride to the Austin ranch, if they built on the northern edge."

Deacon shook his head. "As the crow flies, sure, but that ain't how it works." He pointed to the dark row of triangles on the map that separated the western portion of the BarChi property form the Austin Ranch. "Can't cross the ridge there. Down here by the BarChi, it's low, but out there, it's steep and sheer rock. They'd have had to come back through the BarChi, then go up and around."

"So the land's just sitting there?" Simon asked. The idea excited him.

Deacon shrugged. "Too far out for us to use it, even for grazing. Wouldn't have time to ride out, round up cows and bring them home again before dark. Jeremiah might have sold it, but nobody's wanted to homestead that far west in ages. Too hard to build out there with the wraiths, especially since the wards quit working."

They moved on to other topics, although Aren's fascination with the map never seemed to wane. Eventually, Simon wandered back over the barn for the night, but he couldn't stop thinking about all that available land.

Would Jeremiah sell? That was the first question. Simon had been paid well by Deacon, and even better by Dante, and he'd had very little occasion to spend any of it. He had a good-sized chunk set aside. He hadn't ever quite known what he was saving up for, but suddenly, he couldn't get the idea of having his own ranch out of his mind.

The more important question was, was there any way to build on it? Back when the wards had still worked, it had been easy enough to send out a group of men, put up a shack in a few hours, and make it safe enough to last until something more solid could be built. But now, the wards weren't enough. It would mean putting up not only a shack, but also a generator in the few hours before nightfall. And, of course, if the generator didn't work right on the first try, there would be no second chances. That was why nobody had tried to go further west in years. But Simon refused to believe it was impossible.

Chapter Twelve

Four nights after Simon returned from the BarChi with the new hands, Brighton Ranch was hit by a lightning storm unlike anything Dante had ever seen. He and Cami stood in the living room, watching out the window as it moved across the prairie towards them. It flared over and over, with barely a heartbeat of darkness between the flashes of light. The thunder was a dull, constant roar, echoing across the plain.

"Holy Saints," Cami breathed. "Is this normal?"

"Not even close."

They watched for a while, but it seemed they were both too spooked for casual conversation. Eventually Cami went to her room, and Dante went to his, although he couldn't sleep. He sat by his window, watching as the storm overtook his ranch. Lightning-struck trees burned on the edge of the pasture. The storm brought rain, too, and the fires sputtered and smoked in the downpour. The fury of the storm was right on top of them.

Suddenly, lightning flashed. Thunder boomed. The house quaked. The giant oak tree outside Dante's window flared to life, and with a deafening crack, the trunk sheered in two.

A scream and a crash, this time from down the hall. The sounds chilled him and sent him running down the dark hallway, bright images of lightning bolts still shadowing his sight. The oak was right outside Cami's window, and Dante anticipated finding the window broken, the room open to the night and the wraiths. He threw open her bedroom door. It took him a minute to take stock.

The window was intact, but next to it, the floor was ablaze. Cami stood there, her hair down and her robe flapping loose around her. Her back was to him, and she was striking feebly at the flames with a blanket, trying to put them out.

"What happened?" he asked.

"It startled me, and I dropped the lamp, and it shattered. I'm such a klutz sometimes!"

It was odd to see her so flustered. She was usually so calm and rational. "It's oil. If we can keep it from spreading it will burn out."

She turned to look at him, her eyes big and scared. Her right hand held her robe closed and he saw the dark stains on the fabric. "Are you bleeding?"

"I tried to pick it up, and I cut myself, and…" She stopped, biting her lip as her eyes filled with tears.

"It's fine," he said, finally moving around the bed. The fire had mostly gone out. Dante took the singed blanket she'd been using and smothered the last of the flames. "It's fine," he said again. He was saying it to reassure himself as much as to her. His heart was still racing, his body tingling with adrenaline.

Now that the flames had died, the room was dark except when the lightning flared. He spotted another lantern on the mantel and squeezed past her in the narrow space to light it. His hands shook as he turned up the wick, and he laughed nervously. "Scared the hell out of me."

"It's over now," she said, although she sounded even more frightened than she had before. "I'm fine. You can go."

"Let's check your hand first," he said, turning back to her. She was only an arm's length away, and he reached out to take her wrist.

"No—"

But he'd already grabbed her and pulled her hand down so he could look at her palm. Her robe fell open as he did. He was vaguely aware of her trying to turn away, even as he held her hand, of her fumbling to close it again with her left hand. He didn't want to look. He didn't want to embarrass either one of them by having him see something neither of them wanted him to see. "Don't worry about it." But even as he said it, his eyes betrayed him. It wasn't much. Only a fraction of a second, as a flash of lightning made the room brighter, and in the moment he caught a glimpse of her, without meaning to. Smooth skin. Her navel. A hint of hair. And below that…

He looked up at her face in surprise. "You're a man!"

"I am not!" She yanked her hand away from him and pulled her robe shut.

For a second, he had no idea what to say. He'd seen what was between her legs, and it definitely wasn't what he'd expected. "You are!" he said at last, gesturing futilely towards her groin.

She was trying to tie her robe, but her injured hand stopped her, and she gave up holding it closed. Instead, she threw herself at him, shoving him hard in the chest. "Get out!"

"Cami, what the fuck?"

"Get out, get out, *get out*!"

She shoved him harder with each exclamation, and he was so stunned, he found himself being pushed backward. "Wait!" he said, but he was suddenly in the hallway. Cami slammed the door shut in his face.

He stood there for a moment in the complete darkness of the corridor, staring stupidly at the wood an inch from his nose. Had he imagined it? Could he have been mistaken? There had been so little light, until that moment when the lightning flashed. Could it have been his eyes playing a trick on him? Maybe just a shadow?

He replayed the entire incident in his head, once, and then again, but each time, it ended with that glimpse of skin, and the sudden knowledge that she was not what he'd thought.

"Cami?" he asked.

"Go away!" And then, much to his dismay, she burst into tears.

No matter what he'd just seen, she was female in his mind, and there was nothing worse than trying to deal with a crying woman. He never said the right thing. "Don't cry, Cami. Shit! I'm sorry! I just… I'm confused, that's all."

No answer.

"Cami?"

"Why did you have to see?"

"I didn't mean to!" One minute he'd been trying to help her, and now he was standing outside her door feeling like his whole world had been turned on its ear. "Why are you pretending to be a woman?"

"I'm not pretending."

He threw his hands up in confusion and practically yelled in frustration, "I just saw you naked!"

A heartbeat, and then another. On the other side of the door, he heard nothing but sniffles. He forced himself to take a deep breath. He had to calm down. Yelling at her wasn't going to get him anywhere. "Cami?" he tried again, wondering even as he did if that was really her name.

"Give me a minute," she said quietly. "I'll come out, but I really need a minute."

He was still confused, but the truth was, a minute didn't seem like a bad idea.

And he suddenly, desperately wanted a drink.

* * * *

He waited for Cami in the kitchen. Lightning still crackled outside, but the thunder now came several seconds after the flashes of light. The storm had passed over them. It was moving on, across the prairie, leaving Dante stunned and confused in its wake.

He sipped a glass of whisky while he waited and considered her possible reasons for hiding her true gender. The most likely scenario he could come up with was that she was hiding from somebody. Maybe she'd committed some kind of crime. Here on the plains, there was no formal justice. What there was tended to be vigilante-style. But he knew Cami was from the eastern coast. He'd never been there himself, but they probably had officials of some kind or another. Sheriffs or magistrates or both.

Still, would any of them pursue Cami halfway across Oestend? What kind of crime must she have committed to warrant such a thing? He knew her, and he found it unlikely she could have done anything so terrible. And yet, what other reason did she have for pretending to be a woman?

She finally came in. Yes, *she*. Because despite what Dante had seen in her room, he could not bring himself to think of her as male. She was still wearing her robe. She'd managed to tie it tightly around her. Blood stained the ties at her waist.

"Have a drink," he said, pushing a glass of whisky her way.

Cami's eyes were red, but her cheeks were dry. She watched him with scared eyes.

"Sit down," he said. "Please."

She took the chair opposite him, although she clearly wasn't at ease. She sat straight and rigid, not quite meeting his eyes.

"What did you do?" he asked.

He saw the confusion on her face. She'd obviously expected a question, but not this one. Her eyes moved back and forth as she contemplated what he might mean.

"Did you kill someone?" he asked.

Her confusion seemed to grow. "No. Why would you think that?"

"You're obviously hiding from someone."

"Running, maybe. Not hiding."

"What's the difference?"

"I haven't done anything wrong."

Dante felt they were somehow having two different conversations. He rubbed his forehead with his fingers, trying to figure out what he was missing. "Who are you running from?"

"My dad."

Good. Now they were getting somewhere. "Why?" he asked. "Did you steal something from him?"

"No!" she said, finally meeting his eyes. "It's not like that."

"Then what? Help me understand."

"He wants me to be…" She fidgeted with the sleeves of her robe, pulling them down over her hands as she often did when she was uncomfortable. A single tear rolled down her cheek, and she wiped it angrily away. "He wants me to be a boy."

Just when he thought they were making progress, she said something to confuse him more. "But you *are* a boy!"

"No, I'm not!" Her cheeks were red, but when she met his gaze, he saw the challenge and the anger in her yes. "I'm female."

"I saw you naked!"

"I know how it looks. But what's between my legs is wrong. A mistake. Or a prank by the Saints. I don't know! But it's not who I am."

Dante had to think about that for a minute. It was true that even now, with the memory of Cami's very male body fresh in his mind, he still found himself thinking of her as female. Her face and her movements and her calm, strong, still demeanour.

She had obviously been waiting for him to argue, but when he didn't, she gained some confidence. "I've known all my life I'm a girl. I don't know why I was born the way I am. I only know it's wrong."

He found it confusing, but he didn't know how to argue. She *seemed* like a girl to him.

"You told me you worked in a whorehouse. How is that possible?"

Her cheeks turned an even deeper shade of red. He saw the shame in her eyes, just as he'd seen it the day she'd told him about it.

"Some men like other men. They'd have me wear a skirt, but no blouse. They sold me as a male."

Some men like other men. As if Dante needed to be told that.

When he'd thought before about her time as a whore, he'd thought little of it. But now, knowing what he knew, it made him angry. Somehow, the humiliation of it seemed worse. Not because it was worse for a man to sell his body than for a woman to do so, but because Cami had been forced to reveal to complete strangers a secret she obviously preferred to keep to herself. It was a horrible violation, not to be used sexually, but to be forced to share the body she was so clearly ashamed of.

He felt bad for having discovered her secret. In hindsight, he should have knocked before going into her room, but everything had happened so fast.

Thinking of that made him remember the fire. He looked down at her hands, where they rested on the table between them, wrapped in her long sleeves, one of which was badly stained with blood. It had to hurt, and yet she'd sat here, calmly explaining herself to him. She'd taken the time to justify something he suddenly felt needed no justification.

He stood up and got the salve from the cabinet. He found the strips of cloth they used for bandages. He sat back down across from Cami and held his hand out to her.

"Let's take care of that cut."

She hesitated a moment, still looking scared. He waited—not moving, not speaking—and slowly, her expression changed from wary to cautiously hopeful. She pulled her sleeve up and put her hand in his. He turned it over gently. The cut started at the base of her thumb and ran across her palm. It was smooth and not too deep. It had already stopped bleeding. Her thumb and fingers were burned. They were starting to blister. Dante knew that was good. It meant the skin was still able to heal itself. He hated to think how much worse it could have been.

He began to smear the salve on her injuries, and although he was as gentle as he knew how to be, he heard the sharp intake of her breath as the pain hit her again.

"I'm sorry." He didn't know if he meant for hurting her, or for discovering her secret.

"You're forgiven," she said, and he had a feeling she meant for both things. "Will you let me stay?"

The question surprised him. "Of course. The Saints know I can't run this damn ranch without you."

"Will you let me stay as I am?"

"I don't see why not." Because what would he possibly gain by making her wear pants?

"Will you tell the men?"

That question brought him up short. On one hand, she'd almost be safer if they knew the truth. But he knew that wasn't really the issue. He took a strip of cloth and began to wind it around her burned hand. "Don't see what business it is of theirs what's under your dress. Not unless you choose to make it so."

She was quiet, and with his eyes on his work, he had no way of knowing her reaction, but when he looked up at her, he found her watching him. There were tears in her eyes, but she seemed happy. She smiled at him. "Thank you."

The sentiment made him uncomfortable. He had to look away, back down at her hand. He'd finished wrapping it, and he tucked the end of the bandage under one of the layers and tied a small knot. "We should check that a couple times a day," he said. "If it gets infected, I'll take you to the BarChi so Olsa can fix it."

"It'll be fine."

He thought about Olsa, and the others at the BarChi. "Do they know?" he asked.

It was a strange question, out of nowhere, but he saw in her eyes that she understood. She finally picked up the glass of whisky. She drained it in one swallow. "Aren does," she said as she put down the glass. "He knew right away."

"How?"

She shrugged. "I don't know. He just did."

"So I assume Deacon knows, too?" He wasn't sure why that mattered, but somehow, everything about Deacon mattered.

"Aren said he wouldn't tell."

"Is that why he sent you here?" Because Aren certainly knew about Dante's preference for men. Then again, Cami didn't quite qualify as a man. Still, somehow the idea that Aren had known Cami's secret and then sent her to Dante's ranch felt sneaky and underhanded.

Cami looked confused by the question. "I think he just knew you needed help, and between Olsa and Tama and Alissa, there wasn't much for me to do at the BarChi."

Yes, that had made sense before, and it still made sense now. That hadn't changed.

Dante pushed his unreasonable anger towards Aren out of his mind. It was nothing but his jealousy, tainting his perception as it always did. He thought about their trip to the BarChi, and Olsa saying, "I won't tell them your secret."

"I guess Olsa knows."

"I guess. I sure didn't tell her. I hope Aren didn't."

"I doubt he did. That damn woman knows everything, whether you want her to or not."

She shuddered dramatically. "She gives me the creeps. I'll take care of my hand myself, if it comes to that."

Dante frowned. Maybe it was unfair of him to assume she wouldn't be able to handle it as well as Olsa. After all, she knew about saleratus, and she seemed to know about plants. Still, if the burn did become infected, he'd feel compelled to haul her to the BarChi, whether she liked it or not. Her safety was more important to him than her misgivings about Olsa. Of course, that would mean facing Deacon and Aren again. He hoped for both their sakes it didn't come to that.

* * * *

The next day was unbelievably awkward. Although Dante tried to act as if nothing had happened, Cami was uncooperative. She barely spoke to him. She never looked at him. When he finally did catch a glimpse of her face, he could tell she'd been crying.

After supper, after the generator had been started for the night, he waited for her in the living room. He was used to her joining him there, but this time, she didn't come in. He didn't have to look far for her, though. He found her in the kitchen, chopping vegetables at the counter.

"Still working?" he asked.

"I wanted to get this done."

"I think you're avoiding me."

She didn't answer. She just kept chopping.

"How's your hand?"

"It hurts, but it's fine."

"We should change the bandage." He held his hand out to her, but she shrank away from him, as if she expected to be struck. "You don't need to be afraid of me."

She didn't answer.

He sighed. He didn't want things to be awkward between them, but it was obvious he was scaring her more than he intended. He went to the cabinet and got out the whisky. He poured himself a glass and sat down at the table.

He watched her back. He noticed the long lines of her body, and her lack of curves. The way every skirt she had ended an inch or two short of her ankle. It seemed odd to him now that he hadn't put it all together, and yet, at the same time, she still seemed absolutely female. He almost could have believed he'd imagined the entire thing.

"What's your name?" he asked.

She didn't turn to look at him. Only the fact that her movements seemed to slow gave any indication that she'd heard. "You already know it."

He pondered that answer, realising as he did he'd asked the wrong question. "What does your father call you?"

It took her a minute to answer, and he had the feeling she was debating how much to share. Finally, she said, "Cameron."

He felt better knowing her real name. Not only that, but the names were essentially the same. Somehow, it meant she hadn't ever lied to him. Not about anything that mattered, at any rate.

"And does he know about Cami?"

"He does."

He took a drink of whisky. He was content to let the subject drop, which was what he figured she'd want. "Tell me a story," he said.

He expected her to be evasive, as she so often was. He expected her to tell him one of the fairy tales, about giants and sprites and magical beasts. He was surprised when she said, "I went to the University in Francshire."

Not a fairy tale, then. Something true. It was as if now that her secret had been revealed, she felt the need to share it all. He crossed his arms and leant back in his chair. "I didn't realise women were allowed at universities."

"They're not."

It explained so much—all of the times he'd asked questions and she'd stopped short of answering. "I see."

"My father was annoyed from the beginning because I chose to study plants. He wanted me to be a businessman, and he couldn't see how botany would help with that."

It seemed to Dante one university education was probably as worthless as the next, but he opted to keep his mouth shut.

"It was a big deal, you know. The school's expensive. The students all come from old money. For me to be there, the s-son of a merchant." Dante noticed the way her voice seemed to catch on the word "son", as if she'd had to force it out. "My father hoped I'd make connections there."

"But you didn't?"

She smiled. He couldn't quite see it, but he could hear it in her voice. "Certainly not the type he had in mind."

"So, you were living as a man?"

She stopped chopping and stood staring down at the pile of vegetables on the counter. "I tried," she said quietly. "I really did. During the day, I'd go to school as Cameron. But it was exhausting, pretending to be somebody else. When I came home, I couldn't keep it up."

"So what happened?"

"I'd talked my father into letting me rent a flat downtown. I told him it was because it was closer to the school. And one day, about halfway through my third year, he stopped by to drop off my monthly stipend."

She stopped, as if that were the end of the story, and he had to prod her. "And?"

"And I answered the door like this." She touched her skirt.

"I imagine he was a bit surprised."

She shook her head. "Not as much as you probably think." She picked up the knife again and went back to chopping, but he noticed how her hands shook. Her movements were slow and careful. "I'd always been too much like a girl. I played with dolls instead of playing ball. I liked to wear ribbons in my hair. I spent my time in the kitchen with the maids. When I was a bit older, I found some of my mother's things, and I'd wear them when he was gone. I had stuff the maids had given me, too. He caught me several times."

"What did he say?"

"He hated it. And when I started at the university, he made me promise not to embarrass him."

"But he felt you'd broken that promise?"

She nodded. "He was furious. And I started crying, which made it worse. He told me I could choose to be his son, but he had no use for a daughter." Her voice was shaking, and she stopped to take a deep breath.

"He said a lot of things. Horrible things. But it all boiled down to me having to choose between being his son or being who I wanted to be."

"And being his son wasn't an option?"

"No." She wiped her eyes with the back of her hand. "He never understood. He thought I was pretending to be Cami. He couldn't accept that it was Cameron who was the lie." For the first time, she turned to look at him. She seemed desperate for him to understand. "Do you believe me?"

The question confused him. "About what?"

"That this is me?"

He had to think about what exactly she was asking. He could understand her father's confusion. To have a son who insisted on behaving as a woman had to be upsetting. At the same time, he couldn't imagine a man *choosing* to wear a dress or do women's work. No man would do such a thing willingly—not if he had a choice—and therefore, she must not have had a choice. Which meant she really wasn't a man, regardless of what was between her legs. She claimed to have always known she was female, and how could he argue with that? And yet, he wasn't sure he could put it all into words. What he said was, "I can't imagine you any other way."

He couldn't tell if she was disappointed or relieved. She turned back to her work without a word. Her silence was unnerving. The air felt heavy with emotion. He could practically taste her fear, her embarrassment, and her pain. He almost wanted to cry for her.

"Cami, you don't need to be embarrassed. What happened last night doesn't change anything."

She put her hand over her eyes, and her shoulders shook. He didn't know if her tears meant he was saying the right thing or making things worse.

"I'm sorry," she said. "It's just that I was so happy here, and now I've ruined it."

"You haven't ruined anything. That's what I'm trying to tell you. There's no reason you can't keep on being happy here. This ranch is your home, for as long as you choose to stay."

She didn't respond, but she was very still, and he had a feeling he was finally getting through to her.

"Cami, I want you to stay."

She didn't answer. Not with words, at least. But he saw the deep shuddering breath she took.

He leant back in his chair again and waited. It took her another minute or so to pull herself together, but he could see her becoming more comfortable again—she stood up a bit straighter, like she was no longer trying to hide, and her hands seemed more steady as she went about her work.

Finally, she said, "Have I told you the one about Jonas and Jamus and the castle in the clouds?"

"You haven't."

She smiled shyly at him over her shoulder. "Would you like to hear it?"

"More than anything."

She turned back to her vegetables, but he could tell he'd made her happy. He'd succeeded, to some degree at least, in putting her at ease.

"There once was a very old man, and he had just a little money, but he had two very greedy sons..."

And Dante sipped his whisky and listened, pleased that for once, he seemed to have done something right.

Chapter Thirteen

Winter descended upon the ranch with the sudden brutality Simon had learned to expect of Oestend. One day it was sunny, a shockingly cold wind blowing from the north, and the next day the inhabitants of Brighton awoke to sub-zero temperatures and a world covered in frost.

The best thing that could be said about the arrival of winter was that things at Brighton Ranch were closer to normal. Or at least, the strange occurrences seemed fewer and further between. Maybe it was colder than it had ever been. Maybe the night lasted longer and the wind howled louder, but if there was anything else unusual about the weather, Simon failed to notice.

His relationship with Frances was as easy and casual as it had always been. Frances gave no sign of anything unusual ever having happened between them. Simon might have thought he'd imagined the entire incident. Sometimes he'd go days or even weeks without thinking about it at all, but then suddenly, he'd have one of those days where he couldn't keep his mind off sex, or he'd wake from a dream with his cock hard and aching for release, and he'd inevitably begin to think of Frances.

It wasn't that he desired him. He still didn't find him attractive, any more than he'd ever found any man attractive. It was simply that he now knew how unbelievably good Frances could make him feel. It was with some reluctance and more than a little embarrassment that Simon finally admitted to himself how much he wanted it to happen again.

Even after accepting the truth of his desire, he had no idea how to go about it. It wasn't a matter of seducing Frances or wooing him. That felt wrong on every level imaginable. Frances was his partner. His friend. In many ways, his brother. There was nothing romantic between them, and Simon wanted to keep it that way. But how exactly did one go about asking another man to be his sexual partner?

"What's a hand job between friends?" was a saying commonly heard among ranch hands on the prairie. Still, Simon had no idea how to initiate such a thing. Not only that, he wasn't sure he'd be able to reciprocate.

"What's going on with you?" Frances asked him one day, midway through winter. They were in the loft of the barn, shifting hay from the back, where it was still full, to the front, which had been emptied.

Simon was caught off guard by the question. "What do you mean?"

"Just seems like you've been weird these last few days. You keep looking at me like you're about to say something, but then you just stand there."

Was that true? Simon thought back over the previous week. It was true that several times, he'd almost managed to broach the topic with Frances only to turn craven at the last second. Still, he hadn't realised he'd been so obvious. And now, being confronted by Frances, he found it no easier than he had those other times.

"If it were anybody but you, I'd think you needed money," Frances said. "But I know you hardly spend a dime of your pay, so it can't be that."

"No." Simon's cheeks were burning, his palms suddenly clammy. "It's not money."

"Well, what is it then? You know you can ask me anything."

Frances wasn't looking at him. He was looking down at his work. Simon tried to steady his shaking hands. He'd known for at least a week the words he wanted to say, although now they suddenly seemed like rather stupid words.

Don't be a fool! This is Frances. You can say anything to him.

He took a deep breath and said, "I wondered if you'd be willing to do me one of those favours again?"

Frances stopped working. He was still bent over his pitchfork, but he glanced up at Simon with huge, surprised eyes. "You talking about the kind of favour I think you're talking about?"

Simon felt sure his cheeks had to be at least ten shades of red. He wished he could snap his fingers and make himself disappear. He tipped his head back to stare up at the ceiling, concentrating on the spider webs in the barn rafters so he wouldn't have to meet Frances' eyes. "Uhh, yeah. I think so."

Frances laughed. Not a laugh of mockery or derision, though. It was a sound of pure relief.

"Holy Saints, Simon, I thought you'd never ask!"

And as simply as that, Simon found himself on his back in the hay in the cold, dry loft of the barn, with

Frances' wonderfully warm, wet mouth around his cock. This time, Simon didn't think about women. He didn't think about anything at all except how unbelievably good it felt. He didn't last long, but Frances didn't either.

"Just so you know," Frances joked when they were done, "I'm *always* willing."

After that, it was easy, although still somewhat infrequent. Most of the time, things were as they'd always been between them. There was no flirtation. No casual caresses or new intimacy. But occasionally, when they found themselves alone, Frances would turn to him with a smile and say, "Let me do you a favour."

The third time after the hay loft, they were in one of the windowless outbuildings used for storage. Frances closed the door, leaving them in utter darkness. He pushed Simon back onto a pile of burlap. He greased Simon's cock with saddle oil, and Simon lay back and gave himself up to the feel of being touched by Frances. But then Frances stopped stroking him. There was a rustle of clothing, and then Frances straddled him. The boy was naked from the waist down, his bare legs brushing Simon's hips as he rubbed his perineum on Simon's cock. Feeling Frances' erection against his own was unnerving.

Simon gripped Frances' thighs. "Wait," he said, suddenly unsure. It was one thing to have Frances suck him, but the idea of actually fucking him made him uneasy. He was glad it was too dark to see.

"Shut up, Simon." Frances' voice was thick and breathy with arousal. "It's been way too long since I got to do this."

Frances lifted Simon's erection into position and slowly sank down onto it. He took Simon deep into his warm body and began to move with wild, enthusiastic abandon.

Simon's unease quickly gave way to pleasure. Any other protests he might have uttered died unspoken in his throat. Fucking Frances felt amazing—tighter than any woman, and with none of the guilt—and Simon found himself wondering why he'd ever resisted this type of arrangement in the past. Maybe because he'd never known anyone who was nearly so willing as Frances. Maybe because he'd never trusted anybody enough. Certainly he and Garrett had never even come close to jerking each other off, let alone anything more intimate. But here, with Frances, it seemed logical. Simon was unable to have any kind of normal relationship with women, and Frances was young and horny and willing. They were friends. They were partners. They shared everything else they had. Sharing their bodies seemed like such an obvious solution.

He hoped it wouldn't cause trouble for him later.

* * * *

The deepest heart of an Oestend winter was harsh and bleak. The sky hung low and grey, and the wind blew so cold it made bones ache and skin numb, and seemed to suck the very air from a man's lungs and freeze it upon his lips. It was a dangerous time. Frostbite was common, and hypothermia always a threat. One ranch hand came down with the fever and died a week later. Another fell through the river ice and was swept away before his bunkmate's eyes. The residents of Brighton Ranch wrapped their coats tighter around themselves and ducked their heads against the ever-present wind.

There was still work to be done.

As the temperatures plummeted, Dante worried about Cami. She was so thin and unused to the cold. During the week when she'd cared for the fevered ranch hand, it had been all Dante could do to stand by and let her tend the sick man.

"What do you want me to do?" she'd asked. "Let him die?"

Better him than you, he'd wanted to say. He wanted to keep her safe, and everybody knew women were far more susceptible to the fever than men.

It wasn't until after the man was dead that Dante realised Cami was no more susceptible to it than he was.

As the days crept by, though, Dante began to realise how foolish his concern for her had been. Cami not only survived the winter, she thrived. Whatever light had left the sky seemed to have found its way into her. She was the only person he'd ever met who laughed with joy at the prospect of wrapping oneself in layers to face the day. Certainly it was easier for her than for the men, since only a small portion of her chores were outside. Still, Dante was surprised at how she seemed to bloom in those dark months. The harsh wind made her cheeks red and her eyes bright. More than once when she came in from the cold, Dante found himself thinking she was beautiful.

She spent less time in the evenings mending and more time knitting. She'd found a stash of yarn in the sewing room on the third floor, and she used it to turn out hats and mittens and scarves at a surprising rate. They were bright and cheery, and decidedly un-masculine, but they were warm, and even Dante had to smile when he saw a big rough ranch hand like Simon wearing a purple hat with a garish orange scarf as he went about his chores. Oestend itself may have been grey and bleak, but in attire at least, the residents of Brighton lived up to the ranch's name.

The darkest months of winters were brutal, but the bright side was, the worst part of the season was also blessedly short. Before long, the sky began to glow weakly blue. The shallow sunlight of not-quite-spring warmed the ground and thawed the streams. The wind went from bitter and piercing to merely frigid and brisk.

Dante was also relieved that nothing strange happened during those months. No unexplained cattle deaths or unnatural weather. No buzzards. Nothing that couldn't be blamed on good old-fashioned winter. Nothing out of the ordinary since the lightning storm.

Two weeks after the weather had turned, Dante had his first visitors—Tama, Alissa, and his brother Jay.

"They've been nagging me to bring them for weeks now," Jay said. "It was all I could do to hold them off 'til the thaw."

It pleased Dante to have them there. His last visit home had helped quell his feelings of being an outcast, but having them visit his own ranch gave him a bit of confidence he hadn't quite realised he'd been missing. Yes, it was *his* ranch, not Zed Austin's—not anymore—and it was with a certain amount of pride that he told them of its new name.

"It's fitting," Jay said. "He'd think it was funny."

"He would," Dante agreed. He could imagine Brighton laughing about it. "It was Cami's idea."

"Aren told us to ask if you'd named it," Tama said. "He also wanted us to ask when you'd be back at the BarChi. He says he'd like to talk to you at some point about the books."

"He would, huh?" Dante turned away, trying to decide how that made him feel. Everything always led back to Aren, but for the first time, Dante didn't feel that familiar stab of jealousy behind his ribs. He didn't have to remind himself that Aren wasn't out to get him. Of course Aren wanted to talk to him about the books. That was Aren's job.

"He could have come with you," he said.

He saw the surprise in Tama's eyes at the suggestion and the quick glance that passed between her and her sister.

"Well," Tama said, her tone almost apologetic, "I think he was worried you wouldn't want him here."

It was a fair enough assumption for Aren to make, and Dante regretted having made things so much more difficult than they needed to be. Aren wasn't a bad person. Somewhere deep down, Dante had always known that, but at that moment, it was as clear as the sun shining in the Oestend sky. Aren was just a man who'd fallen in love. He hadn't done it out of spite or any kind of petty desire to hurt Dante. It wasn't as if they'd been in competition for Deacon and Aren had won, because Dante had never had the strength to fight for the man he loved to begin with. He'd hidden away, keeping his feelings secret, afraid to let anybody know, and then he'd had the nerve to be surprised when somebody stronger than him stole the prize out from under him.

But it wasn't Aren's fault.

It wasn't Deacon's either.

It was over, and Dante realised with some surprise that he didn't mind. He had his own ranch now. His own life. It wasn't much, and yet it was enough.

"Tell him he's always welcome here," Dante said. "I'm the one who wronged him, not the other way around. He's got nothing to fear from me."

His brother, it seemed, had simply come to visit for the hell of it, but it quickly became apparent that the women had their own agendas.

"My father wanted to come too, you know," Tama said to him on the third day of their visit. They were sitting in the cool morning light on the steps of the front porch, each of them hugging their coats around them against the cool Oestend breeze.

"Your father? Why?"

"He still wants you to marry Beth."

"Ha!" Dante laughed. "Not a blessed chance."

"That's what I told him you'd say. I don't blame you, but I can't blame him for trying either. He even tried to get your father to marry her."

"Holy Saints! What did my dad say?"

"He politely declined." She shook her head. "I think my father's fed up with her."

"You thought she was pregnant?"

"We wondered, but seems she wasn't. She's just putting on weight, I guess." She laughed. "That's part of the problem."

"That she's getting fat?"

"Well, yes and no." She looked out across the lawn to where Alissa and Cami were putting laundry on the line to dry, fighting to keep the wind from tearing the sheets out of their hands before they could get them hung. "Beth always believed she was better than us. Always thought she was too good to be a rancher's wife. It's hard, you know? It's not like we get to sit around knitting doilies and sipping tea."

"I know you don't." If he hadn't known before, he certainly knew now how much work the women did to keep the ranch running.

"She won't do it. She always thought she'd be able to marry some rich man in town, and she could buy pretty dresses and have parties and hire maids to do the real work." She shook her head. "That's why she tried so hard to get Aren to marry her. She figured she could sit up in that house on the hill and not have to pitch in."

"Makes me glad he said no."

"You and me both. I'd be stuck waiting on her now like I did when we were girls."

"So what does this have to do with her getting fat?"

"I've carried four babies, Dante. Lost two, and have my two boys. And still, I don't have the luxury of getting plump like Beth. Alissa and I, and every maid my daddy hires—we work, all day every day."

"But not Beth?"

"No. Not Beth. She sits around and complains."

"And that's what you want to unload on me?" he joked.

She laughed. "Well, my daddy wants to unload her on anybody he can."

"Well, you tell him I said no way in this Saints-blessed world."

"I'll tell him." She looked out again towards Cami and Alissa. "So, you won't take one sister. What about the other?"

"You asking me to marry Alissa?"

"No. Just hoping you've changed our mind about letting her live here."

He watched the two girls together. Alissa was much as she'd been on their last visit to the BarChi—she seemed to take every opportunity to stand close to

Cami, and to touch her. Cami was a full head taller than Alissa, and Dante watched as the smaller girl reached up to brush Cami's hair out of her eyes. She stepped so close, he thought for a moment she was going to kiss her. It annoyed him. He couldn't see Cami's expression well enough to determine if she appreciated the attention or not.

That annoyed him, too.

"Why the hell would I want her here?" he asked.

Tama looked over at him in surprise. "Why are you mad?"

"I'm not mad!" Although as soon as he'd said it, he realised he was. "I just don't see why I should have to take care of her."

"She's miserable at the BarChi." She gestured out towards the girls again. "Look at her here. I haven't seen her so happy in ages. She's crazy about Cami! It's not like you don't have enough work for her, or room in the house. Cami might appreciate having some help."

Yes, Cami might appreciate it. She might appreciate it a great deal. She might appreciate it so much she'd start to return Alissa's casual touches and flirtatious smiles.

"Just talk to Cami about it, will you?" Tama asked.

He sighed in resignation. "Fine. But if she says no, that's the end of it!"

"What if she says yes?"

Dante chose not to answer.

Chapter Fourteen

Dante hoped to talk to Cami about Alissa that night as they sat in front of the fire, but it wasn't to be. Tama, Jay and Alissa were all there, intruding on his time with Cami, making it impossible for him to broach the subject with her. He tried staying up late, hoping to have time with her after the others had gone to bed, but it was clear Alissa planned to spend every possible moment with Cami. Even after Tama and Jay had gone upstairs, the two sat talking on the couch. Cami kept glancing nervously his way.

He should go. He knew that. He should leave them in privacy. He had no reason to stay there, watching them like some kind of dour old chaperone. He kept his gaze on the fire and tried to decide what was keeping him in his chair. Out of the corner of his eye, he saw Alissa move closer to Cami. Again, Cami glanced his direction, undoubtedly wondering when he'd leave.

He made himself stand up. "I guess I'll wish you gals goodnight."

Cami looked up at him, her eyes wide, but he couldn't read what was in them. Surprise, alarm or relief? He had no idea.

He took himself quickly out of the room and up the stairs. He went to bed, but he didn't sleep. He lay there, listening for noises from downstairs while telling himself that he wasn't. Wondering, yet telling himself he didn't care. It wasn't long before he heard them coming up the stairs. He tried not to pay attention. It wasn't his business which room they slept in. It meant nothing to him if they happened to go into the same one together.

He heard them whispering in the hallway, then the door he knew was Cami's closed. A silent heartbeat, and then light footfalls as Alissa went back down the hall. He heard the door to her room click shut.

He lay there several more minutes, debating. Would he have a chance to speak with Cami the next day? He suspected it wouldn't be any easier than it had been today. He considered going to her room, knocking on the door, asking if he could talk to her. But by now, she'd be undressed. Probably wearing that traitorous robe of hers. It reminded him of the one and only time he'd been in her room. It had been disastrous.

He decided it was better to wait until morning.

He rose early and was inexplicably glad to see that the door to Alissa's room was closed. She was still in bed. Maybe he'd be able to catch Cami alone.

She wasn't in the kitchen, so he pulled on his coat and headed for the barn. It was bitterly cold this early in the morning, and he hugged his arms around him as he walked. Birds were crying overhead.

A lot of birds.

Dante looked up. Above him, flocks of them circled. A few hawks, several jays, some robins, and at least two dozen ravens. Tiny wrens flitted frantically through them all. Dante stopped, watching them.

It seemed like a lot of birds to be there at once. Was that normal? He didn't think so, and yet, he'd never stopped to count birds before. He was usually in the house at this time of morning, and if he wasn't, he was intent on his chores. Maybe it wasn't as odd as it seemed. His determination to find Cami and talk to her before Alissa could interfere kept him from dwelling on the matter for more than a second.

He found Cami in the barn, wearing a garishly striped hat. A bright red scarf hid most of her face. Only her big brown eyes were visible, but he thought she smiled when she saw him.

She leaned away from the cow she was milking to pull the scarf down a bit, revealing cheeks made rosy by the cold. "Isn't it a great day?"

Great? Dante thought about that for half a second. He hadn't noted anything unusual about it, except maybe the birds. It was much like a million other Oestend mornings. But Cami was smiling at him, and he found himself saying, "I suppose it is."

"I love when it's like this. Like winter is trying to hold on, but he's getting old and tired, and spring is sneaking up behind him. It reminds me of the story of the old lady and the winter bears. Have I told you that one?"

"I don't think so."

"Remind me tonight, and I will."

"I will," he said. He was already thinking about being in the living room with her. The fire would be crackling in the hearth, making light dance like magic around the room, and he could watch her sew.

Except they wouldn't be alone.

"I need to talk to you," he said. He grabbed the extra three-legged stool and pulled it over to sit next to her. "About Alissa."

She turned quickly back to her milking. He wished she was still looking at him so he could judge her response, but with her turned away, he had no idea what she was thinking. He could only see the stiff set of her shoulders.

"Tama has asked if I'll let Alissa come and live here."

A short pause, then, "Will you?"

"Well, that's what I'm here to talk to you about. I want to know how you'd feel about having another woman here."

"Are you talking about women in general? Hiring maids instead of hands? Or do you mean just bringing Alissa here?"

Of course he'd meant the latter. He'd never even considered running a maid ranch. But the fact that she would ask such a thing brought him up short. "I don't know," he said. "Does it make a difference?"

She shrugged, but didn't turn to look at him. "If you hired maids instead of hands, I wouldn't have to be so careful."

He thought about that for a minute. On some level he'd known she was uncomfortable around the hands, but it hadn't ever occurred to him to do anything about it. He'd only ever worked male ranches. His first instinct was to stick to what he knew. After all, men could work harder than women, and he knew how to handle them.

On the other hand, women made less money than men, so it wasn't as if he'd be paying equal money for less work. If it made life easier for Cami, would it be worth it?

And what about for himself? Maybe the fact that he wasn't attracted to women meant he'd be better off surrounded by them rather than by men like Frances who knew how to tempt him.

Regardless, a change like that couldn't be made overnight. What he needed to know about right now was Alissa.

"What about the other?" he asked. "What if it was just her?"

Cami looked down at her lap. Her cheeks were turning an even deeper shade of red, and Dante suspected it had nothing to do with the cold. She pulled the sleeves of her coat down over her hands and glanced sidelong at him. "Do you want her here?"

"Only if you do."

She smiled a bit, looking back down at her lap. "She's nice," she said. "It's nice to have somebody to talk to."

Dante's heart fell a bit. "I see."

"I'm glad they came."

"I'll let them know," he said. "We'll have to figure out if I need to go down and get her stuff, or if somebody from the BarChi can bring it up—"

"I don't want her to live here."

Dante's heart skipped a beat, and he stopped short, unsure what to say. There was no reason her words should have made him as happy as they did.

"The thing is," Cami went on, "if she just wanted to come here and work, it would be one thing, but I think…"

She stopped, biting her lip nervously.

"You think what?" he prodded.

She was embarrassed, he could tell, but she answered. "I think she wants to come here for other reasons."

"She wants to be with you."

She nodded and finally turned to face him. "I think letting her come here would give her the wrong idea."

"So you want me to tell her no?"

She fidgeted, pulling her scarf up again to cover her red cheeks. "Maybe," she whispered. "But she's my friend."

It confused him for a second, but then he thought he understood. "You don't want to hurt her feelings, right? You want me to be the bad guy." It was more a statement than a question, but he knew he was right.

She nodded slowly. "I know it's not fair of me—"

Dante found himself smiling. "I don't mind a bit."

Dante whistled as he walked back to the house. He was pleased Cami wanted things to stay as they were. Nobody would be coming to intrude on his home or in his life. Nobody would interfere with him hearing about the old lady and the winter bears. Nobody would take her away from him.

He was so busy planning what to say to Tama, he barely even noticed the birds.

* * * *

By the next day, the unnatural number of birds overhead could no longer be ignored. Tama, Jay and Alissa glanced nervously at the sky as they climbed into the wagon to head home. Even Alissa's disappointment at not being allowed to stay seemed to be overshadowed by the presence of the birds.

They were everywhere. Flocks of them obscured the sky and covered the buildings. The barbed wire of the fences sagged with them, as did the clotheslines. Cami had to string a wire across the kitchen to hang laundry on, because anything hung outside long enough to dry inevitably ended up spotted with bird droppings. The bigger birds attacked the smaller ones. The half-eaten carcasses of robins and house wrens littered the ground. Sometimes the crows and the bluejays attacked the ranch hands as they worked.

Their activity seemed to come in waves. Bunches of them would land and sit quietly for an hour or two on the fences and the tree branches. Then suddenly, something would set them off. They'd take to the air, screeching and chirping and cawing with an unnerving raucousness.

More birds came each day. By the fourth day, even Dante's most stalwart hands seemed shaken. They wore their hoods up and kept their eyes on the ground as they hurried about their chores.

The animals, too, were spooked. Horses rolled their eyes and snorted distrustfully when led out of the barn. The cattle huddled together, moving as a nervous herd back and forth across the pasture as if searching for a patch of earth not shadowed by the flock.

There was none to be found.

A heavy feeling of tension seemed to lie over the ranch. Dante could see it in the hurried steps of his hands. He could hear it in the lowing of the cows. The funny thing was, he couldn't quite feel it. He went about his own chores feeling light and free. He wasn't sure when he'd last felt so content. A few birds in the sky did nothing to quell his happiness. Even the ever-stronger smell of bird shit couldn't bring him down.

He wasn't sure if the birds bothered Cami the way they bothered the hands. She complained about the disruption to her days, yet she did it half-heartedly. She was the only other person on the ranch Dante saw smiling, and he found her smiles unbelievably contagious.

"Why are you so happy?" she asked him on the sixth day, when he came in from his afternoon chores.

"Who says I am?"

He tried to make it sound like a challenge, but Cami wasn't intimated. "I couldn't decide if there were less of them, or if it was wishful thinking."

He leaned his hip against the kitchen counter next to where she stood shelling peas into a bowl. He thought about the flock outside. "Seems about the same to me."

"Your men are spooked, you know."

Yes, he knew. "They're just birds."

"You're the only person on the ranch who still whistles. Either they don't bother you like they do the hands, or you're good at putting up a front."

"They're just birds," he said again.

She smiled. "And the sun is just a star."

He wasn't sure what to say to that, so he said nothing. He stood and watched her instead. He liked the way her long fingers worked the pea pods, pulling the stems so a long green string peeled away, squeezing the pod just right so it opened up, revealing the soft curve of peas nestled inside. The stems and strings went into a pile, peas into one bowl, empty pods into another for Dante knew not what. He liked the way she stood, leaning forward against the countertop. Her skirt stopped an inch short of her boots. She had one foot tucked back behind her other ankle. He liked the bend of her back, as she leaned over her task, and the way her hair fell forward, hiding her face. He wanted to reach out and brush it aside. He actually started to move his hand towards her, but then stopped himself. He wasn't sure he was allowed such an intimacy with her, although he suddenly desperately longed for it.

Cami glanced sideways at him, smiling shyly. "You're making me self-conscious."

"I'm sorry."

"Am I doing something wrong?"

"Of course not."

"Then why are you watching me so closely?"

Because you're beautiful. The words nearly left his mouth before he realised he'd thought them. It surprised him, and yet, it was true. Suddenly, she seemed like the most beautiful person he'd ever seen. He wondered how he'd ever looked at her and thought her to be anything less than stunning. He'd thought her eyebrows a bit too thick, her jaw a bit too wide, her body straight and lean instead of curvy, hips uncharacteristically narrow. They were things that had seemed out of place at the time, but now he realised why. Not only that, but he knew why he no longer found them incongruous. It was because those things hinted at her underlying masculinity. Hidden. Subtle. But undeniably still there.

He'd never really thought of it in those terms before. She was otherwise so utterly feminine—the way she moved, and the notes of her laughter, and the sharp, strong heat of her anger. But in that moment, it came back to him, the memory of seeing her naked. The alluring flatness of her chest, and the softness of her stomach as it dipped down to her groin. And hanging between her legs, the heaviness of a man's cock.

A surge of arousal hit him, so strong, it took his breath away.

She turned to look at him with her eyebrows raised. "Is something wrong?" she asked.

Was something wrong? Other than the fact that he had a raging hard-on? Other than the fact that he wanted her in a way he probably shouldn't? No, nothing was wrong. Nothing, except that his entire world seemed to have turned upside down. All this time he'd lived with her and enjoyed her company and appreciated everything she did. He'd spent time with her, taken meals with her, listened to her stories, and yet he'd never quite realised how strong his feelings for her had become. He'd wanted to think of her only as a woman who shared his home and occupied some small corner of his life. Why had it never occurred to him that she could be more? Maybe because the dress she wore still fooled him more often than not. Maybe because he'd spent months doing nothing but pining for a man he couldn't have and feeling sorry for himself. Whatever the reason, his eyes were open now. And he desperately wanted more of her.

"Dante?" She sounded half amused and half alarmed, probably because he still hadn't answered her. Her eyes were bright with laughter, her full lips parted in a semi-smile, and her voice woke him up and pulled him forward, towards her.

He circled her waist with his hands and pushed her back against the counter, wanting to feel every inch of her body against the length of his, but the look on her face stopped him short. Her smile disappeared, and her eyes widened in what might have been surprise or arousal, or even fear.

Not that, he thought. *Don't let her be afraid of me.*

He stilled himself, forcing himself to be gentle. He raised his hand and brushed her cheek with his fingertips. "I won't hurt you."

She closed her eyes, as if debating his words, but when she opened them again, she smiled flirtatiously. She threw her head back, tossing her hair over her shoulder, as if daring him to kiss her. "You don't scare me."

Whether it was true, or whether it was false bravado, he didn't know, but he found himself smiling at her words. And at what he found in her eyes. Was that wicked invitation he saw in them new, or had it been there all along and he was only now seeing it? Either way, he had no intention of letting it pass him by.

He pulled her close and kissed her. It was the easiest thing he'd ever done. With the few sexual partners he'd had in the past, both men and women, he'd never quite felt at ease, but here, with her, it seemed like the most natural thing he could do. She was sweet and soft and her slim body fit perfectly against his.

What amazed him the most was how eager she was. How absolutely ready she seemed to be, as if she'd known all along this was where they were headed and had only been waiting for him to catch up. He reached for the buttons on her blouse, and she gave him room to undo them, panting impatiently against his lips until at last he had her shirt open to the waist. He slid his hand inside and caressed her, cupping the breast that wasn't there. It was strange, and yet unbelievably arousing. Yes, her chest was flat, but her skin was smooth and soft, her nipple erect, and when he brushed it with his thumb, she moaned. It was the most masculine sound he'd ever heard her make—low and deep in her throat—and it felt as if it went straight to his groin. She put her head back, arching into him as he stroked her. Her neck was pale and slender, but with her head thrown back as it was now, her Adam's apple gave her away. Dante put his lips on it and kissed it. He wanted to celebrate it. Somehow the mix of masculine and feminine he found in her was the most arousing thing he'd ever experienced. Not only that, but it seemed absolutely right. There was nothing that felt out of place. It all made perfect sense—her softness, and the feminine pout of her lips, and her reaction to his touch, and the hardness of the erection underneath her dress. How could she be anything other than she was, the perfect meeting point of both sexes? She was exquisite, beyond anything else he'd ever experienced.

He opened her blouse wider and kissed his way down her neck, ducking his head and halfway lifting her up in his arms so he could feel the bud of her nipple with his lips. He flicked it with his tongue, and smiled at the way she moaned in response. He sucked it into his mouth and felt a shudder move through her body. She made a soft sound, something that was barely more than breathing, and yet was so much more. It spoke volumes. It turned him on even more. He thought he could almost come if she made that sound again.

He sank down to his knees to kiss her stomach. It was perfectly smooth and flat, with only the barest hint of a trail of hair below her navel, leading down to the waistline of her skirt. He reached down to the hem of her dress and lifted it. He put one hand on each of her ankles and slid his hands up her long legs, towards her groin. But as his hands moved upward, she grew still. He gripped her hips, still kissing her stomach, carefully avoiding the bulge that brushed his chin.

She put her hands on his, stopping them on her hips, and when he looked up, he was dismayed to see her expression. Although her cheeks were still flushed, caution and wariness seemed to have replaced arousal.

"What do you want from me?" she asked, her voice a low whisper.

The question confused him. He wanted nothing *from* her. He only wanted things *for* her. He wanted to make her feel as beautiful as she looked. He wanted to see her with that wicked, flirtatious look again. He wanted to hear her moan. He wanted to make her come so hard she saw stars. But how could he say all that?

"I want you to be happy."

Cami blinked at him, then slowly the doubt on her face turned into a shy, hesitant smile. She reached down and put her hand against his cheek. "Really?"

He put his hand over hers and turned towards it to kiss her fingers. He wondered if he could coax her shyness back into the unapologetic arousal he'd felt in her as they'd kissed. But before he could get any further, he heard the door behind him burst open. Cami spun quickly away from him, pulling her blouse tight around her.

"Oh Holy Saints, I'm sorry!"

Dante looked over his shoulder to find Frances in the door, although the boy had turned away, covering as his eyes just as Cami fought to cover her bare chest. Dante wanted to be annoyed, but he knew it was unreasonable. The kitchen was generally considered communal ground. It wasn't Frances' fault Dante and Cami had allowed themselves to get carried away in a place that afforded them no privacy.

Dante sighed as he got to his feet. He had to shift his pants over his erection. No sense in worrying too much about hiding it. Frances still had his back turned. "What do you need?" he asked.

"There's something you should see."

"I'll be right out."

Frances practically ran from the kitchen. Dante might have laughed, except that the erotic heat in his groin was beginning to change into the very un-erotic ache of unfound release. He sighed again and turned back to Cami. She was trying to do up her blouse. Her cheeks were bright red, and when she looked at him over her shoulder, he saw that she was terrified.

"Did he see?" she whispered.

It actually took him a second to realise why she was so upset, but when he did, he could have smacked himself for being such a fool. How could he have exposed her to something so risky? Of course, the answer was simple. It was because he himself saw nothing odd about how she was—both male and female, somehow perfectly balanced. But he also knew that wasn't how others would see it.

He put his arms around her and hugged her, although her back was still to him. She was stiff and tense in his arms. He kissed the side of her head. "Don't you worry about Frances," he said. "I'll slit his throat if he says a word."

She laughed, but it was a brittle, hollow sound. "I don't want that."

Dante doubted it would come to that anyway. Not with Frances at least. He knew he could reason with the boy. His real fear was that Frances might tell some of the others, and they might not be as rational.

"Don't worry," he said again. "I won't let anybody hurt you. Not ever."

* * * *

Dante didn't have to go far to figure out what Frances wanted him to see. He stopped short just out the door, staring in shock.

The birds hadn't left, but they no longer filled the sky. They lay on the ground, unmoving.

"Dead?" Dante asked Frances.

"Every one of them. They just started dropping, one after the other. Didn't take more than a minute or two, start to finish. I'm surprised you didn't hear them hitting the ground."

Dante decided not to point out that he'd been spectacularly distracted up until Frances had burst into the kitchen.

He strode out into the yard. The birds were so thick on the ground, he had to be careful where he stepped, and it was worse as they neared the barn, where so many of them had been concentrated. Dante found himself sliding his feet instead of lifting them, pushing the carcasses ahead of him. It was disturbing, but infinitely better than feeling their lifeless bodies crushed under his boots.

Around the yard, his ranch hands stood, looking unsure of themselves, watching him nervously. Dante wished he had an answer to give them.

Simon came out of the barn, looking grim. "Damnedest thing I've ever seen," he said. "The chickens are dead, too. Every last bird on this Saints-forsaken ranch."

"Any sign of disease?" Dante asked, although he was pretty sure he knew the answer.

Simon shook his head. "Not a thing. It's like each one of them just fell over dead. Even the chicks."

"Just like the cows," Frances said.

"Easier to deal with than the cows, though, thank the Saints," Dante said. "Cami said she'd be burning the trash in the next day or two anyway. May as well do it now. Let's pile it up a bit further out past the house, birds and all, and set a torch to them before they start to stink."

"You got it, boss."

He left, and Dante found himself alone with Frances. They stood together, both of them staring awkwardly down at their boots.

"Listen," Frances said at last, "I'm sorry about earlier."

Dante lifted his gaze to meet the boy's, because he wanted to be able to focus all his attention on what Frances would say. "I suppose it's my own fault for getting carried away in the kitchen."

Frances laughed. "Well, I won't tell anyone."

Dante was pretty sure what he really meant was, he wouldn't tell anyone but Simon. But Simon wouldn't have told anyone but Frances, and so between the four of them, the secret would be safe. But he still wasn't sure exactly how much Frances had seen. "Thank you for that. I know Cami will appreciate your silence."

Frances blushed a bit and looked down to scuff his toe in the dirt. "Tell her I didn't see anything, all right? I mean, she was mostly covered, and I turned away pretty fast." He shrugged. "I don't want her to be embarrassed about anything."

Dante watched him carefully as he said the words. There was no hesitancy over the pronouns. There wasn't any hint of laughter or confusion or mockery in his eyes. Frances had never learned to be duplicitous. If he'd been lying or uncomfortable, Dante would have seen it on his face.

The knot of dread in Dante's gut eased. "I'll tell her."

He had nothing to worry about. Cami's secret was safe.

For the moment, at least.

* * * *

Dealing with the birds took the rest of the day. Through it all, Dante couldn't stop thinking about those stolen moments in the kitchen. He found himself looking for Cami, tracking her movements across the yard when she came out of the kitchen for some chore or another. He had the distinct feeling she was avoiding him, although it was hard to say. Maybe she just didn't want to deal with a pile of dead birds. He couldn't exactly blame her for that.

They debated plucking the birds in order to make use of the feathers, but in the end, nobody wanted to risk it. The trash combined with the carcasses made a tremendous bonfire past the edge of Dante's nearest pasture. It stank of singed feathers and cooked meat, and when it was done, Dante felt grimy. He went to the river. Most of his hands were already there, some of them bathing quietly, some of them splashing and dunking each other like kids. He went downstream and stripped and dove into the bracingly cold water to wash himself clean.

When he finally made it back to the house, Cami wrinkled her nose at him. "Your clothes stink. Leave them on the porch and I'll deal with them tomorrow."

He stripped, halfway self-conscious, but halfway hoping this was just her way of getting him naked. As it turned out, both feelings were moot. Cami didn't even look at him as he went past her and up the stairs to put on clean clothes. By the time he came back down, she was busy feeding the hands their supper. It wasn't until evening, after the generator had been started, that he finally had time with her.

"Have I told you the one about the lost princess and the golden horse?" she asked him from her spot by the lamp.

"No."

She began the story, and although Dante tried to listen, he barely heard a word. He delighted in watching her every move, and the way the firelight played across her skin. He could tell she was nervous by the slight tremor in her voice, and he was sure she dropped more stitches in her knitting than she ever had before. A soft blush remained high on her cheeks, and she never looked at him directly, but glanced at him sidelong through the thick fall of her hair.

He wanted nothing more than to go to her—to kiss her or hold her or even just to get on his knees in front of her and put his head in her lap—but something about her shyness and the stiffness of her shoulders kept him rooted in his chair.

Finally, when her story was done, he stood up. He went to her and held out his hand. She hesitated, then put her hand in his. He pulled her up from the couch, out of the room, up the stairs. But in the upper hallway, she stopped.

"Dante, I can't."

He turned to face her in the dim light. "Why not?"

"You promised when I came here that you wouldn't force me into your bed."

The words hurt him a little—was that what she thought he was trying to do?—but he hid it with a smile. "And I won't." He reached up to touch her cheek. She closed her eyes at his touch. He didn't know if that was a good sign or not. "Didn't occur to me back then at all, but now…" She opened her eyes again, but he could read nothing in them. "Have to admit, I was sort of hoping you'd decide to join me there."

She smiled. But she also took a step backwards, away from him. "Not tonight."

"Does that mean some other night you will?" He'd meant it mostly as a jest, but he saw the way she flinched at his words. He was scaring her, and he felt awful for it. "I'm sorry."

She ducked her head, and he stared at her long dark hair, wondering what he should say. He thought about what had happened in the kitchen that very morning. She'd been so willing. Had he imagined the passion and the abandon?

"I thought I didn't scare you," he said at last.

She raised her head a bit, glancing at him through her lashes. "I think I lied."

Women. He'd never understand them.

He reached out and took her hand. He raised it to his lips and kissed the back of it. He was happy to see her smile at the gesture. He decided to quit while he was ahead.

"Goodnight," he said.

He didn't know if what he saw in her eyes was disappointment or relief.

Chapter Fifteen

It was the dead of night when he heard his bedroom door creak open. He opened his eyes and listened to the light fall of her feet as she entered. He'd been asleep, but only barely. He tracked her paces into the room. Only a few steps, then she stopped. He turned over. He could barely make her out, standing near the wall.

"Did you change your mind?" he asked.

A heartbeat of silence, then, "I can't decide."

Holy Saints, women made things so much more difficult than they needed to be. Yet for the first time in his life, Dante found himself liking that fact. He smiled. "Am I allowed to try to convince you?"

She took a step forward, and in doing so, she came a bit more into the shallow moonlight that fell through the window. What he saw took his breath away. She was only halfway dressed—her feet and calves were bare, her legs hidden from the knee up by the linen shift that probably usually resided under her skirt. Above it, she was naked, except for the loose black sweater she seemed to favour. She held it tight around her chest, but it was short, and her midriff was uncovered and unbelievably sexy.

He sat up on the edge of the bed. He resisted the urge to move any closer, lest he scare her away. "*Please* tell me I'm allowed to convince you."

She laughed—not her normal, happy laugh, but a laugh that spoke of nerves and fear.

He held his hand out to her. Slowly, so slowly he thought it would kill him, she put her hand in his, but when he tried to pull her forward, she resisted.

"I don't know what this means," she said.

He tried not to be frustrated. He wanted very much to be as patient as she needed him to be. But seeing her smooth flat stomach, knowing what was underneath her long, loose shift, he was finding patience very hard to come by. "What *what* means?"

She didn't answer, but she moved closer. She came forward and stopped in front of him, and when he reached up to touch her bare stomach with his hand, she didn't back away.

Her seeming acceptance made him bolder. He practically held his breath as he moved his hand down to caress her hip through her shift. When she still didn't object, he pulled her closer. He put his lips against the smooth, soft skin of her stomach. She was so perfectly lean and supple and beautiful. It was all he could do to keep from grabbing her and throwing her down into his bed.

She cupped his cheek in her hand, and he looked up into her eyes, although the light was too low for him to see anything in them but shadow. She no longer held the sweater tight around her. It hung open, revealing the flatness of her chest, although her nipples were still covered. He wanted nothing more than to reach up and push the thing from her shoulders, but he waited, because he sensed she had something she needed to say.

"I've had men want me as a woman, but then they're appalled when they find what's under my skirt."

He shook his head. "I'm not one of them."

"I've had men who wanted me as a man, too," she said. "But they never want anything to do with me the next day, when I put the dress back on."

He let his lips caress her stomach. He tasted her skin. "I'm not one of them, either." He kissed her again, teasing the hollow above her navel with his tongue.

"There were men who bought me at The Chalice, but they wouldn't ever have faced me otherwise. They couldn't ever respect me as a woman. In the light of day, they wouldn't even have taken my hand to help me from the carriage."

The thought of them might have stirred the horrible rage that dwelled within him, but it was tamed by his need to soothe her. "I'd go back and kill every damn one of them if I could."

"Which do you want me to be?"

"I want you to be you."

She didn't answer. She took her hand away from his cheek, but she didn't move away. He looked up at her again, and found that she'd covered her face with her hands.

"Cami?"

She sniffled, confirming the worst of his suspicions. She pulled her hands down just enough to peek at him over her long fingers. "I don't understand how you can want me the way I am."

"Because you're beautiful." He kissed her smooth flesh again. "And perfect. And sexy as hell."

"I'm not a man or a woman," she said, and her voice caught on her tears.

"You're both."

"I'm a freak."

The word was horrible. He hated it. It sparked that terrible, dark anger in him. "No!" he said, gripping her hips tight and shaking her. "Don't you ever say that word to me again!"

She covered her face again and ducked her head, and although he still hated the word just as much, he recognised that his anger wasn't what she needed. What she needed was reassurance.

He stood up, and she dropped her hands from her face and watched him as he went to the dresser and turned up the lamp, filling the small room with a bit of light. Not enough to be glaring, but enough that he could truly appreciate her long, slim body. Enough that he could see the fear in her dark eyes as he approached.

She was stiff and tense, but she let him step close. He cupped her face in his hands and tilted her head back, forcing her to face him.

"I think you're perfect just how you are. You don't have to pick one or the other. You're both to me."

She started to shake her head, but he didn't give her time to protest. He kissed her instead.

He was careful. He touched her neck and her cheek and her hair, but nothing more. Although it was one of the hardest things he'd ever done, he didn't let his hands stray. He did his best not to push. He just held her and kissed her until she sighed and put her arms around his neck. She finally relaxed and began to truly kiss him back. Only then did he put his arms around her waist and pull her body tight against him.

"I like the dresses," he said quietly against her lips, "and I like what's under them, too. If I had the money, I'd cover you in velvet and silk. I'd put jewels on your fingers and flowers in your hair, just like one of those princesses in your stories. And at the end of the day, I'd bring you here and strip you bare and worship at your feet." He smiled as he thought about her bare feet and then thought about what was at the *other* end of her long legs. "Or anywhere else you'd let me."

She smiled back. A real smile this time, her eyes sparkling and flirtatious. "You're just trying to get me into bed."

"Yes," he said. "But that doesn't mean it's a lie."

She laughed, and he recognised the sound for what it was—a surrender. This time, she came to him willingly, as she had in the kitchen that morning, and he let go of his restraint. He wanted to touch every inch of her. She sighed as he caressed her bare back, and her side. She whimpered when he finally slid his hand up her stomach, under her open sweater to touch her chest. She didn't protest as he unbuttoned her cotton shift and pushed it off her hips, letting it fall to the floor. She let him lay her down on the bed, and then he lost himself in her—the long, lean lines of her neck and her wiry body arching against his, the feel of her nipples on his thumb, the sounds she made as he kissed his way between her ribs, down her stomach, past her navel.

And he had to stop there to catch his breath.

Her cock was smaller than average, lying erect in a patch of pitch black hair, the tip peeking from the folds of her foreskin and crowned with a drop of white. Her scrotum was small and tight to her body, and he lowered his face to it and breathed deep, grinding himself against the bed as he did. He tasted it with his tongue, and she moaned, a deep masculine sound that almost made him come undone.

He loved the way she smelt. More than anything, the thick musk of her groin gave her away as not entirely female. Not the cloying scent he associated with women, but a deeper, darker aroma that made him ache.

"Dante!" It sounded like a command, but he didn't know if she was telling him to stop or go.

He teased his tongue up the side of her scrotum, along the line where it met the inside of her leg, and she made an impatient, hissing sound that almost made him laugh. He longed to touch her cock, to taste it, but he didn't know what the rules were.

She solved his dilemma by grabbing a handful of his hair and guiding him to the end of it. "Dante!" she said again, and this time he understood.

He'd never actually sucked a cock before. He'd seen it done once as he'd watched through a window, but that incident was a distant memory, completely overshadowed by his desire to know every inch of her. In past sexual encounters, he'd wanted only to slake his own lust, but now, his own desire meant nothing. He wanted nothing more than to please her, to make her forget her fears, to erase any ounce of doubt.

He put his lips over the head of her cock and tasted the pearly drop that clung there. It was salty and earth, yet somehow intoxicating, and he moaned as he moved to explore further. He slid his tongue under her foreskin, circling her tip, thrilled by the hint of moisture he found in the soft pocket of flesh.

She twined her fingers into his hair, pushing gently, and he obliged her, sucking her length into his mouth. The sound she made this time was more than a moan.

It was a cry, so utterly feminine, and yet, as she did, she drove her hips forward, pushing deeper into his mouth. So utterly male.

He rose to taste her tip again, longing to draw more from her. He gripped her hips and began to move his mouth up and down on her length. It was easy to swallow her entire cock at once. It was easy to go faster and faster, her ragged cries spurring him along. He ground his erection on the bed as he sucked her, moaning against her cock, practically begging her to come.

And when she did, it was amazing. The sounds she made, and the way she gripped his head and filled his mouth with her seed. He'd never had that experience before, and he found it crazily erotic. It was a wonderful, secret bit of her that nobody else would have. He swallowed fast, sucking hard, wanting more of her, and she gave it. She arched into him again, and it sent him over the edge. He spent himself on his mattress as she came.

"Holy Saints, Dante," she breathed. "I'm glad I let you convince me."

He smiled. He kissed the soft skin of her stomach. He felt unbelievably at peace. Not since those stolen moments in the barn had he known such pure innocent pleasure. Every other sexual experience of his adult life had left him feeling tainted or ashamed or inadequate. He felt none of that with her. For the first time in his life he was with exactly the right person at exactly the right time.

He lay his head on her stomach and stroked her hip with his hand. He wondered how he could possibly love her as much as he did at that moment. How had she gone from being the strange woman who shared his house to the person he loved most in the world?

How could this much emotion have grown in him without him seeing it coming, the way he saw the storms moving across the plain?

He covered her fading erection with his hand. "You're not a freak. You're perfect."

She put her hand on the back of his head, twining her fingers in his hair. "You're the only one who could think that."

He kissed her stomach again. "I guess that means you'll have to stay with me forever."

A tremor ran through her at his words. He could practically feel the weight of her misgivings as she finally let them go. He moved up the bed and pulled her into his arms. She wrapped her arms around his neck and he held while she cried. He stroked her hair and made soft, soothing sounds in her ear. It wasn't the same as when she'd cried before. These tears weren't about fear, or her hatred of herself. These were a form of release and relief. These weren't about falling, but about finding that she'd landed safely after all.

"Please stay with me forever," he whispered.

She didn't say yes.

But she didn't say no, either.

* * * *

They slept snuggled together, and it wasn't until she tried to wiggle away from him at dawn that Dante woke.

"Don't go," he said, tightening his arm around her waist and pulling her backwards against him.

She made a half-hearted effort to break his hold. "I have to start breakfast."

"They're grown men." He brushed her hair aside so he could kiss her shoulder. He slid his hand down her smooth stomach to caress her hip and the inside of her thigh. "They can get their own breakfast today."

"I should get up," she said, but he knew she didn't mean it. Her voice was breathy. Her breathing was speeding up. She pushed her hips back against his groin, and Dante groaned.

"Stay with me," he whispered.

He meant something far more than just staying in bed with him a bit longer, but she didn't ask for clarification.

"Yes," she said.

She let Dante push her gently onto her stomach. There was a jar of salve on his bedside table, and he used it to grease himself and then he pushed into her, as slowly and gently as he could. He couldn't get over how good she felt—how right. She arched into him, moaning, grinding her hips back against him so he was deep inside her. He kissed her shoulders and her neck. He caressed her flat chest. He made love to her in a way he'd never done before with anybody in his life, raging desire and gentle tenderness somehow at odds, and yet, perfectly matched. He fought his own climax, trying to make it as good for her as he knew how. Her slim body fit perfectly against his. She made soft, sweet gasping sounds that were completely feminine, and occasionally she'd moan, low in her throat, in a way that was utterly male. Both sounds drove him crazy. Both spurred him on until he was rocking with her, stroking her cock with his hand, whispering he knew not what into her thick hair, painfully close to climax until her warm body tightened around his cock, and he could finally let go.

They lay there in the wet mess she'd made, locked together, breathing hard. When she'd finally caught her breath, she laughed awkwardly. "I get the feeling I'm going to be washing the sheets a lot more frequently than I have been."

He laughed, but talk of laundry was like a cloud moving over his sun. If only there wasn't work to be done and a ranch to be run. He would have liked to keep her in bed with him all day.

"I suppose having some rags close would be handy."

She pushed him off her, onto his back, then sat across his hips. She leant down so they were eye to eye. Her cheeks were red, her eyes scared and full of doubt. "Did you mean it?" she asked.

"Mean what? About the rags?"

"No." The colour on her cheeks rose higher. "What you said while we were…" Her words trailed away, as if she were unwilling to put words to what had happened.

"What did I say?"

"That you love me."

He didn't remember saying it—he'd been so caught up in their lovemaking—but he didn't have to think about it twice. He brushed his finger down her cheek. "Like a bird loves the sky."

She smiled—a big, bright smile without a hint of doubt. It was the most beautiful smile he'd ever seen, but that wasn't why he liked it so much. It wasn't even because it brightened her face the rest of the day. It was because he knew he was the one who'd put it there.

* * * *

Dante had never been happier than he was the next two days, but his happiness was tainted by the new strangeness that seemed to monopolise Oestend. The first day, Cami tried to make biscuits, but each and every egg she cracked was bad, foul and odorous in its shell. The kitchen reeked of their rottenness. The milk cow once again stopped producing. The ranch dogs slunk around the barn, snarling and snapping at anyone they saw. The haystack began to rot in the field. But worse than all of that were the voices. They were faint. Unintelligible. Little more than whispers drifting on the wind.

"Maybe it's just the wind in the grass," Dante heard Simon say.

"Maybe it's cicadas," another hand suggested.

Dante was sure it was neither of those things, but he kept his opinions to himself.

Through the day, it was easy to pretend the voices were something natural, or that they weren't there at all, but when the chores were done and night fell, the wind seemed to grow louder, and when it did, the voices were there.

"They're tired," Cami whispered one night as they lay in bed. "And really, really sad. Can't you feel it?"

The next day, she pulled him into the pantry to show him a sack of flour split open on the floor. At least, it should have been flour, but there wasn't much flour left. The entire bag was full of dead weevils.

"It was fine two days ago," Cami said. "There's no way it should be this bad now."

That afternoon, one of the dogs attacked a ranch hand. The dog had to be put down, and although the man's injuries were minor, he was badly shaken.

"He was a good dog," he said over and over again. "He was gentle as a mouse."

By the time supper ended, Dante knew his men were barely hanging on. He could see how frazzled they were as they sat at the table eating, hardly speaking at all, their eyes constantly checking the corners of the room. The haunting voices were loud, a strange whispering hiss that drifted around the room. Even Simon looked a bit spooked. Only Frances seemed to be taking it all in stride.

The hands eventually left, walking quickly back to the barracks, but Dante wasn't surprised when Simon hung back.

"We need to talk," Simon said. He pulled a chair over and straddled it backwards, leaning his arms on its back to face Dante. "The men are in a right lather. They're fretting more than a bunch of women at a birthing." He glanced quickly towards Cami. "No offence."

Cami just smiled, the way she'd been doing the last two days, and it took some effort for Dante to pull his attention away from her and focus on Simon.

"What of it?"

"They want to leave," Simon said. "They think Brighton's cursed or unlucky. They're scared, boss. They want to go home. At the very least, they want to go back to the BarChi."

"Just leave the ranch to run itself?"

Simon shrugged, as if to say, *'It's not my fault.'* "They're not too concerned about the ranch, to tell the truth. Most of them think it can't last much longer anyway. Not with animals dropping dead and turning on their masters."

Dante sighed. He crossed his arms over his chest and leant back in his chair to look over at Cami. She was watching him, her smile gone, her eyes wide, but he couldn't tell how she felt about it.

He knew he couldn't force his men to stay. If they wanted to leave, they would, and he'd be left with nobody to work the ranch. On the other hand, the last thing he wanted was to go crawling back to the BarChi to declare himself a failure. He'd grown to love Brighton, and he had no desire to leave it.

"I know it's been rough here lately," he told Simon, "but it'll pass. How about if you take the boys into town in a day or two?" It would mean working awfully short-handed for a bit, but he thought they could manage. "Let them blow off some steam. Let them get drunk and get laid, and by the time they get back, they'll feel better about things."

"They won't come back," Simon said.

"Then we let them go, and we recruit new men—"

"Dante." Simon leant forward to put his hand on the table between them. "This ain't gonna work. You bring men out, they'll be just like these you got, wanting to go back home in a day or a week or a month when the next strange thing happens. I think you got to face the fact that there's something mighty wrong with this here ranch."

"I don't want to give up on it!"

"I get that, boss. The thing is, you may not have a choice."

Dante sighed. He wanted to yell at Simon, to tell him to get out. He wanted to go across the yard to the barracks and take a belt to every one of the quivering hands who thought himself a man. But it wouldn't solve anything.

"Tell them just a few more days. If things don't clear up, I promise we'll go home."

Simon was obviously unsure of the plan, but he didn't argue. Dante wished he could believe the issue was over.

"What do you think?" he asked Cami that night, as they lay in bed.

She didn't have to ask what he meant. "I don't want to go," she said quietly. "But I don't know how long we can live like this, either."

He knew what she meant, even if he was reluctant to admit it. They had no eggs, no chickens, no flour. Even if they went to town and restocked it all, what strangeness would Oestend throw at them next?

"This feels like my home," she said.

"It is your home."

She snuggled against him, and he put his arms around her, holding her close. It pleased him to know that neither of them wanted to leave this haven they had found. Dante was more determined than ever to find a way.

Chapter Sixteen

That night, Simon lay in his bunk listening to the quiet sounds of sleeping men, doing his best to ignore the strange whispers that rode the wind. The hands had taken the news as expected—disgruntled, sceptical, yet in the end willing to wait it out. They were scared. It was that simple. The only person who didn't seem worried was Frances.

Simon smiled at that thought. How Frances could walk around acting as if everything were normal was beyond him, but he did. He shrugged each new incident off as if it didn't matter.

Maybe it didn't.

"Everything here's different," he said, when Simon asked. "It's all the same to me."

Simon was glad he didn't have to worry about Frances' morale, but he still felt protective of the boy. For himself, he would have stayed at Brighton for as long as Dante needed him, but he wanted desperately to get Frances to safety. It was his job to keep Frances out of harm's way. Frances needed him, and the truth was, Simon liked to be needed. That simple fact had been the foundation of his companionship with Garrett for years.

In many ways, he and Garrett had been alike, both of them fighting personal demons, denying themselves something they desperately wanted. For Simon, it was women. For Garrett, it was alcohol. Out of that mutual need for self-control had come trust. Simon kept Garrett out of the taverns, and Garrett kept Simon away from whorehouses and maids. It had worked, and they'd become friends, but in truth, Simon had always known that Garrett's trip to the Oestend prairie was one-way. Garrett had too many demons, and it had been only a matter of time before he gave up running. The fact that the wraiths had taken him before he'd been able to self-destruct had almost been a blessing. Yes, Simon had missed him at first, but he'd never expected to be with Garrett forever.

That was where things with Frances differed. Garrett had died after Miron's death, and after Simon had already taken Frances under his wing. He'd watched Frances transform from a green, scared kid into a bright, determined young man. He'd grown fond of him. He felt protective, but also proud. It didn't matter that maybe Frances had hopes Simon could never fulfil. They were friends, and whenever Simon thought about what might happen down the road—whether it was staying at Brighton or moving on—he'd always assumed Frances would be at his side.

Although not once had that vision included them sharing a bed.

Simon sighed, wondering what the morning would bring. He suddenly wanted to wake Frances up. They'd barely had a chance to talk before they'd crawled into their separate bunks, and Simon wished he knew what the boy thought of Dante's plan.

Of course, thinking of waking Frances up made Simon think of other things. They'd never risked sex in the barracks, but Simon knew everybody else was sleeping.

Frances' arm hung off the side of his bunk, his hand dangling within Simon's reach. Simon glanced around. The curtains to their part of the room were drawn, affording them a tiny bit of privacy.

He took a deep breath and reached up to take Frances' hand. He squeezed his fingers, and heard Frances' breathing hitch as he woke. Simon tugged on his hand, and after a second, Frances slid quietly off the top bunk to the floor. It was so dark in the room, Simon couldn't see his face at all. He could barely make out his shadow as he stood by the bed. Simon tugged his hand again, and Frances came, letting Simon pull him down on to the bed.

"We'll have to be quiet," Frances whispered. Although Simon couldn't see Frances' expression, he knew he was smiling.

"I know."

Frances stood up. Simon could discern just enough to see the boy dropping his pants. Simon wiggled out of his own and Frances crawled into the bed next to him. He felt Frances' warm fingers wrap around his cock.

"How?" Frances' question was barely more than a breath.

"Like before."

Frances rolled away, and for a moment Simon thought he had changed his mind, but then he realised Frances was reaching for the jar of salve tucked under

Simon's bed. He handed it to Simon, then turned onto his belly.

Simon didn't even have to imagine this time that it was a girl he was about to fuck. Just the knowledge of how good it was going to feel was enough. As he stroked himself, spreading the salve on his cock, he had to bite his lip to stifle a moan. He gripped Frances' ass and spread his cheeks. He put more salve on his thumb and ran it up Frances' crack until he found what he sought. He heard Frances' breath catch.

He put the tip of his greased cock against Frances' rim. He froze there, savouring the delay of his pleasure, then slowly pushed inside.

It was unlike any sexual experience he'd ever had. He could barely move, for fear of making the bunk creak. He had to bite his lip to keep from moaning. He hung on with one hand to the underside of the upper bunk, and with the other hand, he gripped Frances' hip. It wasn't thrusting so much as an exquisitely slow rocking motion—deep in then almost all the way out. Frances arched underneath him, moving his hips to maximise his own pleasure. Somehow, the fact that they had to be so quiet seemed to add to the eroticism of it. He could move his hips. He could change his angle. But no matter what he did, he had to be slow, lest the noises of the creaky bunk give them away. They moved together, both of them fighting to remain silent. In the end, Simon came so hard, he couldn't have said if he'd ended up making noise or not.

When they were done, he lay down next to Frances on the narrow bunk. He nudged him. "Better get back in your own bunk."

"Not yet," Frances mumbled sleepily. "Let me stay here for a bit."

Simon smiled and ruffled his hair. "Don't let them see you."

"I won't."

Simon lay there, warm and content in the afterglow of their lovemaking. He heard Frances' breathing slow. He touched the boy's hair again. He wanted to say something. *'Thank you'* seemed wrong. *'I love you'* was worse.

He was still pondering it when he fell asleep. At some point, in the small hours of the night, Frances left for his own bed, and Simon moved into the spot he'd vacated. The sheets were warm from Frances' slim body. His smell was familiar, like sunshine and leather and fresh-cut wheat. Simon smiled and drifted easily into a dream.

It was a day from his past. He was with Lena, walking along the footpath in the park. It was during their courtship, before the attack that had brought it all to an end. They strolled idly around the lake, happy just to be in each other's company. It was warm, and Lena carried a parasol to keep the sun off her face.

No. That part was wrong. She'd never had a parasol. Even in his dream, Simon knew this. She'd *wanted* a parasol. "Do the women still use them back in Lanstead?" she'd asked.

"Only the silly ones," he'd told her.

They walked on. Simon could hear the quacking of the ducks, and the honking of geese. Long, reedy grasses and cattails grew along the bank. He took in the smells—the wet odour of the lake and the ducks, the soft hint of Lena's perfume, and with it, the smell of sunlight and leather and wheat. The scent of the prairie.

The smell of Frances.

Yes, Frances was there, too. And because it was a dream, Simon didn't have to glance over his shoulder to know he was behind them, following quietly. His thumbs were tucked into his belt loops, and he was smiling, his eyes closed, tilting his head back to let the warm sunlight caress his cheeks.

Somehow, in that moment, Frances belonged there as much as Lena, and Simon felt completely at ease. He reached out. He grasped a hand in his. Whether Lena's or Frances' he didn't know.

It was pleasant. Perfect in a way that could never be real, and though he tried to hang on to it, he felt it slipping away. Something else tugged at the edges of his consciousness. A sound, growing louder. Voices.

He resisted opening his eyes for as long as he could, but wakefulness won out.

He wasn't at the park in Holtshire. He was deep in the Oestend prairie, in the barracks at Brighton Ranch. Lena was gone. Frances remained. The wind howled through the tree branches outside.

Real life waited. And it soon became evident that real life was going to be a bit of a bitch.

* * * *

The wind was unbelievable, like nothing Simon had ever seen. It roared around the ranch with a wild destruction that seemed too brutal to be natural. When Frances finally unlocked the barracks door and opened it, the wind blasted into the small building. It ripped the door from Frances' hand, banging it loudly against the outside wall. The door tore free from its hinges with a deafening shriek. Simon and the other men stood and stared in wonder as it tumbled across the prairie, looking as insubstantial as a leaf.

"Holy Saints," Frances said. "Gonna have to fix that by nightfall."

They had to duck their heads and lean into the wind just to get to the main house for breakfast. The door to the kitchen opened the opposite way from the one on the barracks, so it couldn't be torn from its hinges, but they had to fight to open it, and when they let it go, the wind banged it shut behind them.

As they ate, the wind grew worse. The kitchen was silent except for its roar and Cami's quiet humming. In his years in Oestend, Simon had seen hellacious wind, but this was surreal.

The ranch hands fought to do their chores that day. There was no point in taking feed out to the fields. The wind would blow it off the wagon before they made it to where the cows huddled in the sheltering trees on the far side of the pasture. They went around the ranch, securing doors and gates. Three of the men tried to fix the door to the barracks, only to have it ripped off the hinges a second time.

By the time they were eating supper, the storm had reached an all-new level of fury. It was deafening. Dante came downstairs, concern obvious on his face. He went to Cami, who stood at the counter. He put his hand on the small of her back and leant down to say something in her ear. She smiled up at him.

Simon felt himself blush. He looked down at his supper. He wasn't sure when they'd become lovers, but it was obvious now that they were. No wonder they'd both seemed happy despite the fact that Brighton was coming down around their ears.

Crack!

The noise was so loud, Simon jumped. The other men looked up from their plates, faces pale and eyes wide with fear.

Crrrrrack!

The second one was loud as the first. And then a series of them, like gun shots, one right after the other. Simon felt the sounds in his bones, each one harsher than the last. The reverberations seemed to echo in his mind, tingling along his thinly-stretched nerves.

The men jumped up from the table and ran—some to the door, some to the living room to gather around the one window. Simon followed Dante out the door just in time to see the last fence post of the wooden corral snap at its base. The wind lifted the entire fence, yanking it free from the side of the barn, and it flew high into the air like one of the kites Simon had owned as a boy back in Lanstead.

"Mother fuck," Dante swore as it disappeared across the prairie. "It's like a twister, except there's no clouds."

A twister. Simon had seen a couple of them over the years, but only from a distance. Still, the description seemed apt. As they watched, the weather vane tore from the roof of the barn.

The wind gusted stronger. Two more noises boomed from the direction of the barn, similar to the sound of the snapping fence posts, but twice as loud. It was the logs that supported the giant sign over the gate to Brighton. Simon watched in awe as the wood plank fell to the ground and the wind dragged it like a sled across the ground.

Frances came out the front door, and the three men huddled together against the side of the house. "Never going to get that door fixed tonight," Frances yelled above the racket of the wind.

Dante nodded. "Tell the men—"

Whatever he was going to say was lost in a shriek of metal and wood. The ground quaked. Simon knew they should get inside, but he wasn't sure they time. He grabbed Frances and pulled him close, thinking to protect him, although he didn't yet know what the threat was.

Another loud groan that Simon felt in his gut more than heard.

"Holy shit!" Dante yelled. He pointed.

Simon and Frances both followed his gesture, and Simon's jaw dropped open.

Dante was pointing to the giant windmill, situated between the house and the barracks. One blade was gone, and it spun erratically, in bursts and stops, but that wasn't what made Simon's heart begin to pound with fear.

The entire windmill was leaning.

Another gust hit it, and it shook. The ground bucked under Simon's feet.

"We should get inside!" Simon yelled.

He wasn't sure if the other men heard him or not. Neither moved. One more gust. One more screech of metal and wood. With a slowness that seemed unreal, the windmill toppled.

A blade hit the ground first. It snapped in half and was whipped away by the wind. Then the body of the beast slammed to the ground. Simon instinctively turned his back, huddling around Frances to protect them both from flying wood. Debris pelted his back. The crash was deafening. The ground shook, and for one second, Simon was sure the house would come down too.

And then…

Utter silence.

In the blink of an eye, the wind was gone.

Simon took a breath, then another.

"I can't breathe," Frances said, and Simon realised he was still holding the boy tucked against his body, squeezing him as if the tightness of his grip would somehow keep him safe.

He laughed nervously and let Frances go. Next to him, Dante began to curse.

Simon finally turned to survey the damage.

The windmill was no longer recognisable as such. It was nothing but a rat's nest of metal and wood, stretching from the wrecked base across the compound to the barracks.

Or rather, to where the barracks had been.

The building was demolished. Only the back wall, near the privies, still stood.

"Well," Frances said quietly, "at least we don't have to fix the door."

Chapter Seventeen

There was no way Dante could justify staying at Brighton another day. The rest of the evening was spent in preparation—salvaging what they could from the barracks, loading the wagon, rounding up some of the cattle, opening the gates between the pastures so the ones being left behind had room to roam. After that, the only thing they could do was wait for morning.

The windmill had fallen, but the generator was still intact. Dante didn't even consider relying on reserves for the night. He filled it with coal and prayed to both the Saints and Olsa's ancestors that they'd last until morning.

The tension in the house was horrible. With Dante and Cami both now using her room each night, there were enough beds in the house for the men to each have one, as long as they didn't mind doubling up, and yet none of them seemed inclined to leave the warmth of the living room. Dante wondered if any of them would sleep.

"Tell us a story," he said to Cami.

She blushed, looking at the men, who were all suddenly attentive. "They're children's stories."

Dante looked at his ranch hands. Some of them weren't much more than boys. Most of them hadn't led his life, hidden away in the barren reaches of the prairie. They'd probably grown up hearing the stories. He began to feel foolish for having brought them up, but then one of the hands said, "How about Rider and the giant?"

"I haven't heard that since I was a boy," Simon said.

Frances smiled over at him. "Then it's time you heard it again."

So Cami told the story, and the men sat enraptured, as if they really were all boys again. As if magic really existed and giants could be slain by men.

"The way my mom told it, the giant fell to earth and became the mountains," Frances said when it was over. "And the people of Rider's village made a fortress in his bones."

"No," another said. "He turned to smoke and became the clouds, and the rain made the forests grow. They used the trees to make the fortress."

It irked Dante that they'd argue with Cami's story. He wanted to tell them they could go to the wraiths if they were going to be ungrateful like that, but then he caught Cami smiling over at him. She seemed to know what he was thinking, too. "It's like I told you," she said. "The stories were always there, but sometimes they change."

* * * *

Dante and his men rolled into the BarChi two days later, the dogs and the hands driving a herd of cattle in front of them. Tama and his father came out immediately, and Dante began trying to explain what had happened, telling himself the entire time it didn't make him a failure. He was glad Deacon was out in the field. It made it easier.

Alissa and Aren were the next to greet them, although they both ignored Dante and went straight to Cami. It annoyed him. Both of them were smiling at her, touching her, flirting with her. He thought he was over his jealousy of Aren, but watching him with Cami brought it all back in a hurry.

Tama helped him carry his things to his old room. "I'll get the boys' room ready for Cami."

"Don't bother."

She turned to look at him with obvious confusion. "What do you mean?"

"Well…" Dante felt himself blushing under her sudden scrutiny. "I mean, she won't be in the boys' room. She'll be in here with me."

"Sharing a bed with you?"

"Yes."

"But, she's a woman."

Seeing her bewilderment, Dante found himself at a loss for words. He hadn't thought ahead to this moment. Of course Tama was confused. She knew he'd never been attracted to women, and yet here he was, taking one into his bed. Of course, Cami wasn't like other women, but Dante couldn't tell Tama that. It wasn't his secret to share. He'd have to lie to Tama, except he knew once Tama found out, she'd feel betrayed. They were friends, after all.

"Dante?" she prodded.

"Uh…" He stumbled for something to say. "It just happened."

"*What* just happened? Sex? Or are you telling me you're in love with her?"

"Both, I guess."

She was torn, he could tell, part of her wanting to be happy for him, but the other part of her fearing he was lying to himself, and lying to Cami.

"Does she know?" she asked.

He wasn't sure exactly what she meant, but it didn't matter. "I don't have any secrets from her."

Tama sighed as she turned to leave. "It's going to break Alissa's heart."

Tama wasn't wrong. It did indeed seem to break Alissa's heart. The next day, the girl's eyes were red and swollen. She did her best to avoid both Dante and Cami. Dante felt bad about it, and yet, what could he do? Cami didn't want Alissa, even if Dante hadn't been in the picture.

There was one person who took the news of Dante's new relationship well—Dante's father Jeremiah. "I'm glad to finally see you happy," Jeremiah said, patting Dante on the back. After that, he didn't say another word about it, but he seemed to immediately take Cami in as part of the family, joking with her and treating her with the same easy affection he showed all of his daughters-in-law. Dante loved him for his ready acceptance of her.

The next morning, after the hands had eaten and left to do their chores, Dante found Cami alone in the kitchen. She was wearing a pair of wide-legged women's trousers. To the others, it probably meant nothing, but to him, it accentuated the fact that she was male and female both. The narrow angle of her hips and the soft curve of her backside fascinated him. He wrapped his arms around her waist from behind and buried his face in her thick black hair. "We should go upstairs," he whispered.

She shook her head. "I have work to do."

"This isn't your kitchen. Let the others do it."

"I want to help. I don't want to be a burden."

He kissed her neck and as he did, he slid his hand down her stomach. He caressed her groin, letting his fingers play over what was hidden there. She wore a wrap under her clothes to minimise the bulge, and Dante found it unbelievably enticing. "Please?" he whispered.

Cami laughed, although he could tell by the breathless sound that his touch was getting to her. He didn't hear Olsa enter. It wasn't until Cami went stiff in his arms that he noticed the old lady shuffling in.

"Don't be afraid of me, Scia'loh. I'm not your enemy."

Cami's cheeks turned red, but she didn't answer.

"Don't you feel silly for having worried so much about him knowing? It was all for nothing. He knows your secret now, and he loves you for it."

Cami blushed more. She glanced down at where her hands rested on the counter. Dante noticed how they shook. "How did you know?"

"Because I'm Ainuai. My people knew many things. They were smarter than those pale fools from the continent. We made them feel stupid. That's why they wiped us out. But that's not the history you learned in your schools back east, is it, Scia'loh?"

Cami ignored her question and asked one of her own. "What is that word you call me?"

"Scia'loh? It's hard to explain. Your language uses its words on all the wrong things. In my language, there's *leh* for 'he'. And there's *lah*, that means 'she'. And there's *loh*, for the others. The ones like you." She waved her hand in Cami's direction. "For the scia'loh."

Cami's eyes went wide. She took a step towards Olsa, watching her with a rapt expression that might have been horror or might have been love. "What does it mean?"

"You don't have a word. It means man-girl. Or she-he. It means one who's neither. Or it can be one who's both. Or one who's in between. It is one who's other than leh or lah."

Cami turned to Dante, looking for an explanation, but he had none to give. All he could do was shrug. "Olsa?" she said, turning back to the old woman. Her voice shook. "There's truly a word for what I am?"

"Of course there is!"

"But…" Cami's voice caught, and she stopped, covering her mouth with one hand. "I don't understand," she whispered.

Olsa made a vague gesture with her gnarled hands, as if the answer were clear. "Continent people want to make everything sets of two—black and white, man and woman, earth and sky, right and wrong. They're blind to the world in between. But not the Ainuai. We know all things are connected, blending one into the other, all part of a whole. Between black and white are all the shades of the rainbow. Between earth and sky there's wind and rain and clouds and wraiths. Between right and wrong there are a hundred in betweens." She reached out and took Cami's hand. She stared at her with her strange, sightless eyes. "Between man and woman is you, Scia'loh. You are what you were meant to be."

Cami's breath hitched. She looked over at Dante, her eyes brimming with tears. There seemed to be a hundred emotions in her eyes—fear, and relief, and hope. *'Is it true?'* she seemed to be asking. *'Could it really be?'*

He brushed her hair from her eyes. "Makes perfect sense to me."

She covered her face with her hands, and Dante pulled her into his arms. She was quiet, but her shoulders shook from the force of her tears. He rocked her and stroked her hair as she cried. It wasn't grief behind her tears. It was relief, and a lifetime of doubt and shame. It was knowing she'd found a home. Dante wasn't sure he'd ever appreciated Olsa the way he did at that moment. She'd given Cami the one thing nobody else in the world had been able to give her. He glanced at the old woman over Cami's head.

"Thank you," he said.

She waved her hand at him in dismissal. "Bah! Don't thank me. I still think you're a horse's ass."

Chapter Eighteen

There was no room for Simon and Frances in the barracks. In fact, there wasn't even room for the BarChi hands in the barracks, let alone the Brighton hands, too. It seemed that more men had come up from the south, looking not just for work, but for sanctuary. Strange things were happening all over the prairie.

All over, that was, except for at the BarChi.

In town, men talked. Stories spread. Tales grew. They became the ominous, whispered fodder of barkeeps, shopowners, farriers and whores. From them, men learned that the BarChi was somehow immune to whatever plagued Oestend.

"I tried to send them away," Deacon said, "but it ain't like they got anywhere else to go. In the end, I put them in the barn. Pay them a pittance. I keep hoping they'll get fed up and leave, but for every one that does, two more come to take his place."

Simon, Frances, and the rest of the Brighton hands found themselves bedding down in the back room of the barn, along with eight other men they didn't know and one man they did—Foster. He was frightening to look at. The top of his forehead was a mottled band of scar tissue. The right side of his face drooped unnaturally and didn't move when he spoke. Four of the other men appeared to be with him. Simon made sure to bed down as far from the man as he could.

On their third day at the BarChi, things got worse. That was the day Fred McAllen showed up with two daughters, four dairy cows, a flock of maids and a whole herd of swine.

"Couldn't keep my girls safe," Simon heard the man proclaim to Deacon and Jeremiah. "What else could I do?"

Having a dozen maids appear at the BarChi made the ranch hands happy, but Simon suspected they were the only ones. The women were all put up in the house, as were Fred and his daughters, Beth and Uma. He heard Tama, Cami and Alissa complain more than once that it had only given them more people to wait on. Cows and horses had to be moved in order to make room for the pigs. Fences built to hold Oestend cattle didn't necessarily hold hogs, so men were put to work making the field secure. The barn wasn't big enough to hold a dozen men, plus the horses from three different ranches. The dairy cows were crammed so tight into the back barn, Simon wondered how anybody found room to milk.

And over it all, there was *noise*.

Squealing pigs and giggling maids. Men yelling and arguing. Horses stamping and snorting in agitation, wanting out of the barn. It was a nightmare. More than once, Simon wondered about going back to Brighton.

Two days after Fred McAllen's tribe had invaded the BarChi, Simon walked into the barn to find Frances,

Aren and Deacon on their way out of it. The sun was already falling low in the sky. The generators would be turned on soon. It seemed like a strange time to leave the barn.

"Where're you going?" Simon asked.

Frances' ears turned red, but he smiled. "With Aren and Deacon."

Simon had almost forgotten that Aren and Deacon had their own house. A house that wasn't filled with ranch hands or maids. He eyed the back room of the barn. It was crowded and stank of sweat and tobacco. None of those men were his friends. The ones he knew were more like employees. He had a sudden empathy for Deacon, who held himself apart from the men.

All except for Aren. And apparently Frances.

Simon turned back to find Frances watching him expectantly. "Maybe I'll come with you?"

Frances' face lit up. "Really?" he asked.

It seemed like a strange question, and Simon shrugged. "Sure. Why not?"

Frances was practically bouncing. Simon had the feeling he was having to restrain himself from hugging him. "It'll be great," he said. "I promise." But then he turned to Deacon and said, "Is it all right?"

Deacon looked at Simon appraisingly, much the way he looked at new hands who showed up on the ranch, assessing whether or not they'd last and how much trouble they'd cause. "He know how to keep his mouth shut?"

"Of course," Simon said.

Deacon looked at Aren, and Aren shrugged. Deacon sighed. "All right." He pointed a finger at Aren. "No rope."

Aren smiled back. "No rope," he agreed. Then he winked over at Frances. "Unless we use it on him."

Frances laughed. He was happier than Simon had seen him in ages. "Saints, don't tease me! I wouldn't last a minute!"

Rope?

Simon had the distinct feeling he was missing something, but he didn't have time to think about it. The others were already out the door, and Simon had to hurry to catch up. Aren and Frances were further ahead, and Simon fell into step beside Deacon.

"Tell me what's been happening up there at Brighton," Deacon said.

"Didn't Dante tell you?"

Deacon glanced at him sideways. "Dante and I ain't exactly on the friendliest of terms."

Out of Deacon and Aren, Simon hadn't ever known which one of the two Dante had a problem with, or if it was both. He was curious, but he knew better than to ask Deacon. So instead, he started filling him in on what had happened since his last trip the BarChi—the birds, the lightning, the milk cows that wouldn't produce. And the voices. Through it all, Deacon listened, his eyebrows down, his confusion plain on his face.

They arrived at the house, and Simon followed them into the living room. Deacon led him to the bar and poured the two of them each a glass of whisky, as Simon told him about the final windstorm that had sent them packing. "I know this is Oestend, and there's always wind, but I'm telling you, it was like nothing I've ever seen."

Deacon shook his head. "Strong enough to topple a windmill? I've never seen it that strong, either."

"It was unbelievable the way that thing come down. I can't even describe it."

Deacon whistled. "I checked that mill myself. Saints, you know. You were there. No reason to think it was unstable."

"It's been one strange thing after another. Ask Frances about—"

That was as far as he got. He'd had his back to the room as he'd talked to Deacon. At that moment he turned around to find Frances, and what he found stopped him dead in his tracks. Aren was sitting in one of the two chairs in the room. Frances was straddling his lap. And they were kissing.

Not just kissing.

More like, trying to swallow each other's tongue. Frances seemed to be doing his best to get Aren undressed too, and as Simon watched, Aren reached down and began to stroke Frances' erection through his pants.

Simon was stunned. He glanced over at Deacon, expecting to find him angry, but Deacon looked downright amused. He shook his head. "That boy of yours is damn impatient."

Simon felt the world spin, and all the pieces fell heavily into place. All this time, he'd looked at Deacon and Aren as a married couple, and therefore he'd assumed they were both off-limits. Other nights, as they'd passed through the BarChi, Frances had stayed at Aren's house, but it had never occurred to Simon what was really going on. He'd assumed Frances and Aren had just been busy talking and drinking until it was too late to leave. But suddenly, it all made sense. And Frances' excitement about Simon joining them became clear in a whole new way.

Simon wasn't sure how he felt about the idea. He couldn't even decide how he felt watching Aren and Frances together. A bit of jealousy. A hint of arousal.

But over it all, embarrassment and extreme discomfort. He'd learned to allow for sex with Frances, but with Aren too? And Deacon? He glanced again at the man next to him and almost shuddered.

There was no way this was happening.

Except it was. Frances was breathing hard, grinding against Aren as he kissed him. Aren grabbed Frances' wrists, stilling him, pushing Frances away just a bit. "You're never going to last long enough for us to have any real fun," he teased.

Frances laughed breathlessly. "Saints, you don't have to tell me."

Next to Simon, Deacon laughed, his voice deep and booming. "You intend to make a night of this, you best take the edge off now."

Aren smiled over at him. "Good idea."

He pushed Frances off his lap and began to undo Frances' pants.

Deacon looked over at Simon, his eyebrows up, as if to say *you going to help*? Simon felt himself blush up to his hairline. Holy Saints, what exactly were they expecting of him?

Deacon seemed to realise Simon wasn't going to do anything. He shrugged and put his glass of whisky down on the bar and crossed over to them. Aren seemed to be waiting for him.

"Rope?" Aren asked.

He was obviously teasing, but Frances moaned.

"I don't think we need it," Deacon said.

He stood behind Frances. He reached around and grabbed the boy's wrists, pulling his hands behind his back. He held both of Frances' wrists in one hand and wrapped his other arm around Frances' shoulders and leant down to kiss the soft skin on his neck. As he did, Aren pulled Frances' pants out of the way. Frances' eyes were closed. His breathing was shaky. Aren teased his tongue up Frances' erection, and Frances moaned.

Simon felt as if he were made of stone. He couldn't move. He was too uncomfortable to be aroused. He felt awkward for being there, and even more awkward for not being involved. His brain screamed for him to turn away, and yet, he worried he'd feel even more foolish for that in the end, like being the one man in the room who didn't get the punchline to a joke. He stood frozen in his spot as Aren swallowed Frances' erection to the root. Frances moaned again, deeper this time. It was a sound Simon recognised well. Deacon gripped him tighter. Aren's head moved faster. They'd teased him about not lasting long, and he didn't. Simon knew when Frances came by the way his breathing hitched, and the way his hips bucked.

Simon thought his own relief at having it over might have been equal to what Frances felt, albeit for very different reasons.

He turned away from them and drained the last of his whisky in one gulp. His hand shook as he poured himself another glass. Behind him, he could hear all three men laughing as Aren and Deacon teased Frances good naturedly about having a hair trigger.

Simon couldn't face them. He was torn between arousal and disgust and shame and outright fear—not just because they were all men, but because there seemed to be no boundaries. He had no idea what was expected of him or where he fit in. He had no idea if he could even perform with other men in the room. The idea of doing anything sexual with Deacon almost made his bile rise.

He heard Frances come up behind him. He recognised the breathlessness of his laugh. The boy stepped up next to him and reached to pour his own glass of whisky. His cheeks were still flushed, and he looked happy and relaxed. It bothered Simon for no good reason. But when Frances turned and met his eyes, some of the shine disappeared from his face.

"What's wrong?"

Simon was glad to have him ask. "I think I should go."

The disappointment in Frances' eyes was obvious. "No! Why?"

"*Why*?" It seemed like such a stupid question. Did Frances really not know? "Why do you think?"

He saw how the question confused him. Frances' eyes flicked to the side, towards Aren and Deacon.

"Are you mad?"

Was he? He wasn't sure. "I just think I should go."

"You *are* mad!"

"No—"

"Is it because it was Aren? I didn't think you'd mind."

"No." That wasn't it. Or was it? Simon wished he knew. More than that, he wished Frances would stop looking at him with his big, hurt, puppy dog eyes.

"Hey." Deacon suddenly stepped up to them. He leant down and kissed Frances' neck, and Simon thought he'd never seen Frances look so sad. "Let's take this upstairs," Deacon said. "Aren went to turn on the generator."

"Give us a minute," Frances said.

"Take your time. We got all night."

Simon couldn't even look at the man. He listened to Deacon's heavy tread as he went up the stairs, presumably to where their bedroom was. The thought made Simon's heart race, and not in a good way. He had the urge to run.

"Frances, this is too much for me. Really. I can't do this."

If he thought Frances could look more disappointed than he had before, Frances proved him wrong. "All right. I'm sorry. I guess… I don't know. I guess I misunderstood—"

"I didn't realise…" Simon was hesitant to admit how stupid he'd been about exactly what Frances' relationship with Aren and Deacon was. "I didn't realise it would be all four of us."

For some reason, that seemed to cheer Frances up a bit. "If it was just us, would you stay?"

Stay in this nice warm room instead of sleeping in the hay in a draughty barn with nearly a dozen other hands? "Of course."

Frances smiled, his entire expression suddenly changing, as quick and bright as the sun emerging from behind the clouds. He seemed to have to restrain himself from bouncing on his toes. "Thank you!" he said, taking Simon's hand.

"You two coming?" Aren asked from behind him.

"No," Frances told him. "You go ahead."

"Everything all right?"

"It's great," Frances said, and the emotion Simon heard behind that word worried him a bit.

For a while, everything was fine. There was a thick, soft fur hide on the floor by the fire. They sat there together, sipping their whisky. Simon used a stick to stoke the flames, doing his best to ignore the knot of unease in his belly. No matter what had happened earlier, staying at Aren's was going to be infinitely better than sleeping in the barn.

Frances' boots were off, his pants and shirt still undone from earlier. He smiled over at Simon. "I'm glad you came."

It made Simon nervous for a reason he couldn't quite explain. He still felt there was something he was missing.

Frances turned towards him, sitting across his lap so he could look into his eyes. He put his arms around Simon's neck and kissed his cheek.

"I promise it will be worth it."

"I'm not worried," Simon said, although he knew he was lying.

Frances pushed him back onto the rug and began to undo Simon's shirt, kissing his chest as he did. It was a kind of intimacy they'd never shared, and Simon found it disconcerting. Frances caressed Simon's chest and sides. Simon closed his eyes and tried to enjoy as he'd done in the past, but in truth, he wished Frances would hurry up and get on with things. He'd learned to enjoy sex with Frances, but he didn't know how to handle what Frances was doing.

Frances moved his warm mouth from Simon's collarbone to his nipple. He teased it with his tongue, and Simon gasped. He'd never had anybody touch him there—certainly not in a sexual way—and the sensation surprised him. Frances moaned in response. He looked up at Simon. His cheeks were more flushed than before, his eyes heavy with desire.

This was different than anything that happened between them before, and Simon felt something akin to panic stirring in his chest.

"Frances, stop."

Frances shook his head. "No, Simon. Please don't say that." He bent to kiss Simon's chest again. "I'm sorry about Aren. I didn't know you'd be mad, but it's just us now."

"That's not it."

"Then what?"

"This just isn't how we do things."

"I know." Frances moved up so he was looking down into Simon's eyes. "But it's just one night. One night here in front of the fire. Not hiding in a barn, or in some dirty shed. That's all I want. Just one night where I can feel like we have something good."

Simon didn't understand what any of those things had to do with what was going on. All he knew was, their easy arrangement was suddenly looking decidedly less simple. "Wait—" he started to say. But just as he did, Frances kissed him.

It was strange and awkward and not at all erotic, and Simon lost his patience. He pushed Frances backward. "Stop!"

The sudden surprise in Frances' eyes was quickly replaced by something far more painful to see. As if Simon had betrayed him. It should have hurt, but it only made him angrier.

"I don't want this!"

"But…" Frances' voice caught.

If he cries, I'll never forgive him.

"I don't understand. You asked me to stay down here with you."

"Not for this!"

He'd been worried Frances was going to cry, but his eyes suddenly hardened into something more like anger. "Then for what?"

"I don't know! For what we usually do! We have an arrangement."

Frances sat back hard as if he'd been shoved. "An 'arrangement'? Is that how you see it?"

"How should I see it?"

Frances shook his head. He stood up and began buttoning up his shirt and tucking it back into his pants. "I can't believe I was such a fool. You said you wanted to come here to Aren's—"

"Not for this!"

"—and you asked me to stay downstairs with you, and I was stupid enough to believe you actually wanted to be with me."

"Frances, don't be mad."

Frances grabbed his boots and pulled them on, then turned to glare at Simon. "Do you have any idea what it meant to me to think that?"

"I've never lied to you about the way I feel."

Frances' laugh was harsh and bitter. He covered his eyes with one hand. "You really think that's what I'm angry about?"

"Isn't it?"

Frances laughed again. It was a horrible sound, full of heartache and self-recrimination. He looked up at the ceiling, as if searching for answers, then back down at Simon where he still sat on the floor.

"The real problem is I'm a Saints-blessed fool."

He turned and headed for the door, and Simon hurried to get up off the floor and go after him. "Frances, it's full dark out there!"

"Then stay inside."

Frances slammed the door behind him, forcing Simon to fumble it back open and close it again in his haste to catch up. "Frances, wait!"

"Go to the wraiths."

Simon debated the wisdom of pointing out the fact that it was well past sunset, and they were both inviting that exact fate by being outside at all. "I'm sorry, all right?"

Frances stopped in his tracks and turned to face him. "Sorry for what? Do you even know?"

Did he? Not really. Not only that, he wasn't even sure it was true. Underneath it all, he still felt it was Frances who owed *him* an apology, not the other way around. It was Frances who had taken him to Aren's without explaining why. It was Frances who had stood there and let Aren get him off as if it were the most normal thing in the world. It was Frances who had tried to alter the beautiful simplicity of their relationship by making it romantic.

"I don't know why you're pissed at me! This is *your* fault!"

Frances flew at him so fast, Simon barely saw it coming. The boy slammed into his chest with both hands, knocking the wind out of him and shoving him hard enough that he stumbled. He fell and landed hard on his ass.

"Fuck you!" Frances yelled.

Simon tried to stand up, but as he did, Frances punched him in the face. Simon fell back to the ground. He tasted blood and had to turn and spit into the dirt. "Holy Saints, Frances, what the fuck is your problem?"

"Would it have killed you to let me pretend, for just one night?"

"What the fuck are you talking about?"

Frances reeled back and kicked him hard in the thigh. On one hand, Simon recognised that Frances was intentionally aiming for a place that wouldn't do any damage. Saints knew he could have hit him in the gut, or the kidneys, or the head or the nuts. Even in his rage, he was being kind. Still, it hurt like hell.

"Enough!" Simon roared. He pushed himself up and shoved Frances, although not nearly as hard as he could have. "You want to fight me, kid? You really think you can win?"

Frances didn't back down. He stood up straight. He squared his shoulders. Tears were streaming down his cheeks, but he looked Simon right in the eyes. "Go ahead. You can't hurt me any more than you already have."

It was worse than being punched in the gut. Simon wished Frances had hit him instead. He took a step back, trying to understand what the hell had just happened. An hour or two ago, they'd been friends, and everything had been fine. What had brought them to this?

He wanted to erase it all. He wanted to go back to that moment where Frances had so innocently told him, "I'm going with Aren and Deacon." But this time, Simon wanted to let him go.

But he couldn't. He couldn't do anything. He just stood there and watched Frances walk away into the night.

Chapter Nineteen

All the extra people at the ranch were making Dante crazy, and he had to physically be restrained from killing Foster when he saw him. The man made Cami nervous too, and Dante noticed how she stuck close to the house.

More hands had shown up the next day, and so Jay had volunteered to go back to the now-deserted McAllen ranch and turn away anybody else bent on finding sanctuary at the BarChi.

Of course, the hands liked having women around, as did Alissa. Some of the women stayed hidden in the house, which Dante thought was wise, but others delighted in wandering out and flirting with the men. It was becoming all too common to stumble upon couples who thought they'd found a private place on the very crowded ranch.

Despite the hubbub and the fact that she was comfortable with only a few select people, Cami seemed happy. Unfortunately for Dante, one of those people was Aren. And try as he might, Dante couldn't stop being annoyed at how often he saw Aren with her. The boy seemed to make a point of searching her out. Even worse, he couldn't seem to talk to her without touching her too. It made Dante seethe.

After breakfast the next day, Dante took Cami's hand and led her away from the bustle of the ranch. He took her up the hill, towards the fields, into the untamed land of the prairie. It was surprisingly warm. The sun was golden, the Oestend wind a gentle breeze—a hushed, rippling melody that made the long grasses frolic and sway. Cami hugged her sweater around her, smiling, her eyes bright. Dante couldn't believe how happy she looked. He wished he felt the same, but it was tainted by his thoughts about Aren.

"Quit scowling at me and tell me why you're so grumpy."

Was he scowling? Yes, he supposed he was. He thought again about the way Aren had flirted with her, and a familiar feeling bloomed in his chest. "I'm a jealous man."

He wasn't looking at her, but he saw from the corner of his eye the way she turned to him in surprise.

"Jealous? Of what?"

"Of Aren!"

"Because of Deacon?" she asked in a carefully guarded tone.

"No! Not because of Deacon!" Not anymore, at least. "Because of you! I hate the way he touches you!"

"Ah." It was a sound of understanding, but not of sympathy. She sounded sad. He wanted to ask her what that 'ah' had meant, but he wasn't sure how.

"Do you see the way Aren is with the other women?" she asked at last.

"What other women?"

She sighed in exasperation. "What other women do you think, Dante? Any of them. All of them. Have you ever seen him flirt with Tama or Alissa or any one of the McAllen maids the way he does with me?"

He thought about it. Other than Olsa, the only woman he'd ever seen Aren talk to was Tama, and when he did, he certainly never touched her the way he did Cami. It made his jealousy run hotter than before. "No! It's only with you."

"Right. It's not that he dislikes them, but they make him uncomfortable. He doesn't know how to behave around them, so he avoids them whenever he can."

"Yeah. So?"

She sighed again, clearly even more exasperated with him than before that she had to spell it out so completely. "I'm not a woman to him, Dante," she said at last, and he heard the way it hurt her to say it. "He acts that way with me because he knows…" Her voice caught. She took a deep breath, and said, so quietly her voice was nearly lost in the wind, "He flirts with me because he knows I'm a man."

He'd never heard her say those words. He knew how much it pained her. And with that knowledge came real understanding of what she was saying. "It hurts your feelings."

She shrugged. "It reminds me every time that I'm not what people think. Or, I guess I mean it reminds me that what I think I am isn't what other people see."

In the blink of an eye, his jealousy was gone. On one hand, he was happy to hear that even Aren could get things wrong from time to time. But he recognised his self-righteousness was petty. Somebody was hurting her, and he wanted to fix it. "Do you want me to kill him for you?" He was joking, because he knew he could with her, but there was an edge of truth to it, too. He'd do just about anything to make things right.

"Ha!" she laughed. "Yes. Go be a big brute and kill the poor boy for hurting my pride."

He stopped walking, grabbing her as he did so that she turned to face him. "I will if you want."

She shook her head. "He doesn't mean it. I don't think he even knows he's doing it. It's still better than how most people treat me when they find out." She smiled at him, and if it had a hint of sadness behind it, it seemed to have true humour in it as well. "He's a friend. He accepts me, just not quite on the terms I'd like."

He pulled her close and kissed her chin. "So I don't need to kill him?"

She laughed again and put her arms around his neck. "No. And you don't need to be jealous of him, either."

Her laughter was real this time, light and sweet. He loved her eyes, the light in them and the happiness. Knowing he was the one who'd put it there made him feel larger than life. Like he could conquer the world. How could anybody look at her and not see what he saw?

He brushed her cheek with his fingers. "They're all fools."

She nodded as she leaned in to kiss him. "Yep. And you're the biggest fool of all."

Somehow, he couldn't quite bother to be offended.

* * * *

That night, they lay in bed together, tangled in each other's limbs. Cami's legs were wrapped around Dante's waist, and as he pushed against her, he caressed her smooth, flat chest. He sometimes forgot that she didn't really have breasts. Yes, they would have been very small, flat breasts, but she responded when he touched them in a way that implied they were what she wanted them to be.

He sat up, so he could look down at her—her deep, dark eyes, closed now as she succumbed to his touch, her long, lean body, arching into him, and her small, hard cock, lying erect against the flat of her abdomen.

He ran his finger down its length, and she moaned.

"Does it bother you?" he asked.

She opened her eyes, although her lids were heavy with arousal. He loved being able to make her that way. "Does what bother me?" she asked.

Again, he brushed his finger down her length. "That it's wrong." Of course, he didn't think there was anything wrong with it at all, but he knew she believed it shouldn't have been there.

"It used to. There was a time when I wouldn't let myself use it. If I touched myself, it felt like my hand was betraying my heart."

"What changed?"

She smiled at him, that wicked, flirtatious smile he loved so much. She used her legs to pull him tighter against her. "I guess I got horny."

He laughed, and leant down to kiss her chest. But he knew she was evading the question. "It couldn't have been that easy."

It took her a moment to answer, and when he looked into her eyes, he could still see her arousal, but underneath it, he saw the pain of remembering it.

"This is all I have," she said. "It's all I'll ever be. I realised that denying myself any kind of pleasure didn't prove anything. It just meant never feeling as good as I do right now."

Her words warmed him and made him smile. He caressed her cock again, stroking it softly until she closed her eyes and arched into him. "It *is* all you have," he said, and she opened her eyes again to watch him. "It's all you need."

"Sometimes I wonder. Sometimes, when you're inside of me, I close my eyes, and I let myself believe it's different. I imagine things down there are the way I think they should be."

He could tell by the way she said it that she expected that confession to bother him, but it didn't. He leant down to kiss her lips. He loved to watch her. And to hear her. And to taste her. He loved that he could make her moan and writhe. He loved exploring her body and seeing the different ways she responded.

"You imagine anything you want. Just as long as you know I love you the way you are."

He moved his hand down, between her legs, stroking her where her opening would have been if she'd been completely female. For himself, he was glad to feel the smooth skin of her perineum, and the heaviness of her scrotum in his hand. But if it made it better for her, he didn't care what she imagined. He stroked between her legs, letting his fingers play over her flesh as if seeking the opening in the moist folds of a woman's sex, and she responded, gasping and spreading her legs wide. He refrained from touching her cock again, but he caressed every inch of the skin between her thighs. As he did, he kissed her neck, and her collarbone. He teased each of her nipples with his mouth until they were red and swollen.

He moved down her body and put his tongue where his fingers had been. He used his mouth between her legs, sucking and licking her perineum until she was gripping his head, panting and moaning. He moved lower, lapping at her entrance until her rim was slick and wet. And then he slid his finger inside.

She cried out, pushing down hard onto his hand, and like an over-anxious teen, Dante lost control. The warmth of her around his fingers, the smell of her sex, the feel of her bucking towards his hand, it was all so perfect. His orgasm caught him completely by surprise, crashing down onto him far sooner than he might have liked. He came hard, grinding his erection against his bed, marvelling a bit even as he did at just how much she turned him on.

His climax was strong and sudden, but over quickly, and he focused again on her and what he wanted to do. He knew he'd teased her enough. He moved up, and he swallowed the length of her erection, letting it push deep into his throat. He slid a second finger in with the first and moved them in and out, matching the rhythm of his mouth on her cock. He didn't know what she focused on mentally—whether she revelled in having her penis sucked, or whether she imagined that the opening he fingered was really a vagina. Either way, he was just happy to give her what he could. All he cared about was the way she gripped his head, thrusting into his mouth. The way her back arched. The way her body spasmed around his fingers. And the way she cried out his name as she came.

Yes, this was all she would ever have. He planned to make sure she never regretted allowing herself to use it.

* * * *

After their quarrel the night before, Simon had hurried back to the barn, counting himself lucky to have survived a trip outside. He figured he had the combined power of the BarChi generators to thank for it.

He'd lain awake for a long time, waiting for Frances. As the seconds ticked by, he had begun to imagine the worst. He'd never forgive himself if Frances was lost to the wraiths because of their fight.

When the boy had finally come in, Simon breathed a sigh of relief. His bedroll was next to Simon's, but instead of lying down in it, Frances began gathering it all up in his arms.

"Frances, can we talk about this?" Simon had whispered.

Frances hadn't even acknowledged him. He'd gone to the other side of the barn to bed down. By the time Simon woke up in the morning, he was already gone again. He wasn't at breakfast, either, and Cami told him he'd been in early to eat by himself.

Simon tracked Deacon down later that morning, chopping wood behind the barn.

"Can you tell me where Frances is?"

Deacon didn't even stop chopping. "Nope," he said as the axe bit through a log.

"No, you can't tell me, or no, you won't?"

"Frances told me you'd ask. I ain't gonna repeat exactly what he said." He laughed and shook his head as he swung at another log. "I never heard anybody but Red cuss like that. But the short version is, he don't seem to want you to find him."

Simon said a few choice words himself. It annoyed him that Frances would avoid him. Deacon laughed, and in one quick motion, he flipped the axe in his hand to offer it handle-first to Simon. "Why don't you put that energy to good use?"

Simon took his advice. It felt good, actually, to swing the axe and take out his frustration and his anger on the helpless wood. The blade bit through the logs with a satisfying *crack*. It all felt rather therapeutic until Red showed up.

"Need help?" Red asked.

Simon swung the axe again, cleaving a quarter of a log in two. "No."

"Good." Red leaned against the side of the barn to watch him. "Then we'll get along just fine."

Simon had never been fond of Red, and he had no desire to talk to him now. "Go find somebody else to bother."

Red ignored him. "Who punched you?"

Simon stopped chopping long enough to tongue the tender part of his lip where Frances' fist had split it open. He'd mostly forgotten about it. "Frances."

Red laughed. "Really? Feisty little thing, isn't he? Lovers' quarrel?"

The question irked Simon. "We're not lovers!"

Red shrugged, seemingly unbothered by Simon's hostility. "Call it what you like. Partners. Whatever."

"It's not like that!" Except, of course, that it was. Or it had been. He had no idea what they were, now.

Red held his hands up in surrender. "No need to get riled up. We're men, after all. We got needs, and Saints know women are hard to come by."

"Red, mind your own damn business."

But of course, Red didn't oblige him. "Desperate times call for desperate measures, my friend. We've all been there. I've dipped my knob in the chocolate sauce a time or two myself, and I'd do it again, given the chance. I'd fuck my own brother if he'd let me, but he won't. Not to say we ain't given each other a handshake now and then over the years but—"

"Oh, Holy Saints," Simon swore, wondering if the conversation could get any more uncomfortable.

"—I'll tell you what, if Frances offered it up to me, I'd say yes and thank you, too."

He wanted to tell Red to go to the wraiths, but he also knew the man had a point. Everybody knew it happened on occasion. So why was he having such a problem with it? Maybe because he thought he'd understood the terms of their arrangement, and suddenly found himself not knowing what he'd done wrong.

He rubbed his forehead then pinched the bridge of his nose. Red wasn't his friend, but Saints knew he had nobody else to talk to. He took a deep breath and said, "I don't know that we're partners anymore."

Red was silent for a minute. Simon had expected him to make another crude comment, but when one wasn't forthcoming, he looked up.

Red was watching him, looking thoughtful, which he didn't often do. His brother was friendly and hard-working, and Red countered by being a lazy asshole, but it seemed now it really was all an act. Maybe the man saw far more than he let on.

"A wise man once told me he looked for three things in a friend—a man who'd cover his back in a fight, who'd loan him money when he was short, and who'd lend a hand when he was blue in the balls. He told me, you find those three things, you may as well give that man a wedding ring, 'cause you sure as hell won't find all three in a woman. Frances fit that bill?"

Simon didn't answer. He had a feeling he didn't have to.

"Well then," Red said, "the next question you have to ask yourself is, do you?"

* * * *

If anyone had ever told him he'd get wisdom from Red, Simon wouldn't have believed it, but as the day wore on, he found himself watching Frances and pondering Red's words.

Frances had been his friend, and in a way, his lover, but it had always been on Simon's terms. Sex, yes. But little else. Frances usually seemed to get off on it, too, so Simon had figured somehow it was an even trade. But the next day, he saw Frances looking up the hill, watching something with such obvious longing, it hurt Simon to see. He followed Frances' gaze and found Dante and Cami. Their arms were around each other, and even from a distance he could see they were smiling. They kissed, and Simon saw the way Frances turned away as if slapped. Simon had seen Frances interact with both Dante and Cami. He knew the remorse he saw on the boy's face wasn't because he desired either one of them. Which meant the real issue was, he was envious of what they had.

Simon remembered the way Frances had kissed Aren, and afterwards, as Frances and Simon had stood talking, Deacon had leant down and kissed Frances' neck. Simon remembered how sad Frances had seemed at that moment. The fact that Aren and Deacon were attracted to men and Simon wasn't didn't mean they cared for Frances any more than he did. The difference was, they touched him. And they kissed him.

But even that, Simon realised, was on their terms. They invited Frances to their bed when it pleased them to do so, and he went willingly. It seemed unfair to Simon and yet at the same time, Frances probably found a great deal more satisfaction with them than he did with Simon.

It was painful for him to admit, but true. He'd been selfish. In all the times Frances had got Simon off, Simon had never touched Frances back. He might hold his head as Frances sucked him, or grip Frances' hips as he fucked him, but never once had he touched Frances' cock. He'd certainly never kissed him. Never once had he given him anything that might have passed for a caress. Frances allowed Simon to use him sexually, and what was it he wanted in return? Simon had stupidly assumed it was nothing more than friendship, but he could see now that was wrong. What Frances craved from him, what he had *always* craved from Simon, was acceptance and approval. And most of all, affection.

I never claimed to be in love with him!

But he realised as soon as he thought it, that wasn't the point. What had Frances said to him in front of the fire? '*Just one night where I can feel like we have something good.*' And yet Simon had denied him. He'd held onto his assertion that he didn't love Frances—at least, not in the way Frances loved him. But did that really mean withholding all affection?

'Would it have killed you to let me pretend, for just one night?'

No. It wouldn't even have been painful. Strange, maybe, and new. Awkward, even. And yet, such a simple thing to give. It would have been easy to just lie back, and let Frances touch him and kiss him and really make love to him, just that one time. He'd thought it would be a lie to let Frances believe something that wasn't true, but he realised now, Frances knew exactly where things stood. All he'd wanted was one night—*one single night*—where things happened on his terms. And Simon had been too much of an ass to accommodate him.

It was enough to make him wish Frances had punched him harder.

More than a year before, Frances had let his fear get the better of him, and it had cost a man his life. Simon had talked him back from that, coaxing him along, and he'd seen the way Frances had grown from it. Unlike Simon, he hadn't let the shame of the incident rule his life. It wasn't a mark upon his soul. Instead, he'd taken it like bright, sturdy yarn and woven it into his being. He was stronger for it, and more beautiful. And that, Simon realised, was what he himself needed to learn to do with his feelings for Frances. Because the truth was, he did love him. It was a love born of friendship, of shared secrets and of mutual respect. It was a love that felt more fraternal than romantic. It wasn't a love like Dante had found that outshone everything else in his life. But it *was* love, and there was nobody else in the world Simon would have chosen to have at his side.

Could he love Frances as a brother, yet treat him as a lover? Could he learn to give pleasure, too, instead of just taking? It was a strange thing to contemplate, yet not a hard decision to make. The answer was yes, he thought he could. He would teach himself to give Frances what he needed—nothing more than a kind word, or a touch, or a kiss, or the chance to make love on his own terms from time to time. It would be a small thing, really, to take the love he felt, whatever kind of love it was, and turn it into affection. It would be worth it, if it made Frances happy.

The boy was his partner. He'd do whatever it took to keep it that way.

Chapter Twenty

Simon spent all night thinking of a plan. He looked for Frances the next morning, combing every inch of the ranch at least twice. It wasn't that much space, but somehow, the boy seemed to keep eluding him. He finally found Frances in a back stall of the barn, shoving his things into his bag.

"Where you going?" Simon asked.

Frances froze. His back was to Simon, and he didn't turn to face him. "Away."

The words alarmed him. He knew he'd upset Frances, but it had never occurred to him just how much. "'Away' where?"

"What the hell do you care?"

All right. Simon figured he deserved that.

"Can we talk, please?"

"No."

"Frances, I don't want you to go. We're partners, and I don't want that to change."

Frances shook his head. "I don't know, Simon. I don't know if I can." There wasn't much force behind the words, though. Frances still hadn't turned to look at him, but his movements had slowed. He was stalling, waiting for Simon to either leave or to say what he'd come to say.

Simon had expected to have to apologise. He'd known he had to promise to give much more than he had in the past. But somehow, he'd assumed that Frances would want him back.

But instead, Frances wanted to leave him.

Simon couldn't let that happen. Not without trying to make things right. He sat down on bale of hay and thought about what he could say to make Frances give him another chance.

"Years ago, right after Lena died, I worked a farm southwest of Francshire, in the grain belt. The man who ran that farm was real particular about how his horses were paired. He believed you couldn't take any two old draught horses and put them together and expect to get things done. You have to train them in teams.

"The team I used had been together for years, and it showed. A mare and a gelding. Funny thing, you know, 'cause they're just horses. They ain't people. But to see the way they worked together, you could see they're smarter than a man might think.

"There was wild watercress that grew in the stream, and every time we crossed it, that mare wanted a bite. The gelding never cared for it himself, but he knew, and whenever we crossed, he slowed down so she could nip a bit. And along the road there was a hollow, and once, before I ever came there, something in that hollow spooked that gelding, and the mare knew. Didn't matter that the hollow was on his side. When we come to it, she'd always steer to the right and keep herself between her partner and the thing that spooked him."

"Why are you talking to me about horses?"

"Because I realised that partners don't have to be the same. They just have to know how to work together."

Frances still didn't turn, and he didn't say a word. Simon waited, but without being able to see Frances' face, he had no way of knowing if he was even making a dent in the boy's armour, let alone convincing him. "Frances, will you at least look at me?"

Frances shook his head. "I can't," he said, and Simon heard his voice break on the words. He heard the tears Frances was trying so desperately to hide.

"You can."

It took Frances a moment to compose himself. He wiped his face and took a deep breath, but he finally turned. His cheeks were red, and so were his eyes. Frances had always been easy to read, and Simon could see how angry and ashamed he was, both because of his tears, and because of what had happened between them. He could see how hard Frances was working to hang onto his anger, because it helped him keep the pain at bay. It broke Simon's heart to see it. How could he have hurt Frances so much?

"Frances, I'm sorry. I'm so, *so* sorry."

"The thing is, Simon, I can accept the fact that you don't love me. What I can't accept is that even after what's happened between us, you can't even stand to *touch* me."

The words caused a lump to form in Simon's throat. "That's not true." But he could tell Frances didn't believe him.

"It seems true enough to me."

Simon sighed in frustration. It had all been so clear in his head what he needed to do, but somehow, now that he was facing Frances, none of it seemed to be going right.

The problem was, his plan had been about action, not words. It had been all about proving his intent.

He stood up and moved closer to Frances. Frances' expression was wary, but he didn't move. He let Simon reach out and grab his wrist and pull him closer.

"We're not alike. We both know that. I don't think I'll ever be like you. I don't think I'll ever feel for you the way you want me to. But the thing is, I do love you, kid. It may not be the kind of love you want, but it's the only kind I have to give. And I really don't want that to change."

Frances closed his eyes. Simon knew he was making himself think about what Simon was saying. When he opened his eyes again, he looked sad, but somehow less so than before. Simon could tell he was trying to be rational rather than emotional. "And what about the other?" he asked.

Simon didn't have to ask what 'other'. What about the sex? That's what Frances was asking.

"Well, I've been thinking about that. And even though I'm not sure I can ever give you what I think you want, I realise I can still give you more than I have been."

Frances shook his head. "You'll need to be clearer than that."

"I think maybe it's part of being a team. It's part of learning to accommodate each other."

Frances sighed. Amusement and exasperation seemed to war for dominance on his face. "Will you stop talking about horses and tell me what the blessed hell you mean?"

His words made Simon smile. But they also made him realise he was still trying to rely on words when what he needed was action.

It was harder than it should have been to do what he'd planned—harder than Simon had anticipated—but he made himself pull Frances close. He cupped the boy's face in his hands, and he kissed him.

It was awkward at first. Frances didn't kiss him back. He stayed completely still, and Simon pulled back to look into his eyes, wondering at his hesitance.

Frances looked confused, but hopeful. "Are you sure this is what you want?"

Was it? Yes and no. It wasn't what he would have chosen on his own, but what he would have chosen was an awfully selfish, one-sided relationship. Frances deserved better than that. If it was what Frances wanted, then it was something Simon was willing to give. "We're a team, Frances. There's nobody else in the world I want harnessed in next to me."

Frances' smile was hesitant. He reached up and put one hand behind Simon's neck. He moved slowly, watching Simon carefully as he did it, watching to see how Simon would respond. Simon made himself be still as Frances stood on his toes and kissed him.

It wasn't erotic for Simon. It wasn't arousing. But it was something he knew he'd never, ever regret. He knew the very moment when Frances gave in. He felt the shame and the grief disappear, like clouds fleeing before the wind. Frances put his arms around Simon's neck. He parted his lips—not pursuing the kiss, but letting Simon deepen it if he wanted. And Simon did. He pulled Frances tight against him, and he kissed him the way he'd once kissed Lena, and if his own body didn't respond in quite the same way, he found he didn't mind. Frances' response was far more enthusiastic than Lena's had ever been. There was no hesitancy. No holding back. He gave himself up to Simon, and Simon found he loved the way Frances' breathing sped up. He loved that Frances' legs seemed to no longer be able to hold him. He liked the feeling of Frances hanging onto him so tight. He liked it enough that it was easy to move his hand down to the front of Frances' pants. It was easy to caress the growing bulge he found there. He loved the way it made Frances gasp and moan against his lips.

This time it was Frances who broke their kiss. He looked up at Simon, not with shame or embarrassment this time, but with something like awe.

"Tell me you're done being mad," Simon said.

"Holy Saints, Simon, right now I'll tell you anything you want to hear."

Simon smiled. "Then tell me we're a team."

Frances laughed. He pushed Simon gently away. There were no more tears. Frances was bright and smiling and as happy as Simon had ever seen him, and Simon said a prayer of thanks that he'd finally done something right.

Frances held his hand out to Simon, not like a lover, but to shake his hand, as men do when they come to an agreement, and Simon shook it.

"We're a team," Frances said.

Before Simon could answer, he heard a woman's voice coming from the front of the barn. "Frances?"

"I'm here!" Frances called. "I'm almost ready." He turned back to his bag and continued stuffing his belongings into it, as he'd been doing when Simon had first found it.

"What're you doing?" Simon asked in surprise. "You're still leaving?"

Frances laughed. "Yeah, but it's no big deal. Tama wants to take her boys to the McAllen farm. She says it's too crowded here, and she wants to be with Jay. Truth is, I think she's just sick of working her ass off for all these people, and I don't blame her. Anyway, Deacon and Jeremiah don't think she and the kids should go alone, so I said I'd take her." He turned around again to look at Simon. "I'm not exactly the best protection in the world, but I guess I'm better than none at all. And Deacon gave me this." He reached into his bag and pulled out Jeremiah's gun. "Don't really think I know how to shoot it, but I guess as long as it's pointed away from Tama and the kids, I can't screw up too much."

"You'll do fine," Simon said.

"Will you come with us?" Frances asked.

"Do you want me to?"

"If *you* want to."

Simon had to laugh. They were both being far more cautious than they normally were, neither of them wanting to put too much pressure on the other. But now that he knew where Frances was going, Simon didn't even have to think about it. It was a simple choice—stay at the BarChi, which was overly crowded and quickly becoming unbearable, or go with Frances and Tama to the McAllen Ranch, where they'd actually have room to breathe.

"Don't even think about leaving without me. All I need is five minutes to grab my things."

* * * *

The trip to the McAllen Ranch started out pleasant. It was the best kind of spring day—the sun bright and warm, the wind nothing more than a gentle breeze rustling the grass. Simon swore he could almost hear the earth waking from its sleep.

The easy rolling gait of his horse was comfortable and familiar. Almost soothing. Tama and Frances rode ahead of him, talking. The two boys were ahead of them, happy to be trusted with their own horses. They were undoubtedly lost in some make-believe land.

Simon pushed his hat low onto his head and let himself relax completely, confident that his horse would follow the others. He began to drift into sleep, and with sleep came a dream.

It wasn't much of a dream, really. He was still riding a horse through the Oestend prairie, following Frances, but in this dream, Lena was with him. She sat side-saddle on her own horse, trailing slowly along behind Simon. She had her parasol out, and her eyes were closed.

She was smiling.

The perfect weather didn't last, though. The further they got from the BarChi, the worse things seemed to be. The wind picked up. Flies and mosquitoes swarmed around them, biting the men and bothering the horses. Birds swooped down to peck at them. Along the side of the road, they found animals—deer, rodents, and even one coyote—all lying dead. Tama shuddered and was silent. The boys fell back to be near their mom.

"Is this what it's been like?" she asked Simon and Frances.

Simon shrugged uncomfortably. "Let's just say, I won't be surprised if it gets worse."

The blood drained from her face, but it was too late to turn back now.

Other than the wind and the bugs, the rest of the ride passed without incident. Jay came out to greet them as they rode through the front gate of the McAllen farm. He was clearly thrilled to see his family, although worried, too. "Things have been strange," he told her. "I hope you and the boys will be safe here."

"We'll be fine," Tama assured him. "And we won't be packed into the house like hogs in a pen." She turned to Frances and Simon. "You two come on up to the house once the horses are put away. I'll make sure you're fed."

Simon hadn't expected that. Hands weren't usually invited in for supper, but he figured it was her way of repaying them for bringing her and her sons from home.

They were surprised to find a wagon outside the barn. "Well, shit," Frances mumbled. "I know that wagon."

"You do?"

Simon understood Frances' apparent irritation when he saw who it belonged to—Foster. The man sat near the back of the barn, leaning against the closed door to one of the stalls. Two of his men from the BarChi sat with him. If the other two were there, they weren't visible.

Nobody bothered to utter a greeting. Foster continued to watch them as they put the horses away and brushed them down. Simon and Frances went about their work as quickly as possible.

"At least they've left the BarChi," Frances said as they walked back to the house. "I know they were making Cami and Dante nervous."

Tama had managed to throw together a quick supper for them all. Afterwards, Simon and Frances put their hats back on, ready to head back to the barn, but Tama stopped them.

"The whole house is empty. There's no reason you can't sleep here."

"We don't want to be any trouble," Simon told her.

"I just left a house with more than a dozen women in it, including Beth. Believe me, you two are no trouble at all."

She led them upstairs and opened the first door on the left-hand side of the hallway. "This was Alissa's room, once upon a time. One of you can sleep here. The other one can—"

"One room's fine," Simon said. He noticed the way Frances' head whipped around, his eyes wide. He looked even more surprised than Tama.

"Oh," she said as her cheeks turned red. "I didn't realise… Well, I mean, if you're sure…"

"We're sure."

Frances seemed unable to look at him after that. They undressed in silence. Simon pulled back the sheets and climbed in. The mattress was a bit lumpy, but not overly so. The sheets were soft and worn. He lay back with a sigh. "Can't even say the last time I slept in a real bed."

"Me neither," Frances said. "Not since I left Lanstead."

He turned down the lantern. The room didn't have a window, and with the lamp out, it was disturbingly dark. Simon listened as Frances slid into bed and nestled down into the covers. They'd never had this kind of privacy and comfort together before. He lay there, wanting to say something, but unsure what. In the end, it was Frances who broke the silence.

"I'm sorry I kicked you."

Simon laughed. "I deserved it."

"True. But I'm sorry anyway."

It was so much like Frances to not sugar-coat things, yet not hold a grudge, either. It made Simon smile. He reached across the bed. He found Frances' hip. "Come here."

Frances slid willingly into his arms, although Simon could still sense hesitance in him. "Are you sure?" he whispered.

Right or wrong, being in the dark made it easier. Simon let his lips brush over Frances'. "I'm sure."

He'd dreamed many, many times of the ways he might have made love to Lena, if only things had been different. He'd imagined it being slow. He'd imagined stroking her arms, and her back and her sides as he kissed her. He'd imagined the way their bodies might have moved together. In the years since her death, he'd slipped up, and he'd fucked other women, but it had never been like those imagined moments with Lena. It had always been quick, and frantic, and somehow tainted. But being with Frances was different.

For the first time, Simon let himself think about Lena, and for the first time, he didn't feel as if he was betraying her by doing so. It wasn't that he imagined the person in his arms was his dead wife. He knew it was Frances. He was glad for it, even. It was more about finally letting himself relive what he'd felt for her, without the guilt or the remorse. It was about letting the love he'd had for her fill him up, then letting Frances be the receptacle for it all. He kissed Frances, and caressed every inch of him, and as he did, he took all of the affection he'd wanted to give Lena, all of the tenderness they'd never been able to share, all of the gentle touches she'd turned away, everything he had in his heart, and he poured it all into Frances' willing body.

He was clumsy about it, because it was something he'd never done before, but he didn't think Frances minded. Frances was responsive and joyously receptive. Simon found it cleansing, far more than he expected. It felt pure and peaceful. It felt right.

When they were done, he held Frances tight in his arms. He could feel him trembling. He could taste the boy's tears on his lips.

"Holy Saints," Frances whispered at last. "I should have kicked you ages ago."

Chapter Twenty-One

Dante couldn't quite figure out why having extra ranch hands resulted in less work getting done, but somehow it did. With all the new men, and the women too, it seemed the ranch hands got distracted from their work far more often than they actually finished. For every man Deacon scolded and sent back to his chores, two more disappeared into outbuildings with bottles of whisky or willing maids.

Dante knew his own men were part of the problem, and he tried to make up for it by helping out with the chores. He was in the barn mucking stalls that were messier than he'd ever seen stalls at the BarChi get when Deacon came in.

Deacon looked around, as if trying to find anybody he could talk to other than Dante, but there was nobody else there. He sighed and pushed his hat down low onto his head. "Where the hell is everybody?" he asked. "There should be two other men in here doing this. I been looking everywhere, and considering how many ranch hands I'm paying, it's blessed hard to actually track one of the lazy bastards down."

Dante laughed. "I noticed. You need a hand with something?"

Deacon scowled. "Just some trouble out in the south pasture. Nothing I can't handle."

"I can help you."

"Forget it. Stay here and finish this. I'll find somebody else."

For a second Dante was speechless. Deacon was almost out the door before Dante managed to speak. "I'm not trying to cause trouble."

Deacon stopped, but he didn't face him. "I'm not playing this game with you."

"Game? What game?"

Deacon turned to stare at him. "There's nothing you can do that'll change things with Aren."

"Holy Saints, Deacon! I know that! I'm only offering to help with the chores!"

Deacon shook his head. He took a few steps into the barn, pointing his finger accusingly in Dante's direction. "I don't believe it for a second. You think after all these years, you can tell me you've fallen for a woman, and that's the end of it?"

It was understandable that he'd have his doubts about that, but just like with Tama, Dante had no desire to spill Cami's secret just to ease Deacon's mind. "Whether you believe it or not, it's true. I have no reason to mess things up with you and Aren. I'm just trying to help."

"You can help by staying the hell out of my way."

The words stung. They'd known each other their whole lives. How had they come to this? "We were brothers once. Doesn't that mean anything to you?"

Deacon stood taller, putting his shoulders back and his head up. Dante was surprised to see not only anger on his face, but pain as well—pain Dante hadn't ever realised Deacon had felt. "True enough. But then your granddaddy caught us together in this barn. And we might have gone on being brothers, but you turned your back on me."

"It wasn't like that."

"Yes it was."

"I was afraid of him!"

"So was I! Saints, Dante, you were my best friend—my *only* friend—and for years after that, you treated me like I was nothing to you!"

It was true. Dante had been so aware of his granddad's eyes on him, and so eager to have his approval again, and somehow, he'd never realised that Deacon was hurting as well. Even then, the man been so good at hiding his emotions. It had seemed to Dante at the time that Deacon had shaken the whole incident off and moved on without a second thought.

"I wish I hadn't. Do you have any idea how many times I've wished I could change that?"

"It's too late."

He turned his back and started to walk away again. In the past, it would have broken Dante's heart, but this time, it made him angry. "So that's it? Yes, we were brothers, and yet you can't forgive for me for a mistake I made when we were kids?" Deacon stopped again. He didn't turn around, but Dante knew from his stillness that he was listening. "Saints, Deacon, we were *fourteen*!" He felt a familiar tightness in his chest, a lump forming in his throat, but he didn't bother to fight them. There was no point in trying to deny how much this hurt. "I'm sorry! I've always been sorry! How many more years will you make me pay for it?"

Deacon stood there for a moment, stock still and silent. Dante waited for an answer, but Deacon never gave one. He walked away without saying another word.

"Fuck!" Dante punched the wooden wall next to him. It hurt, but as always, the physical pain helped distract him from the emotional pain. Sorrow and grief welled up in his chest, threatening to choke him. He'd lived with it for years, but recently, it had faded. It had been replaced by something new.

He wanted Cami. The sudden realisation that she was there and real and *his* gave him the strength to stand up straight and breathe again. It was like surfacing from a deep pool of water and finally finding air. Yes, he'd lost Deacon, many years ago.

He no longer needed him.

He went first to the kitchen, where he found Alissa and Uma working. "Have you seen Cami?"

Alissa shook her head. "Not since before breakfast."

He was a bit surprised, but not concerned. He made his way through the house, peeking into the various rooms. In each one, he found groups of women—some were sewing, a few were cleaning, a fair number seemed to be doing nothing more than sitting and gossiping—but Cami wasn't with any of them.

Still, he wasn't concerned. She was probably in the one place she could go and be alone, but when he went to their bedroom, he didn't find her sitting in the rocker sewing as he'd expected. The room was empty.

He felt tightness inside his chest. A seed of doubt. A hint of worry.

He made his way back through the house, faster than before. He didn't just look this time. He asked each person he met. "Have you seen Cami?"

No. Nobody had seen her. Not since early that morning.

Back in the kitchen, Uma and Alissa were still chopping at the counter, side by side. "I can't find her."

Alissa turned to look at him in surprise. "Well, she must be around somewhere."

"Are you sure she hasn't been here?"

Alissa looked thoughtfully at her younger sister, who stood next to her. It was Uma who answered. "She went out early to milk the cows."

Alissa frowned. "Are you sure?"

"Yeah. I remember she said, at least the cows in the barn produce milk instead of gossip."

Alissa's frown deepened. "But I had to milk this morning. Celia helped me."

The seed of doubt sprouted into panic. Dante's heart began to pound.

Something had happened to her.

His first thought was Foster, and as he raced to the barn, he swore that if he found Cami safe and sound, he'd scold her up one side and down the other for going outside when that man was around. It was nothing more than a feeble attempt to stay positive. In truth, he was horrified of what he would find. What if Foster or one of the other men had tried to rape her? What would they do when they lifted her skirt and found the sex organs of a man? The thought terrified him.

Just inside the door to the barn, almost hidden in the straw against one wall, he found something that made his blood run cold in his veins—one of her ivory combs.

"Cami?" he called, as he made his made his way through the barn. "Cami, honey, please tell me you're here?"

Fear made his voice weak. He could barely breathe. He expected to find her in the straw, beaten. Bloody. Possibly dead. But in stall after stall, he found only horses, with no sign of Cami. The side barn, where the dairy cows were kept, held nothing but cows who glared disdainfully at him as he ran the length of the building, calling her name.

Back to the main barn, and into the back room, where he found half a dozen men lounging. He didn't recognise any of them. Four were playing cards. Two were doing absolutely nothing.

"Have you seen Cami?"

They all stared blankly at him, as if he were speaking another language.

"Who?" one of them asked.

"A woman! She's tall." He held his hand up to show them. "Dark hair. Have you seen her?"

"Oh yeah," one of them said. "She came in early to milk."

"And then what?"

He shrugged. "I don't know. She went into the milk barn. That's all I know."

Dante was torn. He didn't see anything in any of their faces to indicate that they were lying. Then again, he didn't trust them. He made his way around the room, pushing loose straw out of the way, checking under blankets.

"She ain't here, man."

It seemed to be true. He didn't find anything to indicate Cami had been there.

He checked the rest of the barn, including the loft. Still no Cami.

By the time he left the barn, he was in an outright panic. Somebody should have seen her. There was only one place left he could think of.

He'd never actually knocked on Aren's door before. He'd gone into the house uninvited. He'd spied through windows. At any other time, under any other circumstances, he would have felt self-conscious and uncomfortable knocking now, but his worry was too great. He knew his knock was way too loud, too, for such a small house, but he was scared to death and shaking from adrenaline.

Aren pulled open the door, and Dante didn't even wait for him to speak.

"Is Cami here?"

Aren blinked at him, obviously disconcerted by finding Dante at his front door.

"Is she here?"

"No. Why would she be?"

"Have you seen her?"

"Not since yesterday."

The world seemed to spin. Dante put his head in his hands. "Fuck! Fuckfuckfuck!" He had to lean over and grab Aren's doorframe just to keep from falling. He had to fight to keep from vomiting on Aren's feet.

"What's going on?" Aren asked. Not flippantly. Real concern in his voice.

"I can't find her. Fuck, Aren, I can't find her!"

He felt Aren's hand on his bicep—light and tentative, but there nonetheless. "She has to be here somewhere. Where haven't you looked?"

Dante could have sobbed with relief. He could almost have hugged Aren, or even kissed him. This was Aren, who he'd always resented. Aren, whose house he'd broken into. Whose things he'd destroyed out of selfishness and jealousy. And yet here was Aren, not questioning him. Not doubting him.

It gave him the strength he needed to stand up again and face him. "She's not in the house or the barn. Nobody's seen her since this morning. She went out to milk and didn't come back."

"She wouldn't go anywhere else. Not by herself. She was too afraid of the other men. Especially Foster."

It was exactly what Dante had been thinking, and yet hearing Aren say it out loud caused the bile to rise in his throat.

"Whoever has her, they're still here. They're either in an outbuilding, or out in the fields, but they're still here, Dante. They have to be." He stepped out onto the porch and closed the door to his house. "Come on," he said, heading down the stairs towards the ranch. "You check the buildings. The ones closest to the milk barn first."

"What are you going to do?"

"I'm going to find Deacon."

* * * *

It only took Dante a minute to check the nearest outbuildings, but there was no sign of her. He found Aren and Deacon in the courtyard.

"She's definitely not in the house, or anywhere in the yard," Aren said. "Alissa and Uma have been looking."

Deacon sighed. "I hate to sound like an ass," he said to Aren, his voice low, "but how do we know she didn't leave?" He glanced at Dante, then back to Aren. "Maybe she had her reasons for not wanting to be here."

Just the suggestion filled Dante with rage. Especially coming from Deacon. But Aren jumped in and cut him off before he could protest.

"No," Aren said emphatically. "She loved it here. She said she'd never been happier. She and I talked about how we'd both come west and found a home. She told me how much she loved Dante, and how she couldn't wait to go back to Brighton."

Dante had known all along she wouldn't have left him—not without an explanation at least—but hearing Aren confirm it was still a relief. Deacon looked sceptical. "Maybe she went back to Brighton, then."

"On her own? Without telling Dante?" Aren shook his head. "There's no way."

Deacon stared at Aren. Dante couldn't tell what was passing between them. Only that Deacon seemed to be sizing Aren up, weighing his words. In the end, he sighed. "Fuck. You're right. Tell one of the women to ring the supper bell, and don't stop until the men are here. Somebody has to have seen something."

But nobody had. Even after all the men and women were gathered in the courtyard, nobody could tell them anything. But Dante did notice one thing…

Foster wasn't there.

Once they quit asking about Cami and started asking about Foster, they learned a bit, but nothing helpful. Yes, Foster and his crew had left early that morning. They'd had a wagon. Yes, they seemed to be in a hurry. No, Cami hadn't been with them.

It all seemed to add up to one thing for Dante—Foster had found her. He'd done something to her. And then he'd run. Dante tried to hang onto some shred of hope, but as the sun fell low in the sky, he fell into despair.

He looked out across the prairie, an endless sea of grass. She was somewhere in that expanse, lying on the ground. Beaten. Broken. Dead. It was the only thing that made sense. Whatever Foster had done to her, she hadn't survived. The man had dumped her body somewhere and run.

"We'll find her," Aren said, but Dante could tell by his voice that he didn't expect them to find her alive.

Part of him wanted to get on a horse and hunt Foster down. He wanted to beat it out of him, to make him pay. But he couldn't leave without knowing. What if they found her the moment after he left? What if by some miracle, she was still alive? He couldn't risk it.

He barely slept. The generators whined, and Dante wondered if she could hear them. He wondered if she was within their protective net, somehow near enough to be safe yet still unfound.

No. They'd looked everywhere. Which meant she was out in the prairie. She had nothing to protect her from the wraiths.

As soon as the sun was up, he was back out in the field, searching. He saw the way the men began to glance at him then quickly away, their eyes full of pity. Nobody expected to find her alive.

He went back to the house at midday. Aren made him eat, although it tasted like dirt and nearly made him sick. The chances of finding her alive were negligible and falling fast. One more night, and that slim chance would be reduced to zero. Between the wraiths and the wolves, and thirst and whatever injuries she might have suffered, he knew there was no chance she would survive that long.

Olsa stared at him with her spooky white eyes, but he imagined he could see sympathy in them. "Do you know where she is?" he asked.

"How would I?"

"I don't know! You always know crazy shit you shouldn't."

She shook her head. "I've looked. She's beyond my sight."

"Does that mean she's dead?"

"Nothing is certain."

But he was certain—she was dead. He knew the minute he faced it, he'd break. He'd be lost, and he'd never find his way back. The only thing that kept him going was the idea of finding Foster. His entire world narrowed to a single point—vengeance. He'd take every ounce of his pain out on the man then he'd do it again. He'd already decided that he was leaving in the morning.

He went to his room. He lay down on his bed. He was too exhausted to think about anything. In the morning, he'd go after Foster.

It was the last thought he had before sleep took him.

* * * *

If Simon had worried that things would be different between them, Frances quickly put his doubts at ease in the morning. Everything between them was exactly as it had always been. Frances may have smiled more than usual, but other than that, things were unchanged. It was as if, by mutual agreement, their relationship changed with the sun. During the daytime, they would live on Simon's terms, but the night would be defined by Frances.

Simon felt good about it. He hoped Frances did, too. If the boy's never-ending smile was any indication, he thought they'd be just fine.

Foster and his friends had already left by the time he and Frances made it to the barn to do chores.

"I heard them leave right at sunrise," Frances said as they mucked out the stalls in the barn. "They must have been in a hurry."

"Suits me." Simon hadn't wanted to face them again. He didn't even mind that they'd left the stalls dirty. He was just glad to have them gone. "You in any rush to get back to the BarChi?"

He expected Frances' answer to be an emphatic *no*. After all, at the BarChi, they had to share the barn with more than a dozen other men. Here, they actually had a real bed to sleep in. So he was surprised when the response he received was, "Uh, Simon?"

He sounded scared, which was odd.

"What's up?"

"Oh shit. Oh, fuck!"

"*What*?"

"Holy Saints, Simon. This is bad!"

Simon had rarely heard him sound so alarmed. He went out of his stall and down to the last one, where Frances was. Frances turned around and held out his hands. "Look what I found."

He held a handful of straight, dark hair. Simon's first thought was that it was from a horse's tail, although the texture didn't seem right.

"A lot of it," Frances said. "And this."

What he held in his other hand was an ivory comb. Simon couldn't quite place it, and yet, he knew he'd seen it before.

"It's Cami's," Frances said. "Foster has Cami."

* * * *

It made no sense to Simon at all. Why would Foster have kidnapped Cami, and why would there be four other men in on it? He didn't know, but it hardly seemed to matter. Frances was already saddling the horses.

"You go back to the BarChi. You have to tell Dante. He's probably freaking out, wondering if she left him, or if she got lost. I bet he's out of his mind worrying. Fuck! She was here, Simon, and we didn't do anything!"

"We didn't know."

"We should have!"

There was no point in beating themselves up about it now, and even less point in trying to argue that fact with Frances. "What are you going to do?"

"I'm going after them."

"*What*? Are you insane? No!"

"Don't worry. I'm not stupid enough to try to take on five men at once. But I can at least figure out where they have her, and what they're doing with her."

"Frances, I don't like this."

"Neither do I, but it's the best we can do."

Chapter Twenty-Two

Dante was awakened by somebody pounding on his door.

He'd been deep in sleep, too deep to dream, so deep it felt as if he'd barely laid down at all, but the pounding brought him instantly awake.

Not morning yet. He could tell by the light outside that he'd only been asleep a couple of hours. It was probably just past supper time. He still had time before sunset.

He opened the door and found Aren. "Come quick," he said.

"Did they find her?"

"It's Simon."

Dante was still sleep-addled enough to be confused by his words. "Simon took her?" That didn't make any sense at all.

"No, but I think he knows where she is. He came riding in a few minutes ago from the McAllen Ranch. Almost killed his horse getting here. He's in the barn. He said for you to come."

Dante ran, with Aren at his heels. He found Simon in the barn, just as Aren had said. "The hands are eating," he said. "I didn't think you'd want them to hear."

"Where is she?"

"We think Foster has her."

"You *think*?"

"We didn't see her, but Foster and his men were there. They must have had her in the wagon. This morning, Frances found this." It was one of her combs. Dante recognised it immediately. "Hair, too," Simon said. "They must have cut it in the stall, for some reason."

"She's alive?"

Simon shook his head. "Like I said, we didn't see her. But we didn't see anything to make us think otherwise, either. Her hair and the comb. Nothing else. No blood."

"Are they still there?"

"No. They left for town before we found the comb. Frances went after them. He said he'd wait for you in Milton. If you leave tomorrow morning—"

"Fuck that. I'm leaving now."

Dante went to the strongest horse in the barn and began to saddle it. Simon's horse was still saddled, but Simon had ridden her hard to bring Dante the news. Dante could tell by looking at her that she'd never survive if he tried to ride her full speed back to the McAllens'.

"There's not enough daylight," Simon said. "You'll never make it to the McAllen ranch before dark."

"The wraiths don't want me anyway."

Simon obviously thought it was a bad idea, but he at least quit trying to argue. To Dante's surprise, Aren was actually helpful. He went in the house and came back out with a skin of water, a bundle of dry biscuits, and every knife Dante owned.

"I hope you don't mind that I went in your room," he said as he handed them over.

"I hope you broke a few things while you were in there. I'd feel like things were a bit more right between us."

Aren didn't quite smile, but Dante knew it was only because he was worried about Cami. "I'll get even later."

"I'm looking forward to that." He swung up into the saddle. "If my father asks—"

"If your father asks, I intend to lie through my teeth and say I don't know a damn thing."

"Fair enough."

"I'll send Red and Ronin at dawn."

Dante knew what that meant—just in case the wraiths took him tonight, Red and Ronin would still find Foster. They'd still do whatever they could to get Cami back.

"Thank you."

"Don't thank me, Just bring her home."

* * * *

Considering the odd weather that had been plaguing Oestend, the night was eerily still and silent. Dante rode straight through it. He pushed his horse hard, unafraid of the wraiths, unamazed by the giant expanse of stars overhead. He could do nothing but worry. Why had Foster taken her and what had he done to her while he'd had her? Every time Dante spotted a strange shadow on the road ahead, he grew tense, sure it was Cami's lifeless body, dumped on the road like garbage, but each time, the shadow resolved into something far more benign. Still, he couldn't stop worrying.

He made it to the McAllen ranch sometime in the small hours of the night. He swapped his horse for one of the others in the barn and set out again. It was a shorter trip from there to Milton, and he made it there midmorning. He didn't have to look far for Frances. He was waiting at the edge of town, along with a boy from one of the stables who took Dante's horse and led it way.

"Do you know where she is?"

Frances' cheeks began to turn red, but he levelled a steady gaze on Dante. "Well, maybe."

"What the fuck's that supposed to mean?"

"Dante, don't get mad now, but I have to ask you a question. Is Cami a man?"

Dante's impulse was to be defensive and tell Frances it was none of his business, but he took a deep breath and made himself think. Frances hadn't known, and he wouldn't be asking now if it weren't somehow pertinent.

"Yes."

Frances nodded. "All right. Then yes, I know where they took him."

Dante was too relieved to care about Frances' pronoun blunder. "Thank the Saints. Where is she?"

"This way." He started walking down the street, and Dante hurried to keep up. "I been asking around, and everybody tells me the same thing. There's a man from Francshire here. He was in Milton back in the fall looking for his son, but nobody knew where he was. He came back again a few weeks ago. He's staying down at the inn. He was offering a reward for word of his son, and he must have got it because everybody says he hired a group of men to go get him and bring him back. Nobody's seen the son, but the rumours say those men came back last night."

"And they're at the inn?"

"Yes."

"So we just got to get in there, get her, and get back out. Doesn't sound too hard. Where'd that kid take the horses?"

"I figured we might be trying to leave in a hurry. They'll keep our two at the stable. I already have three fresh horses ready for us at the inn."

"How'd you arrange that?"

Frances smiled. "Your family has good credit. Stablemaster said Aren's the only man in Oestend who pays his debts before they're due."

Dante shook his head. "I guess that's one more thing I have to thank Aren for."

They'd reached the inn, and Frances turned to face Dante. "You should take this, too." He held out a pistol Dante recognised as his father's. He wasn't sure why Frances had it, but he was sure glad to see it. "It's loaded."

"Well, if that don't help them see things my way, nothing will."

Dante took the gun, and Frances reached down and pulled a knife out of his boot. "I was asking enough questions, they probably know we're coming."

"Listen, kid, this ain't your fight. I won't hold it against you if you choose to stay out of it."

Frances didn't even blink. "I'm right behind you."

"All right then," Dante said. "Let's do this."

He pushed open the door and went in, the gun a comfortable weight in his right hand. It was immediately evident that Frances was right—they had known he was coming. Most of the people seemed to be cowering behind the bar at the other end of the room. Two men stood just inside the door, barring his way.

Dante pointed his gun at the first man's forehead. "Where is she?"

The man smirked. "There's no 'she' here."

Dante pulled the trigger. The shot was still resounding in the air when he turned the gun on the second man. "Where is she?"

The man held his hands up in surrender. He looked at the dead man on the floor. A wet stain began to spread across the crotch of his pants.

"Where is she?"

"Up…upstairs," he stammered. "Last room on the right."

"Do yourself a favour, friend, and stay the fuck out of my way."

Dante found another man at the midpoint landing of the staircase. He appeared to be unarmed. He held both hands up defensively. "Look, mister. This really isn't your concern. Cameron's dad is taking him home—"

Dante didn't even slow down. He backhanded the man with the handle of the pistol as he went past, knocking him to the ground.

"Not sure why I thought you needed my help," Frances said from behind him.

"We ain't through yet."

There were only a few rooms upstairs. Another man stood in front of the two at the end of the hall, but Dante didn't even have time to raise his pistol before the man ran into the room on the left. He slammed the door shut and Dante heard the bolt slide home.

"I suggest you stay in there," Dante called to him. He turned to Frances. "Stay back a bit."

Frances nodded his understanding and moved to stand out of sight, with his back against the wall next to the door. Dante turned and kicked it open—

And found himself staring down the barrel of a pistol.

"Well, well, well," Foster said. "Look who's here. Come to save your whore?"

"I should have killed you when I had the chance."

"Probably." Foster backed up, motioning with the piston for Dante to follow. As Dante stepped into the room, Foster took his gun. "Looks like it's my turn, now."

His eyes had a sadistic glint in them. He hadn't pulled the trigger yet, though, which meant he wanted to spend a while gloating and acting superior. It boosted Dante's confidence. In his experience, the longer somebody talked, the less likely they were to actually shoot.

Dante looked around the room. There was a bed against the right wall, and on the other end, a small table, with two chairs. In one sat an older man, dressed in a suit, and in the other was Cami. Her ankles were tied to the legs of her chair and her hands bound in her lap. Her lip was swollen. Her long dark hair had been hacked off and hung in uneven chunks around her face. And she was dressed as a boy.

"You all right?" he asked.

She nodded, but she looked terrified.

"I'm getting you out of here," Dante said.

"Don't you move!" Foster said, but Dante ignored him. He crossed and knelt at her feet. He began undoing the ropes that bound her ankles. He still had knives on him. He could have taken one out and cut her free, but he didn't want to spook Foster too much.

"I could shoot you now," Foster said.

"Dante?" Cami whispered.

"Or maybe I should bash your head in with a chair. How would that be?"

Dante pitched his voice as low as he could. "Is he still pointing the gun at me?"

She nodded.

"Good." That was what he'd hoped. It meant that Foster had turned his back on the door. "Don't watch."

"Or maybe we should try some of the Wild Justice you talk—*grgll…*"

Cami's face had gone white, and her eyes were shut. Dante turned around in time to see Foster fall to the floor. His throat had been cut from ear to ear.

"*That's* why I needed you with me," Dante said to Frances.

"Glad I could help." Frances looked down at the blood on his cuff. "Shit! Son of a bitch has ruined two of my shirts now!"

Dante finished cutting Cami free and pulled her into his arms. He buried his face in her ravaged hair and held her as tight as he could. "Holy hell, honey, you scared me to death. I'm never letting you out of my sight again." He pulled away enough to look into her eyes. "Are you all right?"

"I will be."

"Did they hurt you?"

She touched her swollen lip. "Nothing worse than what you see."

"I'll kill every last one of them—"

"Don't bother. Just take me home."

"You got it." He kissed her once, then let her go. He bent to pick his gun up off the floor where it had landed next to Foster.

There was still one man left in the room, sitting in the chair. He hadn't moved, but he spoke. "Cameron, this is madness! You can't live like this forever!"

Dante turned and pointed his gun at him. "Is this your father?"

"Yes. Don't hurt him."

"I ain't exactly feeling friendly towards him."

"I don't know who you think you are," her father said, "but this is none of your business."

"You send men to *my* family's ranch to kidnap the woman *I* love, and you think it's none of my business?"

"He's not a woman. He's my son, and I'm taking him back to Francshire with me."

"Like hell you are."

"Trust me, young man. He's not what you think." He turned to Cami. "Why don't you show him what you really are, Cameron? Undo those breeches and show him what's between your legs."

"There's no surprises for me there," Dante said. "I've seen every inch of her."

"Then you know he's a man!"

Dante shrugged. "I know she don't look like other women."

"He has a cock! It's called a 'manhood' for a reason!"

"Is that right?" Dante asked. He lowered his gun. "You think it's that simple?"

"Of course it's that simple!"

Dante grinned. He holstered his gun. "In that case, I think I'll let you live." He reached into his boot and pulled out his knife. "As a woman."

"Dante, don't!" Cami said.

"Don't worry." Dante stepped forward to point the blade at the old man's groin. "It won't hurt him much. Just one little cut, and I suppose he'll suddenly be wearing dresses. Maybe a nice man will take him home and make him his wife."

The blood had drained from her father's face, but he didn't say a word.

"Still think it's so simple, old man?"

"Dante," Cami said again. She no longer sounded alarmed. It was more of a scolding tone. "That's enough."

Dante almost laughed. Now that the threat had passed and he knew she was safe, his anger was gone. He found himself feeling reckless and giddy. Almost drunk.

He sheathed his knife. "Well, looks like your daughter's managed to save both your life and your 'manhood'. I hope you appreciate it. And for the record, the next time you send men onto my family's land, I'll send their heads back in a box. Then I'll hunt you down and skin you alive. I don't care how much she begs for your life."

"You can't get away with this. The law will catch up with you."

"What law? This ain't Francshire."

"You can't barge into a hotel and start killing people, and then just walk away!"

"I sure as hell can." Dante gave the man his wickedest smile. "Welcome to the Wild."

Chapter Twenty-Three

Dante had been so focused on finding Cami that he hadn't noticed the changes to Milton when he'd come into town. He noticed now, though. At least a third of the businesses were boarded up. One was burned to the ground.

"Lots of people leaving," Frances said. "Too many weird things going on."

Luckily, nothing unusual seemed to be going on at the moment. The town was still and silent. Dante was fairly certain nobody would try to stop them from leaving, but he didn't see any reason to dally. He figured the longer they stayed in Milton, the more chance there was of having to deal with the repercussions of his actions. He could have kissed Frances for having taken care of the horses ahead of time.

"I don't know how to ride," Cami said when Dante motioned her towards the smallest of them.

"All you got to do is hang on."

He boosted her up into the saddle, and the three of them left a cloud of dust in their wake as they headed to the safety of the prairie. Dante didn't dare ride full-speed with Cami, but they still made it back to the McAllen Ranch by just past supper time.

Red and Ronin were in the barn. They obviously hadn't arrived much before him, because they were still brushing down their horses. "Glad to see we don't have to ride to anyone's rescue," Red said.

"Everyone all right?" Ronin asked.

"Right enough."

They both did a double-take at Cami, but neither of them said anything, for which Dante was grateful. He wasn't surprised when Tama came running out to meet them in the barn. "Dante! Thank the Saints you're safe! When Red and Ronin showed up and said you'd ridden through the night—"

She stopped short and Dante turned to find her staring dumbfounded at Cami.

"I'm fine," Dante said, putting his arm around Cami's shoulder and pulling her close. She wasn't used to riding, and he knew she could barely stand. "We're all fine, other than being a bit saddle sore. If we could just get some supper—"

"Dante?" Tama interrupted him. When she looked at him, he almost winced at the anger and betrayal in her eyes. "Why didn't you tell me?"

"Honey, I ain't slept in nearly three days. Can we save the question and answer session for later?"

"But—"

"It's my fault," Cami said quietly to Tama. "I asked him not to tell."

That wasn't exactly true, but Dante didn't try to contradict her. He could tell Tama couldn't decide if she understood or not, but right or wrong, he was too tired to care. The worry and the riding and the sleepless nights were catching up with him fast and a glance at Frances showed the boy wasn't doing much better. "I promise to spend the rest of our lives making it up to you, but right now, we all just need to rest."

"All right," she relented. "Come on in the house."

Dante couldn't have said what they ate for supper. He was barely conscious when he and Cami finally climbed into bed. He felt like he had a hundred things to say to her, but he only had enough energy to pull her into his arms before he fell asleep.

* * * *

Dante slept until well into the next day. When he finally woke, he found Cami still in the room with him. At first he thought she was looking out the window, but then he realised she was using it as a mirror, looking at her reflection.

"Are you all right?"

She glanced over at him and then quickly away. He could tell she'd been crying. "I'm fine."

"You don't seem fine."

She made a sound that was part laugh, and part hiccup. She sniffed and wiped her face with her sleeve. "I'm being silly."

He sat up on the edge of the bed and waited, wondering if he should prod her or not. In the end, he didn't need to.

She glanced over at him with her big dark eyes. Fresh tears ran down her cheeks. She reached up and touched the rough ends of her hair. "I hate having you see me like this."

"Like what? With short hair, you mean?"

"Looking like a boy."

He laughed. He couldn't help it. And when she put her face in her hands to hide from him, he pulled her into his arms. "Honey, if you had any idea the horrible things I was imagining when I couldn't find you. All the nightmares I had about finding you dead." He hugged her tighter and kissed the side of her head. "I thought I'd lost you, and now I have you back. Believe me when I say, you've never been more beautiful to me than you are right now."

"Everyone will know now."

"Maybe," he admitted. "But it doesn't change anything as far as I'm concerned."

"You say that now, but when you have to explain it to them, you'll change your mind."

"Not a chance."

"It was easy for you when they all thought I was female."

"Not really. If anything, they'll understand more now. Every one of them was wondering how I could suddenly be head over heels for a woman." He kissed her again, but was quickly distracted by a new thought. "Hey, that reminds me!" He picked his pants up off the floor and rifled through his pockets until he found what he sought. He held the ivory combs out to her.

He thought she'd be happy, but instead, tears welled up in her eyes. She reached up again to touch her hair.

"Oh honey, I'm sorry!"

She reached out and brushed her fingertips over the combs. "It's not that. I'm glad you found them."

"Then what's wrong now?"

"You were still asleep, and I went downstairs. I said good morning to Tama, and all she said was, 'I should have known.' And then she just walked away." Her shoulders trembled, and he knew she was fighting tears again. "I can't even face them."

He wasn't sure he'd ever been angry at Tama before, but at that moment, he almost hated her. "Don't you worry," he said to Cami. "Everything's going to be fine."

He dressed quickly and left her there, telling her he had to use the privy. That wasn't a lie, but it also wasn't his only objective. When he was finished there, he went looking for Frances. He found him in the barn, oiling a saddle.

"Not much to do around here," Frances said. "Red and Ronin already left for the BarChi. Only these few horses here. No cattle. Not sure what to do with my time."

"No reason you have to do anything at all."

Frances shrugged. "I guess idleness doesn't suit me." He turned to look at Dante with his big blue eyes. "What's up?"

Dante put his hand on Frances' shoulder. "I can't thank you enough for what you did."

Frances shrugged uncomfortably. "It was nothing."

"No, Frances. I mean it. If it weren't for you…" The thought of having lost Cami and never knowing what had happened to her made his words dry up in his throat. "I owe you, kid. Anything you need *ever*, you just say the word. I'm in your debt."

Frances blushed and scuffed his toe awkwardly in the dirt. "I'm just glad I could help."

"You did more than help. You saved the day, kid. You saved Cami. You saved me." He hooked his hand behind Frances' neck and pulled him close. He kissed the top of his head. "I mean it. Anything. Anytime."

Frances smiled up at him. "I'll remember."

Unfortunately, Dante's next task wasn't nearly so pleasant.

He found Tama outside, taking laundry off the line.

"Would it kill you to be civil?" he asked.

He'd intentionally come up behind her, and he was pleased at the way she jumped at his words. She relaxed quickly, but she didn't turn to face him. "Would it have killed you to tell me the truth?"

"It wasn't my secret to tell."

"I thought I was your friend."

"I thought so, too."

She sighed. There was a hint of shame he saw in her eyes when she finally turned to face him. "I didn't mean to upset him."

"*Her.*"

She shook her head as if it were inconsequential. "I just don't understand. I wouldn't have told anybody!"

"I know that." Now that they were really talking, he softened his tone. "And I felt bad about it, because we *are* friends. But I had to choose between not telling you or betraying her."

"And Cami won?"

He smiled. "I knew you'd forgive me, but I'm still playing things safe with her."

He'd hoped to make her laugh, but it didn't work. "Why is he pretending to be a woman?"

His anger at her had faded while they'd talked, but her question brought it bubbling back up, threatening to destroy his composure. "*She* doesn't feel like she's pretending anything. She says her body doesn't fit what's in her heart."

Tama sighed and shook her head. "That's doesn't make a bit of sense."

"Frankly, I don't give a damn if it makes sense to you or not! It's got nothing to do with you."

"Even though I'm your friend?"

"Don't try to make this all about you! I didn't just ride through the night and risk the wraiths to bring her back because I have a death wish. I did it because I love her."

She hung her head at that. Whether it was because she was ashamed, or because she was hiding her disbelief, he didn't know. He took a deep breath to calm himself. Anger wouldn't get him anywhere with her. He knew that.

"Tama, for the first time in years, I wake up in the morning, and I'm glad to still be alive. I think about my future—a future *without Deacon*—and I'm ready for it. She makes me happy, in a way I don't think I've been since I was a boy. And as *my friend,* that means nothing to you? All you can do is stand there and tell me it don't make sense to you?"

She sniffled and wiped her eyes. He hadn't realised she'd been crying. When she looked up at him, her cheeks were red. "I don't know how to act with hi—her."

He put his hand on her shoulder. "You liked her well enough before, right?'

"Yes."

"Well, she's the same person now she was then. It's only you who's changed."

She thought about that for a second. She dried her face with her apron and nodded. "You're right," she said quietly. "I'm being terrible."

"Not terrible. But I think you can do better."

She moved into his arms and put her head on his chest. "I'm sorry."

"You're forgiven. I'm sorry, too, for what it's worth."

"Do you really love her?"

"Like a bee loves honey."

She laughed. "Oh, Holy Saints. You're going to be unbearable now, aren't you?"

"You mean I wasn't before?"

She smacked him playfully. "You were, but I suspect it's going to get worse before it gets better."

He waited for her to put the last of the laundry in the basket, then picked it up to carry it back into the house for her. When they got there, she reached into the pile of clothes and pulled out a shirt. "Here. I don't have any skirts or slacks that will fit her, but this blouse will probably work. And this." She handed him a little square of lace. "Tell her I'm sorry."

"Thanks, Tama."

The shirt cheered Cami up, but the bit of lace seemed to confuse her. "Is it a handkerchief?"

"It's for your hair," he told her. "It's what the wives wear."

She blushed, but the smile she gave him was teasingly gorgeous. "Am I to be your wife now?"

"I sure wouldn't mind."

She laughed and turned to examine her reflection in the window as she placed the lace over her hair. She didn't have any hairpins to hold it in place, though. "Do you think she'll help me put it on before we go back to the BarChi?"

"I'm sure she will. Will you come down to supper now?"

"I don't really want to, but I suppose I should. I can't hide forever."

"There's no reason you should feel like you have to."

Despite his insistence that everything would be fine, the meal did start out awkward. None of them seemed to know what to say. Cami stared nervously at her plate. Tama and Jay were tense. Their two sons watched Cami carefully.

Finally, as the meal was wrapping up, one of Tama's sons blurted out, "Are you a girl or a boy?"

"Jonas!" Tama scolded. "Don't be rude!"

Jonas looked stunned, and Dante couldn't blame him. It wasn't as if a boy his age could be expected to understand such things.

Cami's cheeks were red, and Dante noticed her hands were clenched in her lap to keep them from shaking, but she answered him. "Olsa says I'm scai'loh. I'm in between."

"So you're both?" the other boy asked.

"Kind of, yes."

"Can you have babies?" Jonas asked.

"Jonas!" Tama scolded again, but Cami actually smiled.

"No. In that way, I'm more like a boy."

"Do you know magic like Olsa?"

"No, I'm not one of the Old People."

"You look like one! Do you know how to make a bow and arrow?"

"I'm afraid not."

Both boys were clearly disappointed by that.

"Nobody knows how to make one," the younger boy said. "Except Olsa, and she won't show us."

"What *can* you do?" Jonas asked.

"Well…" He could see her pondering what she had to offer that they might find interesting.

"She can tell stories," Dante said.

Cami glanced over at him in surprise. The two boys were immediately on the edge of their seats. Even Jay looked intrigued.

"Go ahead," Dante prodded. "Tell us a story."

She smiled at him, and he knew it was her way of saying thank you, and then she turned back to his nephew. "Your name is Jonas?"

"Yes."

"Do you know the one about Jonas and Jamus and the castle in the clouds?"

She was tentative at first, but her audience was enthralled, and she gained confidence as she went. Tama, Jay and the boys loved every minute of it, and Dante breathed a mental sigh of relief. It was only a matter of time before they learned to love her as well.

* * * *

The next day was easier. Tama sat Cami down in the kitchen and took a pair of scissors to her butchered hair. "I can't make it grow any faster, but we can at least make it look like you did it on purpose," she said. After she was done, she used Cami's ivory combs to hold the short sides back, and then showed Cami how to pin the lace over the top. She still seemed more masculine than she had with her long hair, but it did help to soften the effect.

He'd hoped to have a few days to relax, but it wasn't to be. That evening, another BarChi hand showed up to report that the Pane family was in a right lather. Nobody knew if Cami, Dante and Frances were alive or dead. Also, the hand reported, Deacon was threatening to burn the whole blessed ranch to the ground if things didn't get straightened out soon. Dante laughed at that, but he knew his father at least deserved to know he hadn't lost another son. And so the next morning, they saddled up their horses and headed back to the BarChi.

Chapter Twenty-Four

Since parting ways with Frances, Simon had spent his time alternating between confidence and worry. Frances was smart. He was more than capable. Wherever he was, he was fine.

Except that five minutes later, he'd find himself fretting, convinced that something must have happened to the boy and he'd never see him again. He was unbelievably relieved when they finally returned to the BarChi.

"I've been worried," he confessed to Frances as the boy slid down out of his saddle. "I'm glad you're back."

Then he looked over at the other two riders and stopped short. Dante, of course, he recognised, but the other rider surprised him. Instead of the woman he'd come to know as Cami, he found a young man staring back at him. Or was it? It was still Lena's big dark eyes looking out at him, and yet, the angle of her cheekbones…of *his* cheekbones…

"Stop staring," Frances hissed at him as he elbowed him in the ribs. "You're embarrassing her."

Yes, he was. He could tell by the way Cami turned away from him. "I don't understand," he said quietly to Frances.

Frances shrugged. "Not sure I do either, but it's not like it's any of my business."

Simon felt himself blush at the logic of that. "You're right."

Dante was helping Cami down from the saddle, and Simon made himself walk over and face her. "I'm glad you're home safe."

Her cheeks were still bright red, but she smiled at him. "Thank you."

Aren came around the corner of the barn. He didn't seem in the least surprised by Cami's appearance. He hugged her tight, whispering something in her ear, then turned to Dante. "Everybody's been so worried. Deacon's been pacing a trench in our floor, although he'll never admit it." He put his hand on Dante's elbow and leant forward, as if to tell a secret, although Simon still heard what he said. "He was worried about all of you."

This seemed to bother Cami and Dante both, and once again, Simon found himself wondering what exactly had happened between them all. It wasn't the time to ask, though. Aren went to Frances next, and rather than eavesdrop on their conversation, Simon took the reins of Cami's horse and led it into the barn. The others weren't far behind. They were just getting the animals into their stalls when Deacon came in. Like Simon, he stopped short at the sight of Cami.

"Scia'loh?" he asked.

Simon didn't know the word, but Cami seemed to. Her cheeks turned a deeper shade of red, but she said shakily, "That's what Olsa says."

Dante glanced at Aren in surprise. "You didn't tell him?"

Aren shrugged. "He didn't need to know."

Deacon ignored them both. "Not used to riding, are you?"

Cami shook her head. "I was still sore from when we left Milton. I feel like I'll never be able to walk right again."

Deacon laughed, although not unkindly. "It'll pass. That's a promise." He turned to Dante, although he didn't quite meet his eyes. "She's dead on her feet. Take her in. I'll take care of your horse."

Dante looked like he wanted to say something in return, but Deacon didn't give him a chance. He turned away from him to greet Frances.

Dante sighed. He smiled weakly over at Cami, who looked terrified. Simon couldn't imagine how hard it had to be for her to face everybody if they all reacted the way he had.

"It'll be fine," Dante said.

She didn't look as confident as he sounded, but she let him take her hand and lead her out of the barn.

As soon as Dante and Cami were gone, Deacon turned an accusatory glare Aren's way. "You knew?"

"Knew what?"

"About Cami."

"Oh." Aren shrugged. "Yeah. I'm surprised more people couldn't tell."

"That explains *a lot*."

"You mean about Dante?" Aren asked.

"I'm talking about you!"

"Me? What did I do?"

"All the flirting!"

"Whose flirting?"

"Yours!"

Aren actually seemed confused, and Simon wondered if he really hadn't realised he'd been doing it, or if he was just a really good actor. "I've been flirting?" he asked Deacon.

"Yes! You never flirt like that with women!"

"Like what?"

"Don't give me that. You know what I'm talking about."

"I do?"

"I don't want you to flirt with him anymore."

"*Her,*" Frances corrected.

But neither Aren or Deacon gave any sign of having heard him. "You don't mind when it's Frances," Aren said.

Deacon's cheeks began to turn red. "That's different."

"Different how?"

Deacon pointed his finger at Aren. "Stop goading me, Aren. And stop flirting with Cami!"

Aren still seemed baffled, but he smiled, and Simon was fairly sure he was a bit pleased for having made Deacon jealous. "All right. No more flirting."

Deacon made a low noise that sounded suspiciously like a growl. Simon had a hard time not laughing, but Aren didn't even acknowledge it except to smile bigger.

Deacon, Simon and Frances finished tending to the horses in silence. It wasn't until they were done and Deacon was on his way out the door that he turned to Frances.

"Been a while," he said. "Come on up to the house tonight after supper, if you want."

He didn't wait for an answer. He just walked away, leaving Simon with a very red-faced Frances.

"At least with Foster and his men gone, there'll be more room in the barn," Frances said, gesturing awkwardly towards the back room where the Brighton hands had been sleeping. "They were the loud ones anyway. It won't be nearly so bad now."

He was nervous, Simon could tell, and trying to cover it with idle talk.

"It's all right," Simon said. "You can go."

His words didn't seem to make Frances feel any better, though. If anything, he seemed even more upset. "I don't want you to be mad."

"I won't be."

"I don't need to go. It's not fair to you."

"Frances, it's fine."

"I don't want it to be like last time."

"I was a fool last time," Simon said. "It won't happen again."

Frances bit his lip and glanced down at his feet. "I don't want you to be mad. We're partners, right?"

"Partners. But we're not married."

Frances looked up at him, and for exactly the second time in their friendship, Simon couldn't read what was in his eyes. He couldn't tell if Frances was hurt or confused or just scared.

"Listen, I have my own reasons for giving up women. And I have my own reasons for not doing what you and I do with any other men." He blushed when he said that part, but he made himself meet Frances' eyes.

"Still. It feels wrong."

"If it weren't for Lena, and I could still be with women, and I wanted to visit the whorehouse on our trips into town, would you let me?"

Frances shrugged. "Of course. I mean, I might ask you to make sure the one you picked didn't have the rot or something, but I wouldn't mind."

"And I don't mind either."

"But this is different."

"Not for me." He watched Frances, trying to gage his reaction. He thought he was getting through to him. He just had to figure out how to put it all into words. "Frances, I'll give you what I can, but I know it's not a lot. If there's something you get there with Aren and Deacon that I can't give you, then I don't blame you for wanting to go with them now and then."

"I still worry you'll be mad."

"I won't." He could tell by Frances' face that he didn't believe him. Simon laughed. "If I am, you can kick me again. As hard as you want. I promise."

Frances' mischievous smile spread slowly across his face. "I won't be so nice next time. I might aim for a sensitive spot."

Simon laughed. "Fair enough."

They ate supper, and afterwards, as they walked back towards the barn, he sensed Frances growing tense again. Frances glanced sidelong at him, biting his lip. "You sure?" he asked.

Simon laughed. "I'm sure! Go have fun."

Frances didn't answer, but it seemed Simon had finally convinced him. The boy looked a bit embarrassed, but more than a little excited, as he headed through the grass, up the hill to Aren and Deacon's house.

Once he was gone, Simon stood there, wondering what to do for the rest of the evening. He didn't want to go to the barn, where the Brighton hands would be. Those men worked for him, and he didn't count them as friends. Instead, he went to the BarChi barracks. He hadn't been in them since he'd left to work for Dante, but he found them unchanged. Red and Ronin were sitting on their bunks, separate from the rest of the men, drinking and playing poker on a small table set up between them. Simon pulled a chair up to sit with them.

"Where's your boy?" Red asked.

"None of your business."

"You two make up?"

Simon couldn't help but smile. "I don't want to talk about that."

"Good, because I don't want to hear about it."

Simon laughed. He pulled some money out of his pocket and tossed it on the table. "Then stop yakking and deal me in."

* * * *

Dante had worried about Cami's reception at the BarChi, but over the next day he began to realise he'd worried for nothing. Some of the maids stared. Some of them whispered. But some barely batted an eye, and for the most part, the hands were oblivious. Cami wore a wife's headscarf, and that seemed to be enough to keep them from looking any closer.

His own father had taken her hand and said with obvious sincerity, "You gave us a fright. I'm glad to see you home safe." Jeremiah then turned to Dante and pulled him into a hug. "Damn fool boy, riding off into the night! I should take my belt to you for scaring me like that."

He was scolding, yes, but his voice was full of love. More than that, Dante was sure he heard a bit of awe and more than a hint of respect.

"I had to get her back," Dante said.

"I know you did, son."

There was only one person on the ranch who didn't take it well at all, and that was Alissa. Cami told him how when she'd approached Alissa, the girl had slapped her in the face. Dante wanted to chase her down and have a few choice words with her, but Cami begged him not to.

"She's hurt," she said. "She knew from the beginning there was something different about me. She assumed that meant I was like her. Once she found out I was sleeping with you, she was upset, but she still knew on some level that she and I were somehow alike."

"And now?"

"Now, she feels betrayed. And even more alone than she did before. You know what she said to me? She said, 'Men get to do whatever they want, even if it's pretending to be a woman. Those of us who really are women don't have the luxury of living a lie.'"

"What?" Dante asked in exasperation. "That don't make any sense at all!"

"Yes, it does," Cami whispered, turning away. "She didn't give me a chance to tell her she was right."

Much later, after Cami was in bed, Dante found his father in his office. "She was scared to death you'd reject her once you knew," he said, "but you didn't even bat an eye."

"You mean because *she's* not really much of a she?"

Dante did his best not to be annoyed. He knew his father didn't mean it maliciously. "Right."

Jeremiah laughed. "I sort of suspected when I met her that she wasn't quite what she appeared to be. Still, I wasn't *sure* until you brought her home and took her to your bed." He winked at Dante. "I knew then I was right."

Dante looked down at his feet and he made himself ask, "Do you think of less me for it?"

It took his father a moment to answer, and Dante began to worry what he was going to say. Jeremiah crossed the room and put his hand on Dante's shoulder. He ducked down a bit to see Dante's face, forcing him to meet his gaze. Dante was relieved to see that there was no judgement or disgust in his father's eyes.

"I can't say I quite understand it," Jeremiah said. "But I know this—Cami makes you happy. And that's enough for me."

Dante nodded, unsure how else to respond. His father clapped him hard on the shoulder, breaking out of the serious moment into something far more casual and familiar.

"I'm glad you're here," Jeremiah said. "I've been meaning to talk to you. Sit down."

Dante did. He waited while his father poured them both drinks. He handed one to Dante, then went around to the other side of his big oak desk. He sat down and leant forward onto the desk to look at Dante.

"Simon came to see my while you were gone. He wants me to let him build on the vacant land to the west."

"You mean, out past the fields?"

His father nodded.

Dante shrugged. The request surprised him, but he couldn't see what it had to do with him. "How's he plan to build out there with the wraiths?"

"Well, that's the problem, isn't it? But first, he needs my permission, and I won't give it unless I know you agree."

"Why wouldn't I?"

"That land belongs to the Pane family. Now, Simon wants to build on it, and he wants to run a ranch there. He's not buying it, though. He's talking more like a long-term lease. He says he won't ever have an heir of his own, so when he's too old to run it, it'll pass back to the Panes."

Dante laughed, although there was more grief in it than humour. "You have too many ranches and too few heirs. Deacon won't ever have one. Likely I won't, either. Simon don't seem inclined to marry. With Brighton gone, that just leaves Jay's two boys."

Jeremiah nodded. "And the way things look, Jay's likely to end up with Fred McAllen's hog farm. Or half of it, anyway, depending on if and when those other two girls get married."

"You're not too old," Dante teased. "Why don't you marry one of them?"

His father laughed. "Fred keeps telling me the same thing. I'll admit, it gets a bit lonely out here, but I'm not so cruel as to make some young girl like that tie herself to an old man like me."

"I suspect Beth would cause you more than a spot of trouble."

"I suspect you're right." His dad leant back in his chair and put his boots up on his desk. "So, what do you say?"

Dante shrugged. "I got my own ranch. Bit of a mess right now, what with the windmill lying in middle of the barracks, but I'm happy there. I'll be sorry to lose Simon." And Frances, too, if he had his guess.

"That's what I thought you'd say, but I wanted to know for sure."

"You may as well let him get some use out of that land, but I sure don't see how he plans to build on it."

"I don't think he does either, just yet. And he made sure to say he'd help you get Brighton back on its feet before he did anything anyway."

Dante sipped his whisky. "Wish I knew when that was going to be. Things are a bit crowded here at the BarChi."

His dad laughed without much humour. "You're right about that. All these people, yet nothing's getting done. Won't last too much longer, though."

"Oh? Why's that?"

"Deacon. I give that boy one more week before he runs out of patience and starts hanging folks from the nearest tree."

Chapter Twenty-Five

As it turned out, it took far less than a week for Deacon to lose his patience. It took only two days.

The careful schedule of meals at the BarChi had become chaos. The hands ate early, and more often than not, half the maids were in the kitchen with them, flirting and causing trouble. Each meal took twice as long as it should have. Each day, Deacon had to break them up and send them running.

After them came the rest of the maids—the ones who stayed away from the men for whatever their reasons—and after that, the Pane family and the women. Of course by that time, others were showing up looking for dinner. Alissa, Uma, Cami and Olsa had their hands full, barely managing to catch a bite themselves before they were expected to put another meal on the table.

"And those McAllen maids," Cami had said to him the night before. "Some of them are fine, but there are a couple who do nothing but complain. They don't like the cooking, they don't like the food, but they don't do a thing to help, either! Fred McAllen and that oldest daughter of his are the worst of the bunch!"

Dante could see why Tama had opted to leave.

It was the middle of the afternoon, and the house was in chaos as it always seemed to be with so many people. Frances, Simon and Dante had thought to grab dinner before the hands and maids descended on the kitchen for supper. Aren came in from the hallway as they were sitting down, his ledger under his arm.

"Come sit with us, Aren," Dante said. "Have some supper." They hadn't spoken much since he and Cami had returned, but Dante was anxious to settle things with Aren. He wanted to prove he could be a better man than he'd been before, and to show that he was willing to be friends, if Aren would have him.

Aren smiled gratefully. "Maybe I will."

He didn't get the chance, though.

"That's it!" The shout came from the courtyard, and was unmistakably Deacon's voice. "Everybody in the courtyard *now*!"

Dante, Frances and Aren exchanged confused glances. Everybody was rushing for the door, and the three of them followed, although they had to move out of the way to let several of Fred McAllen's maids past. Deacon was standing in the courtyard, glaring and mad as a just-cut bull. He had a tight hold on the upper arm of a very red-faced ranch hand. Behind him was a girl, trying to button up her blouse.

"Maybe you all ain't noticed, but I run a cattle ranch here, not a blessed whorehouse! I'm getting tired of tripping over half-dressed women and rutting ranch hands. So there are about to be some new rules on this ranch!"

He pushed the ranch hand in the general direction of the other men and turned towards the house, where most of the women stood.

"Those of you who came here with Fred McAllen—until we decide what's to be done, every one of you is confined to the house."

This was met by several groans, and a few louder protests.

"You can't do that!" one of them said.

He glared at her, and she took a step back. "This is my ranch. I can do whatever the blessed hell I choose to do. You want to try to fight me on that?"

She glanced around for support, and seeing none, she shook her head.

"Good." He let his gaze move over the rest of them. "And no more meals together, either. From now on, ya'll eat before the hands, and every blessed one of you better be gone by the time my men show up. If you can't follow that rule, you'll not eat. It's that simple.

"This may seem unfair to you, but let me tell you how I see it—Fred McAllen's given me fifteen extra mouths to feed. You're littering up the house, and you're making more work for the BarChi women, and I gotta say, it's starting to piss me right the hell off. I don't know what things are like on Fred McAllen's pig farm, but here at the BarChi, everybody earns their keep. So if you can't find work to do in the house, then have the decency to stay the fuck out of the way. And the next one of you who bitches about the meals is gonna find herself walking back to town, whether it's daylight out or not. Are we clear?"

There was still some grumbling, but they nodded.

He turned to Beth, who stood with her arms crossed and her chin up. "Don't think for a second I don't mean you."

Stunned surprise replaced her arrogant look, but Deacon had already turned towards the gathered ranch hands.

"As for you men—every one of you here is on Jeremiah Pane's payroll and I know for a fact not one of you is getting paid to fuck! I got cows wandering loose, I got woodpiles that ain't been stocked, I got generators that ain't been cleaned and horses and livestock eating dirt in the pasture 'cause nobody's bothered to move them, even though I gave specific orders just yesterday it was to be done! There's horses in my barn standing ankle-deep in soiled straw, pigs that ain't even mine that need to be fed, and my milk cows have been lowing all morning, waiting for somebody to take care of them! I'm docking a week's pay from each and every one of you, and I'm not paying you again until everything on this ranch is back the way it should be."

He looked around at them all, daring them to challenge him, but none of them did. None of them were that stupid. "I don't care if you're male or female, you hear me when I say this—*don't push me on this*. The next time I stumble over a naked maid, I'll drag her out into this courtyard and take my belt to her. I was raised to not hit ladies, but as far as I'm concerned, if you're naked in my barn with your legs in the air, you sure as hell don't qualify anyway.

"And as for you men, the next time you take your pecker out, it better be so you can piss or shake hands with it yourself. 'Cause the next one I see flapping loose I'll cut off and feed to the pigs!"

Dante heard a snort next to him, and turned to see Aren duck his head, hugging his ledger to his chest, obviously trying not laugh.

"Holy Saints, Aren," Frances said with mock gravity. "That sounds like bad news for your pecker."

"Ha!" Aren burst out laughing, but he quickly put his hand over his mouth and turned away from where the hands and maids were gathered. "Don't make me laugh," he whispered to Frances, although Dante could tell he was barely managing to keep from doing so. "He'll be so mad if I laugh when he's being the boss."

"Now get your asses back to work!"

Hands were suddenly scrambling around the ranch, rushing towards the easier of the chores that needed to be done. Maids were pushing past them into the house. Aren leaned against the wall, using his hand to hide his face, obviously trying to compose himself.

The maids were practically running to get through the kitchen and out of the way, and Dante realised why when Deacon came striding in behind them, looking just as pissed as he'd been in the courtyard.

"You and you and you," Deacon said, pointing at Aren, Simon, and Frances, "in the dining room. You"—this time pointing at Cami—"go find Olsa and bring her there."

He didn't wait to see if his instructions were followed. He stalked down the hallway, scattering maids as he went, and Dante, Simon and Frances followed.

Deacon had to kick two more maids out of the dining room in order for them to use it. As soon as the door was closed and they were alone, he turned on Aren.

"Is there something about this situation that you find amusing, Aren?"

To Dante's surprise, Aren didn't flinch. Now that they were out of sight of the hands, he didn't have to act as if he was scared of Deacon as they were. He dropped his ledger on the table and smiled at Deacon. "Well, yeah. A bit."

"Holy Saints! If you can't back me up, then why are you even here? You may as well go home!"

Aren ducked his head, although Dante thought it was more to hide his smile than because he was sorry.

"Yeah, Aren," Frances said. "Just take care you don't let your pecker flap any on the way."

Aren burst out laughing, even harder than before. Dante wasn't sure he saw the same humour in it they obviously did, but Aren's laughter was contagious. He found himself smiling.

Deacon stared for a moment at Aren, who was doubled over laughing, and then at Frances, who was grinning ear to ear. Deacon was still so angry, and Dante knew he wanted to vent it more—to scream and yell and maybe punch somebody in the face—but there was Frances, with his great big smile, and Aren, who had tears running down his face…

"Oh fuck," Deacon said. It was like a surrender, the way he said it. He put his hands on his head and leant back to look up at the ceiling, as if trying to find some balance, and a laugh came bubbling up through his anger. "Holy Saints, I did say that, didn't I?"

"I think you scared them," Simon said. His tone was serious, but his eyes gave him away as joking a bit, too.

"Scared me!" Frances said. "I won't get mine out again for a week!"

Deacon laughed again. He glanced over at Aren, who was finally catching his breath. "Aren?"

Aren shook his head, wiping tears from his eyes. "I might need you to be a bit more clear on just what does or doesn't qualify as 'flapping.'"

Deacon snorted. And then he guffawed. And then he laughed, loud and hard. The sound seemed to fill the room, and it didn't stop. Dante couldn't remember ever seeing Deacon laugh like that, his hand on his stomach, leaning forward a bit, his shoulders shaking with it. It made Aren laugh again, too. Seeing them made Dante smile. In the past, watching Deacon and Aren together would have made him seethe with rage. But now, he found it didn't bother him.

"Oh, holy hell," Deacon finally sighed. He reached over to grab Aren's wrist. He pulled him closer, and smiled down at him. "I promise the flapping pecker rule don't apply to you." He kissed Aren on the head and let him go, then turned to the rest of them who were sitting at the table.

"What about me?" Frances asked. "I'm kinda fond of mine."

Deacon sighed dramatically. "I suppose the rest of you are exempt as well." He sat down and folded his hands in front of him on the table as he looked around at them all. "So, now that you've all quit fearing for your peckers, somebody tell me what the blessed hell we're going to do. 'Cause there's about twenty too many people on this Saints forsaken ranch, and I can't take this shit another damn day."

Cami and Olsa arrived a minute later. Cami didn't seem to know if she should stay or go, so Dante reached out and took her hand, pulling her over to stand next to him.

"It's about time you decided to do something," Olsa said to Deacon.

"Are you gonna be annoying, or are you going to help?"

"Why would I help when you act like that?"

Simon and Frances shifted uncomfortably in their seats, but Dante was used to the way Deacon and Olsa bickered.

"Do you know what's causing all the trouble?" Deacon asked her.

Olsa lowered herself with a groan into a chair. "I know."

"Care to enlighten us?"

Olsa sat thinking for a moment, then she sighed and started to talk. "When the settlers crossed the ocean and found this land, it was full of wild things." She picked up the salt bowl and dumped it out on the table, spreading the rough crystals across the table top with her hand. "There were wolves, like this."

"You're making a hell of a mess," Deacon said.

"Disrespectful brat," she scolded. "Hush and listen."

"Fine. Wolves, all over the blessed table."

"The settlers landed, and they started to build their towns and cities, and they drove the wolves west." She put the flat of her hand on the left edge of the table and began to slowly slide it across the surface, clearing a path through the salt. "Wolves are territorial creatures, and now there were too many packs being pushed into the wild. Do you know what that leads to?"

It was Aren who answered. "Overcrowding," he said.

"Smart boy." She lifted her hand and indicated the pile of salt, forming a small ridge in the centre of the table.

"Overcrowding leads to overhunting," Aren went on. "Which means eventually the food supply runs out."

Olsa nodded. "Then the wolves begin to turn on each other."

"Disease, too," Cami said suddenly.

They all turned to look at her. A blush was creeping its way up her cheeks, and Dante knew this was something she'd learned at the university.

She didn't back down though. "Lack of food means they're weak, which almost always leads to disease."

"Exactly." Olsa sat back, looking with her blind eyes towards Deacon. "That's what's causing it."

Deacon raised his eyebrows at her. "Wolves?"

"No, you blessed fool! Wraiths!"

The word seemed to echo in the small room. It was as if they'd all drawn a breath and were waiting to be told they could relax.

Olsa pointed to the empty spot on the table, where there was no salt. "This is the BarChi," she said. "You've driven them off this land."

Deacon was obviously sceptical, and Dante couldn't blame him. Deacon leant back in his chair, eyeing the salt-covered table thoughtfully. "And how exactly do you think I did that?"

To Dante's surprise, Olsa didn't answer. She looked instead to Aren.

"The brand," Aren said. "You claimed it."

Dante had no idea what that meant, but Cami spoke up before he could ask.

"Animals and ecosystems sort themselves out eventually. Are you saying all we need to do is wait?"

Olsa shook her head. "That's how nature works, but wraiths aren't natural."

"Wait a minute!" Deacon said. "Go back to this." He pointed at the salt on the table, looking back and forth between Olsa and Aren. "You're saying I've driven them off the BarChi, but that don't make any sense! We've had plenty of men killed by wraiths here."

"Yes," Aren said. "But not since you claimed it. Think about it, Deacon. It wasn't until I painted it, and then the night with the wraiths in our house. It wasn't until you sang the marriage song, and then you went to Jeremiah and claimed the BarChi as your own." He glanced apologetically at Dante. "You sent Dante away. That's what did it."

Deacon was thoughtful, but unconvinced. It was Simon who spoke next. "Aren, Frances told me once that when it's just you and Deacon at your house, you don't run the generator?"

Aren blushed, but he answered. "That's true."

"How's it possible you can do that?"

Aren glanced at Deacon, obviously waiting to see if he'd answer himself, but Deacon didn't oblige him. "Deacon is Ainuai."

"Fine," Simon said. "But you aren't."

Aren blushed even more. He glanced again at Deacon, but Deacon seemed to be lost in thought, unaware of Aren's discomfort. "I have a mark."

"The marks you both have?" Frances asked. "The brand with the A?"

Dante had never seen any such mark on either of them, and he wondered briefly how exactly Frances knew about them, but it seemed like an inopportune time to ask.

"Yes." Aren unbuttoned the top of his shirt and pulled it aside to reveal a scar on his chest. Not the thick, mottled scar caused by a brand, but a thin, pale line made by a blade. Even so, the shape of the BarChi brand was easily discernible.

"Holy Saints," Dante said with sudden realisation. "He's right! When I first left the BarChi, I had two nights at the shack without the generator." He didn't bother to mention why. "Wraiths never came. And I rode through the night to get Cami from town and made it fine."

Simon nodded. "That actually makes sense. The other night, Frances and I left Aren's house after dark." Dante noticed how Simon turned beet red as he said that. He turned to face Frances. "You stayed out for hours in the night, and you were fine."

Frances nodded. "That's true."

Deacon looked back and forth between them all, disbelief written on his face. "You're saying anybody with the brand is safe?"

They all looked around at each other as if expecting somebody else to give them a definitive answer.

"If that were the case, Brighton would be alive," Deacon said.

"No," Aren said. "He died before you claimed it."

"Don't you feel guilty about that, either," Olsa said. "His sons and wife would still be dead. Even if you had claimed it before then, having the brand would have saved his life, but not his heart."

"Well," Cami said, "if all this is true, then it's like the wards, right? Everybody just needs to put the BarChi brand on themselves or on their house, and they'll be safe?"

Both Olsa and Deacon were already shaking their heads. "It don't work that way," Olsa said. "Because Deacon's got to mean it. Every boy who comes through here and works this ranch, Deacon takes on as his own, for the time they're here. He takes responsibility for each and every one of them. That brand proves they worked here, and if they worked here, he had them under his wing. It won't work the same for men he has no responsibility for."

Deacon sighed. He leant forward and rubbed his temples with his hands. "Fine," he said. "Let's say I believe you—that I somehow made this safe haven in the middle of the wraiths, and I pushed them off their land. You're saying it's them being pushed away and into each other that's making all this trouble?"

Olsa nodded. "It's the only thing that makes sense."

"If I caused it, then I got to fix it," Deacon said. He turned to Olsa. "So what do we need to do?"

Olsa shrugged. "I told you the problem. I never said I knew the solution."

Deacon groaned and put his head in his hands. "If you don't, then who will?"

Dante looked around the room. Everybody else was watching Deacon or Olsa. Everybody else appeared lost, as if they were waiting for an answer. Everybody, except for Aren.

Aren was chewing his lip thoughtfully. His eyes were moving back and forth, but Dante recognised that his vision was focused inward. He was pondering something. Not only that, he seemed cautiously optimistic about it.

In the past, it might have irritated Dante, but not now. Aren had broken down Deacon's walls. He'd known about Cami. He'd sent her to Brighton. He'd known about the brand. Somehow, Aren had a knack for finding answers.

"What is it, Aren?" Dante asked.

Aren blushed, obviously surprised to find them all suddenly staring at him. He started to shake his head, to say it was nothing, but Dante didn't let him.

"I think you have an idea," he said. "I'd like to hear it."

"The horse's ass is right," Olsa said, and Dante found himself laughing at her reference to him. Somehow, it made him feel loved more than if she'd said his name. "I can't see what you're thinking," she said to Aren, "but I can feel its power. I can feel the strength of your hope, and I don't think it's wrong."

"Symbols have power," he said to her.

"Blessed Saints!" Deacon swore. "Will one of you tell me what the hell you're talking about?"

"Well," Aren began cautiously, "Deacon's claiming of the BarChi was sort of accidental, but I don't see why it couldn't be repeated."

"What exactly does that mean?" Simon asked.

Aren opened his ledger. He flipped quickly to a blank page at the back of the book, then pulled a pencil out of his pocket and handed it to Deacon. "Draw the ward that lays the wraiths to rest."

Deacon took the pencil, but he shook his head at Aren. "It don't matter. You have to do it in the exact place they died. Like Olsa told you before, we'd have to walk the entire length of Oestend."

Aren, who'd been standing up until then, pulled a chair up and sat down to meet Deacon's eyes. "You claimed the BarChi with a painting," he said.

Dante wasn't really sure what that meant, but he could tell Deacon was pondering Aren's words, wondering if it would work.

"We have the map Dante found," Aren said. "I can use it as the canvas. I'll paint the sign. You and Olsa can sing it."

"It won't work, boy," Olsa said. "It's a fine idea, but the magic's not big enough. Not here. We're too far from the ancestors."

"Is there someplace closer, where the magic *is* big enough?" Aren asked.

Olsa pursed her lips and looked away, staring with her white eyes into the far corner of the room. It was Cami who broke the silence.

"What about the lay-en..." She stumbled on the unfamiliar words. "Lay-nah-ro—"

Olsa's chair legs scraped harshly across the floor as she turned on Cami. "How do you know that word?"

"I don't know." Cami's face was pale. She pulled the long sleeves of her sweater over her hands and hugged her stomach as she faced Olsa's frightening gaze. "From the stories."

"What stories?"

Cami glanced around the room as if for help, but nobody seemed to have any to give. "The stories," she said again. "Hasn't everybody heard them?"

Everybody was slowly shaking their heads. Everybody except Deacon.

"Olsa," he said, his voice slow and stern. "What does she mean?"

"Nothing!"

Olsa had practically spat the word at him, but her anger seemed to intrigue him. He sat up straighter in his chair and leaned towards her. "Lai'i n'ahro," he said.

"What does it mean?" Aren asked him.

Deacon kept his gaze on Olsa, but he answered. "It's a twisted phrase. Kind of clever, the way the words overlap. It could mean 'sky table'. It could also mean, 'table for ancestors'."

"It's nothing," Olsa said again.

"You expect me to believe that?"

Olsa turned away from Deacon without a word. Deacon looked to Cami for help. Cami looked back at Dante, her unease clearly visible on her face.

He squeezed her hand. "Tell us about the stories."

She was still unsure, and she spoke to him directly rather than to the table at large. "When Paulus Redmond returned from his expedition, he told a story of the Ainuai. See, the second year of his expedition, there was a drought. Nothing grew. Animals were dropping dead all over the prairie. The Ainuai told Paulus that they were going to appeal to the ancestors to send them rain, but they said for a request so big, they had to go to the lay-ai—"

"Lai'i n'ahro," Deacon said for her.

"Right," Cami said, smiling over at him. "They told him it was a place of great power, where the ancestors where the strongest. Paulus left before they did it, but he said that three days later, the drought broke.

"It's also said that it was there that the warriors made their final pact. The one that allowed them to become wraiths when they died, rather than passing on to be with the ancestors."

"Is that true?" Deacon asked Olsa.

"It doesn't matter," Olsa said. "There's no song for what you want to do."

"Well," Cami said hesitantly, "can't you make a new one?"

Olsa ignored Cami, but she stood up from the table. She turned on Deacon with so much anger, everybody at the table backed up a bit. She pointed a gnarled finger in his face. "H'ailoh rah si'il! Scia'loh ri hai'lou na!"

She walked slowly out of the room. Her steps were hindered by age, but there was somehow still a great deal of dignity in her exit. When she was gone, everybody turned to Deacon for explanation.

Deacon sighed. He ducked his head and rubbed his eyebrows, whether debating Olsa's words or cursing the old woman's stubbornness, Dante didn't know.

"How do you know all this?" he asked Cami.

She shrugged, looking around the table with obvious discomfort. "They're just stories. History. I don't know. I thought everybody knew them."

Deacon shook his head in amazement. "Well, whatever they are, they've got her spooked. And if Olsa's spooked, I think we might be onto something."

He finally turned to the pad Aren had given him. He drew a symbol on it—a circle, with two strangely curving, intersecting lines. "This is the ai'huara," he said to Aren. Then, to the table at large, "It lays wraiths to rest."

"So that's it?" Frances asked. "We go to this sky place, you draw the sign, and it's over?"

Deacon shook his head. "First, you have to do it where they died. The lai'i n'ahro may be where the pact was made, but it's not where their spirits are anchored. Second, like Olsa said, there's no song and no symbol for exactly what we want to do. It's a bit bigger than just laying them to rest."

"You have to claim it, too," Aren said. "Combine the ai'huara and the song you use to claim something." He blushed as he said that.

Deacon smiled at him. "You mean the marriage song?"

Aren didn't answer, but he leaned over to take the pencil from him. He drew a single line through the ward Deacon had drawn. Had it been a clock face, the line would have gone from the nine to the six. Had the other two lines not already existed inside the circle, it would have been the BarChi brand. "Make it yours," he said to Deacon.

"That's good!" Cami said. "Look." She pointed at the symbol they now had. Deacon slid the ledger into the centre of the table so she could easily reach it. "Six is the strongest number for the Ainuia, right?"

Deacon nodded. "Right. Six points on the compass."

"Four," Frances corrected.

Deacon shook his head. "Not for us."

Cami pointed again to the paper. "A circle," she said, "just like the lai'i n'ahro." The Ainuai word came easier to her this time. "It's said to be a tall, round mesa." She pointed to the spots where the three lines touched the edge of the circle. They were evenly spaced around it. "Six points, one for each direction on the compass." She looked around the table at them all. Deacon, Aren, Simon, Frances, Dante and herself. "Six of us. All we need is the song."

Deacon leaned back heavily in his chair. He was staring at the piece of paper on the table, but Dante was sure he wasn't really seeing it.

"Will it work?" Simon asked Deacon.

Deacon shook his head. "Hell if I know." He took the ledger and tore the page from it as he stood up. "Only person who might know for sure is Olsa." He turned to Aren. "Save me some supper, will you? I'm about to piss her off so bad, she won't let me eat for a week."

Chapter Twenty-Six

No one knew what was said between Olsa and Deacon, not because they couldn't hear them, but because they spoke in the language of the Old People. What was known was that when Deacon came back up from her little room in the basement, he was so mad only Aren dared speak to him.

For two days, it went on. Olsa hid away in her room. Several times, Deacon went to talk to her. Sometimes he came away angry, and sometimes resigned, but never with her approval. Dante never tried to ask Deacon what the issue was, but he knew Simon and Frances both asked, and both were told it wasn't their concern. It was Cami who finally got an answer, and she didn't get it from Deacon.

"Does she not think it will work?" Cami asked Aren one afternoon.

They were in the kitchen, sitting together at the table, and Dante noticed how Alissa and Uma fell silent as they strained to listen in.

"It's not that she thinks it won't," Aren said. "I think the problem is, she believes it *will*."

"And she doesn't want that?" Dante asked.

Aren pushed his food around on his plate, contemplating exactly what to say. "The settlers destroyed everything. Her people. Her family. The Ainuai's entire culture. The only thing left is the wraiths."

Dante wasn't sure he understood how that justified letting the wraiths tear the prairie apart, but more of the hands came in then for their supper, and he let the matter drop. He forgot about it until later that evening, when he and Cami were alone in their room. She stood staring out the window, into the night.

"They're so lost," she said.

"Who?"

"The wraiths."

Fear made his gut clench. "How do you know?"

"I don't know. I just do. We can't hear them here, but back at Brighton, when we could hear the voices, I could tell how tired they are. They want to go home."

Dante shivered. "Well, we want that, too, so seems like we're all in agreement. All but Olsa."

"I want to talk to her. Will you come with me?"

Going to see Olsa was about the last thing in the world he wanted to do, but he couldn't find it in him to tell her no.

He led her down the stairs to Olsa's room. Cami knocked quietly on the door.

"Go away, Scia'loh!" Olsa called from inside.

Cami smiled over at Dante. She didn't seem at all surprised that Olsa knew who was at her door. "Can I come in?" she asked.

"What do you think, traitorous brat? I told you to go away!"

Cami ignored her. She glanced nervously at Dante, as if asking for courage, then turned the knob and went in.

The room was tiny. Dante hadn't seen it since he was a boy, and somehow, it had seemed far bigger then. It smelt of herbs and fresh-turned earth. Olsa sat in a wooden rocking chair in the centre of the room. "Go away," she said again.

"I'm not going anywhere." Cami knelt on the floor at Olsa's feet. She tried to take Olsa's hands, but the old lady pulled them away. Cami wasn't dissuaded. She sat there with her hands in Olsa's lap, her gaze locked on Olsa's brown, wrinkled face. Olsa's white eyes continued to stare over Cami's head. Not, Dante knew, because she couldn't see, but because she refused to acknowledge Cami's presence.

"We need your help," Cami said. "You're the only one who can help Deacon make the song."

"You don't know what you're talking about."

"I think I do."

"You're a fool." She glanced Dante's direction. "The two of you deserve each other."

Dante was more offended for Cami than for himself, but Cami didn't seem to mind.

"They want to leave," Cami said. "You must know that."

"They're the only thing left."

"They're so tired. They long to pass over and finally rest."

Olsa sniffed and turned to look in the opposite corner, somehow dismissing Cami without saying a word.

"Olsa, I understand why you don't want this to happen. The settlers destroyed your people, and you think only the wraiths were left to prove they'd been here at all. But the Ainuai will still be here. Their stories will go on."

"Bah!" Olsa said, waving her hand at Cami. "Just words! What good are they?"

"They're a legacy," Cami said. "*Your* legacy."

"It will be the end of the Ainuia."

"I won't let that happen."

"How can you change it?"

Cami took Olsa's wrinkled hand and held it between hers. "With the stories. Every person here will know—all the maids, all the hands—and they'll tell others. We'll all tell the tale, to anybody who will listen. Aren will write it down, and we'll send it to the people I know at the University in Francshire, and the people he knows in Lanstead. It will spread, like stories always do. It will be like fire burning across the prairie, leaving the world changed in its wake. And a thousand years from now, our children's children's children will know that despite everything the settlers did to you and your people, it was *you* who stepped up and saved Oestend."

Olsa's chin trembled, but she shook her head. "It won't matter."

"You'll be remembered," Cami said. "*Deacon* will be remembered."

A single tear ran down Olsa's cheek. Dante saw the way her hands shook.

"Deacon," she whispered. "My Deacon. He's always been a good boy. He deserves it more than I."

"You made him the man he is. You taught him what he needed to know. He is your son in every way that matters. You and he together will be known forever as the Ainuia that freed us from the wraiths."

Olsa ducked her head. Her shoulders shook. Tears spilled down her face.

Cami reached up and cupped the old woman's cheek in her hand. "I won't let them forget," she said. "Not ever."

Olsa took a deep, shuddering breath. Then another. She wiped her tears away with the back of her hand.

"The wraiths don't want to be here anymore. Let's send them home."

"What makes you think any person in Oestend deserves to be saved?"

"Deacon deserves it," Cami said. "And Aren. I know how much you love them. Isn't that enough?"

Olsa sighed. She wiped her eyes again and nodded. When she looked up at Cami with her strange, sightless eyes, she seemed to be almost smiling. She reached out and took Cami's face in her hands. She leant forward, as if she really could see into Cami's eyes.

"You never knew your mother, did you?"

Cami shook her head. "No."

"She was one of us, Scia'loh."

Cami's breath seemed to catch in her throat. "Are you sure?"

"How else would you know the heart of the wraiths? Your mother's Ainuai blood sings in your veins."

Now it was Cami's turn to duck her head and cry. Dante stepped forward, thinking to comfort her, but Olsa looked up at him suddenly, stopping him.

"Go find Deacon," she said. "Tell him to come. It's time for us to make a new song."

* * * *

Three more days while Deacon and Olsa made two new songs—one that Deacon would use and one for them all. Dante had assumed only Deacon would sing, and maybe Cami, but Deacon and Olsa insisted the magic would be stronger if everybody participated, and so part of each day was spent with them all learning the song.

They'd perform the ceremony at night, because that's when the wraiths were the strongest. Olsa and Deacon explained how it would work, the wards Deacon would paint—first on the men who were with them, then on the map—and the chant that would be sung. The song was comprised of three phrases, repeated over and over, which made it easier to learn, but the words were difficult. The vowels were the wrong shape and the inflections unnatural. Still, Olsa and Deacon assured them that their success would not be hindered by a mispronounced word.

At least, not too much.

When they weren't learning the song, Aren and Simon studied the map, trying to estimate how far they had to go to get to the mesa and what the best route might be. Dante and Frances worked the ranch. Things had improved since Deacon's outburst, but there were still too many people and too many animals to contend with. Dante found himself counting down the days until they were to leave.

True to her word, Cami told every hand and every maid about the wraiths, and about the plan. Dante tried to tell her maybe she should wait so they didn't all look like complete fools if they failed, but she ignored him. "It needs to be a story," she told him. "Whether we succeed or not."

There was some debate over whether Cami needed to have the brand before they left. They were all counting on the BarChi mark to keep them safe in the night, but she was the only one without it. Dante wanted her to get one, just to be safe. Olsa and Deacon said if she were full-blood Ainuai, it wouldn't matter, but as a half-blood, they didn't know. In the end, she agreed to be marked. Dante could have done it himself, but he figured it would mean more to the Ainuai ancestors if Deacon did it, so Deacon used Aren's penknife to carve the BarChi brand onto her right shoulder blade, as small as he could make it.

The night before they were to leave, there was a light knock on their bedroom door. Dante was surprised when he opened it to find Alissa there. Her cheeks were red, and she could barely meet his eyes, but she asked, "Can I see her?"

Alissa's anger at Cami had faded since their return, but he knew she hadn't exactly been friendly again, either. Dante was tempted to close the door in her face. He looked over at Cami for guidance. She was surprised, he could tell, but she nodded.

Even after he'd let Alissa in, it took her a minute to start talking. She glanced nervously his way. He was fairly certain she wanted him to leave, but unless Cami indicated the same thing, he had no intention of going anywhere.

"I'm sorry," she said to Cami at last.

"It's fine," Cami said. "You don't need to apologise."

"Yes, I do. I was horrible to you, and it wasn't fair." She shook her head, holding up her hand as if Cami had begun to argue again. "I know it's an awful excuse, but I just feel like things are so unfair. And I know it's not your fault. But I've been angry at everything else. At the rules and my father and my life. So tired of feeling like I'm in a cage. So mad that I can't be like everyone else." She took a deep, shaking breath.

"I know," Cami said, her voice gentle. "I really do know."

"I hate myself." Her voice was a strained whisper, and Dante wished more than anything he'd left the room. He had no right to witness this, but leaving now would only draw attention his way. "I don't want to be me."

Cami reached up and stroked Alissa's hair. "I've felt that way before, too," she said quietly. "It's exhausting, I know. And I'm sorry."

"Uma says I should try harder to be happy, but she doesn't know what it's like. Nobody else understands. That's why I wanted you to like me, because you're the only one who seemed to know."

"I'm sorry I couldn't be what you wanted."

"It's not your fault. I know that. I was just so heartbroken, and I took it out on you, but that wasn't fair of me."

"I don't know," Cami said. "Maybe it was."

Alissa shook her head, but tears were flowing down her cheeks, and she didn't seem able to speak.

"It can be better," Cami said. "I know it feels like nothing will ever change, but it can. You just have to find a way."

Alissa laughed bitterly. "I don't see how."

Cami looked over at Dante. She seemed to be trying to ask him something, but since he had no idea what, he had no way to answer. She turned back to Alissa. "When this is all over, we're going to make Brighton whole again. Maybe you can come there."

Alissa shook her head again. "You don't want me."

"As a lover? No, I don't. I'm sorry. But as a friend? Yes. I'd love very much to have you there. And…" She glanced over at Dante again. She looked unsure of herself. "I think there will be women there," she said, watching Dante carefully for his reaction. "Maids, instead of hands?"

Maids instead of hands? Dante had no idea how to make a ranch of women work, but if that was what she wanted, he'd figure it out.

He smiled at her in answer, and she smiled back, a silent 'thank you' in her eyes. She ducked her head to meet Alissa's eyes. "It's our ranch," she said. "We'll make our own rules."

Alissa looked up at her. She was confused at first, but Dante watched as understanding slowly lit in her eyes. Her long face split into a broad smile. "Really?"

Cami laughed. "Really."

Alissa squealed and threw her arms around Cami's neck, knocking her a step backwards in the process. "Thank you!"

Cami hugged her back, stroking her hair. "We'll make Brighton work. I promise."

Alissa made a sound that might have been laughter, or might have been a hiccup. For a while they stood that way, Cami almost rocking Alissa, rubbing her back, whispering into her ear. Finally, Alissa pulled back enough to look up into Cami's eyes. She glanced Dante's way then slowly stood on her toes and put her lips against Cami's.

Dante stood frozen, watching them kiss. One some level, he felt he should be annoyed, but he wasn't. He couldn't quite decide if he was aroused, or just embarrassed. It only lasted a second. Cami pulled away from Alissa and looked at him over the girl's shoulder, as if asking what he thought.

He shrugged.

She smiled at him, then bent her head and kissed Alissa for real. She pulled Alissa's thin body tight against her.

The kiss lasted longer than he expected. Dante wasn't sure where it was going. More importantly, he didn't know if he should stay or go. He was about to clear his throat to interrupt them when Cami broke the kiss. Her cheeks were flushed and her eyes were bright. She was smiling, but she stepped back decisively, away from Alissa.

"Thank you for coming," Cami said. "I didn't want to leave with things ugly between us."

"Me neither." Alissa looked over at Dante. "Can I really come to Brighton?"

"If Cami says so." He levelled his finger at her. "But that right there was a one-time deal. She's with me, and I don't share."

Alissa laughed. "Fair enough."

"That was about the last thing I expected," Dante said to Cami, once Alissa was gone.

The colour was still high on Cami's cheeks. "Are you mad?"

"Not at all."

"That's the first time I've ever kissed a girl."

"And how was it?"

She shrugged, smiling. "Nice enough, I guess. But I don't think it's for me."

"I'm awful glad to hear that." He took her hand and pulled her into his arms. He bent to kiss her neck. "And the next time she says men can do whatever they want and women can't, you remind her of that kiss. 'Cause if she'd have been a man, I'd have skinned her alive."

Cami laughed. "I'll let her know."

He kissed her neck again. She put her arms around him and sighed happily, melting into him, her thin body warm and supple against his. He reached up and began to undo the buttons on her blouse. "This'll be our last night for a while in a real bed. What do you say we make the most of it?"

"I'd say that's the best idea I've heard all day."

Chapter Twenty-Seven

The day finally arrived for them to leave.

"I should have spent some of that time learning to ride better," Cami said to Dante as she eyed the saddled horses.

Dante secretly agreed with her, but she'd been so busy with Deacon and Olsa, he hadn't wanted to add more to her burden. "You'll be fine."

"Don't you worry," Deacon said from the next stall over. "You can't ride any worse than Aren. I'm laying bets he falls at least twice."

Dante laughed as Aren lifted a certain finger in Deacon's direction. Still, Cami's limited riding skills worried him. He offered up a quick prayer to the Saints that they wouldn't encounter anything along the way that would spook Cami's horse and make it bolt. When he was done doing that, he offered a second prayer to the Ainuai ancestors. For him, they might not listen, but if Cami was one of their own, maybe they would.

They were packed and ready to mount up when Olsa came hobbling slowly out of the kitchen, and over to where they waited.

"Here," she said, shoving a small leather pouch into Deacon's hands. "You know how to brew it. Make it strong. Use it all. Share it between the six of you when you're ready. Then wait. You'll know when to start."

"Will it help?"

"It will make the pieces whole."

Deacon didn't appear to know what she meant, but he nodded. "All right."

"That's the last of it," she said. "I'll be blind without it."

Deacon put his hand on her shoulder. "When fall comes, I'll gather every tea leaf in the prairie—"

Olsa shook her head. She reached up and put her hand on his cheek. "I won't be here that long."

Deacon took a step backwards, as if Olsa's simple words were a force he couldn't bear to stand against. "What? No!"

"Don't you worry—"

"No!" he said. He tried to push the bundle of tea back into her hands. "No, we don't need it. We'll sing without it—"

"Hush, lou'o. It will be my time, with or without the tea."

"But..." Deacon's voice caught on the words. He was fighting to maintain his composure in front of everybody else. Tears escaped his eyes and ran down his dark cheeks. Dante chose to look down at his boots rather than witness the pain on Deacon's face. "I won't go. I won't leave you."

"Yes, you will," she said, her voice stern. "And you won't hurry back, either. You keep your promise to Aren. Take some time. I'll be here when you get back."

"How can you be sure?"

"Because I am. It'll be harder without the tea, but we'll still have time to teach Cami what she needs to know." She reached up to pat his cheek with her gnarled hand. "Be happy, lou'o. You won't have to sing my song alone."

Deacon gathered her carefully into his arms. She was so small and fragile compared to him, and yet, Dante could still picture him as the boy he'd been, running to Olsa for comfort. Deacon whispered quietly into her ear. He kissed her on the cheek and let her go.

Nobody spoke as they mounted up and rode out of the compound, westward, towards the wild, and away from the safety of the BarChi.

For most of the first day, Deacon rode ahead of them all. He eschewed even Aren's company, and so Aren dropped back to ride next to Dante.

"What did Olsa mean about keeping his promise to you?" Dante asked.

Aren looked down at his saddle, a blush creeping up his cheeks.

"I'm sorry," Dante said. "It's not my place. Just trying to make conversation."

"It's fine," Aren said. "I just…" He sighed. "I never know how much I can say to you. I don't want it to seem like I'm rubbing it in."

Dante hated that he'd made things so difficult between them. "Don't worry about that. At one time, it might have bothered me, but now? I'd just like us to be friends. I know that's a lot to ask, after what I've done, but—"

"It's fine. I mean, I think I understand."

"I won't ever cause trouble for you like that again."

"I know." Aren smiled shyly at him. "We're good, right?"

"I hope so."

Aren laughed. "Well anyway, the promise Olsa mentioned, it's nothing big. I just thought it would be nice to be away from the ranch for a while." He looked ahead, to where Deacon rode alone. "The ranch weighs on him. He loves it, but he hates it too. Sometimes it's like a third person in our bed. I just asked him to take a break. Take our time getting home. That's all."

"I don't blame you a bit. What's your plan?"

"We thought we'd ride north to the main branch of the river on Redmond's map. If we follow it, it should lead us right back home." He smiled. "Eventually."

"Home," Dante said. He was surprised to realise the word didn't bring the BarChi to mind. He had a new home now. He looked over at Cami, who rode on his other side, and he knew she shared his thoughts. The smile she gave him was big and bright and possibly the most beautiful thing he'd ever seen.

"I hope you enjoy your time away," she said to Aren. "But for myself? I can't wait to get back to Brighton."

* * * *

Crossing the furthest edge of the BarChi was frightening. It was the halfway point. If they quit now, they could still make it back to the BarChi by nightfall, but past it, there was no turning back. It had been generations since anybody had gone so far. Even Dante and Deacon had to stop for a moment before going on. Only Frances rode on, seemingly unaware. Eventually, the rest of them followed.

The first night away was definitely tense. Deacon watched Aren with a hawk-like vigilance, as if suddenly unsure of his safety. Dante was pretty sure he was watching Cami just as intently. Simon and Frances sat close together, ostensibly playing dice, but Dante suspected their heart wasn't in it. What if they were wrong? How many of them would the wraiths take?

The sun dipped to the horizon. Aren pulled a bottle of whisky out of his pack and began to pass it around. Nobody spoke.

The sky went from brilliant orange, to silver-grey, to black. Pinpricks of light began to appear overhead. Dante lay back on the ground and watched as the stars claimed the sky.

"It's amazing," he said. "Think how few people in Oestend have ever seen this and lived to tell about it."

"We'll fix that," Cami said.

Eventually they curled up in their bed rolls, bundled in pairs. Although the wind gusted and whispers rode its waves, the wraiths didn't come.

Over the next three days they followed a southern branch of the river, and Oestend seemed to fight them every step of the way. It was as if the wraiths knew their intent and did everything they could to make the trip miserable. The six of them rode through wind and rain, hail and even snow. At night, they huddled together, trying to stay warm. The wind buffeted them, stealing their breath, chafing their skin. The voices grew louder, following them even during the day—whether taunting or threatening, Dante didn't know. Deacon was pale and silent, his fists white-knuckled on the reins.

"What are they saying?" Cami asked him.

"Most of it's gibberish, but the part that isn't…" He shook his head. "You were right. They want to go home."

"Then why don't they help us out?" Simon asked. "Quit making things so blessed hard?"

Deacon shook his head. "They can't. It's not their nature."

Nobody spoke for a long time after that.

Twice they passed abandoned homesteads. "What happened?" Aren asked.

Deacon shrugged. "Some people lived out in the wild, before the wraiths. You got to realise, the Ainuai made the pact to stay here after their deaths, but it ain't like they died right away. It wasn't until later, and even then, it was one at a time."

Cami shuddered. "Imagine how it must have been. First only one wraith, and maybe there were rumours, but then slowly more warriors crossed over. More settlers were probably killed. But with so few people out here in the wild, the rumours probably couldn't spread fast enough to save them all."

"Exactly," Deacon said. "Caught a lot of these folks out here in the wild off guard. A generation later, nobody was left. They either went back to civilisation, or they died."

On the fourth day, the rain stopped and the landscape began to change. The long grass of the prairie gave way to barrenness. Deciduous trees still grew along the river, but everywhere else they saw only squat, scrubby evergreens and round puffs of sagebrush. The earth was the colour of rust, and the air was so dry it parched their throats just breathing it in. It should have been hot, but a bitter wind still blew, pelting them with dust and causing their eyes to tear.

"I think we're getting close," Aren said.

They worried the mesa would be hard to find, but on the fifth day, it rose up ahead of them, a tower of reddish-brown earth, surprisingly tall and with a perfectly flat top.

"Nice of them to make it easy for us," Frances said.

As they neared the lai'i n'ahro, the atmosphere somehow became lighter and less oppressive. The wind died down and the temperature seemed to rise a few degrees. By the time they reached the base of the mesa, it was warm and sunny. The light spring breeze was heady with the scent of sage. A row of trees followed the river, leaning over its path like overprotective parents. It was surprisingly peaceful and undeniably beautiful.

"It's hard to believe this, after what we rode through to get here," Simon said.

Deacon answered. "There are no wraiths here. The ancestors are too strong."

The mesa rose above them, and Dante wondered how they'd ever reach the top. They rode around its base, and finally, on the northeast side, they found a path in the rock. It appeared to be partly natural, partly man-made. It was still steep, but was obviously made for the purpose of reaching the summit of the lai'i n'ahro.

They set up camp, tended the horses and ate a quick supper. Afterwards, as the sun began to fall low in the sky, Deacon brewed the tea. The six of them sat in a circle and slowly passed the cup around. It was like no tea Dante had ever tasted, with strong liquorice notes and an aftertaste like wet smoke. It wasn't exactly appetising, but they each drank, passing the tea until the cup was empty.

And then they sat back to wait.

The tea worked quickly. It started as strange pinpricks. A tingling sensation, yet, when Dante tried to locate where on his body he felt it, he couldn't. It was everywhere and nowhere at once. Something teased the periphery of his vision. He felt he should be nervous but instead, his heart seemed to slow. His hands felt unnaturally light. His legs felt a mile away. Somebody laughed, and he was surprised to realise it was him.

"Everybody else feels weird, right?" Simon asked. "It's not just me?"

"Not just you," Dante said.

"Does Olsa feel like this all the time?" Aren asked, his voice full of amusement.

Deacon chuckled. "You'd think she'd be a bit less cranky, wouldn't you?"

They fell silent. Dante's breathing slowed. He closed his eyes and felt himself drifting, a speck of dust on the wind, being carried up and over the prairie. He thought he could see their small campfire a mile below him. Six men, as inconsequential as moths, huddled around it.

"I can feel the river," Frances said suddenly. Simon and Cami started to laugh. "I mean it!" Frances said. "I can feel it, like it's flowing through my soul."

Dante wasn't sure what to think of that. It seemed crazy, and yet, he couldn't dismiss it, either. His perception of himself was blurring. The ends of his consciousness were suddenly hard to define.

"I can feel the birds in the trees," Cami said. "They're watching. I can see us through their eyes."

"I'll be damned," Simon said, his voice full of awe. "I think I feel it, too."

They were silent for a moment, and Dante could sense them all reaching out and up, their consciousness somehow expanding, and stretching, and merging.

"I can feel you guys, too," Frances said. He laughed. "I know Deacon's got a hard-on."

"You would too if you could hear what Aren's been whispering in my ear."

They all laughed at that—even Dante—yet he was distracted. He could feel something pulling at the edges of his mind. Something that was dark and twisted. It swarmed around them, just past the edge of their campsite. Dante knew he wouldn't see it if he turned to look, but it was there, constantly shifting and moving, watching and longing, hating and unbelievably miserable and frustrated.

"Now I can feel y'all trying to listen in," Deacon said. "Mind your own damn business."

They started to laugh again.

"I can feel the wraiths," Dante said.

Their laughter died in an instant, and he felt them all draw breath. He felt their shared consciousness turn its attention upward and outward, afraid and unsure, searching for what he felt.

"Blessed Saints, Dante," Frances breathed. "You sure know how to kill the mood."

Cami had said the wraiths were tired, and sad, and Dante knew now how right she was. They longed to be set free.

"I thought there weren't any wraiths here at the mesa," Simon said.

"They can't get too close," Deacon answered. "But they know we're here. They're going to do all they can to push closer. They may want this to happen, but their nature won't allow them to *let* it happen, if they can help it."

The level of shared anxiety rose a bit, all of them glancing nervously into the dark as if they'd be able to see the wraiths.

Dante knew before Deacon spoke what the man was going to say.

"It's time."

Chapter Twenty-Eight

They gathered what they needed and went single file up the steep trail. Nobody spoke. As they climbed, the mental commotion of the wilderness seemed to fall away. There were no trees here. No birds. No river. Only the sky, brilliant with stars, stretching impossibly far in every direction. When they reached the top, they stood in silence, reaching out with their senses. Although it was full dark out, the array of the stars and the sliver of moon granted the place an eerie silver light. The apex was smooth flat stone, rim to rim. The world lay below. Above them dwelled something vast and awe-inspiring—a quiet sense of peace and of connectedness.

"Is that the ancestors?" Cami whispered. It was so silent atop the mesa, her voice carried despite her hushed tones.

"Yes," Deacon said, and even he sounded amazed. "That's why the mesa is holy."

At another point in his life, Dante might have scoffed at anything so mystical, but there was no denying the wonder of the place.

"Let's get to work," Deacon said.

They'd gone over the steps to the ritual. They all knew what to do. The mesa itself was round, roughly fifty yards across, too big for them to use as their circle. Aren held a piece of string to the ground at the centre of the mesa, and Deacon used it as a guide to paint a smaller circle, six yards in diameter. They used stones to anchor the map in the centre of the circle. When that was done, everybody but Cami removed their shirts. When they'd discussed the process of the ceremony, Cami had balked at being bare-chested, and Deacon had assured her he only needed access to enough skin to paint the ward, so Cami unbuttoned the top few buttons of her blouse instead. They took their places around the circle, Deacon and Cami directly across from each other, Frances and Simon between them on one side, Dante and Aren on the other.

A strange awkwardness suddenly filled their shared consciousness. It felt absurd to be standing together, half naked in the dark in the middle of nowhere. Did they really think this would work?

"Don't doubt now," Deacon said. "Your conviction is important."

Dante took a deep breath. He felt the others doing the same, all of them resolving together to believe in what they were about to do.

"Good," Deacon said.

A heartbeat of silence, and then Deacon began to sing. "Le'ama sa'ahala ma'ana re'ehalo'au roha'ala."

His voice was low, and quiet, and Dante sensed his unease—not because he feared it wouldn't work, but simply because he felt silly singing in front of them all.

"Le'ama sa'ahala ma'ana re'ehalo'au roha'ala."

Immediately, Dante felt a ripple in their shared consciousness. A mental warmth surged from his right. It was Aren, reassuring Deacon. Whether he knew he was doing it, or whether it was only his natural response to Deacon's unease, Dante didn't know, but he felt the way Aren worked to bolster Deacon's confidence. He could almost hear Aren's thoughts. *Don't be ashamed. You're strong. You're amazing. You're sexy as hell.*

Dante smiled. Not on purpose, then.

He took a deep breath, and he threw himself in behind Aren. He was careful not to copy the feeling exactly, but he tried to project absolute faith. A moment later, he felt Cami do the same.

Deacon's voice grew stronger. "Le'ama sa'ahala ma'ana re'ehalo'au roha'ala. Le'ama sa'ahala ma'ana re'ehalo'au roha'ala." The circle seemed to shudder as one.

They had the attention of the ancestors.

The first part of the ceremony was all Deacon. He would draw a ward on each of them as he entreated the ancestors to acknowledge the men who were with him. Deacon and Olsa had explained that in the past, the re'ehalu had been more symbolic than ceremonial. It was the Ainuai's way of declaring friendship or confirming treaties, but it was less than official. It didn't carry the weight of the marriage song, but now, with the first of the songs Deacon and Olsa had created, they asked the ancestors to recognise the men he marked as Ainuai.

Deacon's chant went on. "Le'ama sa'ahala ma'ana re'ehalo'au roha'ala. Le'ama sa'ahala ma'ana re'ehalo'au roha'ala."

He reached down and picked up a jar of paint and a brush. He started with Aren, painting the ward with bright red paint across his chest, singing as he did. Then it was Dante's turn. Dante closed his eyes as Deacon came to him, afraid that whatever passed between them would distract Deacon. The paint was cold. The brush left a wet, tingling trail, and Dante shivered as Deacon made the ward.

"Le'ama sa'ahala ma'ana re'ehalo'au roha'ala."

Next, Deacon went to Cami, who pulled the collar of her blouse open enough for Deacon to paint the ward, then Frances, and finally Simon. Deacon returned to his place in the circle, and his chant continued, the same as before, over and over again. "Le'ama sa'ahala ma'ana re'ehalo'au roha'ala."

Dante waited. His breath caught in his throat. Had he felt something change? Some shift in the cosmic awareness around them, or was he imagining it? He wasn't sure, but he tried to gather his awareness, to pull it close lest he offend the ancestors or distract Deacon with his thoughts.

Deacon stopped. He sang once, almost under his breath, "Sa'ahala nai'alini."

Next to Dante, Aren repeated the words. His intonation was imperfect, but he said it with utter solemnness, and Dante wondered at its meaning, but he knew it wasn't the time to ask.

Deacon took a deep breath, and the next song began. It had three parts, Olsa had explained. First, it claimed the land of Oestend for the living. Second, it asked the ancestors to open the door to the spirit world and to take in those left behind. Third, it asked for healing. Cami had told Dante how she, Deacon and Olsa had debated what kind of healing to ask for. For the wraiths? For the land? For those still alive? In the end, they'd decided that just asking for healing was enough. They'd let the ancestors decide from there.

Deacon's voice was strong and loud. "Ailu jai'roi'o ma'ana sci'holu. Le'ama sa'ahala loai'loma ay'arou. Le'ama aolo'ui ai jai'roi'o, eye'nay."

There was no unease this time. No embarrassment. His voice seemed made for the strange Ainuai words. The vowels took on a depth the rest of them could never achieve. Dante hoped Olsa was right that their belief meant more than their pronunciation.

Cami was the first to join in. "Ailu jai'roi'o ma'ana sci'holu. Le'ama sa'ahala loai'loma ay'arou. Le'ama aolo'ui ai jai'roi'o, eye'nay." Her voice was higher than Deacon's, yet still lower than if she'd been entirely female, blending well with Deacon's deep baritone.

The rest of them began to sing as well, quietly at first, but gaining confidence as they felt their way around the unfamiliar vowels. "Ailu jai'roi'o ma'ana sci'holu. Le'ama sa'ahala loai'loma ay'arou. Le'ama aolo'ui ai jai'roi'o, eye'nay."

Once they were all singing, Deacon moved into the centre of the circle with his paint. He knelt in front of the map. "Ailu jai'roi'o ma'ana sci'holu. Le'ama sa'ahala loai'loma ay'arou. Le'ama aolo'ui ai jai'roi'o, eye'nay." He dipped his brush in the jar then slowly began to draw the new ward on the map.

"Ailu jai'roi'o ma'ana sci'holu. Le'ama sa'ahala loai'loma ay'arou. Le'ama aolo'ui ai jai'roi'o, eye'nay."

Back at the BarChi, Deacon had argued briefly that Aren should be the one to paint it. "You're the one with the art magic," Deacon had said.

Dante wasn't sure what that meant, but Aren had strongly disagreed. "What if I paint it wrong?"

Olsa had backed him up, saying the ward would be stronger coming from the one of them who was full-blooded Ainuai, and so now Deacon sat alone in the circle, making the ward on the ancient piece of parchment.

"Ailu jai'roi'o ma'ana sci'holu. Le'ama sa'ahala loai'loma ay'arou. Le'ama aolo'ui ai jai'roi'o, eye'nay."

When the ward was done, he moved back to his spot at the edge of the circle. The six of them continued to sing.

"Ailu jai'roi'o ma'ana sci'holu. Le'ama sa'ahala loai'loma ay'arou. Le'ama aolo'ui ai jai'roi'o, eye'nay. Ailu jai'roi'o ma'ana sci'holu. Le'ama sa'ahala loai'loma ay'arou. Le'ama aolo'ui ai jai'roi'o, eye'nay."

The air on the mesa grew warmer. A light breeze brushed them all then gusted, strong and unnaturally hot.

"Ailu jai'roi'o ma'ana sci'holu. Le'ama sa'ahala loai'loma ay'arou. Le'ama aolo'ui ai jai'roi'o, eye'nay."

Dante wasn't sure he could breathe. His chest seemed to contract. His pulse raced. Their voices faltered as a wave of unease flowed through them.

All but Deacon. His voice surged on, stronger and louder than before. "Ailu jai'roi'o ma'ana sci'holu. Le'ama sa'ahala loai'loma ay'arou. Le'ama aolo'ui ai jai'roi'o, eye'nay. Ailu jai'roi'o ma'ana sci'holu. Le'ama sa'ahala loai'loma ay'arou. Le'ama aolo'ui ai jai'roi'o, eye'nay."

Then Aren was there, his unfaltering faith in his lover washing over them all. Frances was there, too—a quiet resolve that was less romantic than Aren's feelings, but undeniably worshipful. Dante grabbed onto that feeling. He breathed it in. He swallowed it. He took it in his mind's eye like a mantle and cloaked himself against the onslaught of the wind.

"Ailu jai'roi'o ma'ana sci'holu. Le'ama sa'ahala loai'loma ay'arou. Le'ama aolo'ui ai jai'roi'o, eye'nay."

Their voices were loud now. The wind blasted them, and Dante closed his eyes, knowing in some heart that was not his that this was good. That this thrust of power wasn't a final, pitiful push to remain, but the force of the wraiths, rushing towards peace. Dante reached out to both sides, feeling for the hands of those next to him. Physically, he couldn't reach, but subconsciously, he felt the connection. He felt Cami's calloused fingers in his left hand, Aren's soft warm hand in his right. He felt them all reaching for each other, six men connecting on some unknown level. He felt the power surge around them all, their circle brimming with it, six men and the rocky ground thrumming with something ancient and holy. The strength grew. It rose and expanded up and out, like warm unbaked loaves on a counter, growing fat and thick, and still they sang.

"Ailu jai'roi'o ma'ana sci'holu. Le'ama sa'ahala loai'loma ay'arou. Le'ama aolo'ui ai jai'roi'o, eye'nay. Ailu jai'roi'o ma'ana sci'holu. Le'ama sa'ahala loai'loma ay'arou. Le'ama aolo'ui ai jai'roi'o, eye'nay."

The wind roared to a sudden crescendo, hitting them from all sides at once. The map flew from under the rocks that held it, up into the air, out of sight. The air crackled and snapped—the sound of lightning but with no light.

A tremor ran through them all.

And then there was silence.

The wind had stopped.

"Ailu jai'roi'o ma'ana sci'holu. Le'ama sa'ahala loai'loma ay'arou. Le'ama aolo'ui ai jai'roi'o, eye'nay."

By some unspoken agreement, their song ended. They stood there, looking awkwardly around the circle. They all laughed—a nervous, shaky laugh.

"Is that it?" somebody asked.

Dante felt on edge. The earth seemed to pulse under his feet. The air still crackled with energy.

No, Dante realised, that wasn't it. That may have been what they came to do, but somehow he knew, it wasn't all that needed to be done.

He looked around the circle, all of them but Cami standing there with their chests bare. He could almost see the magic flowing between them.

And then Frances took a step forward.

His was looking straight at Aren, and even Dante could read the blatant invitation he saw in the boy's eyes.

Dante felt the jolt of surprise that touched them all, but then Aren laughed and moved forward, meeting Frances halfway. They kissed and their arousal caused a ripple—a tiny wave that spread from the centre of the circle, growing until it lapped over and around them all.

It was strange. They were so much alike, like two sides of the same coin—Aren a bit older, a bit more scuffed, copper where Frances was golden—but still, as they kissed, Dante began to feel he couldn't tell which one was which. The paint on their chests blended and blurred.

Dante looked at Deacon, wondering if it bothered him to see Aren kiss another man, but Deacon didn't seem bothered at all. He was smiling—a small, knowing smile. Obviously amused. Obviously not surprised. To Deacon's left was Simon, obviously incredibly uncomfortable. When Dante turned to Cami, she met his eyes. The colour was high on her cheeks.

"Oh my," she said.

Frances and Aren broke their kiss, although they still clung to each other. Hands explored bodies as they talked quietly then, moving as one, they both turned his way.

Dante's heart jumped inside his chest. Inside his pants, his cock began to grow hard.

They came straight to him.

No, not just to him. To him and Cami. Frances reached Cami first. He began to undo her blouse. She stopped his hands, looking at Dante in alarm.

"It's fine," Frances said. "We're all friends here." He used his hands on her blouse to pull her into a kiss.

Dante felt he should object, that maybe he should be bothered, but he wasn't. He didn't have time to wonder why, either. Aren was suddenly in front of him, unbuttoning Dante's pants as he stood on his toes to kiss him. He tasted different than Cami. That was Dante's first thought. He was shorter than her, but not quite as thin. Their chests touched, and the power of the blurred wards seemed to pulse. Dante felt his pants slide down his hips and to the ground. Aren's warm hand began to caress Dante's growing erection.

This couldn't be happening.

Dante glanced nervously at Cami, but found her in an equally intimate position with Frances. Her shirt was open, her skirt up around her hips. He felt the confused desire that filled her as Frances deepened their kiss.

Dante left his pants and shoes and let Aren guide him into the centre of the circle. Cami and Frances soon followed. Deacon moved into the circle, already naked. He scooped an arm around Aren and pulled him away from Dante, although not as if he were mad. He winked at Dante as he practically carried Aren over to Cami. "Go ahead," Dante heard him say, and somehow, Dante *felt* the laughter that bubbled up in

Aren's chest. He felt Aren's quiet amusement as he stepped between Frances and Cami. He put his arms around Cami's waist and pulled her close, kissing her while Deacon stood behind him, caressing him and nibbling his neck.

Frances came to Dante. He put his arms around his neck and smiled up at him flirtatiously. "I knew we'd get to do this someday."

Dante heard himself laugh, as if from very far away. Frances was warm in his arms, and when Dante kissed him, he found he tasted divine. It was strange, touching Frances, somehow knowing that Aren and Deacon were touching Cami, and yet there was no jealousy anywhere.

But he realised suddenly that there was still one of them missing.

He pulled away from Frances and found Simon, still alone, still half dressed, still standing on the circle they'd drawn. He looked terrified. Dante looked down at Frances, and he could see the pain in the boy's blue eyes.

"He's not like us," Frances whispered.

Not like us.

The words seemed to echo in Dante's ears. Simon and Frances did everything together, and somehow, Dante knew that Simon needed to join them. He needed to know what this meant.

He turned Frances in his arms, so that the boy faced Simon.

"Look at him," Dante said. Because nobody could look in Frances' eyes and not know what he was feeling. Simon couldn't see Frances' eyes and not know what it meant to his friend.

Simon still hesitated, but suddenly Cami broke from their group. She went to him. Dante couldn't hear what she said. It seemed he should be able to sense what was passing between them, but the combined consciousness of himself, Deacon, Aren and Frances drowned it out. He could only watch. He saw the way Simon stared at her, as if he were half in love and half afraid. She put her fingers on Simon's lips to keep him from talking. She said something to him. Simon turned to look at Frances, his eyes bright with a new understanding. He said something back. Cami nodded, replied. And like a rabbit being lured from his burrow, Simon came. Slowly at first. Then quicker, and then he was there, pulling Frances into his arms and kissing him as though it were the only thing in the world he'd ever wanted to do.

The earth throbbed. The sky shook. The universe seemed to draw its breath and hold it.

Waiting.

Anticipating.

Then plummeting.

Dante fell hard and deep into a raging sea of desire. There were hands, and lips. One minute it was Frances in his arms, then Aren, then Cami. Warmth on his cock, hands gripping his ass, and Dante's perception of himself turned over and upside down. Suddenly he was on the ground, and the whole world was made of gasping mouths and hard, beautiful cocks.

"It's the tea," somebody said, and Dante had to agree.

Whatever was in Olsa's concoction continued to blur the lines of reality. Dante gave up keeping track of who was where. If there was a cock in front of him, he sucked it. A mouth, he kissed it. At one point he felt warm lips on his own cock. When he put his hand down to the head at his groin, he found hair he knew in a heartbeat, even in the drugged state he was in. It was heavy and long and smooth, and Dante knew without looking that it was jet black.

It was Deacon, spread out on the ground in front of him, his head between Dante's legs. Deep in his brain, a voice told Dante this should matter. This should be momentous or miraculous or disastrous. But it was none of those things. It just *was*.

Dante closed his eyes, revelling in what Deacon was giving him. He let himself drift, and he found it wasn't just the lines of reality that were blurred. It was the lines between him and each person he touched, and each person they touched in turn. Somehow, he wasn't just himself, sucking Cami while Deacon sucked him. He was also Cami, who was kissing Frances, stroking the boy's erection, and he was Frances, kissing Cami, while Simon fucked him from behind. He was Deacon, sucking Dante's cock. He was Aren, spreading Deacon's cheeks and using his tongue on Deacon's rim. He somehow knew without using his eyes when Deacon rose up and slid his callused, wet fingers into Cami. He knew the pleasure she felt and the way she arched her back to receive him. He knew when Aren spread his legs and let Simon fuck him. He knew when the tight warm ass his cock sank into belonged to Frances, and he knew the joy Frances felt at being fucked by him.

They were no longer six. They were one, the pieces made whole. One body. One brain. One heartbeat. They were bound by love and friendship. And yes, somewhere between them, there was the sting of betrayal and the ache of loss, but overshadowing it all, there was forgiveness. There was trust. There was healing. More than anything, there was hope. They left themselves behind and became something that was more. Something that was divine. Something that was and holy and ancient and supreme.

One life. One land. One dream. One desire. One gasp away from orgasm, all of them holding a collective breath. Trembling. Straining.

Reaching.

They hung there impossibly long, wonderfully intertwined, the entire universe waiting to exhale.

And then there was release.

It was a climax like no other—six voices crying out as one, one perfect awareness splintering into six separate beings on the cold, hard ground. Six flawed creatures huddling together, a panting, shuddering tangle of limbs. There was cum in Dante's throat, and on his chest, and on his hands. He had no idea who any of it belonged to, and he didn't care.

"Sa'ahala nai'alini," somebody sang quietly, and this time Dante knew it for what it was. It was a song of thanks.

A familiar form found its way into his arms. He knew this lithe, slender body. He pulled Cami tight against him, buried his face in her hair, and gave himself to sleep.

Chapter Twenty-Nine

Simon awoke first. It was a slow, strange awakening. His limbs were heavy, his mind foggy. The sky to the east was just beginning to glow with the hazy light of a distant dawn.

Where am I?

But in the very next moment, he knew the answer. *At the mesa.*

With that thought came a memory of the night before. It was fuzzy and strange. The tea and the chant, the sudden knowledge that the wraiths were gone and the laughter they'd all shared at the end. All of the others had been together, kissing and touching, and Simon had stood alone outside the circle while Frances looked at him with his huge blue eyes, begging him to join them.

He'd been afraid, but then suddenly, Lena had appeared there next to him. He'd struggled, not knowing if he should embrace her or apologise, not knowing if he should rejoice or be afraid.

"Six points," she said. "Three lines. Three couples. It takes us all."

"Lena—"

She'd put her fingers on his lips to hush him. "No more grief, Simon. Grief is just love with no place to go."

He'd looked at Frances then, suddenly understanding. "My grief has a place to go now."

She nodded. "Go over there. Touch him. See how much joy it brings him to be the one to receive it."

And she'd been right. He'd left Lena and gone to Frances, and as he'd kissed him, he'd felt the way Frances' heart soared and raced at Simon's touch, and the way his whole soul seemed to come alive.

After that, there wasn't much he remembered at all. Only the incredible pleasure. It made his cheeks burn and his groin ache to think of it now. He had no idea who all he'd touched, or who exactly he'd fucked.

Well, if he didn't remember, it was a safe bet none of the others did, either.

He took stock of their positions. He was on his back, Frances cuddled comfortably against his side. The boy's head rested on Simon's chest, and Simon put his face into Frances' curls and smiled. *I love you.* Maybe he didn't say the words when he should. Maybe he didn't even mean them quite the way Frances wished, but it didn't make it any less true.

Simon turned his head the other direction. It was still mostly dark, but he was able to make out the shapes of the other four next to them. They were all wrapped up together in a tangle of limbs and hair. Nobody else was awake.

Simon moved out from under Frances, who barely stirred. He scrambled down the side of the mesa to where the horses waited below. He went to the creek to piss and to wash himself. He was a bit embarrassed to realise just how much dried cum he had on him, and where. It was even in his hair. He swam in the near-dark out into the cold water of the river and let it wash him clean. He felt clearer-headed for it. He floated there in the water as the eastern sky began to turn pink.

When he came back out of the river, he found Frances at the bank. The boy was dressed, his hair still wet where he'd apparently dunked his head into the river. He watched as Simon went to his clothes and got dressed.

Simon hated the weight of the boy's gaze. He hated the doubt and the fear in his blue eyes. The light was too low for Simon to actually see it, but he knew it was there. He knew Frances well enough to know what he was thinking. Of course, he understood it, based on how Simon had behaved that evening at Aren and Deacon's house.

"Will you stop looking at me like that?" Simon said. He turned and smiled at Frances, doing his best to be reassuring. "I ain't mad or anything."

Frances sighed in relief and came to stand with Simon. The pale light to the east was just enough to show Simon the hint of embarrassment in Frances' eyes. "I woke up and you were gone. I was worried…"

"Worried that I'd freaked out on you and left?"

Frances nodded.

On some level, Simon wished he could take Frances in his arms and tell him it was fine. He wished he could tell the boy how much he depended on him and how he never wanted them to be apart. But he couldn't do any of that. If Frances had been a girl, he would have, but right or wrong, behaving that way with Frances wasn't his nature. He worried once again that it wasn't enough.

But then he remembered the night before, the way he'd been able to feel what Frances felt as he touched him. The way in that moment he'd known Frances' heart. Didn't that mean Frances had known Simon's too? Frances probably knew Simon's feelings and his doubts, and yet Frances was still here, happy with what Simon offered.

Simon put his hand on Frances' shoulder. "I won't leave you."

Frances' smile was shy and sweet. "I think I know that now." He ran his hand through his wet hair and shook his head, laughing nervously. "Last night was all a bit strange."

Simon laughed. "Saints, that's a nice way of putting it." He was just as glad he couldn't remember it. He didn't want to recall the details. Instead, he turned to the west, where the sky was still the deep indigo of night. "It's all gonna change, you know," he said. "It'll take a while, but eventually word will get out about the wraiths. And all those fools in the east and on the continent will be headed this way."

Frances frowned. "Seems wrong to think of this land being taken over. Almost makes me wish the wraiths were still here."

Simon shrugged. "Whether change is for the good or for ill, makes no difference. A smart man will adjust and learn to survive. A smart man may even thrive."

"I guess that means you have a plan."

"Jeremiah agreed to let me build on the land west of the BarChi."

"Really? You going to start your own cattle ranch?"

"I figure the Pane's got the beef market covered." He'd been thinking about that, but the truth was, there were plenty of other options. He'd worked a lot of different kinds of ranches over the years. He smiled at Frances. "You know anything about sheep?"

"Sure. They're white and fluffy and say 'baa'."

Simon laughed. "Well, it's a start. You're in, right?"

Frances smiled. He moved closer to Simon and looked up at him with his huge blue eyes. "We're a team, aren't we?"

"We are."

Frances smiled. He stood on his toes, and Simon held very still as Frances kissed him. It was sweet. The boy's fingers in his hair, the softness of his breath against Simon's lips. It was still a bit strange to him, but he loved it for what it meant to Frances. They were a team, and like any team, they'd learn to accommodate each other.

That's what it meant to be partners.

* * * *

Dante's first conscious thought was utter confusion. He was lying on something that felt suspiciously like rock. He had no blanket. He had no clothes.

He wasn't sure why that would be.

He sighed and decided he didn't care. Naked on the ground or not, he was content. Somebody rested comfortably in his arms. He didn't need to open his eyes to know it was Cami. He knew the feel of her skin, the shape of her body, the smell of her hair.

Somebody else had their arms around Dante. Somebody big. And warm. Dante could feel the man's genitals nestled against his ass. Not erect, but warm and pleasantly erotic. Dante kept his eyes closed. He settled back into whoever was behind him, happy to share their warmth. He pulled Cami more firmly into his arms.

Wait…

Dante opened his eyes, still unsure what was wrong. Yes, he was asleep on the ground. When he moved his leg, he felt hairs pulling in his groin, and he groaned. Either he'd come in his sleep, or he hadn't cleaned himself off the night before.

He felt the person behind him stir, and suddenly, the strangeness of the situation hit Dante. Exactly whose hard muscular body was that? Dante looked at the arm flung over him, and his heart stopped beating.

Deacon. Nobody else had skin so dark.

Dante turned slowly to look behind him, thinking he had to be mistaken.

No, that was definitely Deacon behind him, still sound asleep. Dante sat up, and as he did, Deacon stirred. He blinked at Dante in confusion, but only once. He turned over onto his other side, where Aren rested. He put his arm over Aren and went right back to sleep.

Dante sat for a moment, replaying the moment in his head. He was sure he should be feeling something much more profound than he was. He'd loved Deacon for so long. He'd longed for them to be lovers. And yet now, he didn't feel elated or validated.

More recently, he'd let that dream go, and he'd embraced a future with Cami. She lay next to him, still asleep, her male body naked and exposed, her smooth, flat chest smeared with red paint. Just looking at her made his chest ache in the most beautiful way. He loved her as much as ever.

He turned again to Deacon and Aren.

Should he feel guilty?

No.

It took him a second to think why that should be, but suddenly he remembered the night before. It was muddled and confusing and completely surreal. It was hard to say which things had really happened and which hadn't, and which had happened, but not to him. But what he knew was—it was over. They had laid the wraiths to rest. They had saved Oestend. And somehow, they'd healed themselves as well.

Dante stood up, wincing as the dried mess at his groin pulled more hair. He found his pants and boots and put them on before going down the hill. He found Simon and Frances in their campsite, playing dice.

"Good morning, sunshine!" Frances called.

Dante waved at him as he headed for the river. He noticed Simon seemed a bit too embarrassed to meet his eyes.

The thought made him laugh.

Eventually, the rest of their group made it down from the mesa and took their turn at the river, washing themselves clean. Simon and Cami were both red-faced and unable to meet anybody's eyes. Aren and Frances seemed to find the entire situation quite funny and took every opportunity to joke about it. Dante laughed with them a bit, as did Deacon, but Dante knew there was one last thing to be done.

They began to break camp. Deacon and Aren were heading north, as Deacon had promised. Frances and Simon would be heading straight back to the BarChi with Dante and Cami.

Dante had just finished saddling his horse when Deacon came up behind him.

"Not even Jay there right now," Deacon said. "Don't you let my ranch fall apart while I'm off with Aren."

"I won't. First thing I'll do is get Fred McAllen and his damn maids to go home."

Deacon laughed. "That'll help a lot."

"Can't promise I'll get any work out of Red, but the rest of them, I'll whip into shape for you."

"I'm pretty sure nobody in the blessed world can get work out of Red."

Dante laughed, but it was an awkward kind of laugh. They stood in silence for a moment, both of them looking down at their boots. Dante had felt for years that there was so much for them to say yet here they were, both of them speechless.

"You know," Deacon said at last, "if we'd been just a bit older, everything would have been different."

Dante didn't have to ask what he meant. "I know. A couple of years later, we wouldn't have cared what he thought."

"And he sure wouldn't have been able to take a horse whip to us."

"Not to you, at any rate," Dante said, laughing. He hadn't grown into his size quite as early as Deacon had.

Deacon nodded. He pushed his hat down low on his head. "He took a lot from us. I'd be lying if I said I didn't think about it once in a while. Can't help but wonder sometimes how different things could have been."

Dante couldn't speak. He swallowed the sudden lump in his throat and nodded.

"Thing is," Deacon went on, "seems like it all got set right."

"It did," Dante agreed. Their prayer for healing had healed more than Oestend. Still, he needed to say the words. "Deacon, I hope you know how sorry I am. About what I did to Aren. And to you. And about Daisy. About everything—"

"Stop," Deacon said, holding his hands up and finally meeting Dante's eyes. "It's over, and you're forgiven."

Dante shook his head. "I don't know that I deserve your forgiveness. I especially don't deserve Aren's."

Deacon looked across the camp, to where Aren seemed to be trying to saddle a horse without getting within arm's reach of the beast. He smiled. "Aren don't know how to hold a grudge."

Dante nodded. "I'm glad for that."

Deacon gestured towards the river, where Cami sat watching them, yet trying to look like she wasn't. "You love her?"

Dante's smile felt so big, he wondered how it could even fit on his face. "Like a fish loves the river."

Deacon laughed, the way he always did—a sudden, loud sound that came from deep inside his chest. Dante wanted to be bothered by Deacon's laughter, but when he turned to look at him, he found he couldn't. Deacon was smiling at him, his face open and friendly. "I'm a better man for having found Aren. I think the same might be said about you and Cami."

"I'm thankful for her every day. And thankful to Aren for thinking to send her my way."

Deacon's smile went from one of laughter to something gentler and almost apologetic. "You were right, you know. When you said we'd once been brothers." He stopped, staring down at his boots, but Dante knew he wasn't done. He waited until Deacon was ready to say the rest. Deacon finally looked up at him again. "It might be nice to try for that again."

The words and the hesitant question in Deacon's eyes made Dante's heart swell. They nearly brought tears to his eyes. It was hard to speak, and when he did, his voice came out hoarse. "I won't let you down like I did before."

"I think that went both ways more than I wanted to admit."

It wasn't quite an apology, but Dante knew the sentiment was there. "We were boys. I think it's fair to see we've both come a long way since then."

Deacon's smile was hesitant. He gripped Dante's shoulder. "I won't let you down again, either."

Deacon pulled him close. Dante closed his eyes as Deacon's big arms closed around him. So many years he'd longed to have Deacon hold him again, and now that it had happened, it felt better than he'd dreamed, yet not for the reasons he'd anticipated. The wounds caused that day in the barn were finally gone. Dante didn't need or want another lover.

But to have one of his brothers returned to him was the greatest gift he'd ever been granted.

"Thank you," he whispered.

Deacon kissed the side of his head. "Don't be a stranger."

He let Dante go and walked away, back to Aren, who still hadn't managed to saddle the horse.

And Dante found, to his surprise, that he wasn't sorry to see him go.

Chapter Thirty

The ride back to the BarChi was peaceful. There was no wind. No snow. The bit of rain they rode through was gentle and warm.

Natural.

At night, Dante and Cami would bed down on the opposite side of the fire as Frances and Simon. He didn't know what happened between the two men, but he and Cami made love as if they'd never have another tomorrow.

During the day, as they rode, the four of them discussed their plans. First, they'd get the BarChi back in shape so it would be ready when Deacon returned. Then, Simon and Frances would go to Brighton with Dante and Cami, and they'd get the barracks ready—for maids this time, instead of hands.

And the windmill? What was left of it would be used for firewood and scrap. They had no need for it now.

Once Brighton was up and running, Dante promised to go with Simon and Frances to the land west of the

BarChi and help them build their own homestead. Simon already had a name for his ranch—Lena.

The four of them weren't quite met with a heroes' welcome upon their return to the BarChi. Most of the men were out in the field. Only Tama and Alissa came running out to greet them. Dante didn't mind.

It turned out he didn't need to send Fred McAllen and his maids home. They'd already left, as had most of the excess hands. Tama reported that Beth was gone, too. Nobody knew where she'd gone or with whom, but Tama told him she'd taken her belongings with her, so they were confident she'd left of her own will.

They found Olsa in the kitchen. Her strange white eyes stared over their heads, somehow more sightless than before. Dante remembered her words to Deacon. *I'll be blind without it.* She still smiled, though, and she wasn't without her wits.

"You may be a hero," she said to Dante, "but you're still a horse's ass."

He laughed. "I know."

"You did well, Scia'loh," she said, turning to Cami. "Your mother would be proud."

"I hope so."

Olsa nodded. "Don't you doubt." She reached out and squeezed Cami's hand. "I have a lot to teach you. If I'd met you earlier, you'd be stronger than I ever was. As it is…" she shook her head. "Still, we'll do our best."

Cami nodded. "I won't let you down."

"I know you won't." Olsa tugged on Cami's hand, pulling her close, and whispered something in her ear. Dante saw Cami's surprise, and her confusion, but Olsa just laughed and walked away.

Dante wasn't sure he'd ever been so happy to see his old room. He moaned out loud at the sight of his bed. "I've decided I'm too old to sleep on the ground."

Cami laughed as she climbed into bed next to him. "Do you mind going back to Brighton without me? I just want to stay with Olsa, until..."

"I understand," he said, putting his arms around her. "I'll miss you like crazy, but I won't mind."

She snuggled into him and gestured towards the rocking chair by the window. "Take that with you when you go."

"You want it?"

She nodded, her cheeks suddenly red. "It'll be good for rocking the baby."

Dante pulled back to look at her in surprise. "What baby?"

She shrugged. "I don't know. But that's what Olsa said, that I'm going to be a wonderful mother."

Nothing could have surprised Dante more than that. Olsa had said she was somehow between male and female. He looked down at her flat stomach. He put his hand on it.

"No, silly," she laughed, pushing his hand away. "I don't know where she'll come from, but I know it won't be from there!"

Dante blushed, feeling a bit foolish for having been confused, even for a moment. He pulled her close and kissed her temple. He wrapped his arms around her.

A baby?

The thought made him smile. He'd always wanted kids. The thought of raising one with Cami filled him with a warm, simple contentment.

He was looking forward to it.

"I don't suppose Olsa was nice enough to tell you *when* this was going to happen."

She laughed. "Of course not."

"Women," he sighed, shaking his head. "You always do cause trouble."

About the Author

Marie Sexton lives in Colorado. She's a fan of just about anything that involves muscular young men piling on top of each other. In particular, she loves the Denver Broncos and enjoys going to the games with her husband. Her imaginary friends often tag along. Marie has one daughter, two cats, and one dog, all of whom seem bent on destroying what remains of her sanity. She loves them anyway.

Marie Sexton loves to hear from readers. You can find her contact information, website details and author profile page at http://www.total-e-bound.com.

CPSIA information can be obtained at www.ICGtesting.com
Printed in the USA
BVOW08s1835310114

343636BV00001B/28/P

9 781781 845127